Midshipman Bolitho

Alexander Kent is the author of twenty-seven acclaimed books featuring Richard Bolitho. Under his own name, Douglas Reeman, and in the course of a career spanning forty-five years, he has written over thirty novels and two non-fiction books.

ALEXANDER
KENT

Midshipman Bolitho

arrow books

Published in the United Kingdom by Arrow Books in 2008

10

Copyright © Bolitho Maritime Productions Ltd 1975, 1978 & 2005

Previously published in three novellas:
Richard Bolitho – Midshipman 1975
Midshipman Bolitho and the 'Avenger' 1978
Band of Brothers 2005

First published in the United Kingdom by Hutchinson in three volumes:
Richard Bolitho – Midshipman 1975
Midshipman Bolitho and the 'Avenger' 1978
Band of Brothers 2005

First published in paperback by Arrow Books in three volumes:
Richard Bolitho – Midshipman 1977
Midshipman Bolitho and the 'Avenger' 1979
Band of Brothers 2006

Arrow Books
The Random House Group Limited
20 Vauxhall Bridge Road, London, SW1V 2SA

www.randomhouse.co.uk

Addresses for companies within The Random House Group Limited can be found at:
www.randomhouse.co.uk/offices.htm

The Random House Group Limited Reg. No. 954009

A CIP catalogue record for this book is available from the British Library

ISBN 9780099504337

Typeset by SX Composing DTP, Rayleigh, Essex

Penguin Random House is committed to a sustainable future for
our business, our readers and our planet. This book is made from
Forest Stewardship Council® certified paper.

MIX
Paper from
responsible sources
FSC® C018179

Printed and bound in Great Britain by Clays Ltd, St Ives plc

Richard Bolitho – Midshipman

For John and Betty Hamilton

Contents

Contents

1

A Ship of the Line

Although only noon, the clouds which scudded busily above Portsmouth harbour made it seem closer to evening. For several days a stiff easterly wind had turned the crowded anchorage into angry criss-crossing patterns of whitecaps, and an attendant drizzle gave each buffeted ship and the stout walls of the harbour defences a glistening, metallic sheen.

On Portsmouth Point itself, solid and uncompromising, stood the Blue Posts Inn. Like inns and hostelries in every busy seaport, it had been added to and altered over the years, but still retained an appearance of a sailor's haunt. In fact, it was used more by young midshipmen than any other seafarers who came and went with the tides, and because of this it held an atmosphere all of its own. Low-beamed, noisy and not particularly clean, it had seen more than one would-be admiral pass through its scarred doors.

On this particular day in mid-October 1772, Richard Bolitho sat wedged in a corner of one of the long rooms half listening to the babble of voices around him, the clatter of plates and tankards and the hiss of rain against the small windows. The air was heavy with mixed aromas. Food and ale, tobacco and tar, and each time the street doors opened to a chorus of curses and complaints the keener tang of salt from the waiting ships.

Bolitho stretched his legs and sighed. After the long and broken coach journey from his home in Falmouth, and a large portion of rabbit pie which was one of the Blue Posts' favourite dishes for the 'young gentlemen', he was feeling drowsy. He glanced curiously at the other midshipmen nearby. Some were very young. Children, no more than twelve years old at the most. He smiled, despite his normal reserve. When he had joined his first ship as midshipman he too had been twelve. Only by thinking back to that time could he appreciate how he had altered. How the Navy had changed him. He had been exactly like one of the boys along the table from him. Frightened, awed by the noise and outward hostility of a man-of-war, yet somehow determined not to show it, and always imagining that everyone else was entirely unimpressed by his surroundings.

And that had been four years ago. It was still difficult to accept. Four years in which he had matured and moulded to the ship around him. At first he had believed he would never be able to learn all that was asked and demanded of him. The bewildering complex of rigging and shrouds. The miles of cordage of every shape and length which made a ship move and obey. Sail drill and gun drill, up aloft on dizzily swaying yards in rain and sleet, or on days when it was so hot he had almost fainted and dropped to the deck far below. He had learned to understand the unwritten laws of the world between decks, the loyalties and rules which made everyday life possible in the overcrowded turbulent existence of a King's ship. He had not only survived, he had come through it better than he had thought possible. But not without some bruises and a few tears to mark his journey.

Now, on this dismal October day, he was joining his second ship, the seventy-four-gun *Gorgon,* which lay somewhere at anchor in the Solent.

He saw a small midshipman wolfing down a huge portion of boiled pork, and smiled grimly. He would live to regret it. It would be a long and lively pull in a boat through this wind.

He thought suddenly of his home in Cornwall, the great grey-stone house below Pendennis Castle where he and his brother and two sisters had grown up together. And where for that matter the Bolitho family had been living for generations. It had been different from what he had expected, from what he had dreamed about as he had endured storm and heat alike. For one thing, only his mother and sisters had been there to greet him. His father, who commanded a ship similar to the one he was joining, had been away in Indian waters. His older brother, Hugh, was senior midshipman in a frigate in the Mediterranean. The house had seemed quiet and very still after a ship of the line.

His new appointment had been delivered on his sixteenth birthday. To proceed with all despatch to His Britannic

Majesty's Ship *Gorgon* at Spithead, which under the command of Captain Beves Conway was recommissioning for duty in the King's name.

His mother had tried to hide her dismay. His sisters had laughed and cried as the fancy took them.

When he had made his way to board the Falmouth coach he had seen the farm workers nod to him as he had passed. But no show of surprise. For many, many years Bolithos had left the grey house to join one ship or another. Some of them had never returned.

And now it was all beginning again for Richard Bolitho. He had vowed that there were mistakes he would never repeat, some lessons he would remember above all else. A midshipman was neither fish nor fowl. He stood between the lieutenants and the true backbone of any vessel, the warrant officers. At one end of the ship, aloof and unreachable like some sort of god, was the captain. Above, around and beyond the overcrowded midshipmen's berth were the ship's company. Seamen and marines, volunteers and pressed men alike, packed together between decks, yet at all times separated by status and experience. Harsh discipline was the rule rather than the exception, danger and death from working the ship in all weathers were too commonplace to mention.

When landsmen saw a King's ship working clear of the shore, her yards alive with sailors and freshly set sails, when they heard the bang of gun-salutes, the lusty voices of those at the capstan joining in a well-tried shanty, they knew nothing of that other world within the deep hull. Which was probably just as well.

'Anyone sitting here?'

Bolitho came out of his thoughts and looked up. Another midshipman, fair-haired and blue-eyed, was smiling at him.

The newcomer added, 'Martyn Dancer. I'm joining the *Gorgon*. The landlord pointed you out to me.'

Bolitho introduced himself and moved along the bench.

'Not your first ship.'

Dancer smiled sadly. 'Almost. I was in the flagship until she went into dock. My experience amounts to three months and two days.' He saw Bolitho's expression. 'I started late. My father was unwilling to let me go to sea.' He shrugged. 'But I had my way in the end.'

Bolitho liked what he saw. Dancer had certainly begun his sea career late. He was about his own age, and had the quiet, cultured voice of a good family. A town family, he decided.

Dancer was saying, 'I have heard that we are sailing for West Africa. But then . . .'

Bolitho grinned. 'It is as good a rumour as any. I heard it too. It will be better than beating back and forth with the Channel Fleet.'

Dancer grimaced. 'The Seven Years War has been over for nine years. I'd have thought the French would be at us again by now, if only to get their Canadian possessions back.'

Bolitho turned as two crippled seamen approached the landlord who was watching one of his girls ladling stew into pewter pots.

No real war for nine years. It was true enough. And yet there were still other conflicts around the world which never stopped. Uprisings and piracy, colonies fighting their new masters, they had claimed as many victims as any line of battle.

The landlord said harshly, 'Be off with you! I want no beggars here!'

One of the sailors, his right arm amputated almost to the shoulder, retorted angrily, 'I'm no bloody beggar! I was in the old *Marlborough,* seventy-four, with Rear-Admiral Rodney!'

There was complete silence in the long room, and Bolitho saw that several of the younger midshipmen were staring at the two cripples with something like horror.

The second man exclaimed anxiously, 'Leave it be, Ted! The devil will give us nothin'!'

Dancer said, 'Give them all they need.' He dropped his eyes, confused and angry. 'I will pay.'

Bolitho looked at him, sharing his concern. His shame.

'That was well said, Martyn.' He touched his sleeve impetuously. 'I am glad we are joining together.'

They both looked up as a shadow fell between them and one of the smoky lanterns.

The one-armed man was staring at them, his face very grim.

He said quietly, 'Thank you, young gentlemen.' He thrust out his hand. 'Good luck go with you. I reckon I'm seeing two captains.'

He moved away as one of the serving girls carried two steaming pots of food to a side table, adding for the room's benefit, 'Some of you take heed of this day. A lesson for you.'

The landlord thrust his large bulk towards the midshipmen as the buzz of conversation slowly returned.

'I'll take your damn money *now*!' He glared at Dancer. 'And after that . . .'

Bolitho said calmly, 'After *that,* landlord, you will bring two glasses of brandy for us.' He watched the man's mounting fury, gauging the moment as he would the fall of a nine-pound shot. 'I would mind your manners if I were you. My friend here is fortunately in good humour. But his father owns most of the land around this point.'

The landlord swallowed hard. 'But, God bless you, sir, I was only teasing! I'll bring the brandy at once. The best I have, and I trust you will allow me to pay for it.' He hurried away, his face suddenly worried.

Dancer said incredulously, 'But my father is a tea merchant in the City of London! I doubt if he has ever seen Portsmouth Point in his life!' He shook his head. 'I think I shall have to sharpen my wits if I am to keep pace with you, Richard!'

Bolitho smiled gravely. '*Dick*, if you don't mind.'

As they were sipping their brandy the street door was flung wide open. This time it did not close. Framed in the entrance was a lieutenant in a streaming tarpaulin coat, his cocked hat sodden from spray and rain.

He barked, 'All midshipmen for the *Gorgon* to muster at the sallyport at once. There is a party of men outside to take your chests to the boat.'

He strode to the fire and snatched a goblet of brandy from the landlord.

'It's blowing like hell outside.' He held his reddened hands above the blaze. 'God help us.'

As an afterthought he added, 'Who is the senior amongst you?'

Bolitho saw the anxious exchange of glances, the way that the snug contentment had given way to something like panic.

He said, 'I think I am, sir. Richard Bolitho.'

The lieutenant eyed him suspiciously. 'So be it. March 'em to the sallyport and report to the boat's cox'n. I will be along shortly.' He raised his voice. 'And when I get there, I want every mother's son of you ready to leave, see?'

The smallest midshipman said desperately, 'I think I'm going to be sick!'

Somebody laughed, but the lieutenant roared, 'You're going to be sick, *sir*! Say *sir* when you address an officer, damn you!'

The landlord's wife watched the untidy cluster of midshipmen hurrying towards the rain.

'Yew'm a bit hard on 'em, Mr Hope, sir.'

The lieutenant grinned. 'We all had to go through it, m'dear. Anyway, the captain's difficult enough as it is, what with one thing and t'other. If I'm adrift with the new midshipmen then *I'll* be in for a broadside!'

Outside on the wet cobbles Bolitho watched some seamen loading the black chests into an assortment of barrows. Burly and tanned, they looked like experienced sailors, and he guessed that the captain was taking no chances by allowing less reliable members of his company ashore in case they deserted.

In weeks, even days, he would know these men and many more. He would not fall into the old traps as in his other ship. He knew now that trust was something you had to earn, not a gift which went with the uniform.

He nodded to the senior hand. 'We will move off directly.'

The man grinned at him. 'Not the first time for you then, sir?'

Bolitho fell in step beside Dancer. 'Or the last.'

At the sallyport they found the boat's coxswain sheltering behind the wall. Beyond it the Solent heaved and broke to endless ranks of cruising wavecrests, and against the leaden sky the few gulls looked like white spindrift.

The coxswain touched his hat. 'I suggest you get 'em all aboard, sir. There's quite a tide runnin' an' the first lieutenant wants the boat to do another trip afore the dog watches.' He dropped his voice. ''Is name is Mr Verling, sir. Be warned. 'E's a mite rough on some young gennlemen. Likes 'em to try their 'ands at everythin' 'e does.' He chuckled unfeelingly. 'Gawd, look at 'em. 'E'll 'ave 'em for breakfast.'

Bolitho snapped, 'And I *you,* if you don't stop gossiping.'

Dancer stared at him as the man hurried away.

Bolitho said, 'I've met his sort before, Martyn. The next minute he'd be asking permission to go off for a quick tot of rum.' He grinned. 'I think the lieutenant back there would be displeased, never mind the formidable Mr Verling.'

The officer in question appeared by the wall, his eyes somewhat glassy.

'Into the boat! Lively there!'

Dancer said quietly, 'I think maybe my father was right!'

Bolitho waited for the others to clamber down the slippery ladder towards the pitching longboat.

'I'm not sorry to go back to sea.' And he was surprised to find that he meant it.

The journey from the sallyport to the anchored two-decker took the best part of an hour. During the trip in the madly leaping longboat the midshipmen who managed to survive being violently sick had plenty of time to study their new home as she grew larger and taller through the relentless rain.

Bolitho had made it his business to learn something about his next appointment. Seventy-fours, as these sturdy two-deckers were nicknamed, made up the bulk of the fleet. In any big sea battle they were always predominant in the line where the fighting was hardest. And yet he knew from experience, and what he had heard old sailors say, that each one was as different from the other as salt from molasses.

While the oarsmen pulled the boat over each angry crest he kept his attention on the ship, seeing the towering masts and crossed yards, the shining black and buff hull with its lines of closed gunports, the scarlet ensign at her high stern and the jack at her bows making patches of colour against the background of grey sea and sky. The oarsmen were getting tired from their hard efforts, and it took the repeated stroke from the coxswain and several threats from the red-faced lieutenant to keep them working in unison.

Around and under the long bowsprit and jib boom, beneath which the brightly gilded figurehead seemed to stare down at the silent midshipmen with something like hatred. It was a splendid if frightening example of a woodcarver's art. The *Gorgon*'s figurehead was a mass of writhing serpents, the face below set in a fierce glare, the eyes very large and edged with red paint to give an added effect of menace.

And then, panting and scrabbling, they were being pushed, hauled and bundled unceremoniously up the ship's side, so that when they arrived on the broad quarterdeck it seemed almost sheltered and calm by comparison.

Bolitho said, 'She looks smart enough, Martyn.'

He ran his eyes quickly along the neat lines of the quarterdeck nine-pounders, their black barrels gleaming in the rain, the trucks freshly painted, every piece of tackle neat and carefully stowed.

Seamen were working aloft on the yards and along the gangways on either beam which joined quarterdeck to forecastle. Beneath the gangways, at the same regular intervals, were the upper deck batteries of eighteen-pounders, while on the deck below them were the ship's main armament of powerful thirty-two-pounders. When required, *Gorgon* could and would speak with loud authority.

The lieutenant shouted, 'Over here!'

The midshipmen hurried to obey, some fearful and already lost. Others wary and careful to watch what was required of them.

'In a moment you will go to your quarters.' The lieutenant had to raise his voice above the hiss of rain, the persistent din of wind through rigging and furled sails. 'I just want to tell you that you are now appointed to one of the finest ships in His Majesty's Navy, one with high standards and no tolerance of laggards. There are twelve midshipmen all told aboard *Gorgon*, including yourselves, so the mother's boys had best work doubly hard to avoid trouble. You will be given postings to gundecks and other parts of the ship until you are able to work with the people without making a poor example to them.'

Bolitho turned as some men hurried past under the control of a tough-looking boatswain's mate. Fresh from the land by the cut of them, he thought. Taken from debtors' prisons and from the Assize Courts where but for the need of men for the fleet they would be held until transportation to the American colonies. The Navy's appetite for men was never satisfied, and with the country at peace it was even harder to supply its needs. As he watched the hurrying party of men Bolitho thought it hardly made sense of what the lieutenant had just said. Not only the midshipmen were new and untrained. Many of the ship's company were little better.

As he slitted his eyes against the rain he found time to marvel at the way a ship like this could swallow such a force of human beings. *Gorgon*, he knew, contained a company of some six hundred officers, seamen and marines in her fat, seventeen-hundred-ton hull, and yet to look along her upper deck it was hard to see more than thirty or so at any one time.

'*You!*'

Bolitho turned as the lieutenant's voice cut into his thoughts.

'I hope I am not boring you?'

Bolitho replied, 'I am sorry, sir.'

'I will be watching you.'

The lieutenant stiffened as another officer approached from the poop.

Bolitho guessed the newcomer to be the first lieutenant. Mr Verling was tall and thin, with an expression so dour that he could have been a judge about to pass sentence of death rather than offering welcome to some new officers. He had a protruding, beaked nose which thrust from beneath his cocked hat as if to seek out some new crime in his ship, and his eyes, as they wandered along the swaying line of midshipmen, were devoid of pity or warmth.

He said, 'I am the senior in this ship.' Even his tone was clipped, with all the compassion honed out of it. 'Whilst on board you will attend to your various duties at all times. You will become so involved with your training and preparation for examination as lieutenants that you will eventually put it before all else, and any sort of leisure will be seen even by you as both selfish and pointless.' He nodded to the other officer. 'Mr Hope is the fifth lieutenant and will be keeping an eye on you until you are settled in your allocated watches. Mr Turnbull, the master, will of course expect a high standard in navigational studies and the general working of the ship at sea.'

His gimlet eyes fastened on the smallest figure at the end of the line, the one who had been violently sick in the longboat, and who looked as if he was about to repeat it.

'And what is *your* name?'

'Eden, s-sir.'

'*Age?*' The word was like a knife cut.

'T-twelve, s-sir.'

Hope said, 'He has a stutter, sir.' Even his earlier belligerence had faded in the presence of his superior.

'Has he indeed. I am certain the boatswain will take care of that before he reaches thirteen years, *if* he lasts that long!'

Verling seemed to tire of the encounter. 'Dismiss them, Mr Hope. We will weigh tomorrow if the wind stays with us. There is much to do.' He strode away without another glance.

Hope said wearily, 'Mr Grenfell will take you below.'

Grenfell, it turned out, was the senior midshipman. A thickset, unsmiling young man of about seventeen, he relaxed as soon as Hope had disappeared.

He said, 'Follow me. Mr Hope is a fair man, but he is worried about his promotion.'

Bolitho smiled. In a ship of the line promotion was always difficult, especially without a war to thin the ranks. As fifth lieutenant Hope had only one officer junior to himself in the wardroom, and unless the lieutenants above him were promoted, sent into other ships or killed he was hard put to find advancement.

Dancer whispered, 'In the flagship we had a sixth lieutenant who was so desperate that he learned to play the flute merely because the admiral's wife liked it!'

They fell silent as they followed the senior midshipman down the first companion ladder to the deck below, and the deck below that. The deeper they went into the hull the more confined it seemed to become. They were surrounded by shadowy figures, faceless and unreal in the half-darkness, their heads bowed beneath deck beams and the carefully slung equipment for each tethered cannon. The smells too seemed to rise to meet them. Salt beef and tar, bilge and packed humanity, while all around them the massive hull creaked and groaned like a live thing, the deckhead lanterns spiralling and throwing shapes across the great timbers and seamen alike, as in part of a vast painting.

The midshipmen's berth was on the orlop deck. Beneath the lower gundeck, and indeed lower than the waterline itself, it had no light other than from the hatches and the swaying lanterns.

Grenfell said offhandedly, 'This is it. We share it with the senior master's mates.' He grimaced towards a white-painted screen. 'Although *they* choose to stay aloof from us.'

Bolitho looked at his companions. Without difficulty he could imagine what they were feeling. He could recall how he had endured the first hours, how he would have given anything for a friendly word when it was most needed.

He said, 'It looks fine. Better than my last ship.'

The boy called Eden asked, *'Really?'*

Grenfell smiled. 'It's what you make it.' He swung round as a diminutive figure scrambled past the screen door. 'This is your servant. His name is Starr, but he doesn't say much. Just tell him what you need and I'll arrange it with the purser.'

Starr was even younger than Eden. Probably about ten, and small for his age. He had the pinched features of a child from the slums, and his arms were so thin they were like sticks.

Bolitho asked quietly, 'Where are you from?'

The boy eyed him warily. 'Newcastle, sir. Me dad was a miner there. He was killed in a fall.' His voice was toneless, as if he was speaking of another world.

'I'll damn well kill *you* if you treat my shirts like this one!'

Bolitho turned as another midshipman, flushed from the wind and rain, strode beneath the low beams. With Grenfell he was obviously one of the ship's three midshipmen remaining from the last commission, and like Grenfell too, still awaiting the chance to sit an examination for lieutenant.

He was in ill humour, and had the sullen good looks of one bred to authority.

Grenfell said, 'Easy, Samuel. The new boys are with us.'

The other one seemed to realise he was surrounded with awkward-looking newcomers and snapped, 'I'm Samuel Marrack. Signals midshipman and captain's messenger.'

Dancer said, 'It sounds important.'

Marrack stared at him. 'It is. And when you appear before our illustrious captain it is best to do it in a clean shirt!' He lashed out at the small servant with his hat and added, 'So remember that in future, you hound!'

He threw himself on to a chest. 'Get me some wine. I'm as dry as dust.'

Bolitho sat down beside Dancer and watched the others opening and shutting their chests like blind men. He had hoped to be appointed to a frigate like his brother. Free of the fleet's heavy authority, able to cover great distances in a third of the time it would take the ponderous *Gorgon,* and with all the possibilities of adventure he had so often dreamed of.

But *Gorgon* was his new home, and he would have to make the best of her for as long as the Navy dictated. A ship of the line.

Richard Bolitho - Midshipman

with all the possibilities of adventure he had so often
dreamed of.

But Gorgon was his new home, and he would have to
make the most of her for as long as the Navy decided. A ship
of the line.

2

Outward Bound

'All hands! All hands aloft to reef tops'ls!'

Like the insistent voice in a nightmare the order was piped
and repeated along the *Gorgon*'s decks until the ship
quivered to the thud of feet as the watch below dashed to
their stations to be mustered.

Bolitho shook Dancer roughly by the shoulder until he
almost fell from his hammock.

'Come on, Martyn! We're shortening sail again!'

He waited as Dancer dragged on his shoes and coat and
then together they ran for the nearest ladder. Three, no nearly
four days it had gone on like this. From the moment the
seventy-four had weighed anchor and started her passage
down-channel towards the Atlantic it had been an endless
turmoil of resetting sails, of dragging weary bodies up the
shrouds to the vibrating yards, and all the while harried and

driven by the first lieutenant's voice from the quarterdeck. Even that had been part of the nightmare, for to make his orders heard above the roar of sea and wind Verling had had to use his speaking trumpet, making his sharp voice a ceaseless goad for the gasping midshipmen.

For the new hands it was always worse, of course. A midshipman had very little status in a King's ship. The common seaman had none at all.

Bolitho knew that to allow any break in discipline at a moment like changing a ship's tack in a heavy wind could be disastrous, but he was sickened to see unnecessary violence used on a man who was perhaps too terrified by working high above the deck to understand what was required of him.

It was no different from the last time. Not yet dawn, but there was a paler hint of grey showing itself in the low clouds, and precious little else to light a way to the shrouds. Lieutenants fretted impatiently as petty officers and master's mates checked their lists of names at the foot of each mast. The marines clumped aft to the mizzen braces, their boots skidding on wet planking, and by the quarterdeck rail the first lieutenant bobbed and pointed, waving his speaking trumpet to emphasise some point or other.

Bolitho peered aft to the big double wheel. Four helmsmen were clinging to the spokes so that he guessed there was still a big swell running to test the thrust of sails and rudder. Beside them he could see old Turnbull, the sailing master, shapeless in his heavy coat, his fists like red crabs as he gestured to his quartermaster.

Quite alone by the weather nettings was the captain. He was

wrapped in a long boatcloak, but his hair blew in the wind while he peered up at the reefed topsails, which with the jib were the only canvas they were able to carry in such a gale.

Bolitho had got no nearer than this to his captain since he had come aboard. In the distance he looked very cool and dignified, apparently untouched by the confusion of hurrying seamen and bawling petty officers.

Dancer gritted his teeth. 'God, I'm near frozen.'

Lieutenant Hope, who was responsible for the foremast, yelled, 'Take 'em aloft, Mr Bolitho! And I want the time cut by minutes before I'm satisfied!'

A whistle shrilled and it all started again. The nimble-footed topmen racing each other up the ratlines while the new hands and less confident followed behind them pursued by threats and not a few blows from the petty officers' rattans to hurry them along.

And above it all Verling's voice, distorted and inhuman through his trumpet, controlling and steering everyone.

'Another pull on the weather forebrace! Mr Tregorren, there's a man in your division who needs starting, damn your eyes, sir! Two more hands aft to the mizzen braces!' He never stopped.

Up those rough, shaking ratlines and around the futtock shrouds, hanging out and down above the hull and creaming sea below, clinging with fingers and toes to keep from falling. Then breathless on to the foretop, with men already scrambling further still to the topsail yard, swarming out on either beam like monkeys, clawing and fisting the thick, half-frozen canvas to control it, to take in another reef while each billowing section did its best to knock the men from their perches and hurl them aside. Curses and sobs, men swearing terrible oaths as fingernails were torn out by the rough heavy-weather canvas; or they fought off their more frightened companions who clung to them for support.

Bolitho gripped a backstay and watched the scene on the other masts. It was almost done, and the ship was answering to the lesser thrust in her sails. Far below, foreshortened like dwarfs, he saw the quarterdeck officers and the afterguard who were securing their halliards and braces. Still by the weather side, the captain was watching the yards. Was he worried? Bolitho wondered. He certainly did not look it.

'*Secure, Mr Hope!*' Verling could not resist adding, 'You seem to have some cripples in your division! I suggest extra sail drill in the forenoon!'

Bolitho and Dancer slid to the deck on a backstay to find Mr Hope fuming again.

'God damn it, I shall swing for that one!' Hope recovered himself and added, 'And for you too, if you don't drive the people harder!'

As Hope strode aft Bolitho said, 'His bark is worse than his bite. Come on, Martyn, let us see what young Starr has saved us for breakfast. There is no point in climbing into a hammock now. They will call the hands directly.'

They found a reedy, severe-looking man in a plain blue coat waiting in the midshipmen's berth when they hurried breathlessly into its damp security. Bolitho already knew his name was Henry Scroggs, the captain's clerk, who messed with their neighbours, the master's mates.

Scroggs snapped, 'Bolitho, is it not?' He did not wait for an answer. 'Report to the captain. Mr Marrack has injured his arm and Mr Grenfell has the morning watch.' He waited, his face impassive. 'Well, sir, jump to it, if you wish to draw breath again!'

Bolitho stared at him, recalling what Marrack had said about clean shirts, conscious of his own dishevelled appearance.

Dancer offered, 'Here, let me help you get dressed.'

The clerk snapped, 'No time. Next to Grenfell and Marrack, you are senior, Bolitho. The captain is very definite about such matters.' He swayed as the ship tilted steeply and sent the sea boiling loudly over the upper deck. 'I suggest you make a move!'

Bolitho reached for his hat and said ruefully, 'Very well.' Then ducking beneath the low deckbeams he made his way aft.

Bolitho stood breathing hard outside a white-painted screen door beneath the poop. After the crowded quarters between decks, the shadowy figures of the seamen returning from the work on the yards, it seemed very quiet. Beside the door, standing rigidly in a pool of light from a deckhead lantern, a marine sentry regarded him coldly before calling, 'Signal midshipman, *sir*!' He further emphasised the introduction by banging the butt of his musket smartly on the deck.

The door opened, and Bolitho saw the captain's servant beckoning him urgently, holding the door open just sufficiently to allow him to enter. Like a footman in a fine house who is not sure of an unwelcome visitor.

'If you would wait 'ere,' pause, 'sir.'

Bolitho waited. It was a fine lobby which opened on to the captain's dining room and which ran the whole breadth of the hull. Glass tinkled quietly in a large mahogany cabinet, while above the long polished table a circular tray of bottles and decanters swung evenly to the ship's motion. The deck was covered in canvas, well painted in black and white squares, and the nine-pounder cannon on either side of the cabin were discreetly hidden under chintz covers.

The door in a further screen opened and the servant said, 'This way, sir.' He was watching Bolitho with something like despair.

The great cabin. Bolitho stood just inside the door, his cocked hat wedged beneath one arm as he stared at the broad expanse of his captain's domain.

The cabin was splendid, and made further so by the huge stern windows which were so streaked with salt and dappled spray that in the grey dawn light they looked like those of a cathedral.

Captain Beves Conway was sitting at a large desk, leafing slowly through a sheaf of papers. A mug of something hot was steaming by his elbow, and as the lantern above the desk swung this way and that Bolitho saw that he was already dressed in a clean shirt and breeches, and his blue coat with its broad white lapels was laid carefully on a bench seat, his hat and boatcloak nearby. There was nothing about the man's face or appearance to suggest he had just returned from the deck and the bitter wind.

He looked up and studied Bolitho without expression.

The captain said, 'Name?'

'Bolitho, sir.' His voice sounded different in the broad cabin.

'Yes.'

The captain half turned as his clerk entered the cabin by another small door. In the lamplight and the angled glow from the stern windows Beves Conway had an alert, intelligent profile, but his eyes were hard and gave nothing away.

He was speaking curtly to Scroggs, his tone clipped, matter of fact, about things which Bolitho could only guess at.

He glanced to one side and saw himself for the first time in a long, gilt-framed mirror. No wonder the cabin servant had looked worried.

Richard Bolitho was tall for his years, tall and slim, with hair so black that it made his tanned features seem pale. In his seagoing coat, one which he had bought eighteen months earlier and had all but grown out of, he looked more like a vagrant than a King's officer.

He realised with a start that the captain was speaking to him.

'Well, Mr Midshipman, er, Bolitho, due to unforeseen circumstances it seems I must rely on your skills to assist my clerk until Mr Marrack is recovered from his, er, injury.' He regarded him calmly. 'What duties have you in my command?'

'Lower gundeck, sir, and with Mr Hope's division for sail drill.'

'Neither of those require that you should look like a

dandy, Mr, er, Bolitho, but in my ship I need all my officers to set a perfect example, no matter what duty they are performing. As a junior officer you will be ready for anything. In this command you *lead,* you set an example, and wherever this ship takes you, you will not only represent the Navy, *you will be the Navy*!'

'I understand, sir.' Bolitho tried again. 'We had been aloft to shorten sail, sir, and . . .'

'Yes.' The captain gave what might have been a wry smile. 'I gave that order. I had been on deck for several hours before I decided it was really necessary.' He pulled a slim gold watch from his breeches. 'Return to your berth on the orlop and put yourself to rights. I want you aft again in ten minutes.' He closed the watch with a snap. 'Precisely.'

They were the shortest ten minutes in Bolitho's memory. Helped by Starr and Midshipman Dancer, and hindered by the luckless Eden, who chose the moment to be sick again, he eventually found his way aft to confront the same sentry by the door, but to discover the great cabin already busy with visitors. Lieutenants with questions or reports on storm damage. The master, who, from what Bolitho could gather, was either for or against the possible promotion of one of his mates. Major Dewar of the ship's marines, his jowls as scarlet as his uniform, even the purser, Mr Poland, a veritable weasel of a man, appeared to be calling on the captain. And it was only dawn.

The clerk led Bolitho unceremoniously to a small desk by the streaming quarter windows. Outside, through the thick glass, he saw the dull grey sea, the long streaks of breaking foam on every crest. A cluster of gulls dipped and wheeled around the *Gorgon*'s high counter, obviously expecting something to be flung overboard by the cook. Bolitho felt his stomach contract. They would be unlucky, he thought. Between them, the cook and the miserly purser left few scraps for gulls.

He heard the captain discussing fresh water with Laidlaw, the surgeon, and something about scouring the empty casks to make them purer for a long voyage.

The surgeon was a tired-looking man with deep, hooded eyes and a permanent stoop. Too long in small ships, or too long bent over his luckless victims, Bolitho could only guess.

He was saying, 'It's a bad bit of coast there, sir.'

The captain replied tersely, 'I know that, damn it. I did not choose to take this ship and all her people to the west coast of Africa just to test your ability at curing ills!'

The clerk leaned over the little desk. He had a dank smell, like unwashed bedding.

He said dourly, 'You can begin by copying these orders for the captain. Five of each. Nice and clear, with a firm hand, or you'll be in trouble.'

Bolitho waited for Scroggs to shuffle away and then cocked his ear towards the little group around the captain. While he had been struggling into one his clean shirts and a fresh neckcloth, he had discovered that his first awe at meeting the captain had begun to shift to resentment. Conway had dismissed his reason for being improperly dressed as unimportant, even trivial. In its place he had presented his own image, that of the captain always on call, tireless, and never without a solution for anything.

But now, as he listened to Conway's calm, unhurried voice, the mention of some four thousand miles to be sailed, the most profitable courses to be used, food, fresh water, and above all the training and efficiency of the company, he could only marvel.

In this cabin, which for a few moments he had regarded as the height of luxury, the captain fought his own private battles. He could share his anxieties with nobody, could divide his responsibility not at all. Bolitho shivered. The great cabin could become a prison for any man who lost his way in doubt.

He recalled his own childhood when he had visited his father's ship on those rare and privileged occasions when she had anchored at Falmouth. How different it had been. His father's officers smiling and friendly, some almost subservient in his presence. Rather different from his later introduction as a midshipman, when lieutenants had appeared bad-tempered and intolerant.

Scroggs was at his side again.

'Take this message to the boatswain and come back immediately.' He thrust a folded piece of paper into his hand.

Bolitho picked up his hat and hurried past the big desk. He was almost through the screen door when the captain's voice halted him in his tracks.

'*What* did you say your name was?'

'Bolitho, sir.'

'Very well. Be off with you, and mark what I said.' Conway looked down at his papers and waited for the door to close.

When he glanced up again at the surgeon he said shortly, 'No better way to inform the people of what we are about than to let a new midshipman overhear.'

The surgeon regarded him gravely. 'I think I know that boy's family, sir. His grandfather was with Wolfe at Quebec.'

'Really.' Conway was already studying the next paper.

The surgeon added softly, 'He was a rear-admiral, sir.'

But Conway was elsewhere in his thoughts, his features set in a small frown.

The surgeon sighed. Captains were quite unreachable.

3

The City of Athens

South-west and then south, day in day out, with barely a pause from backbreaking work. While the *Gorgon* thrust her heavy bulk clear of the English Channel and headed down towards the notorious Bay of Biscay, Bolitho and his new companions drew closer together, as if to use their combined strength against the ship and the sea.

He had heard Turnbull, the master, say that the weather was as bad as he could recall for the time of year, and for someone who had seen some thirty winters in the Navy it was a statement to be taken seriously. Especially now that Bolitho had lost his temporary work in the great cabin. When Marrack had returned to duty after injuring his arm in the first storm, Bolitho had joined Dancer at the foremast whenever the call to make or shorten sail had been piped.

If he found a moment to consider his progress in his new

ship, which was not often, Bolitho thought more of his physical than his mental state. He was always hungry, and every muscle and bone seemed to ache from constant climbs aloft or the other demands of gun drill on the lower batteries of thirty-two-pounders. When the sea and wind moderated, and *Gorgon* headed south under almost a full set of canvas, the ship's company went to quarters to learn, exercise and sweat blood over the heavy and cumbersome tiers of guns. On the lower deck it was made doubly difficult by the lieutenant in charge.

Grenfell, the senior midshipman, had already warned Bolitho about him, and as long days ran into longer weeks, while the ship pushed her beakhead between the Madeiran Islands and the coast of Morocco, all invisible even to the masthead lookouts, the name of Mr Piers Tregorren, the fourth lieutenant and the master of *Gorgon*'s twenty-eight heaviest cannon, took on new importance.

The fourth lieutenant was a massive figure, with the swarthy skin and lank hair more suitable to a Spaniard or gypsy than a sea officer. The beams of the shadowy gundeck were so low that Tregorren had to duck and rise between them as he strode forward or aft to supervise the practice loading and running-out of each weapon. Big, belligerent and impatient, he was a hard man to serve.

Even Dancer, who was usually so busy keeping out of trouble that he saved his strength for eating and sleeping, had noticed that Tregorren seemed to have taken a dislike to Bolitho. It was strange, Bolitho thought, for Tregorren was a fellow Cornishman, and usually that was one bond which survived even the cuts and bruises of discipline.

Because of this animosity Bolitho had received three lots of extra duty, and on another occasion had been sent to the foremast crosstrees in a savage wind until ordered by the officer of the watch to descend. Harsh, unfair, it certainly was, but the punishment brought other sides of shiplife into the open. Young Eden produced a pot of honey which his mother had given him, and which he had been saving for some suitable occasion. Tom Jehan, the gunner, a really unsympathetic warrant officer, who messed beyond the screen and rarely deigned to speak with lowly midshipmen, brought a large mug of brandy from his private stock to restore some life to Bolitho's frozen body.

The endless, unrelenting training on sail and gun took other tolls, too.

Before they had even passed Gibraltar two men were lost overboard, and another died after falling from the mainyard and breaking his back on an eighteen-pounder. He was buried at a brief, but to the new men moving, ceremony, his corpse sewn in a hammock and dropped overboard weighted with roundshot, while the *Gorgon* tilted steeply to a brisk north-easterly.

Further strains showed themselves like cracks in metal. Arguments broke out amongst the seamen, some trivial, some less so. A man turned on a boatswain's mate who had ordered him aloft for the third time in a watch to splice some worn rigging and was consequently taken aft to be awarded punishment.

Bolitho had seen his first flogging at the age of twelve and a half. He had never grown used to it, but he knew what to expect. The newer and younger midshipmen did not.

First came the pipe, 'All hands lay aft to witness punishment!' Next the rigging of a grating on one of the gangways, while the marines trooped athwartships across the poop, their scarlet coats and white crossbelts very clear against the dull, overcast sky. The ship's company seemed to swell out of every hatchway and hiding place, until the decks, shrouds and even the boat tier were crammed with silently watching figures.

And then the little procession wended its way to the rigged grating. Hoggett, the boatswain, and his two mates, Beedle, the unsmiling master-at-arms, Bunn, the ship's corporal, with the prisoner and Laidlaw, the surgeon, bringing up the rear. On the quarterdeck, its pale planking dappled with droplets of spume and spray, the officers and warrant officers took their places in order of seniority and importance. By the lee side the midshipmen, all twelve of them, made two short ranks on their own.

The prisoner was stripped and then seized up on the grating, his muscled back pale against the scrubbed wood, his face hidden as he listened to the captain's austere voice as he read the relevant Articles of War before finishing with, 'Two dozen, Mr Hoggett.'

And so, between the staccato roll of a solitary marine drummer boy, who kept his eyes fixed on the mainyard above his head throughout the flogging, the punishment was carried out. The boatswain's mate who actually used the cat-o'-nine-tails was not a brutal man by nature. But he was powerfully built and had an arm like the branch of an oak. Also, he was well aware that to show leniency would probably invite his changing places with the luckless offender. After eight strokes the seaman's back was a mass of blood. After a dozen it was barely recognisable as human. And so it went on. The roll of the drum and the immediate crack of the lash across the naked back.

The youngest midshipman, Eden, fainted, and the second youngest, a pale-faced youth called Knibb, burst into tears, while the rest and not a few of the watching seamen were stiff-faced with horror.

After what seemed like an age Hoggett called hoarsely, 'Two dozen, sir!'

Bolitho made himself breathe in and out very slowly as he watched the man being cut down from the grating. His back was torn as if mauled by some beast, the skin quite black from the force and weight of the lash. At no time had he cried out, and for a moment Bolitho imagined he had died under punishment. But the surgeon looked up at the quarterdeck as he prised the leather strap from between the man's teeth and reported, 'He's fainted, sir.' Then he beckoned his assistants to carry the man below to the sick-bay. The blood was swabbed from the deck, the grating removed, and as the drummer and two other young marines with fifes struck up a lively jig the company slowly returned to normal life once again.

Bolitho glanced quickly at the captain. He was expressionless, his fingers tapping a little tattoo on his sword-hilt as if in time with the jig.

Dancer exclaimed fiercely, 'What a foul way to treat a man!'

The old sailing master overheard him and rumbled, 'Wait till you've seen a flogging round th' fleet, m'lad, then you will have something to puke on!'

And yet, when the hands went for their mid-meal of salt beef and iron-hard biscuits, washed down with a pint of coarse red wine, Bolitho heard no word of complaint or anger from anyone. It seemed that as in his last ship the rule of the lower deck was that if you got caught you were punished. The fault was being found out.

This acceptance was even showing itself in the midshipmen's berth. The first anxiety and awe at not knowing what to do, and when to do it, had given way to a new unity, a toughness which had touched even Eden.

Food and comfort were paramount, and the uncertainty of the voyage, what they were being ordered to do, took on less importance.

The small compartment which nestled against the ship's curved side had become their home, the space between the white screen door and their heavy chests an area where they ate their crude meals, shared their confidences and fears and learned from one another with each succeeding day.

Apart from the sighting of a few murky islands and two distant ships, *Gorgon* seemed to have the ocean to herself. Daily the midshipmen gathered aft for instruction in navigation under Turnbull's watchful eye. The sun and the stars took on new meaning to some of them, while to the older ones the reality of promotion to lieutenant seemed not so distant and improbable.

After a particularly bad gun drill with the thirty-two-pounders Dancer said angrily, 'That man Tregorren has the devil in him!'

Little Eden surprised all of them by saying, 'He has the g-gout, if that is the d-devil, Martyn.'

They all stared at him as he added in his thin, piping voice, 'My f-father is an apothecary in B-Bristol. He is often c-called to t-treat such cases.' He nodded firmly. 'Mr Tregorren t-takes too much b-brandy for his own g-good.'

With this new knowledge at their disposal they were able to watch the fourth lieutenant's behaviour with more interest. Tregorren would lurch beneath the low deck beams, his shadow crossing the gunports like a massive spectre, while at each great cannon the crew would wait for the order to load and run out, to train or elevate as the lieutenant ordered.

Each gun weighed three tons and had a crew of fifteen hands to control it and its opposite number on the other side of the deck. Every man had to know exactly what to do, and to keep doing it no matter what. As Tregorren had shouted on many occasions, 'I'll make you bleed a bit, but it's nothing to what an enemy will do, so *move yourselves*!'

Bolitho was sitting at the slung table in the midshipmen's berth, a candle flickering in an old oyster shell to add some light to that which filtered from a nearby companionway, and writing a letter to his mother. He had no idea when, if ever, she would read it, but it gave him comfort to retain a link with his home.

From what he had gathered from his privileged position of aiding Turnbull with the navigation lessons, and his daily scrutiny of the master's charts, he knew that the first part of their passage was almost over. Four thousand miles, the captain had said, and as he had studied the wavering lines of the charts, the daily positions fixed by shooting the sun and the usual calculations on speed and course, he knew all the old excitement of an approaching landfall. Six weeks since weighing anchor at Spithead. Changing tack and constantly reducing or making sail. The ship's track wavered over the charts like an injured beetle. A speedy frigate would have covered the distance and been on her way back to England long since, he thought bitterly.

He paused, his pen in mid-air, as he heard muffled shouts from two decks above. He doused the glim and carefully placed it in the chest, and laid the unfinished letter under his next clean shirt.

He reached the upper deck and climbed swiftly to the larboard gangway where Dancer and Grenfell were clinging to the nettings, peering towards the glittering horizon.

Bolitho asked, 'Is it land?'

'No, Dick, a ship!' Dancer grinned at him, his face tanned and alert in the bright sunshine.

It was hard to remember the rain and bitter cold, Bolitho thought. The sea was as blue as the sky, and the crisp wind lacking in bite or menace. High above the decks the topsails and topgallants shone like pale shells, while the masthead pendant licked out towards the larboard bow like a long scarlet lance.

'Deck thar!' They all peered up at the tiny black shape of the masthead lookout. 'She bain't answerin', sir!'

It was then Bolitho realised that this was no ordinary encounter. The captain was by the quarterdeck rail, arms folded, his face in shadow, and nearby Midshipman Marrack and his signalling party were watching their halliards and the bright hoist of flags at the mainyard.

What ship?

Bolitho craned over the nettings and felt the spray touching his face and lips from the wash below. Then he saw the other vessel, a black-hulled barquentine, her sails in disarray against the blinding horizon, her masts swaying steeply in the swell.

Bolitho moved further aft and heard Mr Hope, who had the watch, exclaim, 'By God, sir, if he don't answer our signal he must be up to no good, I say!'

Verling turned towards him, his beaky nose displaying his scorn.

'If he wanted, Mr Hope, he could fly with the wind and leave us far astern within the hour.'

'Aye, sir.' Hope sounded downcast.

The captain ignored both of them.

He said, 'Pass the word to the gunner, if you please. To run out a bow chaser and fire one ball as near as he can. They're either drunk or asleep over there.'

But the solitary crash of a forward nine-pounder brought nothing more than a rush of seamen from below decks in the *Gorgon* herself. The idling barquentine continued to drift, her forward sails almost aback, her big fore-and-aft canvas on main and mizzen shivering in a heat haze.

The captain snapped, 'Shorten sail and heave-to, Mr Verling! And send away the quarter boat. I am uneasy about this one.'

Calls shrilled and twittered along the maindeck, and within minutes of the captain's order *Gorgon* was going about, swinging her heavy hull round into the wind with every sail and shroud quivering and banging in confusion.

Dancer went aft to join Bolitho beneath the hammock nettings.

'D'you think –'

He stopped as Bolitho whispered, 'Keep quiet and stay here.'

Bolitho watched the boatswain mustering a boat's crew on the opposite side of the deck. With *Gorgon* hove-to and groaning into the wind Hoggett, the boatswain, was preparing the quarter boat to be hauled from astern and manhandled alongside.

The captain was speaking to Verling, his words lost in the sullen boom of flapping canvas. Then the first lieutenant turned abruptly, his nose swinging across the quarterdeck like a swivel gun.

'Pass the word! Mr Tregorren lay aft to take boarding party away!' His nose continued to move as his order was yelled forward along the maindeck. *'You two midshipmen! Arm yourselves and accompany the fourth lieutenant!'*

Bolitho touched his hat. 'Aye, aye, sir!' He nudged Dancer. 'I knew he would pick the nearest.'

Dancer grinned, the excitement bright in his eyes. 'It's good to be doing something different!'

Down by the entry port the hastily assembled oarsmen and armed seamen crowded above the blue water, their eyes outboard towards the other vessel which had drifted almost abeam and now lay about half a mile distant.

Mr Hope called, 'I can read her name, sir!' He sounded cautious after Verling's earlier sarcasm. 'She's the *City of Athens*!' He was swaying back and forth in the uncomfortable swell, a big telescope held to his eye. 'No sign of life aboard!'

Lieutenant Tregorren arrived at the entry port, his frame seeming larger and more forceful without the low-beamed gundeck to restrain it. His eyes flashed across his boarding party.

He said bluntly, 'Let no man loose off a pistol or musket by error. Be ready for anything.' His gaze settled on Bolitho and he added, 'As for you –'

He broke off as the captain's voice called from the quarterdeck rail, 'Man your boat, Mr Tregorren.' His eyes were like glass in the bright glare. 'If it's fever aboard I want no part of it. Do what you can and be lively with it.'

Bolitho watched him gravely. He did not know the captain, other than at a distance or seeing him at work with his officers. And yet he was almost certain that Captain Conway was on edge, anxious enough to speak severely to one of his lieutenants in front of the people. He flushed as the cold eyes settled on him.

'You.' The captain half lifted one hand. 'What is your name again?'

'Bolitho, sir.' It was strange that nobody ever seemed to remember a midshipman's name.

'Well, *Bolitho*, when you have quite finished your daydream, or composing a poem for your doxy, I'd be grateful if you would enter the boat!'

Several seamen lounging at the gangway chuckled, and Tregorren rasped angrily, 'If I thought you were trying to show me up!' He gave Bolitho a thrust with his palm. 'I'll deal with you later!'

Once in the quarter boat, one of *Gorgon*'s twenty-eight-foot cutters, the captain's mood, Tregorren's hostility and the discomfort of six weeks at sea were pushed from Bolitho's mind. Crowded in the sternsheets amongst the extra men and weapons, with Tregorren's great shadow swaying over the labouring oars, he turned and glanced quickly astern. How huge and invulnerable *Gorgon* appeared from a low-hulled boat. Standing above her rippling reflection, her masts and yards stark and black against the sky, she looked a symbol of sea power.

He could tell from Dancer's expression that he shared his excitement. He looked leaner than when they had met at the Blue Posts, but tougher and more confident.

Tregorren snapped, 'Give the fellow a hail!' He was standing upright in the boat, oblivious to the lively motion as it lifted and sliced over the wavecrests.

The bowman cupped his hands. *'Ship ahoy!'* His voice seemed to echo back like an acknowledgement.

Dancer whispered, 'What d'you reckon, Dick?'

Bolitho shook his head. 'Not sure.'

He watched the barquentine's masts lifting above the sweating oarsmen, the way the booms on her main and mizzen creaked and shook without purpose.

'Way 'nough!'

The oars stilled and the bowman hurled a grapnel high over the vessel's bulwark.

Tregorren snapped, 'Easy now!' He stood staring up at the bulwark, uncertain, or as if he still expected somebody to appear. Then, 'Boarders away!'

The boatswain had chosen only experienced hands, and within seconds they were all up and over the sun-dried bulwark and clustered close together beneath the batlike sails.

Tregorren said, 'Mr Dancer, take the forrard hatch!' He gestured to a boatswain's mate, the one who had carried out the flogging. 'Thorne, you make certain that the main hatch is secure.' Surprisingly, he drew a pistol from his belt and cocked it carefully. *'Mr* Bolitho, and you two, will come aft to the poop with me.'

Bolitho glanced at his friend who gave a quick shrug before taking his own men to the forward hatch. Nobody was smiling now. It was like a phantom ship, deserted and neglected, her crew spirited away. He looked towards the *Gorgon* but even she seemed further away, her protection less certain.

Tregorren said harshly, 'This bloody ship stinks!' He stood above a companionway, his head on one side as he peered down into darkness. 'Anyone below?'

But there was no sound other than sea noises and the dismal creak of the unattended wheel.

Tregorren looked at Bolitho. 'Down you go.' He seized his wrist and added fiercely, 'Well, attend to your pistol, damn you!'

Bolitho drew the heavy weapon from his belt and stared at it.

The lieutenant said, 'And don't turn your back as you go down the ladder!'

Bolitho slid over the coaming and paused to allow his eyes to become used to the gloom between decks. Once below the poop he heard other shipboard sounds, and he had to tell himself they were quite normal. The sluice of water against the hull, the creak and clatter of loose gear. He could smell candle-grease and damp air, the more rancid stenches of bilge and stale food.

He heard a man yell from above, 'Nothing forrard, sir!' and relaxed very slightly. On the planks above, muffled but recognisable, Tregorren was moving this way and that, probably wondering what to do next. But he remembered Tregorren's haste to send him below first and without aid. If he was concerned about this strange, deserted vessel he was certainly indifferent to his midshipman's safety.

He pushed open a small cabin door and stooped to enter. It was so low beneath the deck beams that he had to shuffle in the darkness like a hunchback, his hands groping to stop the ship from throwing him off balance.

His fingers touched a lantern before his face. It was ice-cold.

At that moment a tiny hatch was flung open overhead and a previously concealed skylight wrenched aside. Framed in the blinding glare, Tregorren's massive head peered down at him.

'What the hell are you doing, *Mr* Bolitho?'

He fell silent, and when Bolitho turned to follow his stare he saw why.

Sprawled in one corner of the cabin was a man, or all there was left of him.

He had received a terrible head wound from cutlass or axe and had taken several more thrusts in chest and side. In the shaft of sunlight his gaze seemed to be slitted against the brightness, his eyes terrified as they fixed on Bolitho.

Tregorren said at length, 'God Almighty!' Then as Bolitho remained stockstill beside the corpse he added roughly, 'On deck with you!'

In the bright sunlight again Bolitho found that his hands were shaking badly, although when he looked at them they seemed as before.

Tregorren ordered, 'Put a hand on the wheel, Thorne. Mr Dancer, take your men to the main hold and search it. The rest of you begin to take in these damned sails!'

He turned as Dancer called, *'Gorgon'*s under way again, sir.'

'Yes.' The lieutenant was frowning with the effort of thinking. 'She'll be dropping down within hailing distance. By that time I want some answers.'

It was like putting together parts of a torn and dismembered book. Dancer's search of the barquentine's main hold revealed that she had been carrying spirits, mostly rum, but the hold, apart from a few broken and upended casks, was empty. By the starboard rail on the poop, and again on the compass box, they found dried blood and the burn marks from discharged pistols.

The solitary corpse in the cabin must have been the vessel's master, running below to arm himself, to save some valuables or merely to hide. It was not clear. What was certain was that he had been brutally murdered.

Bolitho heard Tregorren say to the boatswain's mate, 'Must've been a mutiny and the devils made off after killing the loyal seamen.'

But both of the barquentine's boats were still hoisted inboard and secured.

Then, when *Gorgon*'s great pyramid of sails was running slowly across the vessel's quarter, Heather, one of Dancer's party, discovered something else. Just aft of the main hold a ball had smashed into the timbers, and when the hull dipped across a deep trough it was possible to see where it had struck the outside of the ship. By leaning out from the shrouds Bolitho saw it shining from its jagged socket like a malevolent black eye.

Tregorren said heavily, 'Must have been a pirate of some sort. Put a shot into her when she failed to heave-to and then boarded her.' He ticked off the points on his spatulate fingers. 'Then butchered the hands and pitched 'em overboard. There are sharks a plenty hereabouts. Then they swayed out the cargo to their own ship and cast off.'

He looked round irritably as Dancer asked, 'But why not seize the ship too, sir?'

'I was coming to that,' he replied angrily. But he did not

explain further. Instead, he cupped his hands and began to bellow some of his news towards the *Gorgon*.

Across the narrowing stretch of water Bolitho heard Verling's voice through his speaking trumpet.

'Continue the search and remain under our lee.'

That was probably to give the captain time to examine his own logs and documents about local shipping. The *City of Athens* was obviously not a new vessel, and was probably familiar on the rum trade from the West Indies.

Bolitho shivered, imagining himself alone and suddenly faced with a rush of savage, stabbing boarders.

Tregorren said shortly, 'Down aft again.' He strode to the companion with Bolitho at his heels.

Even though he knew what he would see it was still a shock. Bolitho tried not to look at the dead man's face as Tregorren, after a brief hesitation, began to search his pockets. The *City of Athens*' log and charts had vanished, probably overboard, but in a corner of the littered cabin, almost hidden under a bunk, Tregorren found a canvas envelope. It was empty, but had the vessel's agent's name in Martinique clearly printed on it. It was better than nothing.

The lieutenant righted an upended chair and sat on it heavily, his head still almost brushing the deck beams. He remained in the same position for several minutes, staring at the corpse, his face dark with concentration.

Bolitho said, 'I believe there was a *third* vessel, sir. That the attackers or pirates saw *her* sail and decided to make a run for it, knowing that this one would attract first attention.'

For an instant he thought Tregorren had not heard.

Then the lieutenant said softly, 'When I require aid from you, Mr Bolitho, I will ask for it.' He looked up, his eyes in shadow. 'You may be a post-captain's son, and the grandson of a flag officer, but to me you are a *midshipman*, less than nothing in my book!'

'I – I'm sorry.' Bolitho felt himself tense with anger. 'I meant no offence.'

'Oh yes, I know your family.' Tregorren's chest was lifting with exertion and suppressed fury. 'I've seen the fine house, the tablets on the church wall! Well, *I* had no safe background to help me, and by God I'll see you get no favours in my ship, *understood*?' He swung away, controlling his voice with obvious effort. 'Now tell someone to cast down a line and haul that corpse on deck. Then have 'em clean up the cabin, it stinks like a gallow's-tip down here!'

He touched the leg of his chair. There was dried blood on it, black in the filtered sunlight.

Almost to himself he muttered, 'Probably yesterday. Otherwise the rats would have found their way in here.'

He jammed on his salt-stained hat and ducked out of the cabin.

Later, while Bolitho and Dancer waited by the bulwark and watched the lieutenant being pulled across to *Gorgon*'s side to make his report, Bolitho told his friend something of what had happened between them.

Dancer eyed him sadly. 'I'll wager he intends to put your ideas to the captain, Dick. It would be just like him.'

Bolitho touched his arm, recalling Tregorren's last words before he had dropped into the boat.

'Keep steerage way until told what to do, and send a good lookout aloft.' He had pointed at the corpse by the wheel. 'And throw *that* overboard. It's how some of you'll end up, I shouldn't wonder.'

Bolitho looked now at the empty space where the unknown man had lain. *Callous and senseless.*

He said, 'I've a few more ideas yet.' He smiled, trying to forget his anger. 'At least I know why he dislikes *me*.'

Dancer followed his mood. 'Remember that poor cripple in the Blue Posts, Dick?' He gestured around the deck and at the handful of seamen. 'He said we would both be captains, and, by God, we have a ship of our own already!'

4

'Clear for Action!'

The *Gorgon*'s wardroom, situated directly below the captain's great cabin, and which was approximately the same size, was packed with figures from bulkhead to stern windows. It was lined with small, white-painted cabins and used as a home and dining-space by the lieutenants, the master, the marine officers and Laidlaw, the surgeon.

But in the pink glow of sunset through the stern windows and beneath several spiralling lanterns, the wardroom was filled with almost everyone above the rank of petty officer, except those needed to work the ship.

Bolitho and Dancer found themselves a space on the larboard side by an open window and looked round hopefully for some refreshments. But if the wardroom was required to donate its space for a conference it was not apparently inclined to make its guests welcome.

For most of the day, while *Gorgon* and her small consort had ghosted along under reduced canvas, Bolitho and Dancer had fretted and speculated about what was going to happen, and what their part would be. A boat had eventually been sent for them to rejoin *Gorgon,* the boatswain's mate, Thorne, saying with as much sarcasm as he dared, 'I *think* I can manage to take charge till you young gennlemen get back, sir.' He had served ten years with the fleet.

Now, as they waited with the other midshipmen, ignored by the lieutenants and marine officers, Bolitho and his friend watched the screen door by the trunk of the mizzenmast which pinioned the ship from poop to keel. It was like being in a theatre waiting for the principal actor to appear, or for an Assize judge to take his place and begin a trial.

Bolitho glanced around the wardroom, not for the first time. Different again from the spacious cabin overhead, it was nevertheless a palace after the midshipmen's berth and gunroom. Even the little cabin doors which left the occupants barely more room than a cupboard suggested privacy and something personal. A table and some good chairs were scattered amongst the standing figures and not jammed together against the curved and often dripping side of the orlop.

He turned and leaned over the sill, seeing the froth from the rudder very pink in the sunset, the million dancing mirrors which streamed down from the horizon. It was hard to think of murder and danger, a man being hacked to death in the trim barquentine which sailed under *Gorgon*'s lee.

Another two years and he would share a wardroom like this, Bolitho thought. One more step up the ladder.

He heard feet shuffling around him and Dancer's quick, 'Here they come!'

Verling entered first, holding the screen door aside so that Captain Beves Conway could move aft without taking his hands from behind his back.

When he reached the table Conway said, 'They may sit down if they wish.'

Bolitho watched him, fascinated. Hemmed in by his lieutenants, the warrant officers and midshipmen, he still managed to appear quite removed from all of them. He was wearing a well-pressed blue coat, its white lapels and gilt buttons as fresh as from any London tailor. Breeches and stockings equally clean and neat, and his hair was tied to the nape of his neck with a fresh twist of ribbon. Most of the midshipmen saved their ribbons for special occasions. Bolitho, for instance, had his long black hair tied above his collar with a piece of codline.

Verling said briefly, 'Pay attention. The captain wishes to address you.'

The wardroom seemed to be holding its breath, so that the sigh of sea and wind, the irregular creak of the rudder-head beneath the stern windows intruded forcefully, and Bolitho marvelled at the fact that they had sailed all four thousand miles without any real knowledge of why they were doing it.

The captain said quietly, 'I have brought you all here together to save time. You will return to your messes or your divisions when I have finished and tell the people what we are about, in your own way. Far better than a fine speech from the quarterdeck, I think.' He cleared his throat and looked at their expectant faces. 'My orders were to bring this ship to the west coast of Africa and carry out a patrol, and if necessary land seamen and marines to further those orders. In the last few years there has been a growing menace of piracy along these shores, and many fine ships have been fired on or have disappeared.'

He was speaking without emotion or excitement, and Bolitho wondered how such outward calm was possible. All these miles, with many more yet to sail, with the health and management of a raw company to deal with, the uncertainties of what he might find at the end of each voyage. It could not be so easy to command as he had imagined.

Conway added, 'Information came to the Admiralty some months ago that some of these pirates had made their base on the coast of Senegal.' For a moment his eyes settled on the untidy cluster of midshipmen. 'Which now lies less than thirty miles to lee'rd, Mr Turnbull assures me.'

The ruddy-faced sailing master smiled grimly and nodded. 'Near as dammit, sir.'

'So be it.' The brief touch of humour had gone. 'It is my duty to discover this hiding place, and my intention is then to destroy it and punish all responsible for these crimes.'

Bolitho shivered, despite the oppressive heat in the wardroom, remembering the withered corpses of some captured pirates dangling in irons outside his own town of Falmouth.

The captain said wryly, 'Naturally their lordships, in all their wisdom, chose a seventy-four for the task.'

The master and several of the older men nodded and grinned as he continued, 'A ship too deep-hulled to work close inshore and too slow to catch a pirate vessel on the high seas! However, we do now have the barquentine, which Mr Tregorren has now put into fair shape for use in the King's name.'

Several heads turned to peer at the massive lieutenant as Conway added, 'He has informed me of his observations concerning the vessel's fate, and has suggested that the attackers may have been frightened off by the appearance of another ship. As it was likely this happened yesterday, it may have been *our* topgallants which the pirates saw. If it was near this time, and allowing for wind and current, the *City of Athens* may well have been cloaked in dusk while we still held the sunset as we do now.'

He shrugged, as if tired of speculation. 'Be that as it may, they robbed a peaceful merchantman and no doubt threw the crew to the sharks, or so terrified the survivors that they will hang with their captors when we take them, as take them we must!'

Verling took the hint and asked, 'Questions?'

Dewar, the major of marines, asked bluntly, 'What sort of opposition may we expect, sir?'

The captain eyed him for several seconds. 'There is a small island off the coast which was first discovered about four hundred years ago and which has been occupied by the Dutch, the French, even ourselves for most of the time. It is well sited for defence from the shore. About a mile or so out in shark-infested waters –' He paused, his eyes impatient. *'Well?'*

58

Hope, the fifth lieutenant, asked lamely, 'Why from the shore, sir?'

Surprisingly, Captain Conway offered a small smile. 'A good question, Mr Hope, I am glad someone was paying attention.' He ignored Hope's flush of pleasure and Tregorren's scowl. 'The reason is simple. The island has always been used for gathering slaves for sale and shipment to the Americas.' He sensed the sudden uneasiness amongst his officers and snapped, 'It is a foul trade but not illegal. The slavers assemble their victims for the captivery, and any who do not measure up to the traders' needs are disposed of to the sharks. This "convenience" also prevents friends or relations from saving the wretches from a living hell elsewhere.'

Major Dewar eyed his marine lieutenant and muttered fiercely, 'By God, we'll show 'em, eh? I don't care a fig about slavery one way or t'other, but any pirate is vermin as far as I'm concerned.'

Dancer said softly, 'My father has often said that slavery and piracy go hand in hand. The one section preys on the other, or they work together against authority when it suits them.'

Little Eden murmured excitedly, 'Wait t-till they see the *Gorgon* c-coming for them, eh?' He rubbed his hands. 'J-just you w-wait!'

Verling barked, 'Silence there!'

The captain glanced around the wardroom. 'We will lie-to and then close the land tomorrow. It is a dangerous coastline, and I have no desire to leave the keel on some reef or other.

Our new consort will lead the approach, and landing parties will be detailed at first light.' He moved towards the door. 'Carry on, Mr Verling.'

The first lieutenant waited for the door to shut and said, 'Return to your messes.' He sought out a master's mate. 'Mr Ivey, you are to take charge of the *City of Athens* for the night. I suggest you call away a boat immediately.'

Dancer sighed. 'Tregorren steals your ideas, Dick, and now they've taken our first command.' He grinned. 'But I think I feel a mite safer in this fat old lady!'

Eden grinned. 'I can s-smell f-food!' He hurried from the wardroom, his feet guided by his stomach.

'We may as well go too, Dick.'

They both turned as Tregorren's voice followed them to the gundeck. 'Belay that! I've work for you two. Get aloft to the fore-t'ga'n's'l yard and examine the splicing those lazy devils were supposed to be doing there while we were aboard the prize.' He regarded them calmly. 'Not too dark for you, is it? Or too *dangerous* mebbee?'

Dancer opened his mouth to answer but Bolitho said, 'Aye, aye, sir.'

The lieutenant called after them, 'No skimping now!'

On the darkening gangway by the weather shrouds Bolitho said quietly, 'I wonder if I'm always to be cursed by a fear of heights?'

They stood looking up at the black criss-cross of rigging, the braced foretopsail yard, and the one above it, deep pink in the dying light which had already gone from the decks below.

Dancer said, 'I'll go, Dick. He'll never know.'

Bolitho smiled grimly. '*He'll* know, Martyn. It would be just what he wanted.' He removed his coat and hat and wedged them under a rack of boarding pikes. 'Let's be about it then. At least it will give us an appetite!'

Aft by the big double wheel the helmsmen watched the flickering compass light and eased the spokes very slightly, their bare feet planted on the deck as if they were part of it.

The officer of the watch moved restlessly along the weather side, glancing occasionally to the opposite beam where the barquentine's solitary lantern made a small glow on the sea's face.

From beneath the poop Captain Conway strode past the wheel, his hands behind him, his body angled to the deck.

The senior helmsman nudged his mate and called, 'Steady as she goes, sir! Sou'-east by south!'

The captain nodded and waited for the lieutenant on watch to hurry discreetly to the lee side and leave him the privacy he needed for his nightly walk.

Up and down the weather side, his shoes tapping on the smooth planking. Once he paused to glance through the mainmast rigging to two shadowy figures high up on the foretopgallant yard, like birds on a perch.

But he soon forgot them as he continued pacing and thinking of tomorrow.

On this particular morning all hands were called early from their hammocks to an even hastier meal of oatmeal gruel and toasted ship's biscuit, washed down with a tankard of ale.

As one elderly seaman commented gloomily, 'To get such a good fill-up this early means the cap'n's expectin' trouble!'

Then, as the first hint of dawn showed itself in the eastern sky, and the cooks doused the galley fires, the pipe came from aft, *'Hands to quarters! Hands to quarters and clear for action!'*

Urged on by the frenzied tattoo of the drummer boys as they beat to quarters from the poop, by the additional shouts and threats from warrant officers and senior hands alike, *Gorgon*'s company went into one more drill, one which they had practised and practised until their limbs had ached through sleet and boiling sun alike until they knew where every man, each piece of equipment, every line and halliard should be when the ship was called to action.

Some of the seasoned men took greater care this time, perhaps they expected that today's drill meant more than it showed. Others, and the very young like Eden, went to their stations like excited children, unquenched even by curses from exasperated lieutenants and threats from their companions.

Down on the lower gundeck Bolitho felt his own heart beating faster than usual. In the near-darkness of the low-beamed deck he could see seamen ducking and clambering around each great thirty-two-pounder, heard their bare feet grating on the sand which some ship's boys had sprinkled liberally around the decks to stop them slipping or falling during the drill.

Some light filtered down from the companion on the

upper deck, and he was able to see the gun crews checking their gear and casting off the breechings to check the training tackles and test their handspikes.

High overhead they could hear the muffled squeal of blocks as nets were rigged above the deck and its guns to protect the men underneath from falling spars and broken rigging. How many times had they done it over the four thousand miles?

He felt men hurrying past, guided by the boatswain's thick voice. Screens were still being torn down, chests, tables and unwanted clutter being taken below to the orlop.

Tregorren's voice boomed in the gloom, 'Lively, you scum! It's taken far too long already!'

On the lower gundeck, apart from the mass of seamen needed to work the double battery of thirty-two-pounders, were two lieutenants, Tregorren being in charge, and Mr Wellesley, the ship's junior lieutenant, his assistant, and four midshipmen. The latter were evenly placed along the various divisions of guns, and were supposed to relay orders, fire independently if need be, and carry messages to the quarter-deck. Bolitho and Dancer shared the larboard side, and a sulky youth named Pearce and little Eden had the starboard battery.

Halfway along the deck Tregorren stood with his back to the mainmast trunk, arms folded, his head bent down to peer along his domain. Nearby a marine sentry stood by the companion ladder, as did others at every hatch, so that in the event of battle he could prevent the less brave from running below to hide.

Wellesley, the sixth lieutenant, hurried down the larboard side, his sword flapping against his thigh as he paused by each gun captain just long enough to hear the man snap, 'Ready, sir!'

At last it was all still, and only the gentle heave of the deck, the regular creak of tackles as the guns tugged or nudged to the ship's roll broke the silence.

Bolitho could smell the tension, the men around him, the hull deeper still under his feet. He tried not to think of the midshipmen's berth on the orlop, the after cockpit as it was called, which too had been transformed. There now would be the surgeon and his assistants. Lanterns lit, instruments gleaming in the open cases. Just as they had done it to Captain Conway's orders on countless occasions.

Tregorren yelled, 'Mr Wellesley! What kept you?'

The sixth lieutenant scuttled towards him and almost went sprawling across a ring-bolt.

He gasped, 'Lower battery cleared for action, sir!'

On the deck above they heard a whistle and someone calling, 'Cleared for action, sir!'

Tregorren swore savagely. 'Beaten us again, damn them!' He added harshly, 'Mr Eden! Pass the word, at the double!'

Eden returned, his breath wheezing as he reported, 'The first lieutenant's compliments, sir, and the ship cleared for action in twelve minutes.' He hesitated. 'But –'

'*But what?*'

The boy gulped. 'It took us longer than anyone else, sir.'

More orders were being piped, the calls of the boatswain's mates shrilling like birds on a Norfolk fen.

'Open ports!'

Bolitho leaned forward to restrain one of the gun crews. It was stiflingly hot between decks, but he knew that every port should open as one, here and on the deck above. As the port lids were hoisted upward he felt the cooler air fanning around him, saw the men nearest him take on personality and meaning, their bodies stripped to the waist and shining faintly in the strange dawn light. He glanced aft and saw Dancer give him a quick wave.

During the morning watch *Gorgon* had altered course slightly and was now steering east-south-east, the wind having shifted to the north and held there. The hull tilted and felt steady, and with the wind coming across the larboard quarter, Bolitho's section of guns was pointing high and free from spray. He saw the lively whitecaps, some strange fish leaping like birds along the ship's wash and keeping level with their slow approach. By leaning out and around a gun muzzle he saw a darker shape on the water and guessed it to be the *City of Athens*. He tried to guess what was happening on deck. The prize vessel was obviously leaving her station downwind of her protector and was beating across their line of advance to place herself between *Gorgon* and the land, wherever that was.

A young seaman asked, 'Can you see the land, sir?' He was a good-looking youth who had come from Devon to join the ship. During the night watches and the sweating drill at this same gun he had explained that all his family had worked for their local squire. A hard man, and one taken with abusing the daughters of his tenant farmers and labourers.

That was all he had confided, but Bolitho guessed it likely that he had given the squire a beating and then run to join a ship, any ship, to escape punishment.

Bolitho replied, 'Very near, I'd say, Fairweather. I can see some sea-birds now. Coming out to take a look at us, I shouldn't wonder.'

'Silence on the gundeck!' Tregorren's anger seemed to spread itself to officers and seamen alike.

Someone gave a yelp of pain as a gun captain used a rope's end, and from right aft Wellesley's rather ineffectual voice called, 'Take that man's name, I say!'

Nobody knew what man, or to whom the order was directed, and Bolitho guessed that the lieutenant was merely trying to avoid Tregorren's tongue.

It was strange how cut off from the rest of the ship it felt. More light was painting the sea in black and yellow patterns, but the horizon and sky were still as one. The square gunport cut in the ship's massive oak side was like a picture, Bolitho thought, but as the light strengthened and spilled down the long barrel of the thirty-two-pounder they all seemed to become part of it. Colour stood out now inside the gundeck. The dark red paint which was used on the ship's side, and much of the deck beneath them, showed itself for the first time. It was there to disguise the blood of dead and wounded men, everyone knew that. Bolitho glanced down the sloping deck to the opposite side. Those open gunports were still in darkness, broken here and there by some leaping feathers of spray or a crest breaking close to the hull.

He looked towards Tregorren who was speaking quietly with Jehan, the gunner, silent in his felt slippers which he always wore to prevent striking sparks when he was working in his beloved magazine. He vanished down the nearest ladder by the marine sentry, and Bolitho wondered if Dancer was thinking of the fact that the most dangerous mass of gunpowder in time of action was directly beneath his feet.

There was something like a sigh as the first sheen of sunlight filtered across the water and through each open port.

Bolitho leaned on the gun's breech and watched it transform the horizon into something real and solid. The land.

Fairweather asked excitedly, 'Be that Africa?'

The gun captain showed his uneven teeth. 'Don't matter to you where it be, lad. Just attend to old Freda 'ere and keep 'er fed, no matter what! That's all you need to know!'

A midshipman pattered down from the next deck and sought out Tregorren.

'Mr Verling's compliments, sir.' It was a midshipman named Knibb, a boy as small and as young as Eden, but for a month's difference. 'And we will not be loading just yet.'

Tregorren snapped, 'What's happening then?'

Knibb blinked around him, seeking out his friends. 'The masthead has reported sighting two vessels at anchor around the point, sir.'

His confidence was growing, aided by the knowledge that every shadowy figure was listening to him, trying to discover what was going on in that other world above.

'Our captain has ordered the barquentine to make more sail and investigate, sir.'

The gun captain beside Bolitho was explaining to his crew. 'I know these 'ere waters, lads. Reefs an' shoals everywhere. Our cap'n'll 'ave two good leadsmen in the chains b'now, takin' regular soundins. *Feelin'* our way inshore.'

Bolitho did not hear them. He was thinking of the deserted barquentine, the dead man in her cabin. He wondered if Tregorren's obvious ill humour was because he had not been given command of the *City of Athens*.

The third lieutenant, Tregorren's immediate superior, had been sent instead, and was assisted by Grenfell, the senior midshipman. If all went well, this little piece of extra responsibility would see the midshipman well on his way to promotion. Bolitho was glad for him, if envious of his freedom. Grenfell had done all he could to make him, and the awkward newcomers in his midst, welcome. It was not unusual for midshipmen in Grenfell's place to act like little tyrants.

Two ships at anchor, Knibb had said. Pirates or slavers? Both would get a shock when *Gorgon* made her entrance.

Feet tramped dully overhead and Bolitho heard the squeak of blocks as once again the yards were trimmed, the sails reset while the ship altered course.

He moved inboard and rested his hands on the great capstan which was used for hoisting heavy spars or boats to their allotted positions and listened to Tregorren's harsh voice as he spoke to Wellesley and Midshipman Pearce.

Beyond them the open ports were more sharply defined,

and for a moment Bolitho thought that the light was playing tricks on him. The land was probing out to greet them, which was impossible, for he could see it on his own side. He recalled suddenly what the captain had said about an island. This must be it, with the ship steering into a great arrowhead of water between it and the mainland. The anchored ships must be right ahead and invisible to both gundecks.

Tregorren was saying, 'Look, there's a fort of sorts on the island. Must be as old as bloody Moses.' He chuckled. 'Wait till you cast your eyes on some of these black lasses. They're beautiful, like –' He got no further.

Bolitho had seen what looked like a dolphin skipping across the lively inshore current, and then he heard the far-off boom of an explosion. The line of breaking crests vanished, and there was a chorus of shouts and curses as a great ball slammed down hard alongside the hull.

The old gun captain shouted with disbelief, 'The devils 'ave fired on *us*, be God!'

The whole ship came alive to confused orders and the blare of a marine's trumpet. Tackles squeaked and gun trucks began to move overhead, and then came the cry, 'All guns load and prepare to run out! Starboard battery will engage first!'

Tregorren stared at the messenger's breeches, very white on the companion ladder, apparently unable to believe what he had heard.

Then with a grunt he bellowed, *'All load!* Stand by on the starboard battery!'

The seaman called Fairweather followed Bolitho to the

opposite side as with sudden haste the bare-backed figures began to ram home their bulky cartridges and wads, while each gun captain selected a ball from the garlands, feeling it, testing its shape and even finish before allowing it to be rammed and wadded into his waiting gun.

Hand by hand shot up, and every eye was on the burly lieutenant.

'All loaded, sir!'

'*Run out!*'

They threw themselves on to the tackles and hauled the lumbering guns to the open ports, each truck squealing and protesting like a hog going to market. The guns remained in deep shadow along the starboard side, but the ancient fortress, as it showed itself to each breathless crew, was clear to see. Its rough walls were like gold in the frail light, its shape merging with the rocks which supported it.

Above the ramparts Bolitho saw several dark smudges which he took for an instant to be hovering clouds of mosquitoes.

He heard a seaman mutter between his teeth, 'Them devils is heatin' shot, sir! They got furnaces goin' right the way along!'

Tregorren snarled, 'I'll flog the next man to speak!' But he sounded anxious.

As well he might, Bolitho thought. His father had told him often enough what heated shot could do to a tinder-dry hull with all its top-hamper of tarred rigging and canvas.

A voice yelled, 'Stand by to starboard! Maximum elevation and fire on the uproll!'

A petty officer jabbed a seaman on the shoulder so that he jumped as if he had been shot.

'Wind yer neckcloth round yer ears, man, less you want to be deaf all yer life!'

He winked at Bolitho. The warning had probably been for his benefit, but even midshipmen were allowed some respect.

'Stand by!'

The ship tilted to wind and rudder, and by each gun its captain was crouching inboard, his eye along every black muzzle towards the sky and the fortress.

'Fire!'

5

Change of Fortune

With the order to open fire being yelled from deck to deck, each gun captain thrust his slow-match to the vent and jumped aside. A split second, and yet to Bolitho, who stood between a pair of thirty-two-pounders, it seemed like an age. A long-drawn-out moment when everything was crystal-clear and unmoving, as in a painting. The bare-backed seamen crouching at tackles or holding handspikes. Individual gun captains, grim-faced and concentrating only on their own ports and aim. And through each square port the sunlight on the fortress, the sky very pale without even a puff of cloud.

And then everything changed. The lower gundeck exploded to the thunder of cannon fire, the hull and timbers bucking as if caught beneath an avalanche. Gun by gun crashed inboard on its tackles, its crew running to sponge out, to ram home a charge and another gleaming ball.

Taken by the wind, the dense clouds of smoke drifted away from the hull, shutting out the fortress, masking the sky in brown fog.

Tregorren was yelling, 'Stop your vents! Sponge out! Load!'

But his voice seemed to be coming through a curtain, the first broadside having rendered eardrums and minds almost senseless.

But the effect of firing the starboard battery was plain to see. The first nervousness was gone, instead there was a sort of wildness as gun crews peered at each other, grinned and gestured like children. It was not just another drill, it was real, and they were firing in earnest.

'Run out!'

Once more the trucks squeaked on the deck, the crews hurling themselves on their tackles to be first through the open ports.

Bolitho heard Wellesley say excitedly, 'They'll pipe another tune now, by heaven!'

Tregorren rasped, 'Whoever *they* may be, dammit!'

In the pause, as each crew peered along the angled muzzles, Bolitho heard the clatter of movement from the deck above. *Gorgon* must make a brave sight if there was anyone to care, he thought. Under shortened sail, no doubt, her guns bared to the early sunlight, she must be heading close inshore. He did not even know who had fired on the ship, or why, and he was surprised to discover that it did not seem to matter. In these brief minutes the men around him, the ship around all of them, had become one.

'Stand by! As you bear!' The suspense was breath-stopping. *'Fire!'*

Again the hull shook like a mad thing, the planking jarring under the feet as the guns crashed inboard, their smoke belching like a curtain beyond the ports.

Eden was cheering, despite several angry glances from Tregorren, and some of the seamen were actually laughing.

Dancer called, 'I hope they can see what we are about on the quarterdeck! We could be shooting at the sky!'

He winced as something jarred against the hull, followed immediately by a chorus of shouts from overhead.

Bolitho nodded towards him. It was a direct hit. They, whoever they were, had struck back.

Somewhere a pump began to clatter, and he guessed that a heated ball must have penetrated the timbers and water was needed to quench it before the wood took light.

A seaman near him gestured towards the deckhead. 'Give they lazy dogs summat to do, eh?'

But nobody laughed, and Bolitho saw Wellesley rubbing his chin in quick nervous movements as if he was unable to believe that someone should dare to fire at a King's ship.

'All loaded, sir!'

A messenger appeared on the companion ladder, his voice shrill. 'We are going about, sir! Prepare to engage with the larboard side!' He vanished.

Fairweather peered at Bolitho, his teeth white in the eddying smoke. 'We'm hitting 'em proper, eh, sir? Giving t'other guns a chance!'

The gun captain darted a quick glance at the breechings

and snapped. 'They've got us beat. We're runnin' away, you soft fool!'

Bolitho saw the amazement on Fairweather's face and felt the gun captain's blunt words moving to the other men nearby.

Tregorren strode past, his head dipping between the massive beams.

'Stand to your guns! Prepare to run out!' He paused and glared at Bolitho. 'What th' hell are you staring at?'

'We're coming about, sir.' He kept his voice steady, aware that there was more gunfire from the far distance. Whoever commanded the fortress had plenty of artillery.

'What a *masterly* appraisal, Mr Bolitho!' Tregorren gripped a deckhead beam as *Gorgon* began to tilt steeply, the sea lifting towards the open ports as she swung heavily into the wind. 'Was the din of battle too much for you?'

'No, sir.' He met his hostility and added, 'I think we may have been too close inshore. That fortress has our exact range.'

Men, who seconds earlier had been hurrying to the opposite side, paused to watch. The towering bulk of the lieutenant and the slim midshipman, angled to the deck, their arms at their sides like antagonists meeting for a duel.

Wellesley said nervously, 'The captain knows best.'

Tregorren stared at him. 'Do you *have* to explain to a midshipman?' He looked from one to the other. 'Now stand to your guns!'

But the order to fire the larboard was not given. Instead there was a long and uncertain silence, broken only by the occasional movement of seamen on the upper deck, the twitter of calls as the hands went to braces and halliards for altering course.

The gun captain near Bolitho said darkly, 'Told you. Cap'n's standin' out to sea. Just as well, if you asks me.'

During the long and tiring gun drills Bolitho had never found time to consider how cut off this deck could become. Now, as seamen and their officers stood or lounged beside the ports, he felt a growing sense of apprehension and uncertainty. He could tell from the slant of the sun that the ship was heading away from the land, but apart from that there was nothing to break the frustrating sense of being quite apart from the world above.

'Secure guns!' The messenger's white breeches caught the filtered sunlight on the ladder. 'All officers lay aft, if you please, sir!'

Bolitho said to Dancer, 'I think the captain has been worried all along, Martyn.'

Dancer looked at him grimly. 'But surely he would not run from a damned pirate?'

'Better than be left swimming without a ship, eh?' Bolitho tried to cheer him up. 'I know which I'd rather have.'

But if the lower gundeck was remote and as before, the quarterdeck was not. Bolitho stood blinking in the harsh glare, seeing the two great holes in the main topsail, a streak of scarlet on the planking to mark where a man had fallen, or died. He stared over the rail and saw the land shimmering in a blinding haze. Already the island and its fortress had merged with the mainland and the anchored ships quite lost from sight around the same point which they had so

confidently rounded a few hours earlier. Of the barquentine
there was no sign at all.

Dancer asked anxiously, 'Where is the *City of Athens*, do
you think?'

Little Eden said, 'She's s-standing off t-to keep an eye on
the d-devils.'

Dancer nodded. 'Bit of luck getting hold of her.'

They fell silent as Verling dismissed the hands from the
quarterdeck nine-pounders and beckoned the other officers
to close around him. He appeared as irritable as ever, Bolitho
thought, his beaky nose checking who was present and who
was yet to arrive.

Captain Conway crossed from the weather side and stood
by the quarterdeck rail looking down at the eighteen-
pounders below him, their crews checking their equipment
and refilling the shot garlands.

There was a rank smell of powder in the air, of heated
metal and charred wood.

Verling said, 'All present, sir.'

The captain turned and regarded them thoughtfully, his
back against the rail, his palms resting on the polished
wood.

'We are standing offshore and will anchor further along
the coast. As you know, we were fired on, and fired on with
a confidence I dislike.' He spoke calmly and unhurriedly,
with less emotion than when he had awarded a flogging.
'The enemy is well prepared, and our bombardment, such as
it was, made no impression. But I had to be certain. To gain
some knowledge of what we are against.'

Bolitho could tell from the expressions of some of those nearby, who had been on the upper deck throughout the brief engagement, that there was something more to come.

Captain Conway continued in the same tone, 'Some months ago it was reported that one of our brigs, a new vessel which was employed in these waters, was overdue and therefore presumed lost. There had been some foul weather, and several merchantmen were also wrecked.' He glanced up at the masthead pendant, his eyes shining in the glare. 'When we rounded the point this morning the *City of Athens* was well in the lead. The lookouts reported sighting two vessels at anchor. There may have been more under the island's protection.' His voice hardened for the first time. 'But one of them was the missing brig, His Majesty's Ship *Sandpiper* of fourteen guns. Because of her, the *City of Athens* must have imagined that all was well, that *Sandpiper*'s captain had already done our work for us.'

Dancer gave a gasp as he added, 'The brig was the bait which we, but for our prize, would have taken. We would have laid under the guns of the fortress, and without the speed and agility to beat clear, would have been destroyed. As it was, the barquentine was hit several times. I doubt if any of her people survived.'

There was absolute silence. Bolitho was remembering the din on the lower gundeck, the importance and excitement they had all felt. He recalled the unsmiling face of Midshipman Grenfell, a face which had hidden a warmer and kinder nature than many imagined. And it had all happened without a word being passed from the quarterdeck.

It would have changed nothing, could have done nothing to help. And yet . . .

The captain added slowly, 'When we took the *City of Athens*, Mr Tregorren suggested that the pirates made off upon sighting another vessel. It now seems very possible that the other sail was ours, and the reason for the pirate's haste was that he did not want to be seen for what he is! A captured British man-o'-war. Imagine, gentleman, what havoc he may have been wreaking in *our country's name*?' He spat out the words like poison. 'No master of any peaceful vessel would challenge a ship so obviously British and in the King's service! That is not piracy, it is cold-blooded murder!'

Mr Verling nodded. 'It would be simple, sir. Whoever commands these scum has a sharp mind to attend him!'

The captain did not seem to hear. 'Some of our prize crew may have survived.' He glanced down at the dried blood by his feet. 'We may never know. However, our next task is to seize the brig and discover all we can of what is happening.'

Bolitho looked at the others. *Seize the brig*. Just like that.

'A cutting-out operation must be done tonight. No moon, and the weather favours us at present. The marines will provide a distraction. But I want that vessel retaken, the shame she has been made to endure and promote wiped out!'

He turned as the surgeon appeared on the ladder. 'Well?'

'The lookout died, sir.' Laidlaw's hooded eyes were expressionless. 'Broke his back.'

'I see.' The captain turned to the silent officers. 'The

lookout was the one who first sighted *Sandpiper*. The balls which passed close above us from the battery ashore must have thrown him to the deck.'

Bolitho watched the surgeon for some sign, knowing he was remembering that same lookout was the man who had been flogged.

The captain licked his lips. It was very hot on the quarterdeck, with the worst of the day yet to come.

He said, 'Mr Verling will give you your instructions. There will be two boats for the cutting-out. More would lessen our chances.' He walked away adding, 'Carry on.'

Verling watched him go. 'Two lieutenants and three midshipmen will take charge of the attack.' He eyed Tregorren coldly. 'You will command. Take only trained hands. This is no work for ploughmen.'

Eden whispered, 'What does it m-mean, Dick?' He looked very small beside the others.

The sulky midshipman named Pearce said, 'We board the brig in the darkness and cut 'em down before they return the compliment!' He added harshly, 'Poor John Grenfell. We grew up together in the same town.'

Verling said, 'Return to your duties. The hands can fall out from quarters and secure. Keep 'em busy, I want no bleating and sobbing for what has happened.'

They began to break up, each man wrapped in his own thoughts on the suddenness of death.

Tregorren said, 'Thirty men will be needed –'

He hesitated as Midshipman Pearce called, 'I'd like to volunteer, sir.'

Tregorren regarded him calmly. 'Mr Grenfell was a friend of yours. I had forgotten. A pity that.'

Bolitho watched him, sickened. Despite all that had happened, even the sudden likelihood of his own injury or death, Tregorren still found delight in taunting the grim-faced Pearce.

The lieutenant said abruptly, 'Request denied.' His eyes settled on Eden. '*You* will be one of the lucky midshipmen.' He smiled as Eden paled. 'A real chance to prove yourself.'

Bolitho said, 'He is the youngest, sir. Some of us have had more experience and . . .' He faltered, seeing the trap opening.

Tregorren shook one finger. 'I forgot about that, too. That our Mr Bolitho is always afraid that someone else will steal his thunder, deny him of honour, so that his high-and-mighty family might frown a bit!'

'That is a *lie*, sir. And unfair!'

Tregorren shrugged. 'Is it? No matter. You are also going, *and* the clever Mr Dancer.' He put his huge hands on his hips and looked at each in turn. 'The first lieutenant said only trained hands should be detailed. But we need experienced midshipmen for handling the ship. On a cutting-out raid we only require the right number!'

He took out his pocket watch. 'I want the full party mustered in an hour. Mr Hope will be my subordinate. Report to him when you are ready.'

Dancer said bitterly, 'Better Hope than Wellesley. He is as weak as watered milk.'

They walked along the weather gangway, thinking of

Grenfell and the others who had been lost in the shattered barquentine.

Eden said fiercely, 'I – I'm n-not afraid! R-really I'm not!' He looked at them wretchedly, his eyes filling his face. 'It's just that I d-don't want to go with Mr T-Tregorren! H-he'll be the d-death of us all!'

Dancer looked down at him and tried to smile. 'We'll be with you, Tom. It may not be too bad.' He turned suddenly to Bolitho. 'What *is* it like, Dick? You've done this sort of thing before.'

Bolitho stared across the nettings towards the misty hump of land and the glittering expanse of water.

'It's quick. Everything depends on surprise.'

He did not look at them. What could he say? Tell them of the fearful cries and curses of men fighting with cutlasses and knives, with axes and pikes? Of the touch of an enemy, the feel of his breath and his hatred? It was not like a sea fight, with the enemy just another ship. It was people. Flesh and blood.

Dancer said quietly, 'I can tell from your silence. Let us hope we are lucky.'

Down on the orlop they found Pearce and two other midshipmen restoring the chests and well-used chairs to their proper places, the surgeon's mates having removed their instruments and medicines as soon as the secure was piped.

In its place against one of *Gorgon*'s great frames was Grenfell's chest, his best hat and dirk hanging above it.

Pearce said, 'He always said he'd never rate lieutenant. He never will now.'

Bolitho looked round as Midshipman Marrack entered, impeccable as ever in a clean shirt.

Marrack said shortly, 'Leave his gear alone. There may still be a chance.' He threw his coat on a chair and added, 'You should have seen her go. The *City of Athens* never stood a chance. She was actually shortening sail to close the brig when the fortress battery took her.' He stared at nothing. 'She took fire and then turned turtle. I saw some of our people swimming. Then the sharks came.' He could not go on.

Dancer looked at Bolitho. 'I remember reading something about the *Sandpiper*.'

Marrack said, 'One thing is certain. Our captain will never allow a King's ship to remain in enemy hands, no matter what it costs to recover her.' He reached into his chest and took out a leather case. 'Take my pistols, Dick. They're better than any others aboard. My father gave them to me.' He turned away, as if annoyed at showing a softer side to his nature. 'See what confidence I have in you?'

The small servant scuttled into the berth. 'Beg pardon, sirs, but the fourth lieutenant is lookin' for you, and yellin' murder!'

'That Tregorren!' Dancer was unusually bitter. 'I agree with little Tom here. The damned bully is too full of himself for my liking!'

They made for the companion ladder, and only then realised that Eden was still by the side. He was staring at Grenfell's chest and his dirk which swung easily to the ship's movements.

Bolitho said gently, 'Come on, Tom. There's a lot to be done before sunset.'

To himself he added, *and after.*

6

Face to Face

'Easy there! Watch your stroke!' Hope, the *Gorgon*'s fifth lieutenant, hissed in the darkness, craning forward from the sternsheets as if to seek out the noise.

Bolitho crouched beside him and turned to peer astern. Only an occasional feather of white spray or a trailing glow of phosphorescence around the oars betrayed the position of the other cutter. It was very dark, and after the cloudless day, surprisingly cold. Which was just as well, he thought, for they had come a long way. The boats had been lowered and manned before dusk, and while *Gorgon* made more sail and went about to leave them to their own resources they had settled down to a long, steady pull towards the slab of headland.

When darkness had arrived it had been sudden, like the fall of a curtain, and Bolitho found himself wondering what was going on in the lieutenant's mind. It was a far cry indeed from the time when he had thrown open the door of the Blue Posts at Portsmouth and bellowed at the midshipmen. He remembered what Grenfell had said then about Hope's worries of promotion. The memory saddened him. Grenfell was dead, and Hope would indeed be moving up a place when the captain chose to accept that the lieutenant who had been in charge of the *City of Athens* was also killed.

Eden was leaning against him, his head lowered almost to the gunwale.

Bolitho said quietly, 'Still a way to go yet, Tom.'

It was an eerie sensation. The cutter thrusting jerkily across the inshore currents, the oars rising and falling on either beam like pale bones, their usual noise muffled by rags and thick layers of grease.

Ahead of the boat there was a darker wedge to show the division between sea and sky, and Bolitho thought he could smell the earth, sense its nearness.

In the bows, bent over the stem and a vicious-looking swivel gun, was a leadsman, his boat's lead and line sounding the way above sandbars and hidden rocks.

Turnbull, the master, had explained to the two lieutenants that it was best to creep right inshore, so that once around the headland they would lie somewhere between the beach and the anchored ships.

It had all sounded so easy. Not now, as a man caught his foot in a cutlass and set it clattering across the bottom-boards, and Hope snarled, 'God, Rogers, I'll have you beaten senseless if you make another sound!'

Bolitho looked at his profile, a shadow against the oars' spray alongside. A lieutenant. A man who knew that Tregorren was following close astern, depending on his ability to lead the way. Thirty men. For a press-gang, or for manning a couple of heavy guns, it was ample. For taking a ship against odds, and without surprise, it was disaster.

A strong eddy pushed the hull aside, so that the coxswain had to use his strength at the tiller to bring it back on course. The air felt different again and the sea across the larboard beam looked livelier.

Bolitho ventured, 'We are round the headland, sir.'

Hope swung on him and then said, 'Yes. *You'd* know, of course. You must have grown up with rocks like these in Cornwall.' He seemed to be studying him in the darkness. 'But a long pull yet.'

Bolitho hesitated, unwilling to break the little contact between them. 'Will the marines attack the battery, sir?'

'Some mad scheme like that.' Hope wiped his face as spray lanced into the boat. 'The captain will tack as close as he dares to the seaward end of the island and pretend to attempt a landing. Plenty of noise. Major Dewar will be good at that, he's got plenty to say in the wardroom!'

The whisper came back along the oarsmen. 'Vessel at anchor on th' starboard bow, sir!'

Hope nodded. 'Steer a point or so to larboard.' He twisted round to make sure the other boat was following. 'That must be the first of 'em. The brig is anchored beyond her, a couple of cables yet.'

Someone groaned, more worried apparently at the

prospect of pulling a heavy oar for another four hundred yards than the possible closeness of death.

'Watch out!' The bowman dropped his lead and line and seized a boathook.

The oars went into momentary confusion as something large and black, like a sleeping whale, loomed over the cutter, banging into the blades and making what seemed like a tremendous noise.

Eden murmured shakily, 'It's p-part of the b-barquentine, Dick!'

'Yes.'

Bolitho could smell the charred timbers, could even recognise a part of the *City of Athens*' taffrail before it lurched away into the darkness.

The unexpected appearance of part of the wreck had quite an effect on the steamen. There was something like a low growl, and tired though they were, the oarsmen started putting an extra power into their stroke.

Hope said softly, 'These are seasoned hands, Bolitho. They have been in *Gorgon* together for a long while and had plenty of friends aboard the prize.' He stiffened as the sweeping masts and yards of an anchored vessel passed slowly abeam. 'There she goes. Nary a damn sound.'

Bolitho peered at the darkened ship. Moored alongside the *Gorgon* she would look dwarfed. Out here, and from the cutter, she appeared enormous.

Hope was thinking aloud. 'Small frigate most likely. Not English. Too much rake on her masts.' He sounded completely absorbed. 'This devil has gathered quite a fleet, it seems.'

'Ease the stroke!' the coxswain whispered fiercely. 'Here comes t'other one!'

Hope rose to his feet, steadying himself on Bolitho's shoulder. Bolitho could feel the power of his grip, could imagine his anxieties at this moment.

Hope said, 'If only I could look at my watch.'

The coxswain grinned. 'Might as well send the devils a signal, sir.'

'Aye.' Hope sighed. 'Let's pray that Major Dewar and his bullocks are punctual.'

He peered over the gunwale, watching the swirl of the current, testing the wind against his face.

He seemed satisfied. 'Easy all!'

The oars rose dripping from the water and stayed motionless, the cutter moving steadily ahead in complete silence.

Bolitho saw the anchored brig for the first time. Swinging stern-on, her gilded cabin windows showing more brightly than the lower hull as she pivoted very slowly away from the land.

He could just make out her two masts and furled sails, the blacker angles of her shrouds, before they too merged with the night.

Bolitho tried to put himself in the place of those aboard. They had fought and captured the barquentine, robbed her holds and killed her crew. At the sight of a large man-of-war they had sheered off and come back here to count their gains.

Gorgon's appearance offshore would have caused a lot of speculation, but under the guns of the old fortress they would have felt secure enough. The fortress had been here for a few hundred years, the captain had said. It had changed hands several times by treaty, or because of a trading agreement, but had never been taken by force. Just a few men at those carefully sited guns, some heated shot, and the rest was easy. Even if Captain Conway had commanded several small, agile ships, and ten times as many men, the fortress would still have held the key to victory. And in time of peace it was doubtful if either the Admiralty or the men of Parliament would be prepared to condone a full-scale siege on this tiny pinprick of Africa, with all the losses entailed. Equally, they would expect Captain Conway to do something. To recapture the brig for a beginning.

A shaft of silver ran up the brig's foremast shrouds, and Hope snapped, 'The anchor watch in the bows! Checking the cable!'

The lantern's beam died away just as quickly.

The drift of the current was taking the cutter crabwise towards the brig's counter. Hope must have realised there was no more time left. He said quietly, 'Boat your oars! Stand by, bowman!'

The oars rumbled across the thwarts, but Bolitho knew from experience that the noise which seemed deafening on the cool breeze would be nothing to a man up on the brig's forecastle.

Eden whispered, 'What's Mr T-Tregorren going to do?'

Bolitho could feel his spine chilling under the tension. He heard Hope drawing his sword very carefully from its scabbard, crouching to peer up at the brig's poop as it rose steadily above the boat.

He replied, 'Once we have boarded her, he will attack from the bows, cut the cable and –'

Hope snapped, '*Ready,* lads!'

There was a sudden explosion which seemed to come from far out to sea. A dull red glow spread and glittered on the water, making each part of the swell shine like silk. Another explosion, and still another.

Hope exclaimed, 'Dewar's marines have started already!'

He staggered and all but fell as the cutter ground into the brig's quarter and the bowman hurled his grapnel up and over the rail.

'*At 'em, lads!*' Hope's voice, after the stealth and the suspense, was like a thunderclap. '*Come on!*'

Scrambling and yelling like madmen they swarmed up the side and open gunports in a solid mass of bodies. Someone encountered a loosely rigged boarding net, but even as voices shouted with alarm from below the net was severed, and with Hope and his coxswain in the lead they swept on to the unfamiliar deck.

It was like a scene from an inferno. The British seamen charging across the deck, their faces and wild eyes revealed in the reflected red flashes and the exploding charges at the end of the island.

Two figures ran from the forecastle and a pistol cracked out from a companionway. A seaman fell sobbing, another jabbed down one of the running figures with his cutlass and hacked him across the neck as he fell for good measure.

More shots now, the balls slamming into the planking or hissing away over the sea. The brig's crew were crowding through the two main hatches, and a ragged volley of pistol and musket fire cut down several of Hope's men.

The lieutenant yelled, 'Bring the swivel from the cutter!'

He caught a man who was hurled aside by a musket ball and lowered him roughly to the deck, adding between gasps, 'Where is that bloody Tregorren?'

The forepart of the brig now seemed full of men, pale and crouching. Darting between familiar objects to take cover and fire on the retreating boarding party.

Hope said desperately, 'If we can't get to grips, we're done for!'

With a pistol in his left hand, his curved hanger in the other, he shouted, 'Close quarters, lads!' Then he charged along the deck and threw himself amongst the nearest marksmen. Shouts of surprise gave way to screams and yells as Hope fired his pistol into a man's chest and slashed another with his hanger. Cursing and cheering the remaining boarders followed him, striking out at anything which moved.

Bolitho fired both of Marrack's pistols into the crowd and thrust them into his belt. He drew his own hanger and parried away a pike which plunged towards him like a spear.

Despite all the danger and terror he found he was able to remember his first boarding attack. A lieutenant had taken away his midshipman's dirk and had said scornfully, 'That's only fit for playing games. You need a man's weapon for this kind of work!' He thought of Grenfell's dirk hanging in the *Gorgon.* He had left his behind, too.

A face loomed above him, the man screaming like a fiend, although in what language Bolitho could not tell. He felt a violent blow on the side of his head and saw the man's arm going up, his sword pale against the black sky.

Bolitho twisted his body round and struck upwards with the hanger. He felt the pain of the blow lance up his arm, saw the man and sword fall into the gasping, struggling figures as if swallowed up.

He heard a shrill cry and saw Eden groping on the deck, while above him a figure swung a musket like a club.

A pistol exploded, revealing the man's glaring eyes, his fierce concentration giving way to a distorted mask of agony as a pistol ball flung him down.

Bolitho dragged Eden to his feet, hacking out at a running figure, but feeling the blade slice through the air.

Hope shouted, 'Swivel gun!' He gestured to the little rail across the poop. 'Lively there! Fall back!'

They needed no bidding. Parrying and slashing, dragging the wounded as best they could, the survivors fought their way aft to the poop.

Hope bellowed, 'Down, lads!' He thrust at a charging man with his hanger even as the coxswain put a match to the swivel gun which he had mounted on the rail.

The man cut down by Hope's sword must have been carrying a loaded pistol, for as the swivel let out a savage bang and sent a packed charge of canister shot into the advancing shadows the pistol hit the deck and fired even though its owner was dead. The ball struck the lieutenant in the shoulder and he fell beside the smoking swivel without a sound.

As their ears recovered from the swivel's vicious detonation Bolitho heard the cries and screams of men caught in the deadly canister. No wonder old seamen called a swivel 'the daisy-cutter'.

Then from right forward in the beakhead he heard the familiar harsh tones of Lieutenant Tregorren, the sudden rush of feet and the cheers of the other boat's crew.

It was more than enough for the brig's company. Sharks or not, they were leaping overboard, ignoring the yells and curses of their comrades who were too badly hurt to follow.

Tregorren strode aft, pausing merely to bring a belaying pin down on the skull of someone trying to climb on to the main chains.

He peered at the men by the rail. 'Take care of Mr Hope!' The belaying pin pointed and gestured like an obscene fist. 'Two men on the wheel! Mr Dancer, pass the word to cut the cable!' He rocked back on his heels, his eyes searching amongst the rigging. 'Hands aloft and loose tops'ls! Come along, jump about, my children, if you don't want to run ashore!'

Bolitho knelt beside the wounded lieutenant, feeling his pain, his strength ebbing away.

He said, 'That was a brave thing you did, sir.'

Hope said between his teeth, 'Nothing else I could do.' He tried to pat Bolitho's arm. 'You'll know what I mean one day.'

Tregorren towered above them. 'Mr Eden! Take charge of this officer!' He faced Bolitho. 'So you're still with us, eh?' He shrugged. 'Well, get aloft and chase those laggards!'

The brig was already heeling in the offshore breeze, her hastily released topsails flapping and cracking like musket fire as she tilted free of her severed cable.

'Put up your helm!'

Several shots whimpered overhead, fired by whom, nobody knew.

'Loose the heads'ls!' Tregorren seemed everywhere. 'Lay her on the starboard tack!'

Bolitho clung to the shrouds and stared abeam where a fire was still burning fiercely to show where the marines had created a diversion.

Tiny lanterns moved this way and that, and he realised they were on the other vessel, which had already changed her bearing considerably.

After the long pull around the headland, the apprehension and fear, the actual cutting-out had taken less than twenty minutes. It seemed incredible, and as he paused to think of the nearness of death he felt the sweat like ice-rime on his spine.

He slid down a backstay and found Tregorren bellowing orders down the after companion.

Dancer ran across the deck and said, 'God, I was worried for you! I thought we were never going to engage!'

He turned as a man yelled, 'Sir! There's a whole lot of British seamen battened down 'ere!'

Tregorren snapped, 'See to them! No doubt they are some of the brig's own company.' He caught the man's arm. 'But prisoners, sick or bloody well dying, I want 'em up here on deck!'

He lowered his face to the compass box. 'Hold her steady, Quartermaster. As close to the wind as you can. I want no mauling from that battery!'

'Aye, aye, sir.' The men at the wheel eased the spokes deftly. 'Full an' bye, sir! West by south!'

Bolitho watched the figures emerging from the main hatch. Even in the darkness he could sense their disbelief as they were helped and pushed on to the open deck.

One man lurched aft and touched his forehead.

'Starkie, sir. Master's mate of the *Sandpiper*.' He swayed, and would have fallen but for Bolitho.

Tregorren was watching the released seamen, his chin sunk on his neckcloth.

'You the senior?'

'Aye, sir. Cap'n Wade and the other officers were killed.' He dropped his eyes. 'We have been in hell, sir.'

'Possibly.'

Tregorren strode to the foot of the mainmast and squinted up at the flapping topsail.

'Get some of those hands to work and set the spanker and then the fores'l. I want to get some sea-room.'

He turned and added shortly, 'Well, Mr Starkie, you can take charge aft as you are the best qualified.' He looked him slowly up and down, as if his eyes could pierce the darkness. 'Although it would seem you are less so for defending one of His Majesty's ships, eh?'

He hurried away, shouting for Dancer and thrusting through the dazed seamen like a plough.

The master's mate consulted the compass and the set of

the topsail and said harshly, 'He had no cause to speak like that. We had no chance.' He looked at Bolitho and added, 'You fought well back there. Some of these devils were laughing at what they would do if your ship tried to force home an attack.'

'But who are they?'

Starkie let out a great sigh. 'Pirates, corsairs, call 'em what you will, but I swear I have seen none worse, and I have been at sea all my years.'

Bolitho saw two men carrying Lieutenant Hope to the companion and prayed he would be strong enough to survive. Several seamen had died, and it was a miracle there were not more to be buried.

Starkie said, 'They kept us aboard to crew the poor *Sandpiper*. Like galley slaves we were. Beaten and treated like scum. They had only enough hands for the guns. But enough to keep us cowed, I can tell you.'

Eden had joined them. 'Any midshipmen, w-were there?'

Starkie looked at him for several seconds. 'Two. Only two. Mr Murray died in the attack. Mr Flowers, he was about your age, well, they killed him later.' He turned away. 'Now leave me be, I don't want to think about it.'

Tregorren came aft again. He sounded almost jovial as he called, 'She answers well, Mr Starkie. A fine little vessel. Fourteen guns too, I see.'

Eden said, 'Mr S-Starkie says that the pirates are the worst he's s-seen, sir!'

Tregorren was still studying the brig, his head cocked as

the sails shuddered and banged before the rudder brought the ship back on course again.

'Indeed, indeed. Well, the other pirate vessel has weighed.' He faced Starkie. 'And where would she be going, d'you reckon?'

Starkie shrugged. 'They have another rendezvous to the north of here. Cap'n Wade was searching for it when we were attacked.'

'I see.' Tregorren walked aft to the taffrail. 'Be first light in an hour or so. We will be able to signal *Gorgon*. Put a good man aloft as lookout. We may be able to catch that one and give him a nice dance at the end of a halter.'

He swung angrily on Eden. 'Well, what are *you* gaping at? I hear you were useless during the attack! Weeping for your mother, were you? Nobody to protect you?'

Bolitho said, 'Easy, sir, some of the people are listening.'

'And damn you for your impertinence!' Tregorren's mood had changed like a savage squall. 'I'll have no more of it!'

Bolitho stood his ground. 'Mr Eden was knocked down during the boarding, sir.' He could feel his caution dropping away, his future already in ruins. But he was sick of Tregorren's sarcasm and brutality towards those unable to fight back. 'We were, you recall, outnumbered, sir. We had been expecting some support.'

Tregorren stared at him as if suffering a seizure. 'Are you suggesting –' He tugged at his neckcloth. 'Are you daring to suggest that I was late in boarding?' He leaned forward, his face inches from Bolitho's. *'Well, are you?'*

'I was saying that Mr Eden did well, sir. He had lost his weapon, and he is *twelve years old*, sir.'

They faced each other, oblivious to everything about them.

Then Tregorren nodded very slowly. 'So be it, Mr Bolitho. You will join the masthead lookout until I say differently. When we return to the ship I intend to have you put under arrest for gross insubordination.' He nodded again. 'See how the family likes *that*, eh?'

Bolitho felt his heart pumping against his ribs like a hammer. He had to repeat over and over in his mind: *He wants me to strike him. He wants me to strike him.* It would make Tregorren's actions complete, and for Bolitho final.

'Is that all, sir?' He barely recognised his own voice.

'Aye.' The lieutenant swung away, his sudden move making the mesmerised spectators scatter like rabbits. 'For the present.'

Dancer walked to the main shrouds with him and said hotly, 'That was a foul thing to say! I felt like knocking him to the deck, Dick!'

'So did I.' Bolitho swung himself on to the ratlines and stared up at the mainyard. 'And he knew it.'

Dancer said awkwardly, 'Never mind. We took the brig. That must count for something with Captain Conway.'

'It is all we have.' He started to climb. 'Be off, Martyn, or he'll have you all aback, too.'

'When you have finished, Mr Dancer!' The voice searched him out from the shadows. 'Be so good as to find a cook and have the galley fire lit. These people look like scarecrows, and I can't abide filth!'

Dancer called, 'At once, sir!'

He looked up at the black shrouds, but Bolitho had already vanished.

7

Mr Starkie's Story

Richard Bolitho clung to a stay and watched the sky brightening reluctantly across the horizon. Little more than a grey blur, but in hours it would be almost too hot to think.

He felt the mast shiver and vibrate as the *Sandpiper* responded eagerly to her bulging sails. He wondered how the wounded were getting on, if Lieutenant Hope was better, or giving way to his injury.

A few figures were just visible on the brig's narrow poop and below the mainmast. He thought he could smell food from the galley and felt his stomach contract painfully. He could not remember when he had last eaten, and found himself hating Tregorren for keeping him aloft without relief.

The lieutenant had been right about one thing. When the news reached the Bolitho home in Falmouth it would have lost the unfairness and hostility of the moment. It would be seen only as Tregorren intended. That Bolitho had acted badly and with insubordination against a superior officer.

He heard heavy breathing and saw Dancer hauling himself up to the crosstrees beside him.

He said, 'You'd better watch out, Martyn!'

Dancer shook his head. 'It's all right, Dick. Mr Starkie sent me. He's worried about our lieutenant.'

Bolitho looked at him. 'Mr Hope? Is he worse?'

'He is as before.' Dancer clutched at a stay as the brig heeled violently in a sudden gust. 'It is Tregorren who is causing the concern.' He grinned. 'Although I must say I can't muster much grief!'

Bolitho reached out and stretched his cramped limbs. He was aching from exposure and felt clammy with salt spray.

Dancer added, 'Mr Starkie thinks that he has a fever.'

They slid down to the deck together and found the master's mate by the wheel with the helmsmen.

Starkie said abruptly, 'It'll be dawn soon. I can't understand it. He's like a man possessed down there. I dunno what we'll do if we run into more trouble.' He looked away, his voice brittle. 'I can't take being a prisoner again. Not after what we've suffered, and that's God's truth!'

Bolitho replied, 'We'll go to him.' He touched Dancer's arm. 'But I'm no surgeon.'

In the tiny cabin where *Sandpiper*'s last captain had enjoyed his privacy and suffered his anxieties, they found Tregorren slumped across a table, his face buried in his arms.

The cabin stank of spirits or coarse wine, and as the brig lifted and plunged across the broken water Bolitho heard glass rolling about beneath the cot, and in the glare of a solitary lantern saw that there were many such bottles in a rack against the bulkhead.

Dancer murmured grimly, 'Mr Tregorren has surely found his heaven!'

Bolitho leaned over the table. 'I'll try and rouse him. You keep clear.' He seized the lieutenant's shoulders and heaved him backwards over the chair.

He had been expecting to see a man the worse for drink.

Dancer exclaimed, 'In God's name, Dick, he looks like death!'

Tregorren had a terrible pallor, and more so because his normally ruddy complexion was patchy grey, and when his eyes flickered open very slowly he seemed quite dazed, like someone suffering extreme shock.

He started to speak, but his speech was so thick he had to clear his throat with a series of loud retches.

Bolitho asked, 'Are you ill, sir?' He saw Dancer try to hide a grin and added hastily, 'Mr Starkie was worried for you.'

'Was he?' Tregorren tried to stand but fell back in the chair with a terrible groan. 'Get that bottle!' His fingers were like claws as he seized the bottle and took a long, desperate swallow. 'I don't know what's happening.' He was speaking in a vague, slurred voice. 'Can't control my body.' He retched and tried to rise again. 'Must get to the heads.'

Bolitho and Dancer hauled him to his feet, and for a few

moments the three of them swayed and reeled to the motion as if in a weird dance.

Dancer muttered, 'He's done it this time! What our old doctor would call the *bloody flux*! The man is coming apart!'

As they lurched through the bulkhead door Bolitho saw Eden watching from another small cabin where Hope had been since being carried below.

'Give a hand here, Tom! We have to get him to the heads!'

Eden said brightly, 'He l-looks t-terrible, to be sure.'

When they reached the deck the air was like wine after the overpowering stench in the cabin.

Starkie hurried from the wheel. 'Is it fever then?'

Eden piped, 'H-he has the g-gout, Mr Starkie. I have been s-saying s-so all along. He h-has been taking medicine to ease the pain, but I s-suspect has overindulged.'

They all stared at the diminutive midshipman who had suddenly emerged as their only source of medical knowledge.

'Well, what'll we do?' Starkie sounded lost.

Eden regarded the sagging, groaning figure and replied, 'When he g-gets b-back to the ship the s-surgeon will t-take care of him. There's n-nothing we can d-do.' He grimaced. 'S-serve him right.'

'Be that as it may.' Starkie watched Dancer clinging to the lieutenant's coat to stop him from falling clean across the bulwark. 'We're going to need him shortly.'

Dancer stared at him. 'I don't see that. We can signal *Gorgon* and the captain will know what to do.'

Starkie regarded him bleakly. 'You've not noticed. The

wind has shifted to the nor'-east. It'd take your ship all day to beat up to this position, that is even if your cap'n knows what's happening.'

Dancer persisted, 'Then what is to stop us from running down on her?'

Starkie said, 'I'm only a master's mate, and one right glad to be safe and free again, but I know the Navy, and I know captains. *Sandpiper* is well placed to head off the enemy, or at least follow her to her hiding place.' He shrugged. 'But without an officer, I'm not so sure. You get no reward for empty heroics, and that's for certain in any navy.'

They looked at Eden as he said in a small voice, 'We're *not* going to the *Gorgon*?'

Bolitho noticed that he had even lost his stammer in his anxiety.

He said quietly, 'Come over here, Tom.' He took the boy's arm and asked calmly, 'What did you do to Mr Tregorren?'

Eden stared at the deck, his hands moving in agitation.

'I knew he was t-trying to t-treat himself by p-putting medicine in his w-wine. I s-saw it on a flask in his c-cabin. *Vin Antim,* like my f-father uses in m-matters of g-gout.' He added wretchedly, 'So I p-put a large m-measure in one of his b-bottles. He must have d-drunk all of it, and a full b-bottle of b-brandy as well.'

Bolitho stared at him. 'You might have killed him!'

'B-but I thought we were rejoining the sh-ship, you see. I just w-wanted him to s-suffer for all the things he s-said to you, and to m-me.' He shook his head. 'And now you s-say we'll not be joining *Gorgon* r-right away?'

Bolitho breathed out slowly. 'So it seems.'

Dancer steadied the lieutenant as he staggered away from the bulwark. 'Get some men to help this officer to the cabin!'

Bolitho said, 'What now, I wonder?'

As if in answer he heard the lookout yell, 'Deck there! Sail on the lee bow!'

They ran to the nettings but the sea to leeward was still in deep shadow.

Starkie said bitterly, 'So the devil's downwind of us. He stands between us and safety.'

'How well d'you know this coast?' Bolitho's question seemed to come out all on its own.

'Good enough.' Starkie peered at the compass as if to gather his thoughts. 'It's a bad one to try and outpace a frigate.'

Bolitho thought of the *Gorgon* to the south of their position. Maybe the captain did not even know they had cut out the *Sandpiper,* and believed she had fled with the frigate.

Starkie was saying, 'We'd been searching for pirates for months, and Cap'n Wade got some information from a Genoese trader that there was one such vessel in these waters. At the time, the cap'n thought there was only a small ship, and probably not much of a craft at that. But this pirate is no fool, believe me. They say he is half French and half English, but one thing is certain, he's thrown in his lot with some Algerine corsairs who have come from the Mediterranean to prey on slavers and honest traders alike.'

Bolitho looked at Dancer and asked softly, 'Are there many of them?'

'Enough. They were short-handed when they took *Sandpiper,* but new men are joining their ranks every day. It doesn't matter what race or country they come from. I'm told that if they swear allegiance to Islam they can be anything they like. The frigate was Spanish before they took her off Oran, and she is commanded by this Jean Gauvin. A madman, if ever I saw one, and without fear. The corsair who forced some Senegalese traders to open the fortress for him is Raïs Haddam. He put our officers to death. Slowly, and in front of our people. It was terrible to see and hear it.'

Nobody spoke, and as Bolitho watched Starkie's tanned features he could see him reliving the horror as if it had just happened.

'We anchored just off the fortress. It was a fine day, and the people were in high spirits. And why not, for we were going home in a month more or so. The frigate lay near us, wearing Spanish colours. The fortress too was flying a trading company flag.' He gave a shudder. 'I suppose Cap'n Wade should have known or suspected. But he was only a lieutenant, no more'n twenty-three. We lowered the boats and went ashore to meet the governor of the island. Instead we were surrounded, and the fortress battery put down a few balls around the *Sandpiper* just to let the watch know they had no chance.

'After the killing and the torture was over, this Algerine corsair, Raïs Haddam, spoke to the rest of us. Told us that if we worked the ship for him we might be spared.' He looked away. 'Gauvin was there too, and when one of the midshipmen tried to protest it was Gauvin who ordered him to be killed. They burned him alive on the foreshore!'

Dancer whispered, 'My God!'

'Aye.' Starkie stared past him into the shadows. 'Haddam has gathered the scum of the earth to his banner.'

Bolitho nodded. 'Raïs Haddam. I have heard my father and his friends speak of him. He has raided the Algerian coast for years, and is now looking elsewhere for his corsairs.' He glanced at the paling sky. 'I never expected to meet up with him!'

Starkie said bitterly, 'There is no time left to prepare a defence.'

Bolitho looked at their faces, sensing despair and defeat. Dancer was too new to the Navy to know anything different. Starkie was still too stunned by his captivity to offer advice.

Bolitho said quietly, 'Then we must prepare an attack.'

He thought of Tregorren, filled with pain and drink because of Eden's ruse. Of Hope, barely breathing, a musket ball in his shoulder. Of their seamen, some bewildered at their sudden releases and others quite exhausted from the savage fighting on this same deck.

Starkie exclaimed, 'Gauvin's ship mounts twenty-four guns to our fourteen little squeakers!'

Dancer asked, 'When *Sandpiper* was used to seize the barquentine, what happened to her crew?'

'Over the side.' Starkie looked grim-faced. 'Gutted like pigs.'

Bolitho said, 'So much for the bad side. Now, what can we do against Gauvin?'

He walked to the weather side, feeling the spray pattering across his face and hands.

'He'll know that *Gorgon* is to the south'rd.' Dancer had joined him. 'And will expect us to try and rejoin her.'

Bolitho glanced at Starkie, wondering if his memory could be trusted.

'If we come about, Mr Starkie, how close could we weather the headland?'

Starkie's eyes widened with alarm. 'Back to that damned island, y'mean?'

'*Towards* it. There is a difference.'

'It's dangerous. You should know that, if you rounded the headland under oars. There are reefs aplenty, many not even marked on the charts.'

Bolitho said half to himself, 'Off Cornwall there are some islands called the Scillies. A Bristol trader was being chased by a French privateer in the last war. The trader's master had no chance of outpacing the enemy, but he knew his islands well. He sailed right across one reef and the Frenchie followed him. Ripped out his keel. There were none saved.'

Starkie stared at him with amazement. 'You want to steer a course through the reef? Is that what you're asking me to do?'

A weak ray of sunlight lanced across the upper rigging and made the topgallant yard glitter like a crucifix.

'Do we have a choice?' Bolitho watched him gravely. 'Captivity, and possibly death to make another example, *or* . . .' The word hung in the air.

Starkie nodded firmly. 'We'll probably die anyway, but God, it's a chance I'd rather take.' He rubbed his rough hands together. 'I suggest we call the hands and shorten sail to come about. If the wind goes against us we'll end up on a lee shore.' He chuckled suddenly, dropping the years from his lined face. 'By God, Mr, whatever your name is, I'd hate to serve under you when you're a cap'n. My nerves would give out afore long!'

Bolitho smiled sadly as more light opened up the deck to display the dull stains where men had fought and died, the jagged splinters left by the swivel gun.

He looked at Eden. 'See how Mr Hope is. Try and get him to take some brandy.' He saw the boy flinch. '*Not* Mr Tregorren's bottle, if you please.'

As Eden started for the companion he added, 'And try to find a flag. I want this pirate to recognise *Sandpiper* under her rightful colours today.'

Dancer watched him in silence. Then he said to Starkie, 'I have never seen such a mood in him. He means to fight. It's no deception.'

The master's mate walked to the lee rail and spat on to the creaming wash.

'Well, m'lad, when Gauvin sees the flag, that'll do it right enough. It's not a sight he's very fond of.'

Eden reappeared carrying a roll of bunting. 'Found one, Dick. Hidden under the b-brandy b-bottles in the cabin.'

'How are the lieutenants?' Starkie spoke sharply, perhaps still hoping that someone else would appear to take over responsibility.

Eden pouted. 'M-Mr Hope is breathing a l-little better. Mr Tregorren is in a filthy s-state.'

Starkie sighed. 'Very well. Pipe the hands to the braces. No point in delaying things any more.'

Bolitho gripped the poop rail and watched the seamen hurrying to braces and halliards, their movements jerky, as if they were still shocked and uncertain.

It was like a dream. Of pirates, and brave young men fighting their country's enemies.

But it was fast becoming a nightmare. Only the first part was right, he thought. A little brig, a demoralised company, and some boys to lead them.

He thought of his father, and of Captain Conway, grave-faced and confident behind their guns and their seamanship.

He said, 'Run up the colours, Mr Eden.' Even the formality surprised him. 'Then stand by to come about.'

8

Across the Reef

'Sou'-sou'-east, sir! Full an' bye!'

Bolitho gripped the hammock nettings and watched the
Sandpiper dip her lee bulwark steeply towards the sea. Spray
and drifting foam dashed across the deck, and when he
glanced up at the main yard he saw it was bending like a
huge bow as the seamen worked to set more sail.

Starkie remarked hoarsely, 'The wind's freshening a bit.'
He shaded his eyes to peer at the masthead pendant. 'But it's
holding steady from the nor'-east.' He added grimly, 'So
far.'

Bolitho hardly heard him. He was watching the brig's
efforts as she lifted and smashed down on to each successive
line of whitecaps.

From the moment they had brought the ship about and
turned her gilded figurehead towards the land again he had

sensed the change around him. Even the *Sandpiper*'s original hands, many showing festering cuts and cruel injuries from their captivity, were shouting to each other, doing all they could to set every stitch of canvas short of tearing the masts out of her. Only when they looked aft did they falter. Perhaps, Bolitho thought, they still expected to see their young captain at the rail, as if by hoping they could hold their memories at bay.

Dancer shouted above the din of canvas and wind, 'She's flying, Dick!'

He nodded, seeing the bows dip into a steep-sided roller and hurl the spray high over the beakhead in a solid white sheet.

'Aye.' He looked across the quarter. 'Can you see the frigate?' He gripped Dancer's arm. 'There she is! And she's making more sail.'

As the gloom of the night retreated slowly towards the open sea he saw the topsails and topgallants of the other ship, changing shape as she too changed tack and came end-on in pursuit. He pointed to the flag above his head, making a bright patch against the washed-out sky.

'Mr Starkie was right, it seems. Our enemy is roused!'

Starkie walked up to the weather side, his body leaning against the deck's steep angle.

'I'm holding her as close to the wind as I dare. Bring her up another point and she'll not answer.'

Bolitho took a glass from a rack by the compass box and trained it towards the land. As he steadied it through the maze of shrouds and vibrating halliards he saw the faces of some of the seamen loom towards him, and wondered what they were thinking as the brig headed for the shore, to the place where their pain and humiliation had begun.

Then he saw the headland, jutting out in a welter of breakers like the prow of a Roman galley.

How different it had looked from the cutter, all that while ago. He had to shake himself to realise it was only yesterday.

The sea looked rougher, and driven by the gusty wind was surging amongst a necklace of rocks as if to beckon them all to destruction.

There was a dull bang, and when he swung aft towards the frigate he saw a smear of smoke moving rapidly with the wind.

Starkie said, 'Just a sighting shot. She's too lively to hit us at this range.'

Bolitho did not reply. He was watching the frigate's great foresail writhing and puffing in disorder as her captain brought her up into the wind. She was almost in irons when the foresail filled and hardened again, the lee gunports heeling down until they were awash.

Dancer said, 'She's worked across our stern, Dick.'

'Yes. She intends to take the wind gage from us.' He still kept his eyes on the frigate until they watered painfully. 'But it means she will stand the closer inshore when we pass the headland.'

Dancer stared at him. 'Can we really get through?'

Starkie heard him and called, 'You'll be asking if we can walk on water next!' He seized the wheel and added his own strength to the helmsmen's. 'Watch your head, damn you!'

Another bang. This time Bolitho saw the white feathers of spray kicking across each line of waves as the ball skipped past their stern.

He looked at the *Sandpiper*'s six-pounders. Very suitable for hit-and-run attacks on enemy merchantmen, or for running down pirates and smugglers.

For taking on a frigate they were useless.

'Send another good lookout aloft, Martyn.' He staggered as the deck shook violently in a sudden trough. 'The *Gorgon* may be in sight.'

But there was no sign of the big seventy-four. Just the pursuing frigate, and the first view of the island on the far side of the bay.

As before, it looked pale and strangely tranquil in the early sunlight, and it was hard to accept all that had happened there.

Starkie had said earlier that the island was even now packed with wretched slaves, men and young girls who had been gathered by the traders from all parts of Africa.

And before long many of them would be sailing west to the Americas and the Indies. If they were lucky they might end their days in comfortable captivity, rather like dependent servants. Those less fortunate would eke out their lives like animals. When their usefulness was over, their strength used up, they would be discarded.

Bolitho had heard it said that slave ships, like the oared galleys of Spain, could be traced at sea by their terrible smell. The stench of bodies crammed together, unable to move, incapable of making even the simplest comfort for themselves.

Bang. A ball hissed overhead and slapped through the foretopsail like an iron fist.

'Closer.' Starkie had his thumbs in his belt, his eyes fixed on the frigate. 'He's overhauling us more quickly now.'

'Deck there! Breakers on the lee bow!'

Starkie ran to the rail and snatched a glass. 'Aye, that's 'em. The first line of reefs.' He glared aft at the helmsmen. 'Let her fall off a point!'

The wheel creaked, and brought a protest of flapping canvas from the topgallants.

'Sou' by east, sir!'

'Steady as you go!'

Bolitho could tell from the worsening motion, the way every spar and sail seemed to be quivering in protest, that they were entering shallower water and crossing a fierce undertow.

Starkie said, 'Better shorten sail.'

Bolitho looked at him, his voice almost pleading. 'If we do, he'll take us before *he's* in any danger.'

The master's mate eyed him impassively. 'As you say.'

Eden scrambled through the canting companion, his eyes frightened as he peered astern for the enemy.

'Mr Hope is c-calling for y-you, Dick.'

He ducked as the frigate's bow-chaser hurled a shot close abeam, throwing a waterspout high into the air like a surfacing whale.

Bolitho nodded. 'I'll go to him. Call me if anything happens.'

Starkie was peering through his telescope at the nearest

line of breakers. By allowing his ship to fall downwind just a trifle he had brought the bowsprit and tapering jib boom almost in line with the tell-tale surf.

He said over his shoulder, 'Don't worry. You'll *know*.'

Bolitho groped his way from the companion ladder and entered the small, hutch-like cabin.

Hope was sprawling in a cot, his eyes very bright as Bolitho bent over him.

'I've heard that the fourth lieutenant is unwell?' His face was ashen. 'Damn him, why did he hold off his attack?' He was rambling vaguely. 'My shoulder. Oh God, they'll lop off my arm when we get to the ship.'

The pain and the despair seemed to steady him.

'Are you managing?'

Bolitho forced a smile. 'We have a good master's mate on deck, sir. Mr Dancer and I are trying to look like veterans.'

Another dull bang penetrated the humid cabin, and Bolitho felt the hull tremble as a ball slammed down hard alongside. Too close.

Hope gasped, 'You cannot fight a frigate!'

'Would you have me strike, sir?'

'*No!*' He shut his eyes and groaned with pain. 'I don't know. I only understand that I should be helping you. Doing something. Instead . . .'

Bolitho watched his desperation with new understanding. Hope, the fifth lieutenant, had been closer to him than the other officers. He always pretended not to show his concern for the midshipmen under his charge, displayed an outer skin of hardness which had been taken as brutal on some occasions. But his constant presence amongst them had proved that some of his unsympathetic criticism had been both necessary and beneficial. As he had remarked more than once: *This ship needs officers not children.*

And now he was lying there, broken and helpless.

Bolitho said quietly, 'I will come for advice whenever I can, sir.'

One hand moved out of the bloodstained cot and gripped his.

'Thank you.' Hope was barely able to focus his eyes. 'God be with you!'

'Below there!' It was Dancer's voice. 'The frigate's running out her starboard guns!'

'I'm coming!'

Bolitho ran for the ladder. Thinking of Hope, of all of them.

In the short time he had been below the sunlight had broken from the land and changed the sea into an endless array of leaping wavecrests.

Starkie shouted, 'Wind's backed a piece! Nothing much. But the frigate's going to make a run for us, I reckon!'

Bolitho took a glass from a seaman and trained it over the nettings. The frigate was barely a mile off the larboard quarter, sails braced hard round to hold the wind, her starboard guns showing above the churning wash along her side like black teeth.

He saw her outline alter slightly as she came up a point or so to windward, the sunlight lancing on weapons and telescopes, and on the large black flag at her mainmast truck.

He could even distinguish her name painted on weatherworn scrollwork beneath her beakhead. *Pegaso*. Probably the original name she had carried under the Spanish flag.

'She's fired!'

A stabbing line of orange tongues belched from her gunports, the untimed broadside whipping past *Sandpiper*'s stern and a few moaning above the poop.

Bolitho said, 'Alter course, Mr Starkie. Two points to windward, if you can.'

Starkie opened his mouth to protest and changed his mind. He watched some barely concealed rocks dashing past the starboard side. Well clear, but it meant they were committed. Amongst the sprawling reefs like a fly in a web.

'Man the braces there! Let go and haul!' Dancer hurried to lend a hand. '*Heave,* lads!'

Above the plunging hull every shroud and sail seemed to be booming and creaking in disorder as the bows crept round and then steadied on the next spit of land.

Another ragged broadside, the balls skipping harmlessly astern and bringing a feeble cheer from a watching seaman who did not realise the peril he was in.

Bolitho shouted, 'Get the best gun captain, Martyn! Lively!'

'Sou'-east by south, sir!' The helmsman sounded dazed.

'Very well.'

Starkie turned momentarily to watch as a grizzled old seaman in patched trousers and a check shirt ran aft and knuckled his forehead.

'Taylor, zur.'

'Well, Taylor, I want you to pick your two most reliable crews and man the aftermost six-pounders, starboard side.'

Taylor blinked at the midshipman, probably thinking Bolitho was at last going mad. The enemy, after all, was on the opposite side.

Bolitho was speaking quickly, his mind blank to everything but the frigate and *Sandpiper*'s bearing from her. He tried to remember everything he had learned or had had beaten into him from the age of twelve until this day. 'Double-shotted. I know it's a risk. But I want you to hit the frigate's bows when I give the word.'

Taylor nodded slowly. 'Aye, zur.' He gestured with a tarred thumb. 'I fathom yer meanin', zur.' He ambled away, bawling out names and examining two six-pounders by the poop as he did so.

Bolitho looked at Starkie, his eyes level. 'I want to wear ship and pass out through the reef again. The frigate's bound to follow. He will have all the advantage with the wind under his coat-tails.' He saw Starkie nodding grimly. 'For just a few moments we will have him under our guns.' He smiled, the effort freezing his lips. 'Such as they are. He'll not be expecting us to turn and fight. Not now.'

Starkie stared beyond the bows like a man seeking a way out.

'I think I know a passage. It's not much.' He made a sweeping movement with his fist. 'I'm not sure about the depth. A few fathoms, no more, if I'm any judge.'

Thuds and bangs told Bolitho that Taylor and his men were almost ready.

A sudden roar of cannon fire made him realise that the frigate was still determined to cripple *Sandpiper* and then bring her to close action.

Aloud he murmured, 'Not this time, my friend.'

Starkie lowered his telescope as the frigate's iron shrieked overhead and brought down several lengths of broken rigging and a few blocks. The hull gave a violent jerk, and Bolitho knew they had taken their first direct hit.

He looked at Starkie as the latter called, 'Ready when you are.' He wiped his forehead with his wrist. He was streaming with sweat.

'Man the braces! Stand by to wear ship!' Bolitho nodded to the two gun crews. *'Run out!'*

He gripped his hands behind him until the force of his hold steadied him. He knew Dancer was staring, as were several of the men at the braces and halliards. Perhaps they were trying to see their own fate in his face.

He heard the old gun captain say, 'Don't yew forget, lads. As we goes about we'll be to lee'rd of that bugger. But it'll give your guns a better chance as we 'eels over like.'

There was a brief lull in the wind, so that just for an instant the sounds of sea and canvas faded. Through his racing thoughts Bolitho heard another sound, that of Tregorren groaning like a bull in agony.

The madness of it, the very hopelessness of their position made the lieutenant's discomfort all the more unreal.

He shook himself back to the present.

'Put up your helm! Wear ship!'

*

121

Leaning drunkenly with the wind, her beakhead lifting and smashing down in a welter of criss-crossing waves, *Sandpiper* began to respond to canvas and rudder.

The noise was indescribable, so that when the *Pegaso* fired a solitary shot from a bow-chaser the sound was almost lost in the thundering boom of sails, the protest of blocks and bar-taut rigging.

Bolitho saw that the men at the weather braces were hauling with such effort that their bodies were angled back almost to the deck itself. Others ran to aid their companions at halliards and aloft on the yards as they creaked round still further, the sails hardening and swelling like armour to the wind's thrust.

Bolitho tried not to look for the reefs, or at Starkie who had climbed into the shrouds to gauge better their progress towards the breaking surf.

Weakened by the *Pegaso*'s haphazard shots through the upper rigging, more pieces of severed hemp fell unheeded to the deck and across the rigid shoulders of Taylor, the old gun captain.

Round and still further round, the masts and yards creaking violently as the brig wheeled on to the opposite tack, the sea sluicing up and over the lee bulwark, which minutes earlier had been towards the enemy.

Bang. A ball sliced across the heaving water and slammed savagely into the hull, making several men cry out with alarm.

'Get some hands on the pumps!' Bolitho heard himself yelling orders, but felt like an onlooker, detached from all that was happening.

Ice-cold, he watched the enemy swinging around and across the stern, or so it appeared from *Sandpiper*'s violent alteration of course.

'*Now.*' His voice was lost in the din, and he shouted with sudden urgency, 'As you bear! *Fire!*'

He had seen the *Pegaso*'s big foresail starting to angle round as her captain decided to change tack and follow the brig.

He knew Taylor was crouching behind one of the guns, but could not look at him. He heard the hiss of his slow-match, and started with shock as the gun banged out across the water. He saw the *Pegaso*'s foresail pucker and a large hole appear as if by magic. Explored and strained by the wind and by the sudden alteration of course, the hole spread out in every direction, ripping the sail to fragments.

Starkie yelled, 'He's still coming round, sir!'

A lookout's voice cut across Bolitho's thoughts like a saw. 'Breakers to larboard, sir!'

But all he could think of was failure. The double-shotted gun had destroyed a sail, but under full canvas it could make no difference now.

Once through the reef, and it was strange that he had no doubts now Starkie could do it, the pirate would overhaul and board them.

Taylor loped to the second gun, his face creased in concentration. Fierce gestures with his tarred thumb got a handspike moving here, a tug on a gun tackle there.

He crouched down, his eyes like slits as he wheezed, '*Easy* now! Come on, my little one!'

The match went home, and with a grating crash the gun hurled itself inboard, smoke eddying back through the port like choking fog.

Bolitho watched, mesmerised. It took an age, in fact, only seconds. And then as the carefully aimed shot lifted and dropped across the frigate's bows he saw the bulging jib and staysail tear from top to bottom like old rags.

The effect was instantaneous. Caught in the middle of changing tack, her sails already in confusion, the *Pegaso* wallowed heavily in a deep trough, her gunports buried in the sea as she continued to answer the rudder.

Bolitho heard shouts from the lee side and ran to the nettings, his throat like dust as he saw a green-shouldered rock scudding past the *Sandpiper*'s side, barely yards clear. In those split seconds he saw the worn shape of the rock, and some tiny black fish which had managed to remain motionless, despite the wind and current, sheltering behind the reef which could tear out a ship's keel like the string from an orange.

He darted a glance at Dancer. He looked very pale and wild-eyed, his face and chest soaked with spray as he leaned out to watch the enemy's progress.

The *Pegaso* seemed to stagger, as if taken by an opposite squall, then as she tilted upright her main topgallant mast cracked over and fell straight down to the deck, a tangle of rigging and canvas trailing between the shrouds like weed.

Starkie yelled incredulously, 'See that? She hit a reef!' He was croaking with excitement and awe. '*She struck*, by God!'

Bolitho could not tear his eyes away. The frigate must

have smashed hard against a rock shoulder even as she lost power from her forward sails in the middle of a tack. Just a few yards had made all the difference, and he could picture the confusion on deck, the rush of men below to seek out the extent of the damage.

It had been enough to bring down a topgallant mast, and she must be leaking badly, he thought. And yet the frigate was still coming on, and as he watched, his eyes aching in the glare, he saw a bow-chaser shoot out an orange tongue, and felt the ball shriek past him and crash into the forecastle like a giant's axe.

Broken rigging and whirling splinters were hurled everywhere, and he saw three seamen smashed against the bulwark, their cries lost in the wind, but their convulsions marked by spreading patterns of blood.

Another ball ripped against the hull and ricocheted away over the sea, the deck bucking as if trying to throw the seamen from their feet.

Bolitho yelled, 'Attend the wounded! Tell Mr Eden to put them below!'

He thought suddenly of Eden's father in his little surgery, attending to people with gout and stomach trouble. What would he think if he could see his twelve-year-old son trying to drag a gasping seaman to the companion hatch, every foot of the way marked in pain and blood.

Dancer said despairingly, 'The frigate's closing to board us!' He did not even flinch as a ball whipped above the poop, leaving another hole in the pockmarked sails. 'After all we did!'

Bolitho looked at him and those nearby. The fight, the pathetic determination were going rapidly. And who could blame them? The *Pegaso* had matched their every move, in spite of being surprised. She was through the reef, and he could see the glitter of waving cutlasses as some of the men ran from the guns in readiness to board. He recalled Starkie's description of what had happened to *Sandpiper*'s officers, the torture and the final agony of their deaths.

He drew his hanger and yelled, 'Stand to! Starboard side!' He saw them turn to stare at him incredulously, their eyes dull with despair.

Bolitho jumped to the weather shrouds and waved his hanger at the *Pegaso*.

'They'll not take us without a fight!'

Little cameos stood out from the main picture. A man taking out a knife and honing it back and forth across his hand, his eyes on the frigate. Another crossing the deck to face a man who was probably his best, his only friend. Nothing said. Just an expression which told far more than words. Eden by the companion hatch, his face like chalk, and a man's blood already drying on his shirt, like his own would soon do. Dancer. His hair golden in the sunlight, his chin lifted as he picked up a cutlass and leaned on it. Bolitho saw his other hand gripping into his breeches, like a claw, pinching the flesh to shock him from his fear.

A man, wounded in the attack on the brig, was propped against a six-pounder, his legs in bandages, but his fingers busy as he loaded pistols and passed them to the others.

Something like a baying howl came from the *Pegaso*'s crowded deck as she edged closer abeam, the shadows of her masts and yards reaching across the water as if to snare the brig and engulf her.

Bolitho blinked and dashed the sweat from his eyes as he stared at one of the frigate's open gunports. A man, then another, was clambering out and around the black muzzles, and from other ports he saw figures emerging like rats from a sewer.

Starkie exclaimed, 'They're trying to abandon, sir!' He seized his arm and propelled him to the nettings. 'Will you *look* at that!'

Bolitho stood at his side and said nothing. More and more men were leaping from the gunports and being carried away like shavings on a mill-race.

Gauvin, the *Pegaso*'s fanatical captain, must have put guards on every hatch, and as his ship charged in hopeless, maddened pursuit, he would have known that the hull damage was fatal.

Starkie watched the frigate's bow wave falling away as the great weight of inrushing water slowed her down, the sudden pandemonium on the upper deck as everyone at last realised what was happening.

He said harshly, 'Here, put on your coat.' He even helped Bolitho into it and tugged the collar with its white patches into position.

He pointed to the *Pegaso,* which was starting to head away, the inrush of water playing havoc with the rudder's puny efforts.

'I want him to see you, and I pray to God he'll suffer for what he did.'

When Bolitho looked at him, he added, 'I want him to know he was beaten by a midshipman! A *boy*!'

Bolitho turned away, his ears filled with the sounds of a ship destroying itself, as under full sail she continued to slew round across the glittering crests. He heard guns coming loose from tackles and smashing into the opposite side, and spars falling, trapping the stampeding men under masses of black rigging and canvas.

He heard himself say, 'Shorten sail, Martyn. Call all hands.'

He felt men touching his shoulders, others ran towards him grinning and waving. Not a few were weeping.

'Deck there!' Everyone had forgotten the lonely man at the masthead. 'Sail on th' starboard bow, sir!' The merest pause and then, 'Tis th' *Gorgon*!'

Bolitho waved his hand to the masthead and turned to watch the pirate frigate heeling over, the sea around her filled with flotsam and thrashing, bobbing heads.

Out of the sun's path, across the heaving swell, he also saw a sudden flicker of movement, the knife-edged fins of sharks closing in around the sinking ship. It was over a mile to the nearest beach. It was doubtful if anyone would reach it.

He raised a telescope to look for the *Gorgon*, his eyes misty as he saw her fat black and buff hull, her towering pyramid of canvas rounding the next headland.

In another second he thought he would break, be unable to hide his emotion from those about him.

A great voice bellowed, 'What the *hell* is going on?'

Lieutenant Tregorren was standing half through the companion hatch, and with his blotchy grey face, his hair matted with wine and worse, he looked for all the world like a corpse emerging from a tomb.

Bolitho felt the relief flooding through him like madness. He wanted to laugh and cry all at once, and Tregorren's wild appearance, the realisation that he had been completely helpless throughout the fight, broke down all reserves.

He replied in a shaking voice, 'I am sorry we disturbed you, sir.'

Tregorren faced him and tried to focus a pair of angry red eyes.

'Disturb?'

'Aye, sir. But we have been fighting a battle.'

Starkie said calmly, 'Fetch Mr Eden. I fear the lieutenant is going to be ill again!'

9

Without Honour

Captain Beves Conway stood by an open stern window and held one hand to his eyes to protect them from the fierce, reflected glare. Through the windows of his cabin the recaptured brig roiled untidily in the swell, her tan sails barely moving as she idled above her own reflection.

Within a few hours of *Sandpiper*'s hazardous dash through the reef and the complete destruction of the frigate, the wind had dropped to a mere breath, leaving the heavy *Gorgon* and her small consort almost becalmed.

Like a pale yellow smear along the horizon, twisting and wavering in heat-haze, the shore was still visible, but could have been anywhere.

Conway turned slowly and studied the group by the bulkhead.

Tregorren, massive and red-eyed, his body swaying to the heavy motion, his face still the colour of ashes.

The three midshipmen, and the master's mate, Mr Starkie, standing slighly apart.

Verling, the first lieutenant, was also present, his nose disapproving as the captain's servant filled glasses of madeira for the crumpled and dishevelled visitors.

The captain took a beautifully cut glass from a tray and held it to the filtered sunlight.

'Your health, gentlemen.' He regarded each of them in turn. 'I do not have to say how gratified I am that *Sandpiper* is again with the fleet.' He turned to listen to the distant tap of hammers across the water as work continued to put right the damage from *Pegaso*'s cannon fire. 'Eventually I will be sending her to report to the admiral at Gibraltar with my despatches.' His gaze rested momentarily on Tregorren. 'To cut out a vessel at anchor is never easy. To do it, and to find the extra agility and skill to run an enemy frigate to ground, is worthy of their lordships' attention.'

Tregorren stared at some point above the captain's shoulder.

'Thank you, sir.'

The captain's eyes moved to the midshipmen. 'To have survived all this will give you scope for putting the experience to work, both for your own advancement and for the Navy in general.'

Bolitho darted a quick glance at Tregorren. The man was still staring at the deckhead, and he looked close to another violent attack of vomiting.

The captain said in the same matter-of-fact tone, 'At first light, while you were entering the reefs, I was searching to the south'rd. Quite by chance we came on a heavy dhow, loaded to the gunwales with black ivory.'

Starkie exclaimed, 'Slaves, sir?'

The captain regarded him coldly. *'Slaves.'* He gestured with his glass. 'I put a boarding party into the vessel, and she is now anchored around the next headland.' He gave a thin smile. 'The slaves I put ashore, although I know not if I have done them a favour.' The smile vanished.

'We have wasted too much time, and lost too many good men. It would take an army to lay siege to the island, and even then it is doubtful how the attack would go.'

He paused as the marine sentry beyond the door shouted, 'Surgeon, sir!'

The servant hurried to open the door as Laidlaw entered, wiping his hands carefully on a scrap of cloth.

'Yes?' The captain sounded sharp.

'You wished to know, sir. Mr Hope is sleeping. I took out the ball, and although I doubt if he'll ever be rid of discomfort, he'll not lose an arm.'

Bolitho looked at Dancer and Eden and smiled. It was something. The rest was over, part of a nightmare which even Tregorren's failure to admit that he had had no hand in the final action could not spoil.

He glanced at Starkie, who was studying Tregorren with something like hatred.

The captain added, 'At dusk, provided the wind returns, which Mr Turnbull *assures* me will, we will make contact with our new prize. At dawn I intend to send *Sandpiper* to chase the dhow towards the fortress. *Gorgon* will, of course, supply full support.'

Bolitho swallowed another glass of madeira, barely realising that the cabin servant had refilled it more than once. His stomach was quite empty, and the wine was making him feel light-headed and dizzy.

One fact stood out. The captain had no intention of giving in to the pirates who occupied the island. By retaking *Sandpiper* they had added another arm to their reach, and the watchers on the fortress's battery would have been able to see quite clearly how the brig had lured their one major vessel on to the reefs.

Verling snapped, 'Understood?'

Bolitho exclaimed, 'They'll think we're chasing a cargo of slaves, and be too busy firing at *Sandpiper* to watch the dhow, sir?'

The captain looked at him and then glanced across at Tregorren.

'What *d'you* think, Mr Tregorren?'

The lieutenant seemed to come out of a trance. 'Yes, sir. That is . . .'

The captain nodded. 'Quite.'

He walked aft again and studied the brig for some time.

'Mr Starkie will return to his ship and be prepared to assist whichever officers I appoint to take charge, and to sail eventually with my despatches.' He swung round, his eyes hard in the light. 'Had I thought that you had any part in losing *Sandpiper* in the first place, by negligence or lack of courage, I can assure you that you would not be here now, and your chances of advancement would have been smashed.' He smiled, the effort making him older rather than the opposite. 'You did very well, Mr Starkie. I only wish I could keep you in my command. But I think that when you reach higher authority your efforts will be better rewarded.' He nodded. 'Carry on, gentlemen.'

They left the cabin in a daze, the captain already in conference with Verling and the surgeon.

Bolitho shook Starkie's rough hand and exclaimed, 'I'm glad for you! But for your skill, and accepting an idea which to most people would have seemed quite mad, we would not be here at all!'

Starkie studied him gravely, as if searching for something he could not understand.

'But for *you,* I'd still be in irons and awaiting death.'

He turned as Tregorren strode to the companion ladder on his way down to the wardroom.

'I wanted to speak out.' Starkie's eyes were bitter. 'But as you said nothing, I thought it best to hold my peace. He is without honour!'

Eden stammered, 'It's n-not r-right, D-Dick! H-he'll get the c-credit!' He was almost weeping. 'He j-just stood th-there and t-took it all!'

Dancer smiled. 'I think the captain knows more than he's prepared to admit. I watched him. He is balancing the value of the victory against damaging it with envy and shame.' He grinned at Eden. '*And* midshipmen who go round trying to poison their betters!'

Bolitho nodded. 'I agree. Now let us go and eat. Anything, even a ship's rat, will do for me.'

They turned towards the companion ladder and froze.

A figure in an ill-fitting uniform, that of a lieutenant, blocked their way.

He said, 'Nothing to do, eh? Midshipmen are not what they were in my day!'

They crowded round him, and Bolitho said, 'John Grenfell! We thought you dead!'

Grenfell gripped his hand, his face very grim. 'When *City of Athens* was destroyed, some of us managed to find safety on drifting spars. We hauled them together like a little raft, not knowing what was happening.' He dropped his gaze. 'Most of our people were killed. The lucky ones in the cannon fire, the rest when the sharks tore amongst us. The third lieutenant, oh, so many old faces, were slashed to fragments before our eyes.' He shrugged, as if to free himself of the memory. 'But we drifted ashore, and as we made our way along the coast, there, as large as life, was the ship standing in to the beach, and Dewar's bullocks with a dhow full of screaming slaves, an Arab crew and two Portuguese merchants who were so terrified that I think they believed their end had come.' He plucked at his borrowed coat. 'So I have been made acting sixth lieutenant. It will do no harm when my examination is called.' He looked into the distance. 'But I got the chance at a price I would dearly repay if it were possible.'

Bolitho said quietly, 'But *you* are safe.'

Starkie yawned. 'I could sleep for a year.' He grinned at Grenfell. *'Sir.'*

Grenfell walked with them to the ladder. 'I suggest you all get some rest. I have a feeling it will be all the hotter tomorrow, in more ways than one!'

Mr Turnbull's knowledge of weather did not desert him. By the time the first dog watch had run its course both vessels were under way again, their sails filling to the breeze. An hour later the wind had steadied to a fresh northerly, and when the hands were assembled aft the air was like a tonic after the sweaty furnace between decks.

The lieutenants and marine officers were by the poop ladder, watching the captain, who was conferring with Verling and the sailing master.

Petty officers moved amongst the assembled seamen, checking their muster lists and calling out names, while from the lower gundeck Bolitho could hear the screech of a grindstone as the gunner's mates attended to the sharpening of cutlasses and boarding axes. The very sound made him shiver, as it always had.

A lookout bawled, 'Deck there! Vessel at anchor off the larboard bow!'

Dancer had been peering across at *Sandpiper*'s sails. They were creamy in the fading light, and there was nothing visible of the shot holes and patches.

Dallas, the second lieutenant, had taken charge of her for the attack. A man Bolitho knew nothing of, and had barely heard utter more than a few necessary orders since he had joined the ship. But the captain's choice showed that he trusted Dallas for the task. It also suggested he was not entirely satisfied with Tregorren's part in the cutting-out.

When Bolitho had seen Starkie over the side to be taken back to the brig, the master's mate had stared aft towards the captain's slowly pacing figure. He had grinned.

'It's how you gets to *be* a post-captain, young feller, knowing them things!'

'All midshipmen lay aft to the quarterdeck!'

They hurried along the gangway and found Verling waiting by the lee nettings, one foot tapping with impatience.

'Three of you will be required for the attack.' He scowled as Marrack made to speak. 'Not you. You will be needed for the signal party.' His cold eyes rested on Bolitho. 'As you have just returned to your proper duties with us, I cannot order you to take part either. Mr Pearce,' he turned to the sulky-looking midshipman from the lower gundeck, 'and . . .'

Bolitho glanced at Dancer who gave the briefest nod.

He called, 'Mr Dancer and I would like to volunteer, sir. We sailed very close to the island. It might be of some use.'

Verling smiled wryly. 'Now that Mr Grenfell has placed his foot on the bottom rung of promotion, you three, apart from Mr Marrack, are the oldest. So I suppose I'd better allow you to go.'

Eden stepped smartly from the rank of midshipmen.

'S-sir! I'd l-like to v-volunteer, too!'

Verling glared down at him. 'Don't you stutter at me, you urchin! Get back in line and hold your noise!'

Eden retreated, beaten before he had started.

Verling nodded, apparently satisfied.

'Boats will be lowered as soon as we heave-to. All the marines and sixty seamen will transfer to that floating hell yonder.'

Dancer whispered, 'The captain is sending everyone he can spare.'

Verling rasped, 'After the raid, should you be spared, Mr Dancer, you will be awarded five days' extra duty. *Be silent!*'

The captain walked aft towards the poop, as if on a stroll ashore.

He paused and asked evenly, 'All well, Mr Verling?'

'Aye, sir.'

The captain glanced at the three midshipmen who stood where they had been called.

'Be vigilant.' He looked at his first lieutenant. 'Mr Verling will command the attack, so he will expect your best support, as will I.' He leaned forward, seeking out Eden's small shape. 'You, er, Mr er, will probably be useful assisting the surgeon in your new and er, surprising capacity.'

Neither he nor Verling gave even the hint of a smile.

It was almost dark by the time the transfer of men and weapons had been completed.

Even before they reached the large dhow Bolitho could smell the stench of slavery. Once on board it was almost overpowering as the seamen and marines clambered below, stooping beneath the crude deck beams and slithering on filth and broken manacles.

Major Dewar's corporals were spaced at intervals along the hull to lead or push the new arrivals into the proper places where they would remain until the actual moment of attack. It was as well Eden had been left behind, Bolitho thought. This stench, and the cramped journey, would have made him as sick as a dog.

Several swivel guns were swayed up from the longboats and mounted on the bulwarks and aft by the high poop.

There was a smell of rum in the air too, and Bolitho guessed that the captain had thought it prudent to give the attackers something to sustain them.

Bolitho and the other two midshipmen made their way aft to the poop to report that all the extra seamen and marines were crammed below like pork in a barrel.

In the half-darkness the marines' cross-belts stood out very white, their coats merging with the background.

Hoggett, the *Gorgon*'s leather-lunged boatswain, was in charge of the dhow's sails and steering, and Bolitho heard one seaman mutter unkindly, ''E'd be right at 'ome on a blessed slaver, 'e would!'

Verling snapped, 'Break out the anchor and get this vessel under way, Mr Hoggett! Perhaps the wind will take the stench out of her!'

He turned as another shadowy figure climbed to the poop. 'All ready, Mr Tregorren?'

Dancer said, 'So he's coming too, damn him!'

'Anchor's aweigh, sir!'

Bolitho watched the two seamen using the great sweep oar which stood in place of wheel or tiller. The strange lateen sails creaked up the masts, the sailors slipping and cursing with unfamiliar and, to them, crude rigging.

Verling had brought a small boat's compass, and handed it to the boatswain.

'We will take our time. Stand well offshore. I'd rather not finish the attack like that frigate ended her life, eh, Mr Tregorren? It must have been quite a moment.'

Tregorren sounded as if his breathing was hurting him.

He replied thickly, 'It was, sir.'

Verling dropped the matter.

'Mr Pearce, show the lantern to *Gorgon*.'

Bolitho saw the light blink briefly as Pearce lifted the shutter. Captain Conway would know they had started. In the small glow from the compass Bolitho saw Verling's beaky profile, and was suddenly glad he was in command.

He wondered what Tregorren would say to him when next they spoke. If he would continue his deception, or admit that he was not responsible for *Pegaso*'s destruction.

Verling's voice bit into his thoughts.

'If you have nothing to do, I suggest you sleep until you are called. Otherwise I will discover a task of some enormity for you, even in this vessel!'

Hidden by the deepening darkness, Bolitho grinned broadly.

'Aye, aye, sir. Thank you, sir.'

He settled down against an ancient bronze cannon and rested his chin on his knees. Dancer joined him, and together they stared up at the tiny, pale stars, against which the dhow's great sails showed like wings.

'Here we go again, Martyn.'

Dancer sighed. 'But we kept together. That's the main thing.'

10

A Name to Remember

'Wind's backed again, sir!'

The boatswain's hoarse voice made Bolitho nudge Dancer with his elbow and rouse him.

He saw Verling and Tregorren consulting the compass, and when he looked up at the ragged mainmast pendant he saw it was lifting and whipping to a new thrust of wind. The sky was paler, and as he struggled to his feet he felt every muscle throbbing with cramp.

Verling commented flatly, 'We will beat clear of the headland nevertheless.' His arm shot out, black against the sky. 'There! I can see surf below the point!' The arm darted round. 'You midshipmen, get below and rouse the people. My compliments to Major Dewar, and tell him we will pass very close inshore. I want no marine or seaman on deck who has not been so ordered.'

A block squeaked, and Bolitho saw a large flag jerking up to the foremost lateen sail. In daylight it would be seen as a black one, similar to that worn by the *Pegaso*. He shivered, despite his excitement.

'Come on, Martyn, we'd better hurry.'

He retched and covered his mouth with his sleeve as he plunged down into the fat-bellied hold. In the glitter of a solitary lantern the crowded seamen and marines could have been another slave cargo. The realisation came like an ice-cold shock. If this attack failed, the survivors would end as no better than the poor wretches released by Captain Conway. Although the corsair, Raïs Haddam, recruited many white mercenaries to man his ships and expand his grip across the trade routes, he had little love or respect for them. If half of what was said of him was true, it was more than likely he would keep captured British seamen to replace those very same slaves.

Dewar listened to his message and grunted.

''Bout time. I'm aching like a sick cow.'

Dancer coughed and gasped, 'I am glad *we* were on deck, sir.'

The marines exchanged glances and Dewar said, 'Spoiled young devils! It is the discomfort I object to. The smell is no worse than any field of battle.' He grinned at Dancer's nausea. 'Especially after a few days, when the crows have been at work, eh?'

He stood up, ducking under the beams. 'Marines, stand-to! Sar'nt Halse, inspect the weapons!'

Bolitho returned to the poop, and found to his surprise that it was already bright enough to see the land drifting abeam, the dancing spray amongst some angry-looking rocks.

Dancer murmured, 'A lee shore. If the first lieutenant had taken an hour longer we'd have been hard put to beat clear.'

'Sir! I can see someone on the point!'

Verling raised a telescope. 'Yes. He's gone from view now. Probably a lookout of some kind. He won't get across to the island, but the cosair may have a sort of signalling arrangement.' He was thinking aloud.

The wind made the great sails bang noisily, and the poorly made rigging looked as if it might tear apart at any second. But it must be stronger than it appeared, Bolitho decided. He watched Hoggett supervising the helmsmen, the easy way the dhow turned to starboard to let the nearest rocks slip past the quarter with a bare twenty feet to spare. The dhow handled well. He smiled tightly. So it should. Arab sailors were using them long before ships like *Gorgon* were even dreamed of.

Pearce said, 'There's the fortress.' He grimaced. 'God, it looks a mite larger from this side!'

It was still shrouded in gloom, with only the upper tower and battery catching the first feeble light.

There was a sharp bang, and for an instant Bolitho imagined the fortress had seen through Captain Conway's ruse and could not restrain the gunners from firing.

He ducked as a ball whipped high overhead and threw a fanlike waterspout amongst the rocks.

'*Sandpiper*, sir!' A seaman almost prodded Verling in his excitement to point across the larboard beam. '*She* fired!'

Verling lowered his glass and studied him coldly.

'Thank you. I did not imagine it was an act of God!'

Another shot banged out, and this time the ball smashed down across the bows in direct line with their approach.

Verling gave a thin smile. 'Let her fall off, Mr Hoggett. I *know* Mr Dallas has an excellent gun captain with him in *Sandpiper*, but we'll not take too many chances.'

The dhow tilted steeply as the helmsmen brought her further round towards the island.

'Fire the er, stern-chaser.'

Verling stood aside as some seamen who had been working on one of the old bronze cannons plunged a slow-match into the pitted touch-hole and jumped clear.

The ancient bronze barrel was almost worn out, but the resonant bang was far louder than anyone had expected.

Verling said, 'That should do it. If we fire it again, I fear it will explode in our midst.'

Bolitho saw the brig for the first time. Close-hauled on a converging tack, she was heeling well over to the wind, her sails merged into one pale pyramid in the dawn light.

He saw the flash of another gun, and winced as the ball pounded close to the waterline, dousing seamen and crouching marines in falling spray.

Verling remarked angrily, 'Mr Dallas is too good an actor. A few more like that and I will have to take him to task.' He smiled at the boatswain. '*Later*, of course.'

'He's worried.' Dancer peered through the bulwark. 'I've never heard him make jokes before.'

'Listen!' Verling held up his hand. 'A trumpet! We've roused them at last!'

He became serious. 'Divide up the people, Mr Tregorren. You know what to do. There is some kind of jetty on the eastern side, right beneath the fortress. I am told it is where the traders bring the slaves, and from whence they ferry them to seagoing vessels.'

He placed his hat on the deck and glanced quickly at the others around him.

'Remove any items of uniform which might be recognised, and keep out of sight as much as possible. Pass the word to the marines to stand fast and wait for the order. *No matter what.*'

The brig was closing fast, several of her snappy six-pounders loosing off shot, some of which fell dangerously near to the dhow.

A great boom shattered the air, and seconds later Bolitho saw a waterspout shoot skywards just beyond *Sandpiper*'s bowsprit.

Her sails were in disarray as Lieutenant Dallas brought her even closer, running up his ensign to the gaff as if to further infuriate the enemy.

Several more flashes lit the battery wall, and the splashes, although as big as the first, were haphazard and nowhere near the brig.

Bolitho supposed that the gun crews were still half asleep, or could not believe that a vessel so frail, one which had already been seized below these same cannon, would dare press any nearer.

He bit his lip as another heavy ball passed between the brig's two masts. It was a miracle that neither was hit, but he saw several lengths of cut rigging drifting in the wind like jungle creeper.

One direct hit in a vital spot was all the battery needed to render the *Sandpiper* helpless. At least long enough for her to drive ashore and be taken.

Verling's voice was right in his ear.

'Don't keep staring at *Sandpiper*. Keep your eyes and mind ahead. We could be quite wrong about the entrance. Mr Starkie's memory may have played tricks on him.'

Bolitho darted a quick glance at Verling. Without his hat to balance it, the nose looked even beakier and larger. He saw something else on his face. Determination, anxiety, both were there. But also a kind of recklessness.

Bolitho looked away. He had seen a similar expression on the face of a highwayman as he had been driven to the gibbet.

Sunlight felt its way gingerly over the land and played across the fortress walls. There were several heads peering from the weathered embrasures, and then Bolitho saw what appeared to be a flagstaff poking out of the ground at the foot of the furthest wall.

Verling had already seen it.

'The entrance.' He turned to Hoggett. 'That must be a mast, just inside. Another dhow most likely.' He wiped his narrow face with the back of his arm. 'Steer for it.'

Tregorren hurried aft, hard put to hide his great bulk beneath the litter of spare sails and fishing gear which covered the slaver's filthy deck from side to side.

'All ready, sir.'

He saw Bolitho and met his gaze without blinking. Defiance? It was difficult to see any emotion in the man. Even his colour was returning, and Bolitho wondered what would happen if he found time to take more drink before the attack.

'*Sandpiper*'s going about, sir. She's going to try another attack.'

Bolitho held his breath as two balls fell on either side of the brig's sleek hull, as with sails flapping and banging she turned across the wind's eye for another attempt to head off the dhow.

He saw the first sunlight shining on weapons above the battery wall and imagined the defenders jeering at the brig's retreat. Small she might be, and recaptured from them was a hard fact to swallow. But she was still a symbol of power of the world's greatest navy. And now, against their massive cannon, she was as helpless as a sick horse.

'There are men on the jetty, sir!' Pearce was in the bows, kneeling beside one of the swivels. 'They're watching us.'

Bolitho saw Hoggett's weatherbeaten face harden. The next minutes were vital. If the pirates suspected what was happening, the guns would soon be firing down on them. At this range there was no escape. And in a few more moments the island would lie between them and safety.

He felt his stomach rumbling noisily and glanced quickly at Dancer. His friend was breathing very quickly, and jumped as Bolitho gripped his shoulder and pulled him down to the deck.

Bolitho tried to smile. 'If they see your fair hair, they'll know we are not likely to be friendly!'

He turned as Verling snapped, 'Well said. I should have thought of that myself.' He turned away, already thinking far ahead of the slow-moving dhow.

The guns were firing again, but the sound was muffled, for the brig was hidden now by the fortress.

Nearer, and nearer. Bolitho tried to lick his lips as the top of the main fortress showed itself above the bulwark where he lay. Did the enemy recognise the dhow? Had she been here before?

He glanced up at Verling, who was standing with his arms folded beside the helmsmen. One of the latter was a Negro, of whom there were several in *Gorgon*'s company. It would make the little group seem genuine, he thought, and Verling certainly looked every inch a slaver.

'Take in the mains'l.'

Sunlight flooded into the deck as the mass of patched canvas and leather lashings came tumbling into the hull.

There were a dozen or more figures at the end of the jetty. Motionless, with only their long white robes lifting to the wind as the dhow edged round the crumbling stonework. Beyond the jetty there was a high, cavelike entrance, directly below the main wall. Several small vessels were moored there, and the largest one, a dhow, very like their prize, was tied up at the outer end, unable to dip her masts beneath the curved archway.

Thirty feet. Twenty.

Then a man yelled something and a figure ran to the steps to peer down at the dhow with sudden alarm.

Verling called tightly, 'Put her alongside! They're on to us!'

Then he tore his sword from its scabbard and was leaping long-legged from the poop before Hoggett's men had begun to lever their great oar.

Everything seemed to happen at once. From the bows and the bulwark the swivel guns were bared and fired at extreme angle into the men on the jetty. Those in the front fell kicking and screaming before a torrent of canister shot, and others caught on the end of the wall were cut down by the swivel on the poop.

Bolitho found his legs were taking him after the lieutenant, although he did not remember moving from the bulwark. Seamen surged from the hatches, cheering and yelling as they hurled themselves over the side and began to run for the entrance. Muskets banged from the wall and a few seamen fell before they had gone twenty yards.

But shock and surprise were taking effect. Perhaps the defenders had grown complacent and careless. Too long treated to the spectacle of terrified, beaten slaves being driven up this same jetty. The charging mob of seamen, the lethal glitter of cutlass blades and axes, held some of them spellbound, so that when the *Gorgon*'s men swept amongst them they were cut down where they stood.

'Follow me, Gorgons!' Verling's voice needed no trumpet. *'At 'em!'*

As they ran haphazardly beneath the archway and past some smaller boats there was a rattle of musket fire from the fortress itself, as at long last the defenders were made to realise what was happening.

Gasping and cursing, their legs apart, chests heaving painfully, the attacking sailors were slowly compressed by two adjoining walls, their advance steadily reduced as more and more men came from the wall above.

Bolitho locked swords with a great giant, who mouthed and screamed with every savage slash of his heavy blade. He felt something slide against his ribs and heard the seaman, Fairweather, gasp, 'Take *that* then!'

The touch had been Fairweather's pike, which was almost dragged from his grasp as the pirate toppled shrieking over the side of the stairs.

But other seamen were falling. Bolitho could feel his shoes catching on sprawled limbs as he lurched shoulder to shoulder with Dancer and Hoggett, their arms aching, their swords and hangers as heavy as lead.

Someone pitched sideways and was trampled underfoot.

Bolitho only got one glance. It was Midshipman Pearce, his eyes already dull and without recognition as blood ran from his mouth.

'Verling was yelling, *'Stand fast, lads!'* There was blood on his neck and chest, and he was almost separated from the bulk of his men by slashing, screaming pirates.

Bolitho turned as Dancer let out a cry and dropped amongst the others. He had slipped on some blood, and as he fell his hanger clattered away out of reach.

He rolled over, staring wide-eyed as a robed figure ran at him with a raised scimitar.

Bolitho tried to cut a man down to reach him, but was in turn knocked aside as Tregorren charged through the mob like a bull and slashed the pirate across the face, opening it from ear to chin.

Then above the cries and clash of steel Bolitho heard the blare of a trumpet, followed instantly by Major Dewar's thick, familiar tones.

'Marines! Advance!'

Bolitho dragged his friend away from the interlocked figures, holding him clear of thrusting blades, his mind cringing from noise and hate.

Verling's reckless attack had been for one thing only. To lure down the bulk of the pirates from the wall to defend the entrance from the dhow's crew. What it must have been like for the marines, crouching in the hold, hearing their messmates and friends being butchered while they waited for the signal to advance, Bolitho could barely imagine.

But they were coming now. Their scarlet coats and white cross-belts shone in the sunlight as if on parade, and as Verling waved his sword to call his seamen back from the stairs, Major Dewar bellowed, 'Front rank, *fire!*'

The musket balls swept through the packed bodies on the stairs, and as the marines paused to reload, their ramrods rising and falling as one, the next rank marched through them, knelt, took aim and fired.

It was more than enough, the defenders broke and stampeded through the entrance.

Dewar lifted his sword. 'Fix bayonets! Marines, *charge!*'

Yelling like madmen, his men forgot their discipline and lunged for the entrance.

'Huzza! Huzza!' The seamen, breathless and bleeding, lowered their weapons as the marines charged past.

Dancer said, 'Let's get George out of the way.'

Together they dragged Pearce's spreadeagled body into the shadow of the wall. He was staring straight up at the sky, the shock of death frozen on his face.

Hoggett was shouting, 'Through 'ere, sir!' He gestured at some great iron-studded doors. 'It's full of slaves!'

Bolitho stood up shakily and took a firmer grip on his curved hanger. He caught Tregorren's eye, and the lieutenant asked curtly, 'You all right?'

He replied shakily, 'Aye, sir.'

Tregorren nodded. 'Right. Take some hands and follow the marines –' He paused as a sound like distant thunder rolled across the bay and against the headland. Then came the crash of iron, the clatter of falling stonework.

Verling wrapped a rag around one bloodied wrist and tightened the knot with his teeth.

'Gorgon has arrived.' It was all he said.

Again and again, the seventy-four poured a broadside into the island fortress. The bombardment made little difference to the defences, but attacked and harried from within by the jubilant marines, and with two ships-of-war sailing unhampered below the wall, it was enough.

Major Dewar appeared at the top of the steps, his hat gone, a deep cut above one eye. But he was able to grin as he reported that the defence had crumbled.

To prove his words, the black flag above the battery

floated down like a dying bird, and was replaced, to wild cheering, by one of the ship's ensigns.

Their minds still shocked by the savage fighting, they climbed the steps to the high ramparts where the unmanned guns pointed impotently across the blue water. There were dead and dying everywhere, and too many red coats sprawled amongst the rest.

Bolitho and Dancer stood on the wall and watched the ships far below. The little brig was already quivering in the early haze, but *Gorgon* was clear-cut and splendid as she tacked ponderously towards the island, her depleted topmen shortening sail, but pausing to wave and shout towards the figures on the wall, their cheers lost in distance.

It was very quiet, and when Bolitho looked at Dancer he saw there were tears cutting through the grime on his cheeks.

Bolitho said, 'Easy, Martyn.'

'I was thinking of George Pearce. How it was nearly me. And you.'

Bolitho turned to watch as *Gorgon*'s great anchor plummeted into the placid water.

He said quietly, 'I know. But we are alive, and must be grateful.'

Verling's shadow merged with theirs.

'God blast your eyes!' He glared at the pair of them. 'Do you think I can do everything on my own?' He looked past them at the ship and gave a tired smile. 'But I know how you feel.' The strain dropped from his sharp features like a shadow. 'I never thought I'd live to see that old lady again!' He swung away, already barking orders.

Bolitho watched him gravely. 'Well, it shows you never really know a man.'

They pushed themselves from the wall, as wearily, obediently, the seamen and marines began to muster beneath the flag.

When Verling spoke again to the assembled men his tone was as usual.

'Smarten yourselves up. Remember this, and remember it well. You are Gorgons. It is a reputation hard to live by.' For the briefest instant his glance fell on Bolitho. 'Often easy to die for. Now, clap the prisoners in irons and attend to our wounded. After that' – he looked up and beyond the gently flapping flag, as if surprised to be able to see either – 'we will take care of those who were less fortunate.'

By evening most of the wounded had been ferried across to the anchored *Gorgon*. The dead were buried on the island beneath the wall, where Bolitho heard an old seaman say as he leaned on his spade, 'I reckon this place'll be fought over again an' again. These poor lads will get the best view of it next time.'

As shadow hid the scars of *Gorgon*'s bombardment, Dancer and Bolitho stood side by side on the larboard gangway watching the last rays holding on to the drooping flag above the battery.

Despite a careful search, they had found no trace of Raïs Haddam. Perhaps he had escaped, or had never been in the fortress at all. The pirates would say nothing about him, or betray his whereabouts. They were more frightened of Haddam than they were of their captors. The latter offered only death by hanging.

It would all have to be sorted out by Captain Conway, Bolitho throught wearily, his eyelids drooping. The slaves to be ferried ashore, the battery spiked and thrown into the sea. So many things.

A step fell on the deck behind them and they turned, lurching upright as the captain paused to speak. He was impeccably dressed. The same as if nothing had happened, and none had died.

He examined them impassively. 'The first lieutenant informs me that you all did very well. I am glad to know it.' His gaze shifted slightly. 'Mr Bolitho, he told me that you in particular acted with the finest qualities of a King's officer. I shall mention as much in my report to the admiral.'

He nodded curtly and strode aft towards the poop.

Dancer turned, his smile fading as he saw Bolitho bent over the nettings, his shoulders shaking uncontrollably.

But Bolitho faced him again, gripping his friend's arm to reassure him.

Between gasps he managed to explain. 'Things *have* changed, Martyn. *The captain remembered my name!*'

Midshipman Bolitho and the Avenger

To All Midshipmen
Past and Present

Contents

Contents

1

Home from the Sea

With an impressive clatter of wheels the stage-coach shivered to a halt beside the inn's courtyard and its handful of weary passengers gave a sigh of relief. It was early December, the year 1773, and Falmouth, like most of Cornwall, was covered in a blanket of snow and slush. Standing in the dull afternoon light, with its four horses steaming from their hard drive, the coach seemed to have no colour, as it was coated with mud from axles to roof.

Midshipman Richard Bolitho jumped down and stood for a few moments just staring at the old, familiar inn and the weathered buildings beyond. It had been a painful ride. Only fifty-five miles from Plymouth to here, but it had taken two days. The coach had gone inland, almost into Bodmin Moor, to avoid flooding from the River Fowey, and the coachman had firmly refused to move at night because of the treacherous roads. Bolitho suspected he was more afraid of highwaymen than weather. Those *gentlemen* found it much easier to prey on coaches bogged down on muddy, rutted tracks than to match shots with an eagle-eyed guard on the King's highway.

He forgot the journey, the bustling ostlers who were releasing the horses from their harness, also the other passengers as they hurried towards the inn's inviting warmth, and savoured the moment.

It had been a year and two months since he had left Falmouth to join the seventy-four-gun ship of the line *Gorgon* at Spithead. Now she lay at Plymouth for a much-needed refit and overhaul, and he, Richard Bolitho, had come home for a well-earned leave.

Bolitho held out his hand to steady his travelling companion as he climbed down to join him in the bitter wind. Midshipman Martyn Dancer had joined *Gorgon* on the same day as himself, and like Bolitho was seventeen years old.

'Well, Martyn, we have *arrived*.'

Bolitho smiled, glad Dancer had come with him. His home was in London, and quite different in a thousand ways from his own. Whereas the Bolithos had been sea officers for generations, Dancer's father was a rich City of London tea merchant. But if their worlds were miles apart, Bolitho felt towards Martyn Dancer as he would to a brother.

When *Gorgon* had anchored, and the mail had been brought aboard, Dancer had discovered that his parents were abroad. He had immediately suggested that Bolitho should keep him company in London, but *Gorgon*'s first lieutenant, the ever-watchful Mr Verling, had said icily, 'I should think not indeed. Alone in *that* city, your father would see me damned for it!'

So Dancer had readily accepted Bolitho's invitation. Bolitho was secretly glad. And he was eager to see his family again, for them to see him, and the change that fourteen months of hard service had offered him. Like his friend, he was leaner, if that were possible, more confident, and above all grateful to have survived both storm and shot.

The coach guard touched his hat and took the coins which Bolitho thrust into his gloved fist.

'Don't 'ee fear, zur. I'll tell the innkeeper to send your chests up to the house directly.' He jerked his thumb at the inn windows, already glowing with lantern light. 'Now I'll join me fellow travellers for an hour, then on to Penzance.' He walked away, adding, 'Good luck to 'ee, young gennlemen.'

Bolitho watched him thoughtfully. So many Bolithos had mounted or dismounted from coaches here. On their way to far-off places, returning from one ship or another. Some never came back at all.

He threw his blue boatcloak round his shoulders and said, 'We'll walk. Get the blood alive again, eh?'

Dancer nodded, his teeth chattering uncontrollably. Like Bolitho, he was very tanned, and was still unable to accept the violent change of weather and climate after a year in and around the African coastline.

Now, as they strode through the mud and slush, past the

old church and ancient trees, it was hard to believe it had ever happened. Searching for corsairs, retaking the brig *Sandpiper* and using her to destroy a pirate's ship after a chase through dangerous reefs. Men had died, many more had suffered from all the countless burdens which beset sailors everywhere. Bolitho had fought hand to hand, had been made to kill, had watched one of the *Gorgon*'s midshipmen fall dead during an attack on a slaver's stronghold. They were no longer boys. They had become young men together.

'There it is.' Bolitho pointed at the big grey house, square and uncompromising, almost the same colour as the low, scudding clouds and the headland beyond.

Through the gates and up to the broad doorway. He did not even have to reach for one of the massive iron-ringed handles, for the doors swung inwards and he saw Mrs Tremayne, the housekeeper, rushing to meet him, her red face beaming with pleasure.

She hugged him to her, overwhelming him, bringing back even more memories. Her smell of clean linen and lavender, of kitchens and hung bacon. She was well over sixty-five, and was as much a part of the house as its foundations.

She rocked him back and forth like a child, although he was a head taller than she.

'Oh, young Master Dick, what have they done to 'ee?' She was almost in tears. 'You'm as thin as a reed, nothin' to 'ee at all. I'll soon put some meat on your bones.'

She saw Dancer for the first time and released him reluctantly.

Bolitho grinned, embarrassed but pleased at her concern. She had been far worse when he had first gone to sea at the age of twelve.

'This is my friend, Martyn Dancer. He's to stay with us.'

They all turned as Bolitho's mother appeared on the great stairway.

'And you will be most welcome.'

Dancer watched her, entranced. He had heard plenty about Harriet Bolitho during the long sea-watches and the rare moments of peace between decks. But she was like no woman in his imaginary picture. She seemed too young to be Richard's mother, too fragile even to be left so often alone in this great stone house below the Pendennis Castle headland.

'Mother.'

Bolitho went to her and they embraced for a long moment. And still Dancer watched. Richard, his friend, whom he had come to know so well, usually so good at hiding his feelings behind an impassive face and those calm grey eyes. Whose hair was as black as his own was fair, who could show emotion at the death of a friend, but who had become a lion in battle, looked more like her suitor than a son.

She said to Dancer, 'How long?'

It was calmly put, but he sensed the edge in her question. Bolitho replied for him. 'Four weeks. Maybe longer if . . .'

She reached up and touched his hair.

'I know, Dick. That word *if*. The Navy must have invented it.'

She put her hands through their arms and linked them together.

'But you will be home for Christmas. And you have a friend. That is good. Your father is still away in India.' She sighed. 'And I am afraid Felicity is married and with her husband's regiment in Canterbury.'

Bolitho turned and studied her gravely. He had been thinking only of himself. Of his homecoming, his own pride at what he had done. And she had been made to face everything alone, as was too often the case with the women who married into the Bolitho family.

His sister, Felicity, who was now nineteen, had been very happy to receive one of the young officers from the local garrison. While he was away she had married him, and had gone.

Bolitho had guessed that his only brother, Hugh, would be away. He was four years his senior, the apple of his father's eye, and at present a lieutenant aboard a frigate.

He asked awkwardly, 'And Nancy? Is she well, Mother?'

Her face lit up, making her appear her old self again.

'Indeed she is, Dick, although she is out visiting, despite the weather.'

Dancer felt strangely relieved. He had heard a good deal about Nancy, the youngest of the family. She would be about sixteen, and something of a beauty, if her mother was anything to judge by.

Bolitho saw his friend's expression and said, 'That is good news.'

She looked from one to the other and laughed. 'I see your point.'

'I'll take Martyn to his room, Mother.'

She nodded, watching them as they climbed the stairway, past the watching portraits of long-dead Bolithos.

'When the post-boy told us that the *Gorgon* was in Plymouth, I knew you would come home, Dick. I'd never forgive your Captain Conway if he'd denied me that pleasure!'

Bolitho thought of the captain, aloof, impressively calm no matter what the hazards. He had never really pictured him as a ladies' man.

Dancer was studying one portrait at the turn of the stairway.

Bolitho said quietly, 'My grandfather Denziel. He was with Wolfe at Quebec. Grand old man, I think. Sometimes I can't remember if I really knew him, or if it was what my father told me about him which remains.'

Dancer grinned. 'He looks a lively sort. And Rear Admiral, no less!'

He followed Bolitho along the landing, hearing the wind and sleet against the windows. It felt strange after a ship's constant movement, the sounds and smells of a crowded man-of-war.

It was always the same with midshipmen. They were constantly hungry, and being chased and harried in every direction. Now, if only for a few days, he would find peace, and if Mrs Tremayne had anything to do with it, a full stomach too.

Bolitho opened a door for him. 'One of the maids will bring your things, Martyn.' He faltered, his eyes like the sea beyond the headland. 'I'm glad you came. Once or twice,' he hesitated, '. . . back over the months, I thought I would never be coming here again. Having you with me makes it feel complete.'

He swung away, and Dancer closed the door quietly behind him.

Dancer knew exactly what he had meant, and was moved to have shared the moment with him.

He crossed to a window and peered through the streaming glass. Almost lost in the winter's gloom the sea was lively and criss-crossed with angry crests.

It was out there waiting for them to return.

He smiled and started to undress.

Well, it could damned well wait a bit longer!

'So, Martyn, what did you think of your first free evening?'

The two midshipmen sat on either side of a roaring log fire, legs outstretched, eyes drooping from the heat and the biggest meal Mrs Tremayne had prepared for some time.

Dancer raised his goblet and watched the flames change colour through the ruby port and smiled contentedly.

'Something akin to a miracle.'

It had been a lengthy meal, with Bolitho's mother and his young sister Nancy both eager and willing just to let them talk. Bolitho had found himself wondering how many tales had been passed across that same table, some embroidered no doubt, but all true.

Nancy had worn a new gown for the occasion, which she apparently had made in Truro. *'The latest thing in France.'* It had been low-cut, and although her mother had frowned once or twice, it made her look younger rather than wanton.

She was much more like her mother than her sister, who took after the Bolitho side of the family, with the same ready smile which had charmed Captain James Bolitho when he had taken a Scottish girl for his wife.

Nancy had made a great impression on Dancer, and Bolitho guessed it was probably mutual.

Outside the curtained windows it was quieter, the sleet having given way to snow, which had already covered the outbuildings and stables in a thick, glistening blanket. No one would be moving very far tonight, Bolitho thought, and he pitied the coach on its way to Penzance.

How still the house seemed, the servants having gone to bed long since, leaving the two friends to drowse or yarn as so inclined.

'Tomorrow we'll go to the harbour, Martyn, although Mr Tremayne tells me there's little anchored in the Roads at present worth looking at.'

The male half of the Tremayne family was the household steward and general handyman. Like the other retainers he was old. Although the Seven Years War had ended ten years back, it had left a lot of unfilled gaps in the villages and hamlets. Some young men had fallen in battle, others had liked the outside world better than their own rural communities and had stayed away. In Falmouth you were usually a sailor or a farm worker, and that was how it had always been.

'Maybe it will be clear enough for us to ride, eh?'

Bolitho smiled. *'Ride?'*

'We don't go everywhere in London by coach, you know!'

Their laughter stopped in mid-air as two loud bangs echoed from the front doorway.

'Who is abroad at this hour?' Dancer was already on his feet.

Bolitho held up his hand. 'Wait.' He strode to a cupboard and took out a pistol. 'It is well to be careful, even here.'

Together they opened the big double doors, feeling the cold wind wrap around their overheated bodies like a shroud.

Bolitho saw it was his father's gamekeeper, John Pendrith, who had a cottage close to the house. He was a powerfully built, morose sort of man, who was much feared by the local poachers. And there were quite a few of them.

'Oi be sorry to disturb you, zur.' He gestured vaguely with his long-barrelled musket. 'But one o' the lads come up from the town. Old Reverend Walmsley said it were the best thing to do.'

'Come in, John.'

Bolitho closed the doors after them. The big gamekeeper's presence, let alone his air of mystery, had made him uneasy in some way.

Pendrith took a glass of brandy and warmed himself by the fire, the steam rising from his thick coat like a carthorse.

Whatever it was, it must be important for old Walmsley, the rector, to send a messenger here.

'This lad found a corpse, zur. Down on the foreshore. Bin in the water for some while, 'e reckons.' He looked up, his eyes bleak. 'It were Tom Morgan, zur.'

Bolitho bit his lip. 'The revenue officer?'

'Aye. 'E'd bin done in afore 'e went into the water, so the lad says.'

There were sounds on the stairway, and then Bolitho's mother, wrapped in a green velvet cloak, hurried down towards them, her eyes questioning.

Bolitho said, 'I can deal with it, Mother. They've found Tom Morgan on the foreshore.'

'Dead?'

Pendrith said bluntly, 'Murdered, ma'am.' To Bolitho he explained, 'Y'see, zur, with the soldiers away, an' the squire in Bath, the old Reverend turned to you like.' He grimaced. 'You bein' a King's officer, so to speak.'

Dancer exclaimed, 'Surely there's somebody else?'

Bolitho's mother was already pulling at the bell-rope, her face pale but determined.

'No. They always come to the house. I'll tell Corker to saddle two horses. You go with them, John.'

Bolitho said quietly, 'I'd rather he was here, with you.' He squeezed her arm. 'It's all right. Really. I'm not the boy who went off to sea with an apple in his pocket. Not any more.'

It was strange how easily it came to him. One minute he had been ready for bed. Now he was alert, every nerve keen to sudden danger. From the look on Dancer's face, he knew he was equally affected.

Pendrith said, 'I sent the lad back to watch over the body. You'll remember the place, zur. The cove where you an' your brother overturned that dory an' took a good beatin' for it!' He gave a slow grin.

One of the maids appeared, and listened to her instructions before hurrying away to tell Corker, the coachman, what to do.

Bolitho said, 'No time to change into uniform, Martyn. We'll go as we are.'

Both he and his friend were dressed in mixed clothing which they had borrowed from chests and cupboards throughout the house. In a house which was, and had always been, a home for sea officers, there was naturally a plentiful supply of spare coats and breeches.

They were ready to leave in fifteen minutes. From drowsy relaxation to crisp preparedness. If the Navy had given them nothing else, it had taught them that. The only way to stay alive in a ship-of-war was to stay vigilant.

Horses clattered on the stones outside the doors, and Bolitho asked, 'Who is the lad who found the body, John?'

Pendrith shrugged. 'The smith's son.' He made a motion with his finger to his forehead. 'Not all there. Moonstruck.'

Bolitho kissed his mother on the cheek. Her skin was like ice.

'Go to bed. I'll be back soon. Tomorrow we'll send someone to the magistrate in Truro, or to the dragoons.'

They were out and mounted before the swirling snow made their journey more difficult.

There were few lights to be seen in the town, and Bolitho guessed that most sensible folk were in bed.

Dancer called, 'I suppose you know most people hereabouts, or they know you? That's the difference 'twixt here and London!'

Bolitho tucked his chin into his collar and urged the horse through the snow. Fancy Pendrith remembering about the dory. He and his brother had been competing with each other. Hugh had been a midshipman then, while he had been waiting the chance to join his first ship. Their father had been beside himself with anger, which was unusual. Not for what they had done, but because of the worry they had given their mother. It was true too that he had beaten them both to make them remember it.

Soon they heard the sea, rumbling and hissing against the headland and the necklace of rocks below. It was eerie under this mantle of snow. Strange shapes loomed through the darkness, while trees shed great pieces of their white burden to make sounds like a footpad running through the night.

It took all of an hour to discover the cove, which was little more than a cleft in the solid rock with a small, sloping beach. The smith's son waited for them with a lantern, humming to himself and stamping his feet on the wet sand for comfort.

Bolitho dismounted and said, 'Hold my horse, Martyn.' The animal was nervous and restless, as horses often are in the presence of death.

The corpse lay on its back, arms outflung, mouth open.

Bolitho forced himself to kneel beside the dead revenue man.

'Was he like this, Tim?'

'Aye, zur.' The youth giggled. 'I was a-lookin' for . . .' He shrugged. 'Anythin'.'

Bolitho knew all about the local blacksmith. His wife had left him long ago, and he sent his weak-minded son out of his cottage whenever he was entertaining one of his many female visitors. It was said that he had caused the boy's mind to go by hitting him as a baby in a fit of rage.

The youth said as an afterthought, ''Is pockets is empty, zur. Nary a coin.'

Dancer called, 'Is it the man, Dick?'

Bolitho stood up. 'Aye. His throat's been cut.'

The Cornish coast was renowned for its smugglers. But the revenue men were seldom injured in their efforts to find and catch them. With the squire away, and without his additional support as local magistrate, it would mean sending for aid from Truro or elsewhere.

He recalled the gamekeeper's words and said to Dancer, 'Well, my friend, it seems we are not free of our duty after all.'

Dancer soothed the restless horses. 'I thought it too good to last.'

Bolitho said to the youth, 'Go to the inn and tell the landlord to rouse some men. We'll need a hand-cart.' He waited for his words to sink in. 'Can you manage that?'

He nodded jerkily. 'Oi think so, zur.' He scratched his head. 'Oi bin 'ere a long time.'

Dancer reached down and handed him some money. 'That's for all your trouble, er, Tim.'

As the youth stumbled away, chattering to himself, Bolitho shouted after him, 'And don't give it to your father!'

Then he said, 'Better tether the horses and give me a hand.

The tide's on the make and we'll lose the body in a half-hour otherwise.'

They pulled the sodden corpse up the shelving beach, and Bolitho thought of other men he had seen die, yelling and cursing in the heat and din of battle. That had been terrible. But to die like this man, alone and terrified, and then to be thrown in the sea like some discarded rubbish seemed far worse.

By the time help arrived and the corpse was taken to the church, and then they had all gone to the inn to sustain themselves, it was almost dawn.

The horses made little noise as they returned to the house, but Bolitho knew his mother would hear and be waiting.

As she hurried to greet them he said firmly, 'No, Mother. You must go back to bed.'

She looked at him strangely and then smiled. 'It is *good* to have a man in the house once again.'

2

The Avenger

Bolitho and Dancer entered the front door, stamping their boots free of mud and snow, their faces and limbs tingling from a brisk ride across the headland.

It had all but stopped snowing, and here and there gorse or shrub were poking through, like stuffing from a torn mattress.

Bolitho said quietly, 'We have company, Martyn.'

He had already seen the coach in the yard where Corker and his assistant were tending to a fine pair of horses. He had recognised the crest on the coach door, that of Sir Henry Vyvyan, whose sprawling estates lay some ten miles to the west of Falmouth. A rich and powerful man, and one of the country's most respected magistrates as well.

He was standing by the crackling fire, watching Mrs Tremayne as she put the finishing touches to a tankard of mulled wine. She had her own recipe for it, with carefully measured ingredients of sugar, spice and beaten egg yolk.

Vyvyan was an impressive figure, and when Bolitho had been much younger he had been more than a little frightened of the man. Tall, broad-shouldered, with a large hooked nose, his countenance was dominated by a black patch over his left eye. From above his nose, diagonally across the eye socket and deep into the cheekbone was a terrible scar. Whatever had done it must have clawed out the eye like a hook.

The remaining eye fixed on the two midshipmen, and Vyvyan said loudly, 'Glad to see you, young Richard, an' your friend.' He glanced at Bolitho's mother who was sitting by the far window. 'You must be right proud, ma'am.'

Bolitho knew that Vyvyan rarely spent his time on useless visits. He was something of a mystery, although his swift justice against footpads and highwaymen on and around his estates was well known and generally respected. He was said to have made his fortune privateering against the French and along the Spanish Main. Others hinted at slavery and the rum trade. They were all probably wrong, Bolitho thought.

It was strange how unreal the revenue man's death had seemed as they had ridden hard along the rutted coast road. It had been two nights since they had stood by the corpse with the smith's moonstruck son, and now with a bright sky to drive the shadows away from the snow and the hillsides, it had all become like part of a bad dream.

Vyvyan was saying in his deep voice, 'So I says to meself, ma'am, with Squire Roxby an' his family enjoyin' themselves in Bath, an' the military away disportin' themselves like dandies at our purses' expense, who better than meself to get over to Falmouth an' take the strain? I see it as me duty, especially as poor Tom Morgan was a tenant of mine. He lived just outside Helston, a stout, reliable yeoman. He'll be sorely missed, not least by his family, I'm thinkin'.'

Bolitho watched his mother, seeing her hands gripping the arms of her chair, the relief on her even features. She was glad Sir Henry had come. To restore security and kill the dangers of rumour. Bolitho had heard plenty of that on their two days of leave. Tales of smugglers, and spine-chilling talk of witchcraft near some of the smaller fishing villages. She was also relieved that Vyvyan and not her youngest son was to carry the responsibility.

Vyvyan took the steaming tankard from Mrs Tremayne and said approvingly, 'God swamp me, ma'am, if I didn't hold Mrs Bolitho as a dear friend I'd lure you to Vyvyan Manor all for meself! There's none in the whole county who can mull wine like you.'

Dancer cleared his throat. 'What do you intend, sir?'

The solitary eye swivelled towards him and held steady.

'All done, me boy.' He spoke cheerfully and offhandedly, like one who is used to making and following through decisions. 'Soon as I heard the news I sent word to Plymouth. The port admiral is a friend.' The eyelid dropped in a wink. 'And I'd heard that your people have been active of late against the smugglin' *gentry*.'

Bolitho pictured the big two-decker, *Gorgon*, laid up for repairs, her decks probably covered in snow. It would take longer than anticipated. Captain Conway might well see fit to grant extended leave to his junior officers. After all, when she put to sea again it could be several years before the *Gorgon* touched England once more.

Vyvyan added, 'The admiral will send a ship to deal with this matter. I'll have no murderin' scum working *my* coast!'

Bolitho remembered that some of Vyvyan's land ran down to the sea itself, from the dreaded Lizard to somewhere near the Manacles. A dangerous and cruel coastline. It would take a brave smuggler to try and land a catch there and face Vyvyan's rough justice at the end of it.

Bolitho turned as his mother said softly, 'I'm grateful for your trouble, Sir Henry.' She looked pale, more so in the reflected glare from the snow outside.

Vyvyan regarded her affectionately. 'But for that damned husband of yours, ma'am, I'd have set me cap at you, even if I am a cut-about old villain!'

She laughed. 'I'll tell him when he returns. It may make him quit the sea.'

Vyvyan downed the last of the wine and waved another ladle aside. 'No, I must be off now. Tell that fool of a coachman to get ready, if you please!' To the room at large he added, 'No, don't do that, ma'am. England will need all her sailors again afore long. Neither the Dons nor the French Court will rest until they have bared their metal against us for another attempt.' He laughed loudly. 'Well, let 'em!' He faced the two midshipmen. 'With lads like these, I think we can rest easy at night!'

With a hug for Mrs Bolitho and heavy slaps on the back

for the midshipmen he stamped out into the hall, bellowing for his coachman.

Dancer grinned. 'His man must be deaf!'

Bolitho asked, 'Is it time to eat, Mother? We're starving!'

She smiled at them warmly. 'Soon now. Sir Henry's visit was unexpected.'

Two more days passed, each full of interest, and neither spoiling their escape from discipline and the routine life of shipboard.

Then the postboy, as he called at the house for something hot to drink, confided that a vessel had been sighted standing inshore towards the entrance to Carrick Roads.

The wind had veered considerably, and Bolitho knew it would take all of an hour for the incoming vessel to reach an anchorage.

He asked the postboy what she was, and he replied with a grimace, 'King's ship, sir. Cutter by the looks of 'er.'

A cutter. Probably one of those used by the Revenue Service, or better still, under naval command.

He said quickly, 'Shall we go and see her?'

Dancer was already looking for his coat. 'I'm ready.'

Bolitho's mother threw up her hands. 'No sooner back and you want to go looking at ships again! Just like your father!'

The air was keen-edged, like ice, but by the time they had walked through the town to the harbour they were glowing like stoves. Good food, with regular sleep and exercise, had worked wonders for both of them.

Together they stood on the jetty and watched the slow-moving vessel tacking towards her anchorage. She was some seventy feet in length, with a massive beam of over twenty. Single-masted, and with a rounded, blunt bow, she looked cumbersome and heavy, but Bolitho knew from what he had seen elsewhere that properly handled cutters could use their great sail area to tack within five points of the wind and in most weathers. She carried a vast, loose-footed mainsail, and also a squared topsail. A jib and fore completed her display of canvas, although Bolitho knew she could set more, even studding sails if required.

She was now turning lazily into the wind, her canvas vanishing deftly as her hands prepared to drop anchor. A red ensign and masthead pendant made the only colour against the pewter sky, and Bolitho felt the same old feeling he always did when seeing a part, even a small part, of his own world.

Blunt and clumsy she might appear, lacking the glinting broadsides and proud figureheads of larger men-of-war, she was nevertheless somebody's own command.

He saw the anchor splash down, the usual bustle at the tackles to sway the jolly boat up and over the bulwark.

Across the choppy water they both heard the twitter of calls, and pictured the scene on board. In that seventy feet of hull they carried a company of nearly sixty souls, although how they managed to sleep, eat and work in such cramped space was hard to fathom. They shared the hull with anchor cables, water, provisions, powder and shot. It left few inches for comfort.

The jolly boat was in the water now, and Bolitho saw the gleam of white breeches beneath a blue coat as the vessel's commander climbed down to be pulled ashore.

As the tide and wind swung the cutter to her cable Bolitho saw her name painted across her raked quarter. *Avenger*. The dead revenue man would have approved, he thought grimly.

A small knot of onlookers had gathered on the wall to watch the newcomer. But not too many. People who lived by and off the sea were always wary of a King's ship, no matter how small.

Bolitho started as the boat hooked on to the jetty stairs and a burly seaman hurried towards him and knuckled his forehead.

'Mr Midshipman Bolitho, sir?'

Dancer chuckled. 'Even out of uniform you are recognised, Dick!'

The seaman added, 'My cap'n wishes a word, sir.'

Mystified, they walked to the stairs as the cocked hat and shoulders of *Avenger*'s commander appeared above the wet stones.

Bolitho stared with amazement. *'Hugh!'*

His brother regarded him impassively. 'Aye, Richard.' He nodded to Dancer, and then called to his coxswain, 'Return to the ship. My compliments to Mr Gloag, and tell him I will signal when I require the boat.'

Bolitho watched him, his feelings mixed and confused. Hugh was supposed to be in a frigate, or so he thought. He had changed quite a lot since their last meeting. The lines at his mouth and jaw were deeper, and his voice carried the rasp of authority. But the rest was unchanged. The black hair like his own, and like some of the portraits in the house, tied above his collar with a neat bow. Steady eyes, strained after long hours of sea duty, and the same old air of supreme confidence which had brought them to blows in the past.

They fell in step, Hugh thrusting past the onlookers with barely a glance.

As they walked he said, 'Is Mother well?' But he sounded distant, his mind elsewhere.

'She'll be glad to see you, Hugh. It will make it a real Christmas.'

Hugh glanced at Dancer. 'You've all been having a time for yourselves in the old *Gorgon*, I believe?'

Bolitho hid a smile. There it was again. The barb, the hint of disbelief.

Dancer nodded. 'You read of it, sir?'

'Some.' Hugh quickened his pace. 'Also I saw the admiral at Plymouth and spoke with your captain.' He stopped by the broad gateway, his eyes examining the house as if for the first time. 'I may as well tell you now. You have been placed under my orders until this local matter is cleared up, or my vacancies have been filled.'

Bolitho stared at him, angered by his abruptness, sorry for Dancer's position.

'Vacancies?'

Hugh regarded him calmly. 'Aye. I had to send my senior and some good hands aboard a prize last week. The Navy is hard put for spare officers and men, Richard, although you would not know about that, of course. It may be sunshine in Africa, but it is icy reality here!'

'Did you *ask* for us?'

Hugh shrugged. 'Your captain told me you would both be here. Availability and local knowledge decided the rest, right? He approved the transfer.'

The expression on their mother's face as they entered the house made up for some of the sudden hurt.

Dancer said softly, 'It may be fun, Dick. Your brother has the cut of an experienced officer.'

Bolitho replied grudgingly, 'He has that, damn it!'

Bolitho watched Hugh leading their mother into an adjoining room. When she came out again she was no longer smiling.

'I am so sorry, Dick, and more so for you, Martyn.'

Dancer said firmly, 'You need not be, ma'am. We have both become used to the unexpected.'

'Nevertheless . . .'

She turned as Hugh entered the room, a glass of brandy in one hand.

'*Nevertheless*, dear family, it is a serious affair. This is just the tip of the berg. God knows what that fool Morgan was about when he was killed, but no revenue man should act alone.' His eyes moved to Bolitho. 'It is far worse than smuggling. At first we believed it was the foul weather. Wrecks are common enough on this coast.'

Bolitho chilled. So that was it. Wreckers. The worst crime of all.

His brother continued in his clipped tones, 'But we have received news of too many rich cargoes lost of late. Silver and gold, spirits and valuable spices. Enough to feed a city, or raise an army.' He shrugged, as if weary of confidences.

'But my duty is to seek out these murderers and hand them to the authorities. The whys and wherefores are not for a King's officer to determine.'

His mother said huskily, 'But wreckers! How could they? Loot and rob helpless seamen . . .'

Hugh smiled gently. 'They see their betters reaping a rich bounty from ships run ashore on their private land. Reason soon flies out of the window, Mother.'

Dancer protested, 'But an accidental wreck is a far cry from being lured aground, sir!'

Hugh looked away. 'Possibly. But not to the leeches who live off the trade.'

Dancer said, 'Your presence here will be well known by now, sir.'

Hugh nodded. 'I will warm a few palms, make a few promises. Some will give information just to send the *Avenger* somewhere else!'

Bolitho looked at his friend. This was a different kind of navy. Where a commanding officer could use bribery to gain information, and then act independently without waiting for ponderous authority to give him its blessing.

The door flew open and Nancy rushed across the room and threw her arms around her brother's neck.

'Hugh! This really is a gathering of the clan!'

He held her away and studied her for several seconds.

'You are a lady now, well *almost*.' He raised his guard again. 'We'll sail on the tide. I suggest you make your way to the harbour and hail a boat.' His tone hardened. 'Don't fret, Mother, I have become very swift in matters of this sort.

We shall have Christmas together if I have anything to say on it!'

As Bolitho closed the door to go to his room he heard his mother's voice.

'But *why*, Hugh? You were doing so well aboard your ship! Everyone said your captain was pleased with your behaviour!'

Bolitho hesitated. Unwilling to eavesdrop, but needing to know what was happening.

Hugh replied shortly, 'I left the *Laertes* and was offered this command. *Avenger*'s not much, but she's mine. I can lend weight and authority to the revenue cutters and excise-men, and do much as I please. I have few regrets.'

'But why did you decide so?'

'Very well, Mother. It was a convenience, if you must know. I had a disagreement . . .'

Bolitho heard his mother sob and wanted to go to her.

He heard Hugh add, 'A matter of honour.'

'Did you kill someone in a duel? Oh, Hugh, what will your father say?'

Hugh gave a short laugh. 'No, I did not kill him. Just cut him a trifle.'

He must have taken her in his arms for the sobs were quieter and muffled,

'And Father will *not* know. Unless you tell him, eh?'

Dancer waited at the top of the stairs.

'What is it?'

Bolitho sighed. 'My brother has a quick temper. I think he has been in trouble over an *affair*.'

Dancer smiled. 'In St James's there is always someone getting nicked or killed in duels. The King forbids it.' He shrugged. 'But it goes on just the same.'

They helped each other to pack their chests again. Mrs Tremayne would only burst into tears if they asked her to do it, even at the promise of a quick return.

When they went downstairs again Hugh had disappeared.

Bolitho kissed his mother, and Dancer took her hand before saying gently, 'If I never returned here, ma'am, this one visit would have been a great gift to me.'

Her chin lifted. 'Thank you, Martyn. You are a good boy. Take care, both of you.'

Two seamen were at the gates, waiting to carry their chests to the boat.

Bolitho smiled to himself. Hugh had been that certain. Confident as ever. *In control.*

As they crossed the square by the inn Dancer exclaimed, 'Look, Dick, the coach!'

They both stopped and stared at it as it rumbled off the cobbles and the horn gave a lively blare.

Back to Plymouth. It was even the same coachman and guard.

Bolitho gave a great sigh. 'We had best get aboard the *Avenger.* I am afraid Mrs Tremayne's cooking has blunted my eagerness for duty.'

They turned towards the sea, and heads bowed made their way on to the jetty.

3

Like a Bird

After a lively crossing to the anchored cutter Bolitho found the *Avenger* surprisingly steady for her size. Holding his hat clapped to his head in the icy wind, he paused by the small companionway while he studied the vessel's solitary mast and the broad deck which shone in the grey light like metal. The bulwarks were pierced on either beam to take ten six-pounders, while both forward and right aft by the taffrail he noticed additional mountings for swivel guns. Small she might be, but no slouch in a fight, he decided.

A figure loomed through a busy throng of working seamen and confronted the two midshipmen. He was a giant in height and girth, with a face so weather-beaten he looked more like a Spaniard than any Briton.

He said loudly, ' 'Eard about you.' He thrust out a big, scarred hand. 'Andrew Gloag, actin'-master o' this vessel.'

Bolitho introduced Dancer and watched them together. The slim, fair midshipman, the great, unshakable figure in the patched blue coat. Gloag may have begun life in Scotland with a name like his, but his dialect was as Devonian as you could imagine.

'Better lay aft, young gennlemen.' Gloag squinted towards the shore. 'We'll be weighin' presently, if the cap'n is anything to judge by.' He grinned, revealing several gaps in his teeth. 'I 'opes you're not too much like *'im.* I can't stand a brace o' you!' He laughed and pushed them towards the companion. 'Get below an' see to yer gear.' He swung away, cupping his hands to bellow, 'Look alive, you idle bugger! Catch a turn with that line or I'll skin you for supper!'

Bolitho and Dancer clambered breathlessly down a short ladder and groped their way to a small stern cabin, banging their heads more than once on the low deckhead beams. The *Avenger* seemed to enfold them with her own sounds and smells. Some familiar and some less so. She felt like a workboat more than a man-of-war. In a class all of her own. Like Andrew Gloag, whose loud voice carried easily through wind and stout timbers alike. A master's mate and acting master. He might never command the quarterdeck of a ship like *Gorgon,* but here he was a king.

It was hard to picture him working with Hugh. He thought suddenly of his brother, wondering, as he often did, why he felt that he never really knew him.

Hugh was changed in some ways. Harder, more confident, if that were possible. More to the point, he was unhappy.

Dancer pushed his chest into a vacant corner and sat on it, his head almost reaching one of the deck beams.

'What do you make of it all, Dick?'

Bolitho listened to the creak and groan of timbers, the rattle and slap of wet rigging somewhere overhead. It would get more lively once they cleared the Roads.

'Wrecking, smuggling, I believe the two always go hand in hand, Martyn. But the port admiral at Plymouth must have heard more than we, if he's so willing to send the *Avenger*.'

'I heard your brother say that he had lost his senior by putting him in a prize, Dick. I wonder what happened to the cutter's last commander?' He smiled. 'Your brother seems to have a way of getting rid of people.' The smile vanished. 'I am sorry. That was a stupid thing to say!'

Bolitho touched his sleeve. 'No. You're right. He does have that way with him.'

Oars thrashed alongside, accompanied by more curses and threats from Mr Gloag.

'Jolly boat's away again.' Bolitho grimaced. 'Hugh'll be coming aboard now.'

It took Lieutenant Hugh Bolitho longer than expected to return to his command. When he did arrive he was drenched in spray, grim-faced and obviously in ill humour.

In the cabin he threw himself down on a bench and snapped, 'When I come aboard I expect to be met by my officers.' He glared at the midshipmen. 'This is no ship of the line with ten men for each trivial task. This is . . .' He swung round on the bench as a frightened-looking seaman peered in at them. 'Where the *hell* have you been,

Warwick?' He did not wait for a reply. 'Bring some brandy and something hot to go with it.' The man fled.

In a calmer tone he continued, 'In a King's ship, no matter how small, you must always keep up an example.'

Bolitho said, 'I'm sorry. I thought as we are only *attached* to your command . . .'

Hugh smiled. 'Attached, pressed, volunteered, I don't care which. You're both my officers until the word says otherwise. There's work to do.'

He looked up as Gloag came through the door, his great frame doubled over like a weird hunchback.

'Sit you down, Mr Gloag. We'll take a glass before we set sail. All well?'

The master removed his battered hat, and Bolitho saw with surprise he was quite bald, like a brown egg, with the hair at his neck and cheeks as thick as spunyarn as if to compensate for his loss.

Hugh said, 'You will assume duties of second-in-command, Richard. Mr Dancer will assist you. Two halves to make the whole, eh?' He smiled at his joke.

Gloag seemed to sense the atmosphere and rumbled, 'I 'eard that you took command of a brig, the pair of you, when your lieutenants were too sick or injured to be of use?'

Dancer nodded, his eyes shining. 'Aye, sir. The *Sandpiper*. Dick took command like a veteran!'

Hugh said, 'Good, here's the brandy.' Half to himself he added, 'We want no heroes cluttering *these* decks, thank you.'

Bolitho looked at his friend and winked. They had scored a small victory over Hugh's sarcasm.

He asked, 'What about the smugglers, Mr Gloag?'

'Oh, this an' that. Spirits and spices, silks and other such nonsense for them with too much money. Mr Pyke says we'll soon 'ave 'em by the 'eels.'

Dancer looked at him. 'Pyke?'

Hugh Bolitho pushed some goblets across a low table. 'Pyke's my boatswain. Used to be a preventative officer himself before he got more sense and signed to wear the King's coat.' He held up his goblet. 'Welcome, gentlemen.'

The nervous seaman named Warwick, who was also the cabin servant, carried in a lighted lantern and hung it carefully on a beam.

Bolitho had his goblet to his lips when he saw Dancer's eyes flash a quick warning. He looked down and saw a dark stain on Hugh's stocking. He had seen too much of it in the last year not to recognise blood. For an instant longer he imagined Hugh was injured, or had snared his leg climbing aboard. Then he saw his brother meeting his gaze with a mixture of defiance and need.

Feet thudded overhead, and then Hugh placed his goblet very carefully on the table.

'You will work watch-and-watch. Once we have cleared the headland we will run to the south'rd and find some sea-room. I have information, but not enough. Show no lights and pass no unnecessary commands. My people know their work, and most of them are ex-fishermen and the like, as sure-footed as cats. I want to run these smugglers or wreckers to ground without delay, before it becomes catching hereabouts. It has happened in the past. Even in times of war the *trade* has been busy in both directions, they tell me.'

Gloag groped for his hat and went stooping towards the door. 'I'll get things ready, sir.'

Hugh glanced at Dancer. 'Go with him. Learn your way around the deck. She's no *Gorgon*.' As Dancer made his way towards the door, his shadow swaying about with the pitching lantern, he added softly, 'Or *Sandpiper* either, for that matter!'

Alone for the first time the brothers studied each other.

Bolitho thought he could see through Hugh's scornful guard. He was stiff with the authority of his first, if perhaps temporary, command. But at twenty-one, with only himself to answer, that was understandable. But there was anxiety there also, a defensive hardness in his eyes.

He did not have to wait for long.

Hugh said offhandedly, 'You saw this stain? Pity. But can't be helped, I suppose. I can trust you to stay silent?'

Bolitho matched his mood, keeping his face and tone level and impassive.

'Need you ask?'

'No. I'm sorry.' He reached for the brandy and poured another goblet, the movement without conscious thought. 'A matter I had to settle.'

'Here? In Falmouth?' Bolitho almost got to his feet. 'What about Mother?'

Hugh sighed. 'It was partly because of her. It was some fool who wanted revenge over another affair.'

'The *affair* which had you removed from *Laertes*?'

'Yes.' His eyes were distant. 'He wanted money. So I answered his insults in the only honourable way.'

'You provoked him.' He watched for some hint of guilt. 'Then you killed him.'

Hugh took out his watch and held it to the lantern.

'Well, the second part is correct, damn him!'

Bolitho shook his head. 'One day you'll put a foot wrong.'

Hugh smiled fully for the first time. It was as if he were glad, relieved to have shared his secret.

'Well, until that sad day, young Richard, there is work to be done. So get yourself on deck and rouse the hands. We'll up-anchor before we lose the light. I don't want to end up in splinters across St Anthony Head because of you!'

The weather had worsened considerably, and as Bolitho climbed up through the hatch he felt the punch of the wind like a fist. Figures bustled this way and that, bare feet slapping on the wet planking like so many seals. Despite the wind and soaking spray, the men wore only their checkered shirts and white, flapping trousers, and were apparently unmoved by the bitter weather.

Bolitho ducked aside as the jolly boat was swayed up and over the lee bulwark, showering the men who worked the tackles with more icy water. He saw the boatswain, Pyke, directing the operations until the boat was securely made fast on her tier, and could well imagine him as a revenue man. He had a furtive, even sly, look, and was quite unlike any boatswain he had ever seen.

It would take some getting used to, he thought. Men everywhere, loosening belaying pins and checking the many flaked lines and halliards as if expecting them to be frozen.

It would be dark early, and the nearest land looked indistinct and blurred, the ramparts at Pendennis and St Mawes already without shape or identity.

Gloag was shouting, 'Three men to the tiller! She'll be lively as a parson's daughter when she comes about, lads!'

Bolitho heard someone laugh. That was always a good sign. Gloag might be fearsome, but he was quite obviously respected too.

Dancer said quickly, 'Here comes our captain, Dick.'

Bolitho turned as his brother came on deck. In spite of the weather he was without a cloak or even a tarpaulin coat to protect himself. The lapels of his lieutenant's coat were very white in the dull murk around him, and he wore his cocked hat at a slightly rakish angle, like a figure in an unnamed painting.

Bolitho touched his hat. 'The master informs me we are ready to get under way, sir.' He was surprised the formality came so easily. But it was the Navy speaking. Not one brother to another.

'Very well. Break out the anchor, if you please. Send the hands to their stations. We'll get the main and fore on her as soon as we weigh and see how she takes 'em. Once clear of the headland I'll want jib and tops'l set.'

'Reefed, sir?'

The eyes steadied on him for a moment. 'We shall see.'

Bolitho hurried towards the blunt bows. It seemed incredible that *Avenger* could set so much canvas on one mast and in this sort of wind.

He listened to the metallic clink of pawls as the men at the capstan threw their weight on the bars. He pictured the anchor, it's fluke biting into the sea bed, waiting to break free, free of the land. He often thought of it at times like this.

He jerked out of his thoughts as his brother called sharply, 'Mr Bolitho! More hands to the mains'l! It will be fierce work directly!'

Gloag was banging his big hands together like boards. 'Wind's backed a piece, sir!' He was grinning into the blown spray, his cheeks streaming. 'That'll help!'

Bolitho climbed over unfamiliar gun tackles and thick snakes of cordage. Past unknown seamen and petty officers, until he was right above the stem. He saw the straining cable, jerking inboard through the hawse-hole as more men took the strain, while on either side of the stem the tide surged past as if the *Avenger* herself was already moving ahead.

The boatswain dashed forward to join him. 'A good night for it, sir!' He did not bother to explain but made a circling motion with his fist and yelled, *'Hove short, sir!'*

Then everything seemed to happen at once. As the anchor started to drag free of the ground the hands on deck threw themselves to the big boomed mainsail as if their lives depended on it. Bolitho had to jump clear as the foresail was broken free and started to billow into the wind, only to be knocked aside again as Pyke yelled, *'Anchor's aweigh, sir!'*

The effect was immediate and startling. With her fore and main filling out like mad things, and the deck canting steeply to the thrust of wind and current, the *Avenger* seemed to be sliding beam-on towards sure destruction.

Gloag called hoarsely, 'Sheet 'em 'ome *'ard*, Mr Pyke! Lively now.'

Bolitho felt at a loss and totally in the way as men darted hither and thither, oblivious to the water which surged as high as the lee gunports.

And then, just as suddenly, it was done. Bolitho made his way aft to where three straddle-legged seamen stood by the long tiller-bar, their eyes squinting in concentration as they watched both helm and sails. The *Avenger* was standing as close to the wind as any vessel he had ever seen, with her big mainsail and the fin-shaped foresail sheeted home as Gloag had ordered, until they were almost fore and aft along the cutter's centre line.

Foam boiled under the counter, and Bolitho saw Dancer watching him from the foredeck, grinning like a boy with a new plaything.

Hugh was eyeing him too, his mouth compressed in a tight line.

'Well?' One word. Question and threat together.

Bolitho nodded. 'She's a lady, sir! Like a bird!'

The boatswain stumped to the weather rail and peered at the blurred shoreline.

'Aye, Mr Bolitho, sir. An' I'll wager some devils are watchin' this bird right now!'

The land was edging past, and Bolitho saw the spray whipped off the wave crests like spume as they approached the dangerous turn of the headland.

Pyke cupped his hands. 'Stand by to get aloft, there!' He glanced at his commander's set features as if expecting him to cancel his demands for more canvas. When no word was uttered he added heartily, 'An' mebbe a tot for the first one down afterwards!'

Bolitho made himself take in the darkening deck section by section, until he could match what he already knew with the bustling seamen and the jumble of rigging and blocks which went to make a vessel stay alive.

Hugh and the master seemed satisfied, he thought, watching the men at work, the set of the sails, with an occasional glance at the compass to confirm some point or other.

What a step I have yet to make, Bolitho thought. From midshipman to a place on the quarterdeck. Like his brother, who at twenty-one was already on another plane. In a few years this first, tiny command would probably be forgotten, and Hugh might have his own frigate. But she would have played her vital part for him all the same. Provided, that was, he kept out of trouble and held his sword in its scabbard.

'Mr Bolitho!'

Hugh's voice made him start.

'I said earlier, we have no passengers in my command! So stir yourself and put more hands forrard to the jib. We'll set it as soon as the topmen are aloft.'

As dusk yielded to a deeper darkness the *Avenger* threw herself across the stiffer crests of open sea. Lifting and plunging, throwing up great sheets of spray from her bows, she changed tack to point her stem towards the south.

Hour after hour, Hugh Bolitho drove everyone until he was ready to drop. Wet, freezing canvas, iron-hard and unyielding to the fingers of salt-blinded men, drowned even the sea's noise with its constant boom and thunder. The screech of blocks as swollen cordage was hauled through, the stamp of feet on deck, an occasional cry from the poop, all joined in one chorus of effort and pain.

Even the cutter's young commander had to admit that too much canvas was too much, and reluctantly he ordered the topsail and jib to be taken in for the remainder of the night.

Eventually the watch below, gasping and bruised, groped their way down for a short respite. Some swore they would never set foot aboard again once they put into port. They always said it. They usually came back.

Others were too tired even to think, but fell on their cramped messdeck to lie amongst the sluicing mixture of sea water and oddments of clothing or loose tackle until the next call from the deck.

'All hands! All hands on deck to shorten sail!' They never had to wait long for that either.

As he lay in a makeshift cot, pitching and swaying with the savage motion, Bolitho found time to wonder what might have happened if he had gone to London as Dancer had suggested.

There was a smile on his lips as he fell into a deep sleep. It would certainly have been totally different from this, he thought.

4

No Choice

Lieutenant Hugh Bolitho sat wedged into a corner of the *Avenger*'s low cabin, one foot against a frame to hold himself steady. The cutter was alive with creaks and rattles as she drifted sluggishly downwind through a curtain of sleet and snow.

The midshipmen, Gloag, the acting-master, and Pyke, the cutter's sly-faced boatswain, completed the gathering, and the confined space was heavy with damp and the richer tang of brandy.

Bolitho felt as if he had never worn a shred of dry clothing in his life. For over two days, while the *Avenger* had tacked or beaten her way down the Cornish coastline, he had barely slept for more than minutes at a time. Hugh never seemed to rest. He was always calling for extra vigilance, although who but a madman would be abroad in this weather was hard to fathom. Now, around the dreaded Lizard and its great sprawl of reefs, they lay to under the lee of the shore. And although it was pitch dark and no land in view, they sensed it, felt it not as a friend but as a treacherous enemy waiting to rip out their keel if they made just one mistake.

Bolitho was impressed by his brother's outward calm, the way he outlined his ideas without any sign of uncertainty. He could tell that Gloag trusted his judgement, although he was old enough to be his father.

He was saying, 'I had intended to put a party ashore, or go myself to meet this informant. However, the weather has other ideas. Any boat might lose her way, and the advantage of surprise would also be lost.'

Bolitho glanced at Dancer, wondering if he was as mystified as himself. Informants, stealthy rendezvous in the dark, it was a different sort of navy.

Pyke said abruptly, 'I knows the place well, sir. It would be where Morgan, the revenue man, was done in. A real likely spot for runnin' a cargo ashore.'

Hugh's eyes settled on him curiously. 'D'you think you could meet this fellow? After all, if he says the birds have flown there's no damn point in my hanging about here.'

Pyke spread his hands. 'I can try, sir.'

'*Try*, dammit, that's not good enough!'

Bolitho watched. Again, Hugh's latent temper was getting the better of him. He saw the almost physical effort as reason took over.

The lieutenant added, 'You do see what I mean?'

'Aye, sir. If we gets ashore without stovin' the boat's bottom in, we could reach 'is cottage as you wanted in the first place.'

Hugh nodded briskly. 'Very well. I want you to land the party as soon as you can. Find out what the man knows, but pay him nothing. We've got to be sure.' He looked at his brother. 'You, Richard, will go with Mr Pyke. The presence of my, er, second-in-command will add something, eh?'

Gloag rubbed his bald pate. 'I'll go an' check the set o' the tide, sir. We don't want to lose your brother on 'is first affray, does we?' He went out chuckling to himself.

His chuckling stopped as a voice called, 'Breakers on the lee bow, sir!' That was Truscott, the gunner, standing a watch alone while his betters pondered on matters of strategy.

Hugh Bolitho said, 'Too many reefs about here. Take yourself on deck, Mr Dancer. Have the jolly boat swayed out and muster the landing party. See that they are armed, but ensure that nobody steps into the boat with a loaded piece. I want no eager hands loosing off a pistol by mistake.' His eyes flashed. 'You'll be answerable to me.'

He relaxed slightly. 'It is all we can do. They say that a cargo of smuggled goods has been dropped in the next cove to the nor'-west of where I am putting you ashore. They say it will stay there until everyone believes the *Avenger* elsewhere.' He banged the table. 'They *say* a lot of things, but tell me nothing of value!'

Pyke grinned. 'It sounds right, sir. I'll take the centipedes, just in case.'

Another voice called, 'Boat ready, zur! Mr Gloag's respects, an' could the young gentleman make haste?'

Hugh nodded. 'Immediately.' He led the way on deck.

Bolitho felt the damp biting into his bones. Easy living for a few days at home had had its effects, he thought ruefully. Now, tired and weary from the sea and wind, he was feeling very low indeed.

He peered at the tossing boat alongside. It was so dark he could barely make out its outline, just a pitching shape in a welter of white spray.

Dancer hurried to his side. 'I wish I was going with you.'

Bolitho gripped his arm. 'Me too. I feel a complete novice amongst these people.'

His brother lurched across the slippery planking.

'Be off with you. Carry on, Bosun.' He waited for Pyke to vanish over the side and added quietly, 'Keep your eyes wide open. I will lie to when I can, but in any case will be nearby at first light. If there is any truth in my information we may stand a chance.'

Bolitho threw his leg over the bulwark and waited for his eyes to adjust to the darkness. One false step and he would be swept away like a wood chip on a mill-race.

The boat cast off and veered away from the *Avenger* almost before he had regained his breath, while Pyke swung the tiller-bar and peered above the oarsmen's heads as if to seek a way through the nearest line of leaping breakers.

To calm his nerves Bolitho asked, 'What are the centipedes, Mr Pyke?'

The stroke oarsman grinned, his teeth very white in the

darkness. '´Ere, sir!' He kicked out with his foot as he leaned aft for another pull at his oar.

Bolitho reached down and felt two enormous grapnels. They were unlike any he had seen, with several sets of flukes like legs.

Pyke did not take his eyes from the shore as he said, 'The smugglers usually sink their booty to wait until the coast is clear. Then they lifts it when they'm good and ready. My little centipedes can drag the stuff off the bottom.' He laughed quietly, a humourless sound. 'I've done a few in me time.'

The bowman called, 'Land ahead, sir!'

The boat was planing forward, the spray hissing between the oar blades to beat across the already dripping inmates.

'Easy, all!'

A tall, slab-sided rock rushed down the starboard side, muffling the sound of breakers like a huge door.

With a lurch and a violent shudder the boat grounded on hard sand, and as men fell cursing in the water and tried to steady the impact, others leapt on to the beach to guide the bows clear of fallen rocks.

Bolitho tried to stop his teeth chattering. He had to assume Gloag and Pyke knew what they were doing, that his brother's plan made sense. This was the cove, but to Bolitho it could have been anywhere.

Pyke regarded him through the gloom. 'Well, sir?'

'You know this business better than me.'

Bolitho knew some of the men were listening, but this was no time to stand on dignity at the expense of safety. He was *Avenger*'s second-in-command. But he was a lowly midshipman for all that.

Pyke grunted, satisfied or contemptuous it was impossible to say.

He said, 'Two men stand by the boat. Load your weapons now.' He gestured upwards into the darkness. 'Ashmore, you stand guard. Watch out for any nosey bugger hanging around.'

The invisible Ashmore asked, 'An' if I does, sir?'

'Crack 'is 'ead, for Gawd's sake!'

Pyke adjusted his belt. 'The rest of you, come with us.' To Bolitho he added, 'Night like this, should be all right.'

The snow swirled around them as they fumbled their way up a winding, treacherous pathway. Once, Bolitho paused to give a seaman his hand on a slippery piece of the track and saw the sea reaching out far below him. Impenetrable black lined with broken crests of incoming rollers.

He thought of his mother. It was unreal to know that she was only twelve miles or so away from where he was standing. But there was a world of difference between a straight bird's flight and the *Avenger*'s meandering track to this particular point.

Pyke was tireless, and his long, thin legs were taking him up the path as if they did it every single day.

Bolitho tried to ignore the cold and the blinding sleet. It was like walking into oblivion.

He collided with Pyke's back as the boatswain hissed, '*Still!* Th' cottage is up 'ere, somewhere.'

Bolitho fingered his sheathed hanger and strained his ears, expecting to hear something.

Pyke nodded. 'This way.' He hurried on again, the track levelling off as the little group of men left the sea behind them.

The cottage loomed out of the sleet like a pale rock. It was little more than the size of a large room, Bolitho thought, with very low walls, some kind of thatched roof and small, sightless windows.

Who would want to live here? he wondered. It must be quite a walk to the nearest hamlet or village.

Pyke was peering at the little cottage with professional interest. To Bolitho he said, 'Man's name is Portlock. Bit of everything 'e is. Poacher, crimp for the press gangs, 'e can turn 'is 'and to most trades.' He laughed shortly. ''Ow 'e's escaped the noose all these years I'll not know.' He sighed. 'Robins, go 'alf a cable along the track and watch out. Coote, round the back. There's no door, but you never knows.' He looked at Bolitho. 'Better if you knocks the door.'

'But I thought we were supposed to be quiet about it?'

'Up to a point. We've come this far safe an' sound.' He approached the cottage calmly. 'But if we are bein' watched, Mr Bolitho, we got to make it look good, or Mister bloody Portlock will soon be gutted like a fish!'

Bolitho nodded. He was learning.

Then he drew his curved hanger and after a further hesitation he banged it sharply on the door.

For a moment longer nothing happened. Just the patter of

sleet across the thatch and their wet clothing, the irregular breathing of the seamen.

Then a voice called, 'W-who be it at this hour?'

Bolitho swallowed hard. He had been expecting a gruff voice to match Pyke's description. But it was a female. Young by the sound of her, and frightened too.

He heard the rustle of expectancy from the sailors and said firmly, 'Open the door, ma'am. In the King's name!'

Slowly and reluctantly the door was pulled back, a shuttered lantern barely making more than a soft orange glow across their feet.

Pyke pushed past impatiently and said, 'One of you stay outside.' He snatched the lantern and fiddled with it, adding, 'Like a bloody tomb!'

Bolitho held his breath as the light spread out from the lantern and laid the cottage bare.

Even in the poor light he could see it was filthy. Old casks and boxes littered the floor, while pieces of flotsam and driftwood were piled against the walls and around the dying fire like a barricade.

Bolitho looked at the girl who had opened the door. She was dressed in little more than rags, and her feet, despite the cold earth floor, were bare. He felt sick. She was about Nancy's age, he thought.

The man, whom he guessed was Portlock, was standing near the rear wall. He was exactly as Bolitho had imagined. Brutal, coarse-featured, a man who would do anything for money.

He exclaimed thickly, 'Oi done nothin'! What right be yours to come a-burstin' in 'ere?'

When nobody answered he became braver and seemingly larger.

He shouted, 'An' what sort o' officer are *you*?'

He glared at Bolitho, his eyes filled with such hatred and evil that he could almost feel the man's strength.

'Oi'll not take such from no *boy*!'

Pyke crossed the room like a shadow. The first blow brought Portlock gasping to his knees, the second knocked him on to his side, a thread of scarlet running from his chin.

Pyke was not even out of breath. 'There now. We understand each other, eh?' He stood back, balanced on his toes, as Portlock rose groaning from the floor. 'In future you will treat a King's officer with respect, no matter what age 'e's at, see?'

Bolitho felt that things were getting beyond him. 'You know why we are here.' He saw the eyes watching him, changing from fury to servility in seconds.

'Oi 'ad to be *certain*, young sir.'

Bolitho turned away, angry and sickened. 'Oh, ask him, for God's sake.'

He looked down as a hand touched his arm. It was the girl, feeling his sodden coat, crooning to herself like a mother to a child.

A seaman said harshly, 'Stand away, girl!' To Bolitho he added vehemently, 'I seen that look afore, sir. When they strips the clothes off the poor devils on the gibbet!'

Pyke said smoothly, 'Or off those unlucky enough to be shipwrecked, eh?'

Portlock said, 'Oi don't know nothin' about that, sir!'

'We shall see.' Pyke regarded the man coldly. 'Tell me, is the cargo still there?'

Portlock nodded, his gaze on the boatswain like a stricken rabbit. 'Aye.'

'Good. And when will they come for it?' His tone sharpened. 'No lies now.'

'Tomorrow mornin'. On th' ebb.'

Pyke looked at Bolitho. 'I believe him. At low tide it's easier to get the cargo 'ooked.' He grimaced. 'Also, it keeps the revenue boats in deeper water.'

Bolitho said, 'We had better get the men together.'

But Pyke was still watching the other man. Eventually he said, 'You will stay 'ere.'

Portlock protested, 'But me money! I was promised . . .'

'Damn your money!' Bolitho could not stop himself even though he knew Pyke was looking at him with something like amusement. 'If you betray us your fate will be as certain as that meted out by those you are betraying now!'

He looked at the girl, seeing the bruise on her cheek, the cold sores on her mouth. But when he reached out to comfort her she recoiled, and would have spat at him but for a burly seaman's intervention.

Pyke walked out of the cottage and mopped his face. 'Save yer sympathy, Mr Bolitho. Scum breeds on scum.'

Bolitho fell in step beside him. Broadsides and towering pyramids of canvas in a ship of the line seemed even further away now. This was squalor at its lowest, where even the smallest decency was regarded as weakness.

He heard himself say, 'Let us be about it then. I want no more of this place.'

The sleety snow swirled down to greet them, and when he glanced back Bolitho saw that the cottage had disappeared.

'This be as good a place to wait as any.' Pyke rubbed his hands together and then blew on them. It was the first time he had shown any discomfort.

Bolitho felt his shoes sinking into slush and half-frozen grass, and tried not to think of Mrs Tremayne's hot soup or one of her bedtime possets. Only this was real now. For over two hours they had wended their way along the cliffs, conscious of the wind as it tried to push them into some unknown darkness, of the wretched cold, of their complete dependence on Pyke.

Pyke said, 'The cove is yonder. Not much to look at, but 'tis well sheltered, an' some big rocks 'ide the entrance from all but the nosiest. At low water it'll be firm an' shelvin'.' He nodded, his mind made up. 'That's when it will be. Or another day.'

One of the seamen groaned, and the boatswain snarled, 'What d'you expect? A warm 'ammock and a gallon o' beer?'

Bolitho steeled himself and sat down on a hummock of earth. On either side his small party of seamen, seven in all, arranged themselves as best they could. Three more with the jolly boat somewhere behind them. It was not much of a force if things went wrong. On the other hand, these were all professional seamen. Hard, disciplined, ready for a fight.

Pyke took out a bottle from his coat and passed it to Bolitho. 'Brandy.' He shook with a silent laugh. 'Yer brother took it off a smuggler a while back.'

Bolitho swallowed and held his breath. It was like fire, but found just the right place.

Pyke offered, 'You can pass it along. We've quite a wait yet.'

Bolitho heard the bottle going from hand to hand, the grunts of approval with each swallow.

He forgot the discomfort instantly as he exclaimed, 'I heard a shot!'

Pyke snatched the bottle and thrusting it into his coat said uneasily, 'Aye. A small piece.' He blinked into the darkness. 'A vessel. Out there somewheres. Must be in distress.'

Bolitho chilled even more. Wrecks dotted this shoreline in plenty. Ships from the Caribbean, from the Mediterranean, everywhere. All those leagues of ocean, and then on the last part of the voyage home, Cornwall.

Rocks to rip out a keel, angry cliffs to deny safety to even the strongest swimmer.

And now, after what he had heard, the additional horror of wreckers.

Perhaps he had been mistaken, but even as he tried to draw comfort from the thought another bang echoed against the cliffs and around the hidden cove.

A seaman whispered fiercely, 'Lost 'er way most like. Mistook the Lizard for Land's End. It's 'appened afore, sir.'

Pyke grunted, 'Poor devils.'

'What will we do?' Bolitho tried to see his face. 'We can't just leave them to die.'

'We don't *know* she'll come aground. An' if she does, we can't be sure she'll sink. She might beach 'erself up at Porthleven, or drift free of danger.'

Bolitho turned away. God, Pyke does not care. All he is interested in is this job. A quick capture with the booty.

He pictured the unknown vessel. Probably carrying passengers. He might even know some of them.

He stood up. 'We will go round the cove, Mr Pyke. We can stand by on the other headland. She'll most likely be in sight very soon.'

Pyke jumped to his feet. 'It's no use, I tell you!' He was almost beside himself with anger. 'What's done is done. The cap'n gave us orders. We must obey 'em.'

Bolitho swallowed hard, feeling them all looking at him.

'Robins, go and tell the men at the boat what we are doing. Can you find the way?'

It only needed Robins to say no, to proclaim ignorance, and it was over before it had started. He could barely recall the other men's names.

But Robins said brightly, 'Aye, sir. I knows it.' He hesitated. 'What then, sir?'

Bolitho said, 'Remain with them. If you sight *Avenger* at daybreak you must make some effort to tell my, er, the captain what we are about.'

It was done. He had disobeyed Hugh's orders, overruled Pyke and taken it on himself to look for the drifting vessel.

They had nothing but their weapons, not even one of Pyke's centipedes to grapple the vessel into safer waters.

Pyke said scornfully, 'Follow me then. But I want it understood. I'm dead against it.'

They started to scramble along another narrow path, each wrapped in his own thoughts.

Bolitho thought of the brig *Sandpiper* where he and Dancer had faced a pirate ship twice her size. This was entirely different, and he wished yet again his friend was with him.

As they rounded a great pile of broken rocks a seaman said hoarsely, 'There, sir! Lights!'

Bolitho looked, stunned even though he had been expecting it. Two lanterns, far apart and lower down the sloping side of the headland. They were moving, but only slowly, one hardly at all.

Pyke said, 'Got 'em tied to ponies, I expect. That ship's master out there will think they're ridin' lights.' He spat out the words. 'A safe anchorage.'

Bolitho could see it. As if it had happened. As if he were there. The ship, which seconds before had been beset with doubts and near panic. Then the sight of the two riding lights. Other vessels safely at anchor.

When in fact there was nothing but rocks, and the only hands waiting on the shore would be gripping knives and clubs.

He said, 'We must get to those lights. There may still be time.'

Pyke retorted, 'You must be mad! There's no doubt a

bloody army o' the devils down there! What chance do we 'ave?'

Bolitho faced him, surprised at his own voice. Calm, while his whole body was shaking. 'Probably none, Mr Pyke. But we have no choice either.'

As they started to descend towards the cove even the night seemed to become quieter. Holding its breath for all of them.

'How long before dawn?'

Pyke glanced at him briefly. 'Too far off to 'elp us.'

Bolitho felt for his pistol and wondered if it would fire. Pyke had read his thoughts. Hoping against hope that with daylight they might see the cutter standing inshore to help them.

He thought of Hugh. What he would have done. He would certainly have had a plan.

He said quietly, 'I'll need two men. We'll go for the lights, while you, Mr Pyke, can take the remaining hands to the hill and cause a diversion.'

Just like that.

Pyke stared at him. 'You don't even know this beach! There's not an inch o' cover. They'll cut you down afore you've gone a pace or two!'

Bolitho waited, feeling his skin sticking to his wet shirt. He would be still colder very shortly. And quite dead.

Pyke had sensed his despair, his determination to do the impossible.

He said abruptly, 'Babbage an' Trillo will be best. They knows these parts. They got no cause to die though.'

The one called Babbage drew his heavy cutlass and ran his

thumb along the edge. The second seaman, Trillo, was small and wiry, and favoured a wicked-looking boarding axe.

They both moved away from their companions and stood beside the midshipman. They were used to obeying orders. It was senseless to protest.

Bolitho looked at Pyke and said simply, 'Thank you.'

'Huh!' Pyke beckoned to the others. 'Follow me, men.' To Bolitho he added, 'I'll do what I can.'

Bolitho set his hat firmly on his head, and with his hanger in one hand and the heavy pistol in the other he walked clear of the fallen rocks and on to the wet, firm sand.

He could hear the two seamen squelching along at his heels, but the sounds were almost drowned by his own heartbeats against his ribs.

Then he saw the nearest light, the shadowy outline of a tethered horse, and further along the beach another animal with a lantern tied across its back on a long spar.

It seemed impossible that such a crude ruse would deceive anybody, but from experience Bolitho knew a ship's lookouts often only saw what they wanted to see.

He could see several moving figures, briefly silhouetted against the hissing spray around the nearest rocks. His heart sank, there must be twenty or thirty of them.

The puny crackle of pistol shots echoed down into the cove, and Bolitho guessed that Pyke and his men were doing their part. He heard startled cries from the beach, the clatter of steel as someone dropped a weapon amidst the rocks.

Bolitho said, 'Now, fast as we can!'

He dashed towards the horse, hacking the lantern from its

spar so that it fell burning on the wet sand. The horse reared away, kicking with terror, as more shots whined overhead.

Bolitho heard his companions yelling like madmen, saw the seaman, Babbage, hack down a charging figure with his cutlass before running on to cut away the next lantern.

A voice yelled, 'Shoot those buggers down!' Someone else screamed in pain as a stray ball found a mark.

Figures fanned out on every side, advancing slowly, hampered and probably confused by Pyke's pistol fire from the hillside.

One dashed forward, and Bolitho fired, seeing the man's contorted face as the ball flung him backwards on to the beach.

Others pressed in, more daring now that they realised there were only three facing them.

Bolitho locked blades with one, while Babbage, slashing and hacking with his heavy cutlass, fought two men single-handed.

Bolitho could feel his adversary's fury, but found time to hear Trillo give just one frantic cry as he was struck down by a whole group of slashing weapons.

'Damn your eyes!' The man was gasping between his teeth. 'Now you die, you bloody rummager!'

Dazed, his mind and body cringing to the inevitability of death, Bolitho was shocked at his own anger. To die was one thing, but to be mistaken for a revenue man was like the final insult.

He remembered with stark clarity how his father had taught him to defend himself. Twisting his wrist with all his

strength he plucked the other man's sword from his hand. As
he blundered past him he pointed his hanger and then laid it
across his neck and shoulder.

Then something struck the side of his head and he was on
his knees, dimly aware that Babbage was trying to stand
guard above him, his cutlass hissing through the air like an
arrow.

But darkness was closing across his mind, and he felt his
cheek grind into the wet sand as he pitched headlong,
his body exposed to the nearest thrusting blades.

Soon now. He could hear horses and more shouts through
the painful blur in his brain.

His last conscious thought was that he hoped his mother
would not see him like this.

5

Bait

Bolitho opened his eyes very slowly. As he did so he groaned, the sound thrusting straight through his aching body, as if from the soles of his feet.

He struggled to remember what had happened, and as realisation, like the returning pain in his skull, came flooding back, he stared round with dazed bewilderment.

He was lying on a thick fur rug in front of a roaring log fire, still wearing his soiled uniform, which in the great heat was steaming as if about to burst into flames.

Someone was kneeling behind him, and he saw a girl's scrubbed hands reaching round to support his head, which he knew was bandaged.

She murmured, 'Rest easy, zur.' Over her shoulder she called, 'He's awake!'

Bolitho heard a familiar, booming voice, and saw Sir

Henry Vyvyan standing above him, his one eye peering down as he said, '*Awake,* girl, he damn near died on us!'

He bellowed at some invisible servants and then added more calmly, 'God swamp me, boy, that was a damn fool thing to do. Another second and those ruffians would have had your liver on the sand!' He handed a goblet to the girl. 'Give him some of this.' He shook his head as Bolitho tried to swallow the hot drink. 'What *would* I have told yer mother, eh?'

'The others, sir?' Bolitho tried to think clearly, remembering Trillo's cry, his last sound on earth.

Vyvyan shrugged. 'One dead. A damned miracle.' He sounded as if he could still not believe it. 'A handful of men against those devils!'

'I thank you, sir. For saving our lives.'

'Nothin' to it, m'boy.' Vyvyan smiled crookedly, the scar across his face looking even more savage in the shadows. 'I came with my men because I heard the gun. I was out with 'em anyway. The Navy isn't the only intelligence round here, y'know!'

Bolitho lay still and looked straight up at the high ceiling. He could see the girl watching him, her eyes very blue, frowning with concern.

So Vyvyan had known all about it. Hugh should have guessed. But for him they would all be dead.

He asked, 'And the ship, sir?'

'Aground. But safe enough 'til mornin'. I sent your boatswain to take charge.' He tapped his big nose. 'Nice bit of salvage there, I shouldn't wonder, eh?'

A door opened somewhere and a voice said harshly, 'Most of 'em got away, sir. We cut down two, but the rest scattered amongst the rocks an' caves. They'll be miles away by dawn.' He chuckled. 'Caught one of 'em though.'

Vyvyan sounded thoughtful. 'But for the ship, and the need to help these sailors, we might have caught the lot.' He rubbed his chin. 'But still, we'll have a hangin' all the same. Show these scum the old fox is not asleep, eh?'

The door closed just as silently.

'I am sorry, sir. I feel it is all my fault.'

'Nonsense! Did yer duty. Quite right too. Only way.' He added grimly, 'But I'll be havin' a sharp word with yer brother, make no mistake on it!'

The heat of the fire, his exhaustion and the effect of something in the drink made Bolitho fall into a deep sleep. When he awoke again it was morning, the hard wintry light streaming in through the windows of Vyvyan Manor.

Freeing himself from two thick blankets he got gingerly to his feet and stared at himself in a wall mirror. He looked more like a survivor than a victor.

He saw Vyvyan watching him from one of the doorways.

Vyvyan asked, 'Ready, boy? My steward tells me that your vessel is anchored off the cove. I've been up most of the night m'self, so I know how you're feelin'.' He grinned. 'But still, nothin' broken. Just a headache for a few days, eh?'

Bolitho put on his coat and hat. He noticed that both had been cleaned, and someone had mended a rent in one of the sleeves where a blade had missed his arm by less than an inch.

It was a cold, bright morning, with the snow changed to slush and the sky without a trace of cloud. Had the night been like this the ship would have seen the danger and the smugglers would have picked up their cargo from the cove.

If . . . if . . . if . . . It was too late now.

Vyvyan's coach dropped him on the narrow coast road above the headland, and to his astonishment he saw Dancer and some seamen waiting for him, and far below, a boat drawn up on the beach.

How different it looked in daylight. He almost expected to see some corpses, but the beach was silky smooth, and beyond the cove the anchored *Avenger* tugged at her cable with barely a roll.

'Dick! Thank God you're safe!' Dancer ran to meet him and gripped his arm. 'You look terrible!'

Bolitho gave a painful smile. 'Thanks.'

Together they walked down that same steep path, and Bolitho saw several burly-looking men examining the two lanterns and some discarded weapons. Excisemen, or merely Vyvyan's retainers, it was hard to say.

Dancer said, 'The captain sent us to get you, Dick.'

'How is his temper?'

'Surprisingly good. I think the vessel you warned away from the rocks had a lot to do with it. She's beached a mile or so from here. Your brother, er, *induced* her people to come off, then he put a prize crew aboard. I think her master was so glad to save his skin he forgot the matter of prize money!'

By the boat Bolitho saw some seamen replacing Pyke's centipedes in the sternsheets.

Dancer explained, 'We made a drag along the seabed but found nothing. They must have come in the night after Vyvyan's men had driven away the wreckers.'

Avenger's other boat was already alongside when Bolitho returned on board. The man he had chosen to warn the jolly boat had done well, he thought. Poor Trillo had been their one loss.

Hugh was watching him as he climbed up over the side, hands on hips, hat at the same rakish angle.

'Quite the little fire-brand, aren't you?' He strode across the broad deck and gripped his hand. 'Young idiot. But I guessed you'd disobey my orders as soon as I heard that distress cannon. I had a prize crew aboard before they could say knife.' He smiled. 'Nice little Dutch brig bound for Cork. Spirits and tobacco. Fetch a good price.'

'Sir Henry said the wreckers got away. All but one.'

'Wreckers, smugglers, I believe they're one and the same. Pyke thinks he may have wounded a few with his pistol shots, so they may turn up somewhere. No Cornish jury will ever convict a smuggler, but a wrecker is something else.'

Bolitho faced his brother. 'The loss of the smugglers' cargo was my fault. But I couldn't help myself. A few kegs of brandy against the value of a vessel and her people made me act as I did.'

Hugh nodded gravely. 'As I knew it would. But brandy? I think not. My men found some oiled wrapping hidden away in one of the caves while they were looking for clues. That drop was not for drinking, my brother. It was made up of good French muskets, if I'm any judge.'

Bolitho stared at him. 'Muskets?'

'Aye. For rebellion somewhere, who can say. Ireland, America, there's money aplenty for anyone who can supply weapons in these troubled times.'

Bolitho shook his head and immediately regretted it. 'It is beyond me.'

His brother rubbed his hands. 'Mr Dancer! My compliments to the master, and tell him to get the vessel under way. If weapons are the bait we need, then weapons we will have.'

Dancer watched him warily. 'And where are we bound, sir?'

'*Bound?* Falmouth of course. I'll not run back to the admiral now. This is getting interesting.' He paused beside the companionway. 'Now get yourself washed and properly turned out, *Mr* Bolitho. I daresay you had a quieter night than some.'

Avenger returned to Falmouth without anything further unusual happening. Once at anchor, Hugh Bolitho went ashore, while Gloag and the midshipmen prepared to take on stores and ward off the curious and others who had obviously been sent out to discover as much information as they could.

Bolitho began to imagine a smuggler at each corner and behind every cask. The news of a shipwreck, and Vyvyan's chase of the would-be wreckers, had preceded *Avenger*'s arrival, and there would be plenty of speculation as to what would happen next.

When the cutter's young commander returned he was in unusual good humour.

In the cabin he said, 'All done. I have had words with certain people in town. The story will be that *Avenger* is out searching for another arms runner in the channel. By this ruse, the smugglers on this side will know we have discovered about the muskets, even though we did not find any ourselves.' He looked cheerfully from Gloag to his brother and then to Dancer. 'Well? Don't you see? It's almost perfect.'

Gloag rubbed his bald head as he always did when he was considering something doubtful, and answered, 'I can well see that nobody'll know for certain about another cargo, sir. The Frenchies will keep sendin' 'em once they've a buyer. But where will *we* get such a haul?'

'We won't.' His smile grew broader. 'We'll sail into Penzance and land a cargo of our own. Load it into waggons and send it overland to Truro to the garrison there. The governor of Pendennis has agreed to lend us a tempting cargo of muskets, powder and shot. Along the way to Truro someone will attempt to seize the lot of it. With the roads as they are, how could they resist the temptation?'

Bolitho asked quietly, 'Wouldn't it be wiser to tell the port admiral at Plymouth what you are about first?'

Hugh glared at him. 'From you that is priceless! You know what would happen. He'd either say no, or take so long the whole country would know what we were doing. No, we'll do this quickly and do it well.' He smiled briefly. 'This time.'

Bolitho looked at the deck. An ambush, the anticipation of quick spoils giving way to panic as the attackers realised they were the ones in the trap. And no escape into little caves this time.

Hugh said, 'I have sent word to Truro. The dragoons will be back by now. The colonel is a friend of Father's. He'll enjoy this sort of thing. Like pig-sticking!'

There was a sudden silence, and Bolitho found himself thinking of the dead Trillo. They were all here safe and busy. He was already buried and forgotten.

Dancer said, 'I think it would work, sir. It would depend a lot on the people who were watching for an attack.'

'Quite. On a lot of luck too. But we'll have lost nothing by trying. If all else fails, we'll stir up such a hornets' nest that we may push somebody into laying information just to get rid of us!'

A boat grated alongside, and minutes later Pyke entered the cabin.

He took a goblet of brandy with an appreciative nod and said, 'The prize is in the 'ands of the chief revenue officer, sir. All taken care of.' He glanced at Bolitho and added, 'That informer, Portlock. 'E's dead, by the way, sir. Somebody talked too loud.'

Hugh Bolitho asked, 'Another glass of brandy, anybody?'

Bolitho looked at him grimly. Hugh knew already. Must have known all along that the man would be killed.

He asked, 'What of the girl?'

Pyke was still studying him. 'Gawn. Good riddance too. Like I said. Scum breeds on scum.'

Hornets' nest, his brother had predicted. It was stirring already by the sound of it.

The bell chimed overhead and Hugh Bolitho said, 'I'm for the shore. I'll be dining at the house, Richard.'

He glanced at Dancer. 'Care to join me? I think my brother had best remain aboard until he's free of that bandage. Mother will have vapours if she sees our hero like that!'

Dancer looked at Bolitho. 'No, sir. I'll remain here.'

'Good. Stand a good watch at all times. There'll be quite a few tongues wagging in the Falmouth ale houses tonight, I shouldn't wonder.'

As he climbed up from the cabin and left the two midshipmen alone, Bolitho said, 'You should have gone, Martyn. Nancy would have liked it.'

Dancer smiled ruefully. 'We came together. We'll stay that way. After last night, I think you need a bodyguard, Dick!'

Gloag came back from seeing his captain over the side and picked up his goblet. In his fist it looked like a thimble.

'What I want to know is,' he eyed them fiercely, 'what 'appens if they knows what we're up to? If they've got ears and eyes amongst us already?'

Bolitho stared at him, but Dancer answered first.

'Then, Mr Gloag, sir, I fear the loss of government arms and powder will take more explaining than we are capable of.'

Gloag nodded heavily. 'My thought too.' He took another swallow and smacked his lips. 'Very nasty it could be.'

Bolitho thought of what the admiral at Plymouth and his own captain in the *Gorgon* would have to say about it.

The careers of James Bolitho's two sons might come to a speedy end.

6

A Plain Duty

Bolitho wandered up and down the high stone jetty and watched the activity of Penzance harbour. But for the bitter cold it could almost have been spring, he thought. The colours of the moored fishing boats and grubby coasting vessels, the rooftops and church spires of the town beyond the anchorage seemed brighter and more cheerful than they should have been.

He looked down at the *Avenger* tied to the jetty. She seemed even less a King's ship from this angle. Her broad deck was strewn with ropes and alive with bustling seamen. But here and there he saw the occasional motionless figure. Watchful, despite the casual atmosphere, ready to seek out any suspicious loiterer nearby.

Even their departure had been well planned and executed with stealth. The cargo of borrowed arms and powder had been swayed aboard in total darkness, while Pyke and over twenty hands had patrolled the nearest jetty and street, just to be sure that nobody had seen what they were about.

Then, taking good care to avoid local shipping, *Avenger* had stood away from the land before heading down-channel again, towards Penzance.

Hugh was ashore now, as usual leaving neither explanation nor destination.

Bolitho studied the passing men and women, seamen and fisherfolk, traders and idlers. Had the rumour gone out yet? Was someone already plotting a way of ambushing Hugh's fictitious capture?

Dancer clambered up from the cutter and stood beside him, rubbing his hands to ward off the cold.

Bolitho said, 'It *seems* very peaceful, Martyn.'

His friend nodded cheerfully. 'Your brother has thought of everything. The chief revenue officer has been here, and I'm told that waggons are being sent to collect our precious hoard!' His mouth widened to a grin. 'I didn't know the Navy ever got mixed up in this kind of game.'

A seaman called, 'Cap'n's a-comin', sir!'

Bolitho waved to the man. He had grown to like the friendly way that forecastle and afterguard shared their confidences when one might expect such an overcrowded hull to drive them further apart.

Hugh Bolitho, wearing his sword and looking very sure of himself, climbed swiftly down to the deck, the midshipmen following at a respectful distance.

Hugh touched his hat to the poop and briskly flapping ensign and said, 'Waggons will be here presently. They've done well. The whole town's agog with news of our little enterprise. Good muskets and powder, seized from a potential enemy.'

He ran his glance swiftly over the large bundles of muskets which were already being swayed up from the hold under the gunner's watchful eye.

He sniffed the air. 'Good day to begin too. No hanging about. It's what they will be watching. Probably right now. To see if we're really intent on getting the cargo ashore and into safe hands, or are trailing our coats as a ruse.'

Gloag, who had been listening, said admiringly, 'You've a clever mind an' no mistake, sir. I can see you in your own flagship afore too long!'

'Maybe.' Hugh walked to the companionway. 'The waggons will be loaded and under guard from the moment they arrive. There'll be a party of revenue men as additional escort.' His eyes fixed on Dancer. 'You will be in charge. The senior revenue man will know what to do, but I want a King's officer *in charge.*'

Bolitho said quickly, 'I'll go, sir. It doesn't seem right to send him. It was because of me he is here at all.'

'The matter is closed.' Hugh smiled. 'Besides, it will all be over before you know it. A few bloody heads and the sight of the dragoons will be sufficient. Sir Henry Vyvyan can have all the hangings he wants after that!'

As he vanished below Dancer said, 'It's no matter, Dick. We've done far worse in the old *Gorgon.* And this may stand us in good stead when our examinations come due, whenever that wretched day will be!'

By noon the waggons had arrived and were loaded without delay. Again, Hugh Bolitho had planned it well. Not enough fuss to make the preparations appear false, but enough to suggest the genuine pride of a young commander's capture.

If it went well, Gloag's remark would make good sense. The prize money from the stranded Dutch vessel and the destruction of a gang of smugglers or wreckers would do much to push Hugh's other problems to one side.

'You there! Give me a hand down with my bag!'

Bolitho turned to see a seaman helping a tall, loose-limbed man in a plain blue coat and hat down on to the cutter's bulwark.

The seaman seemed to know him well and grinned. 'Welcome back, Mr Whiffin, sir!'

Bolitho hurried aft, raking through his mind to place where he had heard the name. He had now been aboard the cutter for ten days and had learned the names and duties of most of the men, but Whiffin's role eluded him.

The tall man regarded him calmly. A mournful, expressionless face.

He said, 'Whiffin. Clerk-in-charge.'

Bolitho touched his hat. Of course, that was it. These cutters carried a senior clerk to do several jobs in one. To act as purser, captain's clerk, in some cases even to try their hand at surgery, and Whiffin looked as if he could do all of them. Bolitho remembered hearing his brother mention vaguely he had put Whiffin ashore for some reason or other. Anyway, now he was back.

'Captain aboard?' He was studying Bolitho curiously. 'You'll be the brother then.'

Wherever he had been, Whiffin was remarkably well informed.

'Aft.'

'Very well. I'd better see him.'

Shooting another glance at Dancer he went below, twisting himself around and down the companion like a weasel.

'Well now.' Dancer pursed his lips in a whistle. 'He's a strange one.'

The boatswain's mate of the watch called, 'Cap'n wants you below, sir!'

Bolitho hurried to the ladder, wondering if Whiffin's return had changed something. Perhaps he and not Dancer was going with the waggons after all.

His brother looked up sharply as he entered the cabin. Whiffin was sitting near him, filling the air with smoke from a long clay pipe.

'Sir?'

'Slight alteration, Richard.' He gave a small smile. 'I want you to get ashore and find the chief revenue officer. Hand him this letter, and bring me a signature for it.'

Bolitho nodded. 'I see, sir.'

'I doubt it, but no matter, so off you go.'

Bolitho looked at the address scrawled on the wax-sealed envelope and then returned to the deck.

He led Dancer to the side and said, 'If I'm not back aboard before you leave, good luck, Martyn.' He touched his arm and smiled, surprised at his sudden uneasiness. 'And take care.'

Then he climbed on to the jetty and strode quickly towards the town.

It took over an hour to find the revenue officer in question. He seemed out of sorts, probably because of the extra work he was being given, and also at having to sign for the letter, as if he was not to be trusted.

When Bolitho returned to the jetty nothing seemed to have changed. Not at first glance. But as he drew nearer to the *Avenger*'s tall mast and furled sails he realised that the waggons had already gone.

As he lowered himself to the deck Truscott, the gunner, said, 'You're wanted below, sir.'

Again? It never stopped. He was still a midshipman, no matter what title Hugh had chosen for him.

Hugh Bolitho was seated at the table, as if he had not moved. The air was still wreathed in smoke, and it gave the impression that Whiffin had only just left.

'You didn't take long, Richard.' He sounded preoccupied. 'Good. You can tell Mr Gloag to call the hands and prepare to get under way. We'll be short-handed, so see that they know what they are doing.'

'The waggons are gone.'

His brother watched him for several seconds. 'Yes. Soon after you left.' He raised one eyebrow. 'Well?'

'Is something wrong?' Bolitho stood his ground as he recognised the quick flash of impatience.

'Whiffin brought news. There is to be an ambush. The waggons will take the road to the east'rd towards Helston, then nor'-east to Truro. Whiffin has made good use of his time ashore and a few guineas in the right palms. If all goes as expected, the attack will be between here and Helston. The coast road is within easy reach of a dozen coves and beaches. *Avenger* will get under way now and be ready and waiting to offer assistance.'

Bolitho waited for more. His brother was explaining crisply, confidently, but there was a difference. He sounded as if he was speaking his thoughts aloud to convince himself of something.

Bolitho said, 'And the letter I carried was for the dragoons?'

Hugh Bolitho leaned back against the curved timbers and said bitterly, 'There are no dragoons. They're not coming.'

Bolitho could not speak for several moments, seeing only his friend's face as they had parted, recalling Hugh's remark about *Avenger* being short-handed. The plan had been for ten seamen to go with Dancer, while the rest of the escort would be some revenue officers. The dragoons from Truro, superbly trained and experienced, were to have been the main force.

The fact that Hugh had sent more seamen than intended showed he had known for some while.

He said, 'You knew. Just as you did about the informant Portlock.'

'Yes. If I had told you, what would you have done, eh?' He looked away. 'You'd have passed the news to

Mr Dancer, frightened him half to death before he'd even started.'

'As it is, you might be sending him to his death.'

'Don't be so bloody insolent!' Hugh stood up, stooping automatically between the deckhead beams. It made him look as if he was about to spring at his younger brother. 'Or so self-righteous!'

'I could ride after them.' He could hear his own voice. Pleading, knowing at the same time it was wasted. 'There'll be other ways of catching the smugglers, other times.'

'It is settled. We sail on the tide. The wind has veered and is in our favour.' Hugh lowered his voice. 'Rest easy. We'll manage.'

As Bolitho made for the door he added, 'Mr Dancer is your friend, and we are brothers. But to all else we are authority, with a plain duty to carry out.' He nodded. 'So be about it, eh?'

Standing aft by the taffrail as he watched the *Avenger*'s depleted company preparing to take in the mooring lines, Bolitho tried to see it as his brother had suggested. Detached. Uninvolved. It would be simple to recall the waggons. A fast horse would be up to them in less than two hours. But Hugh was not prepared to risk his plan, no matter what chance it had of success without the dragoons' aid. He would rather put Dancer and two dozen of his own men in mortal danger.

Standing out of harbour almost into the eye of the wind, the *Avenger* made a leisurely exit.

Bolitho watched his brother by the compass, seeking some sign, a hint of his true feelings.

He heard Gloag say, 'Damn this fair weather, I say, sir. We'll not be able to change tack till we're hid from the land by dusk.' He sounded anxious, which was unusual. 'Time's runnin' out.'

Then Bolitho saw through his brother's guard as he thrust himself away from the compass with a sharp retort. 'Keep your miseries to yourself, Mr Gloag! I'm in no mood for them!'

He went below, and Bolitho heard the cabin door slam shut.

The acting-master remarked to the deck at large, 'Squalls ahead.'

Darkness had closed over the choppy waters of Mounts Bay when Hugh Bolitho came on deck again.

He nodded to Gloag and the watchkeepers on the lee side and said, 'Tell Mr Pyke and the gunner to attend to both boats. They must be armed and ready for hoisting outboard at short notice.' He peered at the feeble compass light. 'Call the hands and bring her about. Steer due east, if you please.'

As the word was passed between decks, and the seamen came hurrying once more to their stations, he crossed to where Bolitho stood beside the helmsmen.

'It'll be a clear night. Wind's brisk, but no need to take in a reef.'

Bolitho barely heard him. He was picturing the cutter's progress, as if he were a sea-bird high overhead.

From the calculations on the chart, and the new course, he knew that they would be heading inshore again, to dangerous shoal waters, towards the very coastline where the

Dutchman had gone aground, and many more fine ships before.

If Whiffin's information was correct there would be an attack on the slow-moving waggons. If the attackers already knew of the deception they would be beside themselves with glee. If not, it would still make little difference unless *Dancer* and his men received help.

He looked up at the hard-bellied sails, the long whipping tongue of the masthead pendant.

His brother called, 'Very well. Stand by to come about.'

When order had replaced the confusion of changing tack, and *Avenger*'s long, pole-like bowsprit was pointing towards the east, the gunner came aft, leaning over to a steeper angle as the wind pushed the hull over.

'Boats checked an' ready, sir. An' I've got a good man by the arms chest in case we . . .'

He swung round as a voice called hoarsely, 'Light, sir! On th' larboard bow!'

Dark figures slithered down across the tilting deck to the lee side to search for the light.

Someone said, 'Wreckers, mebbe?'

But Gloag, who had also seen it, said, 'No. It was too regular.' He pointed. 'See? There it be again!'

Bolitho snatched a telescope and tried to train it across the creaming wash of crests and spray. Two flashes. A shuttered lantern. A signal.

He felt Hugh at his side, heard his telescope squeak as he closed it and said, 'Where is that, d'you reckon, Mr Gloag?' Calm again. In charge.

' 'Ard t' tell, sir.'

Bolitho heard Gloag breathing heavily, any animosity between him and his youthful captain momentarily forgotten.

Pyke suggested, 'Round the point, towards Prah Sands, is my guess, sir.'

The light blinked out twice like a malevolent eye against the black shoreline.

Pyke said with disbelief, 'God damn their eyes, they're runnin' a cargo tonight, the buggers!'

Bolitho chilled, imagining the unknown vessel, somewhere ahead of the lightless cutter. If they sighted the *Avenger* they might sheer off. Then again, they might raise an alarm which in turn would warn the ambush. The attack would be brought forward and there would be no hope of quarter.

'We will shorten sail, Mr Gloag. Mr Truscott, have the guns loaded with grape and canister.' The sharpness in his tone held the gunner motionless. 'But do it piece by piece. I don't want to hear a sound!' Hugh peered round for a boatswain's mate. 'Pass the word forrard. A flogging for the first man to alert the enemy. A golden guinea for the first man to sight him!'

Bolitho crossed the deck before he knew what he was doing.

'You're not going after her?'

His brother faced him, although his face was hidden in the gloom.

'What did you expect? If I let her slip away we could lose both. This way we might do for all the devils at once!'

He swung away as the hands ran to the braces and halliards.

'I've no choice.'

7

A Tragedy

As the *Avenger* ploughed her way through each succession of wave crests, Bolitho found it harder to contain his anxiety. The cutter seemed to be making an incredible noise, and although he knew it would not be heard beyond half a cable, he could find no comfort. The sluice of water against the hull, the boom of heavy canvas with the attendant strains and rattles in the rigging, all joined in an ever-changing crescendo.

The topsail had been taken in, as had the jib, but even under fore and mainsail alone *Avenger* would stand out to any watchful smuggler.

As Gloag had mentioned, it was a fair night. Now that their eyes had become accustomed to it, it seemed even brighter. No clouds, a million glittering stars to reflect on the frothing waves and spume, and when you looked up the sails were like great quivering wings.

A man craned over a stocky six-pounder and thrust out his arm.

'There, sir! Fine on th' lee bow!'

Figures moved about the decks, as if taking part in a well-practised dance. Here and there a telescope squealed or a man whispered to his companion. Some in speculation, others probably in envy for the man who would receive a golden guinea.

Hugh Bolitho said, 'Schooner, showing no lights. Under full sail too.' He shut his glass with a snap. 'Bit of luck. He'll be making more din than we are.' He dispensed with conjecture and added shortly, 'Bring her up a point, Mr Gloag. I don't want the devil to slip past us. We'll hold the wind-gage if we can.'

Voices passed hushed orders, and cordage squeaked through the sheaves while overhead the big mainsail shivered violently before filling again to the alteration of course.

Bolitho glanced at the compass as the helmsman said hoarsely, 'East by south, sir.'

'Man the larboard battery.' Hugh sounded completely absorbed. 'Open the ports.'

Bolitho watched the port lids being hauled open to reveal the glistening mane of water alongside. *Avenger* was heeling so far over that spray came leaping inboard over the six-pounders and deadly-looking swivels.

Normally Bolitho would have felt like the rest of the men around him. Tense, committed, slightly wild at the prospect of a fight. But he could not lose himself this time, and kept thinking of the waggons, the outnumbered escort, the sudden horror of an ambush.

A light spurted in the darkness, and for an instant he thought some careless seaman had dropped a lantern on the other vessel. Then he heard a distant crack, like a man breaking a nut in his palms, and knew it was a pistol shot. A warning, a signal. Now it did not matter which.

'Put up your helm, Mr Gloag!' Hugh's voice, loud now that caution was pointless, made the men at the tiller start. 'Stand by on deck!'

There were more flashes, doing more to reveal the other vessel's size and sail plan than to harm the crouching seamen.

The distance was rapidly falling away, the big sails sweeping the cutter downwind like a bird of prey, and then they saw the schooner rising through the darkness, her canvas in confusion as she tried to change tack and beat clear.

Bolitho watched his brother as he stood by the weather rail, one foot on a bollard, as if he was watching a race.

'As you bear, Mr Truscott! On the uproll!'

A further pause, and across the choppy water Bolitho heard muffled shouts, a vague rasp of metal.

Then, *'Fire!'*

At a range of less than seventy yards the larboard battery hurled themselves inboard on their tackles, their long orange tongues as blinding as their explosions were deafening. Unlike the heavy artillery of a ship of the line, or even a frigate, *Avenger*'s little six-pounders had voices which scraped the insides of the brain.

Bolitho pictured the effect of the sweeping hail of grape and close-packed canister as it cut into the other vessel's deck. He heard a spar fall, saw splashes alongside the darkened schooner as rigging and perhaps men dropped from the masts like dead fruit.

'Sponge out! Load!'

Hugh Bolitho had drawn his sword, and in the misty starlight it shone in his hand like a piece of thin ice. The same one he had used to settle a matter of honour. Probably many others too, Bolitho thought despairingly.

'*Fire!*'

Even as the small broadside crashed out again, shaking the hull like a giant fist, a few cracks and flashes showed that the smugglers were not ready to surrender.

Hugh Bolitho yelled, 'Stand by to board!' He did not even look round as a man fell kicking on the deck with a musket ball in his neck.

How many times they must have drilled and practised this, Bolitho thought as he dragged out his hanger. The gun crews left their smoking charges and seized up cutlasses and pikes, axes and dirks, while the remainder of the hands threw themselves on sheets and halliards. At the moment of collision between the two hulls, *Avenger*'s sails seemed to vanish like magic, so that with the way off her heavy, downwind plunge she came alongside the other vessel with one heart-stopping lurch.

But stripping off her sails had lessened the chance of dismasting her, likewise she did not rebound away from her adversary, so that as grapnels soared through the darkness and more shots and cries echoed between the hulls, the first boarders swarmed across the bulwark.

Pyke yelled, 'Back, lads!'

Even that was like part of a rehearsed dance. As the cheering boarders threw themselves inboard again, two swivels exploded from the forecastle, scything through a crowd of screaming figures who seconds earlier had been rushing to repel the attack.

Hugh Bolitho pointed his sword. *'Now!* At 'em, lads!' Then he was up and over, slashing at a man as he did so, and catching one of his own as he all but fell between the two grinding hulls.

Bolitho ran to the forecastle, waving his hanger to the last party of boarders.

Yelling and cheering like demons they clambered over the gap. One man fell beside Bolitho without a sound, another threw his hand to his face and screamed, the sound ending with a sharp gasp as a boarding pike came out of the darkness and impaled him.

Shoulder to shoulder Bolitho's men advanced along the schooner's deck, while from the cutter alongside the remaining seamen yelled advice and warnings, accompanied by pistol-fire and a few well-aimed missiles.

Bolitho felt his shoes slithering on the remains left by the swivels' murderous onslaught. He shut his mind to all else but the faces which loomed and faded before him, the jarring ache of steel as he kept up his guard and probed for weakness in an opponent's defence.

Across the heads and shoulders of the yelling, cursing men he saw his brother's white lapels, heard his voice as he urged his party forward, separating and dividing the defenders into smaller and smaller groups.

Someone yelled, *'That's* for Jackie Trillo, you bugger!' A cutlass swung like a scythe, almost cutting a man's head from his shoulders.

'Strike! Throw down your arms!'

But a few more were to fall before the cutlasses and pikes clattered on the planking amongst the corpses and groaning wounded.

Then Bolitho saw his brother point his sword at a man by the untended wheel.

'Have your people anchor. If you desist or try to scuttle, I will have you seized up and flogged.' He sheathed his sword. 'Then hanged.'

Bolitho hurried to his side. "The whole of Cornwall will have heard this!'

Hugh did not seem to be listening. 'Not Frenchies as I suspected. They sound like Colonists.' He turned abruptly and nodded. 'Yes, I agree. We will leave the prize anchored here, under guard. Have two swivels hoisted across and trained on the prisoners. Then put a petty officer in charge. He'll know how to deal with them. He'd rather die than face me after letting them escape!'

Bolitho followed him, his mind awhirl as he watched his brother's progress. Passing orders, answering questions, his hands moving to emphasise a point or to indicate what he wanted done.

Pyke shouted, 'Anchor's down, sir!'

'Good.' Hugh Bolitho strode to the side. 'The rest of you, come with me. Mr Gloag! Cast off and get the ship under way, if you please!'

Blocks squeaked, and like rearing spectres the sails rose above the listing, pock-marked schooner. Reluctantly at first, and then with gathering speed, the *Avenger* jerked and bumped her way free of the other vessel's side, the sails filling immediately to carry her clear.

'Where to, sir?' Gloag was peering at the sails. 'It's a mite more dangerous 'ere.'

'Put a good leadsman in the chains, please. Sounding all the way. We'll anchor in four fathoms and sway out the boats.' He looked at his brother. 'We'll head inland in two groups and cut the road.'

'Aye, aye, sir.'

Surprisingly, Hugh clapped him on the arm. 'Cheer up, man! A fine prize, full of smuggled booty, I shouldn't wonder, and no more than a few men killed! We can only take one step at a time!'

As the cutter groped her way closer and closer to the land, the leadsman's dreary chant recorded the growing danger. Eventually, with surf to starboard, and a dark hint of land beyond, they dropped anchor. But for Gloag's anxiety and repeated warnings, Bolitho suspected his brother would have gone even nearer.

Even now, he did not envy Gloag's responsibility. Anchored amidst sand-bars and jagged rocks, without sufficient hands to work her clear if the wind rose again, he would be hard put to stop *Avenger* dragging and being pushed ashore.

If Hugh Bolitho was also conscious of it he concealed his fears well.

The two boats were lowered, and taking all but a handful of men, they headed for the nearest beach. The boats were filled to the gunwales, and each man was armed to the teeth.

But as the oars rose and fell, and the land thrust out to enfold them, Bolitho could feel the emptiness. The sounds of gunfire would have been enough. The people who had been making the signals, and any others involved, would be in their cottages by now, or galloping to some hiding-place as fast as they could manage.

Once assembled on the small beach, with the sea pushing and then receding noisily through the rocks, Hugh said, 'We will divide here, Richard. I'll take the right side, you the left. Anybody who fails to stop when challenged will be fired on.' He nodded to his men. 'Lead on.'

In two long files the sailors started up the slope from the beach, at first expecting a shot or two, and then finally accepting that they were alone.

Bolitho crossed the narrow coast road, the wind whipping around his legs, as his men hurried out on either side. The waggons might be safe. Could already have passed on their way. There were certainly no wheel tracks to mark where the heavily loaded waggons had gone by.

The seaman named Robins held up his hand. *'Sir!'* Bolitho hurried to his side. 'Someone's comin'!'

The seamen scattered and vanished on either side of the rough track, and Bolitho heard the soft click of metal as they cocked their weapons in readiness.

Robins and Bolitho remained very still beside a wind-twisted bush.

The seaman said softly, 'Just th' one, sir. Drunk, by th' sound of it.' He grinned. 'Not been as busy as th' rest of us!' His grin froze as they heard a man sobbing and gasping with pain.

Then they saw him reeling back and forth across the road, almost falling in his pitiful efforts to hurry. No wonder Robins had thought him drunk.

Robins exclaimed, 'Oh God, sir! It's one of our lads! It's Billy Snow!'

Before Bolitho could stop him he ran towards the lurching figure and caught him in his arms.

'What is it, Billy?'

The man swayed and gasped, 'Where was you, Tom? Where *was* you?'

Bolitho and some of the others helped Robins to lay the man down. How he had got this far was a miracle. He was cut and bleeding from several wounds and his clothing was sodden with blood.

As they tried to cover his injuries, Snow said in a small voice, 'We was doin' very well, sir, an' then we sees the soldiers, comin' down the road like a cavalry charge!'

He whimpered, and someone said harshly, 'Easy with that wound, Tom!'

Snow muttered vaguely, 'Some of the lads gave a huzza,

just for a joke, like, an' young Mr Dancer went on ahead to greet them.'

Bolitho stooped lower, feeling the man's despair, the nearness of death.

'Then, an' then . . .'

Bolitho touched his shoulder. 'Easy now. Take your time.'

'Aye, sir.' In the strange star-glow his face looked like wax, and his eyes were tightly shut. He tried again. 'They rode straight amongst us, hackin' an' slashin', not givin' us a chance. It was all done in a minute.'

He coughed, and Robins whispered huskily, ''E's goin', sir.'

Bolitho asked, 'What about the others?'

The head jerked painfully. Like a puppet's. 'Back there. Up th' road. All dead, I think, though some ran towards the sea.'

Bolitho turned away, his eyes smarting. Sailors would run towards the sea. Feeling betrayed and lost, it was all they knew.

''E's dead, sir.'

They all stood round looking at the dead man. Where had he been going? What had he hoped to do in his last moments?

'The cap'n's comin', sir.'

Hugh Bolitho, with his men at his back, came out of the darkness, so that the road seemed suddenly crowded. They all looked at the corpse.

'So we were too late.' Hugh Bolitho bent over the dead

man. 'Snow. A good hand.' He straightened up and added abruptly, 'Better get it over with.' He walked down the middle of the road, straight-backed. Completely alone.

It did not take long to find the others. They were scattered over the road, the rocky slope beyond, or apparently hurled bodily over the edge on to the hillside.

There was blood everywhere, and as the seamen lit their lanterns the dead eyes lit up in the gloom as if to follow their efforts, to curse them for their betrayal.

The waggons and the escort's own weapons had all gone. Not all the men were there who should have been, and Bolitho guessed they had either fled into the darkness or been taken prisoners for some terrible reason. And this was Cornwall. His own home. No more than fifteen miles from Falmouth. On this wild coastline it could just as easily have been a hundred.

A man Bolitho recognised as Mumford, a boatswain's mate, came from the roadside. He held out a cocked hat and said awkwardly, 'I think this is Mr Dancer's, sir.'

Bolitho took it and felt it. It was cold and wet.

A cry brought more men running as a wounded seaman was found hiding in a fold of rocks above the road.

Bolitho went to see if he could help and then stopped, frozen in his tracks. As Robins held up his lantern to assist the others with the wounded and barely conscious man, he saw something pale through the wet grass.

Robins said fiercely, ' 'Ere, sir, I'll look.'

They clambered up the slippery grass together, the lantern's beam shining feebly on a sprawled body. It was the fair hair Bolitho had seen, but now that he was nearer he could see the blood mingling with it as well.

'Stay here.'

He took the lantern and ran the rest of the way. Gripping the blue coat he turned the body over, so that the dead eyes seemed to stare at him with sudden anger.

He released his grip, ashamed of his relief. It was not Dancer, but a dead revenue man, cut down as he had tried to escape the slaughter.

He heard Robins ask, 'All right, sir?'

He controlled the nausea and nodded. 'Give me a hand with this poor fellow.'

Hours later, dispirited and worn out, they reassembled on the beach in the first grey light of dawn.

Seven more survivors had been found, or had emerged from various hiding places at the sound of their voices. Martyn Dancer was not one of them.

As he climbed aboard the cutter Gloag said gruffly, 'If 'e's alive, then there's 'ope, Mr Bolitho.'

Bolitho watched the jolly boat pulling ashore again, Peploe, the sailmaker, and his mate sitting grimly in the sternsheets, going to sew up the corpses for burial.

There would be hell to pay for this night's work, Bolitho thought wretchedly. He thought of the fair-headed corpse, the sick despair giving way to hope as he realised it was not his friend.

But now as he watched the bleak shoreline, the small figures on the beach, he felt there was not much hope either.

8

Voice in the Dark

Harriet Bolitho entered the room, her velvet gown noiseless against the door. For a few seconds she stood watching her son silhouetted against the fire, his hands outstretched towards the flames. Nearby, her youngest daughter Nancy sat on a rug, her knees drawn up to her chin as she watched him, as if willing him to speak.

Through another set of double doors she could hear the rumble of voices, blurred and indistinct. They had been in the old library for over an hour. Sir Henry Vyvyan, Colonel de Crespigny of the dragoons, and of course Hugh.

As was often the case, the news of the ambush and the capture of a suspected smuggler had reached Falmouth overland long before the *Avenger* and her prize had anchored in the Roads.

She had been expecting something to happen, to go

wrong. Hugh had always been headstrong, unwilling to take advice. His command, no matter how junior, had been the worst thing which could have happened. He needed a firm hand, like Richard's captain.

She straightened her back and crossed the room, smiling for him. They needed their father here and now more than anyone.

Richard looked up at her, his face lined with strain.

'How long will they be?'

She shrugged. 'The colonel has tried to explain why his men were not on the road. They were ordered to Bodmin at the last moment. Something to do with bullion being moved across the country. De Crespigny is making a full inquiry, and our squire has been sent for too.'

Bolitho looked at his hands. He was only feet from the fire but was still cold. His brother's hornets' nest was here, amongst them.

Like the dazed and bewildered survivors of the ambush, he had found himself hating the dragoons for not riding to their aid. But he had had time to think about it, and could see the colonel's dilemma. An unlikely scheme to catch some smugglers set against his rigid orders for escorting a fortune in gold was barely worth considering. He would also have assumed that Hugh would call off the attempt once he had been told about the change of circumstances.

He blurted out, 'But what will they do about Martyn?'

She stood behind him and touched his hair.

'All they can, Richard. Poor boy, I keep thinking of him too.'

The library doors opened and the three men entered the room.

What an ill-assorted trio, Bolitho thought. His brother, tight-lipped, and shabby in his sea-going uniform. Vyvyan, massive and grim, his terrible scar adding to his appearance of strength, and the dragoons' colonel, as neat and as elegant as a King's guard. It was hard to believe he had ridden many miles without dismounting.

Harriet Bolitho's chin lifted. 'Well, Sir Henry? What do *you* think about it?'

Vyvyan rubbed his chin. 'I believe, ma'am, that these devils have taken young Dancer as hostage, so to speak. What for, I can't guess, but it looks bad, and we must face up to it.'

De Crespigny said, 'Had I more men, another two troops of horses at least, I might do more, but . . .' He did not finish.

Bolitho watched them wearily. Each was protecting himself. Getting ready to lay the blame elsewhere when the real authorities heard what had happened. He looked at his brother. There was no doubt whose head would be on the block this time.

Nancy whispered, 'I shall pray for him, Dick.'

He looked at her and smiled. She was holding Martyn's hat, drying it by the fire. Keeping it like a talisman.

Vyvyan continued, 'It's no use acceptin' defeat. We'll have to put our ideas together.'

Voices murmured in the hallway, and moments later Mrs Tremayne peered into the room. Behind her Bolitho could see Pendrith, the gamekeeper, hovering with obvious impatience.

His mother asked, 'What is it, Pendrith?'

Pendrith came into the room, smelling of damp and earth. He knuckled his forehead to the standing figures and nodded to Nancy.

He said in his harsh voice, 'One of the colonel's men is outside with a message, ma'am.' As the colonel made his excuses and bustled outside, Pendrith added quickly, 'An' I've got this, sir.' He thrust out his fist with a small roll of paper for Vyvyan to read.

Vyvyan's solitary eye scanned the crude handwriting and he exclaimed, '*To whom it may concern* . . . what the hell?' The eye moved more quickly and he said suddenly, 'It's a demand. As I thought. They've taken young Dancer as hostage.'

Bolitho asked, 'For what?' His heart was beating painfully and he could barely breathe.

Vyvyan handed the letter to Mrs Bolitho and said heavily, 'The one wrecker that my men were able to capture. They want to exchange Dancer for him. Otherwise . . .' He looked away.

Hugh Bolitho stared at him. 'Even if we were allowed to bargain . . .' He got no further.

Vyvyan swung round, his shadow filling the room. '*Allowed?* What are you sayin', man? This is a life at stake. If we hang that rascal in chains at some crossroads gibbet they will kill young Dancer, and we all know it. They may do so anyway, but I think they will keep their word. A revenue man is one thing, a King's officer another.'

Hugh Bolitho met his gaze, his face stiff with resentment.

'He was doing his duty.'

Vyvyan took a few paces from the fire. He sounded impatient, exasperated.

'See it this way. We know the wrecker's identity. We may well catch him again, when there'll be no escape from the hangman. But Dancer's life is valuable, to his family and to his country.' He hardened his tone. 'Besides which, it will look better.'

'I don't see that, sir.'

Hugh Bolitho was pale with tiredness but showed no sign of weakening.

'You don't, eh? Then let me explain it for you. How will it sound at a court of inquiry later on? A midshipman's loss is bad enough, the deaths of all those sailors and revenue officers hard to explain, let alone those damned muskets which are now in the wrong hands. But who got clean away without hurt? The *Avenger*'s two officers, *both of this family*!'

For the first time Hugh Bolitho looked shocked.

'That was not how it was, sir. But for the schooner, we would have been well placed to assist, dragoons or no dragoons.'

The colonel entered at that moment and said quietly, 'I have just had word that the schooner's crew are ashore and under close guard. They will be taken to Truro.'

Vyvyan handed him the crumpled letter and watched his face.

The colonel said savagely, 'I guessed it would not end there, damn them!'

Hugh Bolitho persisted stubbornly, 'That schooner was carrying gold coin by the box-load. The crew are all American Colonists. I have no doubt they intended to use the money to buy muskets, here in Cornwall. Then they would likely transfer them to a larger vessel at some safe rendezvous elsewhere.'

The colonel eyed him coldly. 'The schooner's master insists he is innocent. That he was lost, and that you fired on him without warning. He took you for a pirate.' He raised one hand wearily. 'I *know*, Mr Bolitho, but it is what everyone will believe who wants to. You lost your muskets, failed to capture any of the smugglers, and several men have died for no good reason. I know there is talk of unrest in the American Colony, but it is only talk at present. What y*ou* have done is very real.'

Vyvyan said gruffly, 'Be easy on him. We were all youngsters once. I told him we should agree to exchange our prisoners. After all, we have a good prize in the harbour, if the magistrates can prove she was after the guns. And when we get Dancer back safe and sound he might tell us more.' He gave a crooked smile. 'What say you, Colonel?'

De Crespigny sighed. 'It is no matter for a landowner or a young lieutenant to dabble with. Even I will need to be directed in this case.' He looked round to make certain that the gamekeeper had gone. 'However, if your captured felon should escape, I see no reason to report it just yet, eh?'

Vyvyan grinned. 'Spoken like a true soldier! Well done. I'll have my men deal with it.' His eye moved across the Bolitho family. 'But if I am wrong, and they harm young

Dancer, they will eventually be very sorry for what they have done.'

Hugh Bolitho nodded. 'Very well. I accept the plan, sir. But after this I will stand no chance of success in these waters. My command and all in her will be laughed into oblivion.'

Bolitho looked at his brother and felt sorry for him. But there was no other way.

The others eventually left the house and Hugh said vehemently, 'If I could have laid hands on just one of them. I'd have finished this damned affair once and for all!'

The next two days were filled with suspense and anxiety at the Bolitho house. There was silence from Dancer's captors, although no further proof was needed as to the value of the letter. Some gilt buttons, cut from a midshipman's coat, and a neckcloth which Bolitho recognised as Dancer's were found outside the gates as a blunt warning.

On the second night the two brothers were alone by the fire, each unwilling to break the silence.

Then Hugh said suddenly, 'I shall go down to the *Avenger.* You had better remain here until we hear something. One way or the other.'

Bolitho asked, 'After this, what will you do?'

'Do?' He laughed. 'Go back to some damned ship as a junior lieutenant, I expect. Promotion went through the window when I failed to finish what I came to do.'

Bolitho stood up as horses clattered in the yard. A door banged open and he saw Mrs Tremayne staring at him, her eyes filling her face.

'They've got him, Master Richard! They've *found* him!'

In the next instant the room seemed to be full. Servants, some troopers and Pendrith, the gamekeeper, who said, 'The soldiers discovered 'im walkin' along the road, sir. 'Is 'ands were tied behind 'is back and 'e was blindfolded. Wonder 'e didn't go 'ead-first off the cliff!'

They all fell silent as Dancer, covered from head to foot in a long cloak, came into the room, supported on either side by two of de Crespigny's dragoons.

Bolitho strode forward and gripped his shoulders. He could barely speak, and they looked at each other for several more seconds until Dancer said simply, 'Near thing that time, Dick.'

Harriet Bolitho pushed through the watching figures and lifted the cloak from Dancer's shoulders. Then she took him in her arms, pulling his head to her shoulder, tears running unheeded down her cheeks.

'Oh, you poor boy!'

Dancer's captors had stripped him of all but his breeches. Blindfolded and stumbling barefoot along a road unknown to him, had he fallen, he would certainly have died of the bitter cold. Someone had beaten him too, and Bolitho saw weals on his back like rope burns.

Mrs Bolitho said huskily, 'Mrs Tremayne, take these good men to the kitchen. Give them anything they want, money too.'

The soldiers beamed and shuffled their boots. 'Thankee, ma'am. It was a real pleasure to be sure.'

Dancer lowered himself in front of the fire and said

quietly, 'I was carried to a small village. I heard someone say it was supposed to be a witches' place. That nobody would dare come looking for me there. They laughed about it. Told me how they were going to kill me if you didn't release their man.'

He looked up at Hugh Bolitho. 'I am sorry I failed you, sir. But our attackers looked like real soldiers, and acted without mercy.' He shuddered and touched his arm as if to hide his nakedness.

Hugh replied, 'What's done is done, Mr Dancer. But I'm glad you are safe. I mean it.'

Mrs Bolitho brought a cup of hot soup. 'Drink this, Martyn. Then bed.' She sounded composed again.

Dancer looked at Bolitho. 'I was blindfolded all the time. When I tried to get it off I felt them holding a hot iron close to my face. One of them said that if I did it again I would not need a blindfold. The iron would take care of my sight.'

He shivered as Nancy covered his shoulders with a woollen shawl.

Hugh Bolitho banged his fist against the wall. 'They were clever. They knew you'd not recognise their faces, but thought you might recall where you were being held!'

Dancer got painfully to his feet and grimaced. He had cut them badly along the way before the troopers had found him. 'I know one of them.'

They all stared at him, thinking he was about to break down.

Dancer looked at Mrs Bolitho and held out his hands until she took them in hers.

'It was the first day, I was lying in the darkness, waiting to die, when I heard him. I don't think they'd told him I was there.' He tightened his grip on her hands. 'It was the man I saw here, ma'am. The one called Vyvyan.'

She nodded slowly, her face full of sympathy.

'You've suffered enough, Martyn, and we have been very worried for you.' She kissed him gently on the lips. 'Now to bed with you. You'll find everything you need.'

Hugh Bolitho was still staring at him as if he had misheard.

'Sir Henry? Are you *certain*?'

She exclaimed, 'Leave it, Hugh! There's been harm enough done to this boy!'

Bolitho watched his brother's strength returning, like a sudden squall approaching a becalmed ship.

'A boy to you, Mother. But he is still one of my officers.' Hugh could barely conceal his excitement. 'Right here under our noses. No wonder Vyvyan's men were always nearby and we never caught anyone. He had to rid himself of his so-called prisoner before an examining judge arrived. The man would have informed on him to save his own life.'

Bolitho felt his mouth go dry. Vyvyan had even had some of his own men shot down to make it look perfect. He was a monster, not a man at all. And it had nearly worked, might still work if Dancer's story was not believed.

Wrecker, smuggler and an important part of some planned uprising in America, it was like a growing nightmare.

Vyvyan had planned all of it, outwitted the authorities

from the very beginning. He had even put the idea of exchanging hostages in their minds.

To his brother Bolitho said, 'What will you do?'

He gave him a bitter smile. 'I am inclined to send word to the admiral. But now we will try to determine where this village is. It cannot be far from the sea.' His eyes shone like fires. 'Next time, Richard, *next* time he will be less fortunate!'

Bolitho followed Dancer up the stairs, past the watching portraits and into his room.

'In future, Martyn, I will never complain about serving in a ship of the line.'

Dancer sat on the edge of the bed and cocked his head to listen to the wind against a window.

'Nor I.' He rolled over, worn out with exhaustion.

As his head lay in the glow of some candles, Bolitho thought of that other one, dead in the wet grass, and was suddenly grateful.

9

The Devil's Hand

Colonel de Crespigny sat stiffly in the *Avenger*'s stern cabin looking around with a mixture of curiosity and distaste.

He said, 'As I have just explained to your, er, captain, I cannot take a risk on such meagre evidence.'

As both the midshipmen made to protest he added hastily, 'I am not saying I disbelieve what you heard, or what you *thought* you heard. But in a court of law, and make no mistake, a man in Sir Henry's position and authority would go to the highest advocates, it would sound less than convincing.'

He leaned towards Dancer, his polished boots creaking on the deck.

'Think of it yourself. A good advocate from London, an experienced assize judge and a biased jury, your word would be the only voice of protest. The schooner's crew can be held upon suspicion, although there is nothing so far to connect them with Sir Henry or any evil purpose. I am certain that fresh evidence will come to hand, but against them, and not the man we are after.'

Hugh Bolitho lay with his shoulders against the cutter's side, his eyes half closed as he said, 'It seems we are in irons.'

The colonel picked up a goblet and filled it carefully before saying, 'If you can discover the village, and some good, strong evidence, then you will have a case. Otherwise you may have to rely on Sir Henry's *support* at any court of inquiry. Cruel and unjust it may be, but you must think of yourselves now.'

Bolitho watched his brother, sharing his sense of defeat and injustice. If Vyvyan was to suspect what they were doing, he might already have put some further plan into motion to disgrace or implicate them.

Gloag, who had been invited to the little meeting because of his experience if not for his authority, said gruffly, 'There be a 'undred such villages an' 'amlets within five miles of us, sir. It might take months.'

Hugh Bolitho said harshly, 'By which time the word will have penetrated the admiral's ear and *Avenger* will have been sent elsewhere, no doubt with a new commander!'

De Crespigny nodded. 'Likely so. I have served in the Army for a long while and I am still surprised by the ways of my superiors.'

Hugh Bolitho reached for a goblet and then changed his mind.

'I have made my written report for the admiral, and to the

senior officer of Customs and Excise at Penzance. Whiffin, my clerk-in-charge, is making the copies now. I have sent word to the relatives of the dead and arranged for the sale of their belongings within the vessel.' He spread his hands. 'I feel at a loss as to what else to do.'

Bolitho looked at him closely, seeing him as a far different person from the confident, sometimes arrogant brother he had come to expect.

He said, 'We must find the village. Before they move the muskets and any other booty they've seized by robbing or wrecking. There must be a clue. There has to be.'

De Crespigny sighed. 'I agree. But if I send every man and horse under my command, I'd discover nothing. The thieves would go to earth like foxes, and Sir Henry would guess we were on to him. But "capturing" that wrecker and then exchanging him was a master-stroke. It would convince any jury, let alone a Cornish one.'

Dancer exclaimed, 'Sir Henry Vyvyan told you he *knew* the prisoner and would catch up with him one day.'

De Crespigny shook his head. 'If you are right about Sir Henry, he will have killed that man, or sent him far away where he can do no harm.'

But Hugh Bolitho snapped, 'No, Mr Dancer has made the only sort of sense I have heard today.' He looked about the cabin as if to escape. 'Vyvyan is too clever, too shrewd to falsify something which could be checked. If we can find out who the man was, and where he came from, we may be on our way to success!' He seemed to come alive again. 'It is all we have, for God's sake!'

Gloag nodded with approval. ''E'll be from one of Sir 'Enry's farms, I'll bet odds on it.'

Bolitho could feel the flicker of hope moving around the cabin, frail, but better than a minute earlier.

He said, 'We'll send to the house. Ask Hardy. He used to work for Vyvyan before he came to us.'

De Crespigny stared. 'Your head gardener? I'd need a higher trust than that if I had so much in the balance!'

Hugh Bolitho smiled. 'But with respect, sir, you do not. It is my career in the scales, and the good name of my family.'

Avenger rolled lazily at her cable, as if she too was eager to be at sea again, to play her part.

Bolitho asked, 'Well? Shall we try?'

Bill Hardy was an old man whose touch with his plants and flowers was better than his fading eyesight. But he had lived all his life within ten square miles and knew a great deal about everyone. He kept to himself, and Bolitho suspected that his father had taken him on because he was sorry for him, or because Vyvyan had never tried to hide his admiration for and interest in Mrs Bolitho.

Hugh Bolitho said, 'As soon as we can. Carefully though. An alarm now would be a disaster.'

Surprisingly, he allowed his brother and Dancer to return to the house with the mission. To keep it as simple as possible, or to avoid the risk of losing his temper, Bolitho was unsure.

As they hurried across the cobbled square Dancer said breathlessly, 'I am beginning to feel free again! Whatever happens next, I think I am ready for it!'

Bolitho looked at him and smiled. They had been looking forward to Christmas together and facing one of Mrs Tremayne's fantastic dinners. But the immediate future, like the grey weather and hint of rain, was less encouraging than it had seemed in *Avenger*'s cabin. It seemed likely they would be facing the table of a court of inquiry rather than Mrs Tremayne's.

Bolitho found his mother in the library writing a letter. One of the many to her husband. There must be a dozen or more at sea at any one time, he thought. Or lying under the seal of some port admiral awaiting his ship's arrival.

She listened to their idea and offered without hesitation, 'I will speak with him.'

'Hugh said no,' Bolitho protested. 'None of us want you implicated.'

She smiled. 'I became implicated when I met your father.' She threw a shawl over her head and added quietly, 'Old Hardy was to be transported to the colonies for stealing fish and food for his family. It had been a bad year, a poor harvest and much illness. In Falmouth alone we had some fifty people die of fever. Old Hardy lost his wife and child. His sacrifice, for he was a proud man, was for nothing.'

Bolitho nodded. Sir Henry Vyvyan could have saved him. But Hardy had made the additional mistake of stealing from him. It was another glimpse of his own father too. The stern, disciplined sea captain, who to please his wife had taken pity on the poor-sighted gardener and brought him here to Falmouth.

Dancer sat down and looked at the fireplace. 'She never

fails to amaze me, Dick. I feel I know her better than my own mother!'

She returned within a quarter-hour and sat down at the desk again as if nothing had happened.

'The man's name is Blount, Arthur Blount. He has been in trouble before with the revenue men, but this is the first time he has been taken. He's never in honest work for long, and when he is it is of little value. In and around farms, repairing walls, digging ditches. Nothing for any length of time.'

Bolitho thought of the dead informant, Portlock. Like the man Blount, a scavenger, getting what he could, where he could.

She added, 'My advice is to return to your ship. I'll send word when I hear something.' She reached out and rested her hand on her son's shoulder, searching his face with her eyes as she said, 'But take care. Vyvyan is a very powerful man. Had it been anyone but Martyn here, I might have disbelieved he could do all these terrible things.' She smiled sadly at the fair-haired midshipman and said, 'But now that I know you, I am surprised I did not realise it for myself far earlier! He has links with the Americas and may well have further ambitions there. Force of arms? It is the way he has always lived, so why should he have changed now? It has taken a newcomer like Martyn to reveal him, that is all.'

The midshipmen made their way back to the anchored cutter, feeling the freshening edge to the wind, and noting that several of the smaller fishing boats had already returned to the shelter of Carrick Roads.

Hugh Bolitho listened to their story, then said, 'I have had a bellyful of waiting, but I can see no choice this time.'

Later, when it was dark, and the anchorage alive with tossing white crests, Bolitho heard the watch on deck challenge an approaching boat.

Dancer, who had been in charge of the anchor-watch, clattered down the ladder and struck his head against a deckhead beam without apparently noticing.

He said excitedly, 'It's your mother, Dick!' To the cutter's commander he added in a more sober tone, 'Mrs Bolitho, sir.'

She entered the cabin, her cloak and hair glistening with blown spray. If anything it made her look younger than ever.

She said, 'Old Hardy knows the place, and so should I! You remember the terrible fever I was telling you about? There was some wild talk that it was a punishment for some witchcraft which was being performed in a tiny hamlet to the south of here. A mob dragged two poor women from their homes and burned them at the stake as witches. The wind, drunkenness, or just a mob getting out of hand, nobody really knew what happened, but the flames from the two pyres spread to the cottages, and soon the whole place was a furnace. When the military arrived, it was all over. But most of the people who lived in and around the hamlet believed it was powerful witchcraft which had destroyed their homes as punishment for what they had done to two of their own.' She shivered. 'It is foolish of course, but simple folk live by simple laws.'

Hugh Bolitho let out a long breath. 'And Blount defied the

beliefs and made his home there.' He looked at Dancer. 'And certain others shared his sanctuary, it seems.'

He stepped around his mother, shouting, 'Pass the word for my clerk!' To the others he said, 'I'll send a despatch to de Crespigny. We may need to search a big area.'

Dancer stared at him. 'Are *we* going?'

Hugh Bolitho smiled grimly. 'Aye. If it's another false lead, I need to know it before Vyvyan. And if it's true, I want to be in at the kill!' He lowered his voice and said to his mother, 'You should not have come yourself. You have done enough.'

Whiffin bowed through the door, staring at the woman as if he could not believe his eyes.

'A letter to the commandant at Truro, Whiffin. Then we will need horses and some good men who can ride as well as fight.'

'I have partly dealt with that, Hugh.' His mother watched his surprise with amusement. 'Horses, and three of our own men are on the jetty.'

Gloag said anxiously, 'Bless you, ma'am, I've not been in a saddle since I were a little lad.'

Hugh Bolitho was already buckling on his sword.

'You stay here. This is a young man's game.'

Within half an hour the party had assembled on the jetty. Three farm labourers, Hugh and his midshipmen, and six sailors who had sworn they could ride as well as any gentlemen. The latter included the resourceful Robins.

Hugh Bolitho faced them through a growing downpour.

'Keep together, men, and be ready.'

He turned as another rider galloped away into the darkness with the letter for Colonel de Crespigny.

'And if we meet the devils, I want no revenge killings, no *take this for cutting down our friends*. It is justice we need now.' He wheeled his mount on the wet stones. 'So be it!'

Once clear of the town the horses had to slow their pace because of the rain and the treacherous, deeply rutted road. But before long they were met by a solitary horseman, a long musket resting across his saddle like an ancient warrior.

'This way, Mr Hugh, sir.' It was Pendrith, the gamekeeper. 'I got wind of what you was about, sir.' He sounded as if he was grinning. 'Thought you might need a good forester.'

They hurried on in silence. Just the wet drumming of hoofs, the deep panting of horses and riders alike, with an occasional jingle of stirrup or cutlass.

Bolitho thought of his ride with Dancer, when they had joined the witless boy at the cove, with the corpse of Tom Morgan, the revenue man. Was it only weeks and days ago? It seemed like months.

As they drew nearer the burned-out village Bolitho remembered something about it. How his mother had scolded him when as a small child he had borrowed a pony and gone there alone but for a dog.

This night she had described the superstition as foolish. Then, she had not sounded quite of the same mind.

The horses milled together as Pendrith dismounted and said, ''Alf a mile, sir, an' no more, at a guess. I think it best to go on foot.'

Hugh Bolitho jumped down. 'Tether the horses. Detail two men to stand guard.' He drew his pistol and wiped it free of rain with his sleeve. 'Lead on, Pendrith, I'm more used to the quarterdeck than chasing poachers!'

Bolitho noticed that some of the men chuckled at the remark. He was learning all the time.

Pendrith and one of the farmhands moved on ahead. There was no moon, but a diamond-shaped gap in the racing clouds gave a brief and eerie outline to a small, pointed roof.

Bolitho whispered to his friend, 'They still build these little witch houses in some villages here. To guard the entrances from evil.'

Dancer shifted uncomfortably in his borrowed clothing and hissed, 'They didn't have much success in this place, Dick!'

Pendrith's untidy shape came bounding amongst them, and Bolitho imagined he was being chased, or that some of the legends were true after all.

But the gamekeeper said urgently, 'There's a fire of sorts, sir! T'other side of the place!'

He turned, his face glowing red as a great tongue of flame soared skyward, the sparks whirling and carrying on the wind like a million spiteful fireflies.

Several of the men cried out with fear, and even Bolitho, who was used to tales of local witches and their covens, felt ice running up his spine.

Hugh Bolitho charged through the bushes, all caution thrown aside as he yelled, 'They've fired a cottage! Lively, lads!'

When they reached the tiny cottage it was already blazing

like an inferno. Great plumes of sparks swirled down amongst the smoke-blinded seamen, stinging them, trying to hold them at bay.

'Mr Dancer! Take two men and get around to the far side!'

In the fast-spreading flames, the crouching seamen and farmhands stood out clearly against the backcloth of trees and rain. Bolitho wrapped his neckcloth around his mouth and nose and kicked at the sagging door with all his strength. More flames and sparks seared his legs, as with a rumbling crash the remains of the thatched roof and timbers collapsed within the cottage.

Pendrith was bawling, 'Come back, d'you hear, Master Richard! Ain't no use!'

Bolitho turned away and then saw his brother's face. He was staring at the flames, oblivious to the heat and the hissing sparks. In those few seconds it was all laid bare. His brother saw his own hopes and future burning with the cottage. Somebody had set it alight, no ordinary fire could burst out like this in the middle of a downpour. Equally quickly, he made up his mind.

He threw himself against the door again, shutting his mind to everything but the need to get inside.

It toppled before him like a charred drawbridge, and as the smoke billowed aside he saw a man's body twisting and kicking amongst burning furniture and black fragments of fallen thatch.

It all swept through his mind as he ran forward, stooping to grip the man's shoulders and drag him back towards the door. The man was kicking like a madman, and above a gag his eyes rolled with agony and terror. He was trussed hand and foot, and Bolitho was as sickened by the stench as by the act of leaving a man to burn alive.

Voices came and went through the roar of flames like the souls of dead witches returning for a final curse.

Then others were seizing his arms, taking the load and pulling them both out into the torrential, beautiful rain.

Dancer came running through the glare and shouted, 'It's the same place, Dick! I'm certain of it. The shape of the rear wall . . .' He stopped to stare at the struggling, seared man on the ground.

Pendrith knelt down on the mud and embers and asked hoarsely, ''Oo done this thing to you?'

The man, whom Pendrith had already recognised as the missing Blount, gasped, 'They left me 'ere to burn!' He was writhing, his teeth bared in agony. 'They wouldn't listen to me!' He seemed to realise that there were sailors present and added brokenly, 'After all I done for 'im.'

Hugh bent over him, his face like stone as he asked, 'Who, man? Who did it? *We must know!*' He stiffened as one of the man's blackened hands reached out to seize his lapel. 'You are dying. Do this thing before it is too late.'

The man's head lolled, and Bolitho could almost feel the release from pain as death crept over him.

'Vyvyan.' For a brief instant some strength rebelled, and with it came another agony. Blount screamed the name, '*Vyvyan!*'

Hugh Bolitho stood up and removed his hat. As if to allow the rain to wash away what he had seen.

Robins whispered, 'That last shout done for him, sir.'

Hugh Bolitho heard him and turned away from the corpse. 'For more than one man.'

As he brushed past, Bolitho saw the claw-like stain on his white lapel, left there by the dying man. In the flickering light it looked like the mark of Satan.

10

'On the Uproll!'

Bolitho and Dancer trained their telescopes on the jetty and watched the sudden activity amongst the jolly boat's crew which had been waiting there for over an hour.

'We shall soon know, Dick.' Dancer sounded anxious.

Bolitho lowered the telescope and wiped his face free of rain. He was soaking wet, but like Dancer and most of the *Avenger*'s company had been unable to relax, to be patient while he awaited his brother's return.

That first horror of finding the man who had been left to die, the excitement of knowing Dancer had been right about Vyvyan's implications, had already gone sour. Colonel de Crespigny himself and a troop of dragoons had ridden hard to Vyvyan Manor, only to be told that Sir Henry had left on an important mission, and no, they did not know where, or when he might return. Sensing the colonel's uncertainty, the steward had added coldly that Sir Henry was unused to having his movements queried by the military.

So there was no evidence after all. Apart from that last, desperate accusation of a dying man, they had nothing. No stolen cargo, no muskets, brandy or anything else. There were plenty of signs that people had been there. Hoof-marks, wheel-tracks and traces of casks and loads being hauled about in a great hurry. But what remained would soon be washed away in the continuous downpour. In any case it was not evidence.

Dancer said quietly, 'It will be Christmas Day tomorrow, Dick. It may not be a happy one.'

Bolitho looked at him warmly. Dancer was the one who would be spared all inquiry but the briefest statement. His position, to say nothing of his father's importance in the City of London, would see to that. And yet he felt just as vulnerable as the Bolitho family which had got him involved in the first place.

The boatswain's mate of the watch called, 'Cap'n's boat 'as just shoved off, sir!'

'Very well. Call the side party. Stand by to receive him.'

It might well be the last time Hugh Bolitho was received aboard in command, here or anywhere else, he thought. Hugh Bolitho clambered over the side and touched his hat to the side party.

'Call the hands and hoist the boats inboard.' He squinted up at the flapping masthead pendant. 'We will get under way within the hour.' He looked at the midshipmen for the first time and added bitterly, 'I'll be glad to be rid of this place, home or not!'

Bolitho tensed. So there was no last-minute hope, no reprieve.

As Dancer and the boatswain's mate hurried forward, Hugh Bolitho said in a calmer tone, 'I am required to make passage to Plymouth forthwith. The members of my company I put aboard a prize are assembled there, so your appointment as my senior will no longer be needed.'

'Did you hear anything about Sir Henry Vyvyan?'

He saw his brother give a shrug as he answered, 'De Crespigny was duped like the rest of us. You remember that bullion which the dragoons were suddenly and mysteriously required to escort at Bodmin? Well, we have now learned that it was Vyvyan's property. So while the revenue men and our people were being set upon by his ruffians, and cut to pieces, Vyvyan's booty was coolly being put aboard a vessel at Looe, after being escorted by the very soldiers who have since been searching for him!' He turned and looked at him, his face strained and seemingly older. 'So as he slips away to France, probably to negotiate for more weapons for his private wars, I will have to face the consequences. I thought I could run before I could walk. But I was outwitted, and beaten without knowing it!'

'And Sir Henry is *known* to be aboard this vessel?' He could picture the man even as he spoke.

It would be a triumph for Vyvyan, who had led a dangerous but rewarding life before coming to Cornwall. And when it had all quietened down he would come back. It was unlikely he would be challenged by the authorities again.

Hugh Bolitho nodded. 'Aye. The vessel is the *Virago*, a new and handy ketch-rigged sloop. Vyvyan has apparently owned her for a year or so.' He swung away, the rain pouring unheeded down his features. 'She might be anywhere by now. My orders from the port admiral *suggest* that a King's ship may be required to investigate, but nothing more than that.' He slapped his hands together, despairing, final. 'But *Virago* is fast, and will outsail anything in this weather.'

Gloag came clumping on deck, his jaw working on some salt beef.

'Sir?'

'We are getting under way, Mr Gloag. Plymouth.'

No wonder Hugh wished to be rid of the place. Danger from an enemy, or across the marks of a duelling pitch, he could take with ease. Scorn and contempt he could not.

Bolitho watched the dripping boats being swayed inboard, the seamen's bodies shining like metal in the heavy rain.

To Plymouth, and a court of inquiry. It was not much of a way to end a year.

He thought of the nearness of success, the callous way Vyvyan had directed the deaths and the plunder of wrecked ships. He thought too of Dancer's face as the troopers had aided him into the house, the livid bruises on his shoulders. How his captors had threatened to put out his eyes. All the time they had been on the fringe of things. Now it was over, and they were as much in the dark as ever.

His brother said, 'I'm going below. Inform me when the anchor is hove short.'

His head was almost at deck level when Bolitho stopped him.

'What is it?'

Bolitho said quietly, 'I was thinking of what we did achieve, what we *do* know.' He saw his brother's features soften slightly and hurried on, 'No, I'm not saying it to sugar the pill. Suppose the others are wrong, de Crespigny, the port admiral, all of them?'

Hugh Bolitho climbed up the companion ladder very slowly, his eyes fixed on him.

'Go on.'

'Perhaps we have overestimated Sir Henry's confidence. Or maybe he was intending to quit England anyway?' He saw the understanding on his brother's face and added quickly, 'He would certainly not be sailing to France!'

Hugh Bolitho stepped over the coaming and stared across the darkened harbour, at the choppy white crests, and the town's glittering lights beyond.

'To America?' He gripped his brother's shoulder until he winced. 'By God, you may be right. The *Virago* could be standing down-channel at this very instant, with nothing between her and the Atlantic but –' he looked along his broad-beamed command, '– my *Avenger*.'

Bolitho was almost sorry for what he had said and done. Another false hope perhaps? One more barb to anger the admiral and hasten a court martial.

Gloag was watching him anxiously. 'It will be rough outside, sir. Misty too, if th' rain eases.'

'What are you saying, Mr Gloag? That I give in now? Admit to failure?'

Gloag beamed. He had made his point and was content.

'I says go after 'im, sir, take the devil back for the 'angman.'

As if to put doubt over the side the cry came from the bows, 'Anchor's hove short, sir!'

Hugh Bolitho bit his lip, measuring the chances as he looked from the tense helmsmen to the hands at the braces and halliards, from his grey-eyed brother to Gloag, Pyke and the rest.

Then he nodded. 'Carry on, Mr Gloag. Get the vessel under way and lay a course to weather the headland as close as you dare.'

Dancer looked at Bolitho and gave a reckless grin. Christmas had become just part of a dream.

Bolitho waited for the *Avenger* to complete another staggering lunge and then crossed the deck to peer at the compass. The motion was sickening, with the sturdy hull lifting across each rearing wavecrest before sliding heavily again into a waiting trough. And it had been going on for nearly twelve hours, although it felt much longer.

One of the helmsmen said wearily, 'West by north, sir.' Like the rest of them he sounded tired and dispirited.

Seven bells chimed out from the forecastle, and Bolitho made his way to the weather rail, seeking a handhold before the cutter began another one of her dizzy plunges. In half an hour it would be noon, Christmas Day. But it meant a lot more than that to his brother, perhaps to them all. Maybe it had been a foolish gesture after all, a last desperate attempt to settle the score. They had sighted nothing, not even an overzealous fisherman. Which was hardly surprising on this of all days, Bolitho thought bitterly.

He squinted through the rain, his stomach queasy as it rebelled against the liberal ration of rum which had been sent round the vessel. Trimming sails, reeling from one tack to another, left little chance for lighting the galley fire and getting something hot for all hands. Bolitho had decided he would never drink rum again if he could help it.

Gloag had been right about the weather too, as he always seemed to be. The rain was still falling steadily, cutting the face and hands like icy needles. But it had lessened in strength, and with the slight easing had come a strange mist which had joined sea to sky in one blurred grey curtain.

Bolitho thought of his mother, picturing the preparations for the Christmas fare. The usual visitors from surrounding farms and estates. Vyvyan's absence would be noticed. They would all be watching Harriet Bolitho, wondering, questioning.

He stiffened as he heard his brother coming on deck again. He had barely been absent for more than one half-hour at a time since leaving Falmouth.

Bolitho touched his salt-stained hat. 'Wind's holding steady, sir. Still southerly.'

It had backed during the night and was pounding into the *Avenger*'s great mainsail from almost hard abeam, thrusting her over until the lee scuppers were awash.

Gloag's untidy shape detached itself from the opposite side and muttered, 'If it rises again or veers, sir, we'll 'ave to be thinkin' about changin' tack.' He pouted doubtfully, unwilling to add to his commander's worries, but knowing his responsibility was for them all.

Bolitho watched the uncertainty and the stubbornness fighting one another on his brother's wind-reddened face. The cutter was about ten miles due south of the feared Lizard, and as Gloag had said, with a rising gale they could find themselves on a lee shore when they eventually went about, if they did not take care.

Hugh Bolitho crossed to the weather side and stared fixedly into the stinging rain.

Partly to himself he said, 'Damn them. They've done for me this time.'

The deck lifted and slithered away again, men falling in sodden bundles, cursing despite fierce looks from their petty officers. Soon now. They were late already in responding to the admiral's summons. If Hugh Bolitho delayed much longer the wind might decide to play a last cruel trick on him and shift direction altogether.

He looked at his younger brother and gave a bleak smile. 'You are thinking too hard again, Richard. It shows.'

Bolitho tried to shrug it off. 'It was my suggestion to make this search. I merely thought . . .'

'Don't blame yourself. It is almost over. On the noon bell we'll bring her about. And it *was* a good idea of yours. Any other day the channel would be dense with shipping and it would have been like a needle in a haystack. But Christmas

Day?' He sighed. 'If the fates had been kinder, and we could *see*, who knows?'

He added, 'We had better see to our extra canvas, in case the weather worsens presently.' It was his duty to attend to the vessel's needs, but his voice showed that his thoughts were elsewhere, still seeking his enemy. 'Get aloft to the yard and check the stuns'l booms, and tell Mr Pyke we'll need to take in a reef shortly.' He peered up at the wind-hardened topsail, the angry jerking of shrouds and braces as his command met the challenge of sea and tiller.

Dancer had also come on deck, looking pale and dishevelled.

'I'll go, sir.'

Hugh Bolitho gave a tired smile. 'Still no head for heights, Richard?'

The brothers looked at each other, and Dancer, who knew only one of them, could sense they were closer than they had been for a long time.

As Dancer clambered into the weather shrouds, Bolitho said, 'I'm glad you asked me to join *Avenger*.' He looked away, embarrassed that it was so hard to speak like this.

Hugh Bolitho nodded slowly. 'Aboard the old *Gorgon* I expect they're envying you at ease beside a full table. If they only knew . . .'

He looked up, showing his anxiety, as Dancer yelled, 'Deck there! Sail on the weather bow.'

Even as his cry faded, eight bells chimed out from the forecastle. They had been following the other vessel all this time without being able to see her. She could only be the

Virago. Had to be. Another few minutes and *Avenger* would have come about, allowing her prey to slip away once and for all.

Pyke and Truscott, the gunner, came hurrying aft, their hair ragged with spray, their bodies so steeply angled to the deck they looked like drunken sailors with three sheets to the wind.

Pyke shouted, 'I'll go aloft to be sure, sir!' His teeth were bared, as if this was too personal to be shared.

Hugh Bolitho handed his hat to a seaman and snapped, 'No. I will go myself.'

They all watched in silence. If Dancer had not gone aloft they would have sailed to Plymouth in ignorance. Hugh Bolitho, his coat-tails flapping around his white breeches like twin pendants, paused merely briefly beside the midshipman before continuing up and further still until his shape was blurred in mist and rain. When he reached the topsail yard he stopped, and with his arms wrapped around the madly vibrating mast peered ahead.

In two minutes he returned to the deck, his face expressionless as he said, 'She's *Virago*. No doubt about it. Two masts, ketch-rigged, carrying a lot of canvas.' Only his eyes were alive, bright like little fires as he thought it out. 'She has the wind-gage of course, but no matter.' He took a few paces to the compass and then eyed each sail in turn. 'Set the jib, Mr Pyke, and then send the hands aloft and run out the booms from the yard. With stuns'ls she'll even outpace that sloop.' His eyes flashed as he added sharply, 'Or someone will answer to me!'

Dancer was called down to the deck, and an experienced seaman sent aloft to take his place. As he arrived, breathless and soaked in rain and spray, he exclaimed, 'A change of luck, sir!'

Hugh Bolitho tightened his jaw. 'We need skill today, Mr Dancer, but I'll grant you I'll not send any luck away!'

Straining and pitching, her sails booming under the pressure, *Avenger* responded to their combined efforts. Like huge ears, the studdingsails were run out on either beam, so that with the yards braced round she presented a tremendous pyramid of canvas before the wind.

It was a strange sensation, and sometimes frightening, Bolitho thought, as the cutter battered her way through crests and troughs alike, the spray bursting over the weather bulwark in solid sheets. There was still no sign of the *Virago,* and from what Dancer had described, there was little to see, even from the yards. Her hull was lost in sea mist, while like disembodied fins her sails towered above it, an easy task for the keen-eyed lookout.

Bolitho thought it unlikely that Vyvyan's sailing master was bothered at the possibility of a sea chase. Not at this stage. Vyvyan probably knew more about local ship movements even than the Admiralty, and would imagine *Avenger* snug in harbour, or tail between legs on her way back to face the admiral's wrath.

They were probably celebrating, somewhere up ahead. Christmas, victory over the King's authority, and a booty Bolitho could not even begin to imagine. And why not?

Vyvyan had won all the tricks. And now he was safely around the Lizard and would be well clear of the Scillies when he eventually broke into the vast desert of the Atlantic.

He heard Truscott ask, 'What pieces will she be carryin', sir?'

Hugh Bolitho sounded preoccupied as he scanned the sails again, searching for some possible danger or weakness.

'Much as ourselves normally. My guess is that Sir Henry Vyvyan will have a few extra surprises however, so be vigilant, Mr Truscott. I want no haphazard shooting today.' His tone hardened. 'This is not a mere fight. It is a matter of honour.'

Bolitho heard him. He sounded as if it was another duel. Something to be settled in the only way he knew. Perhaps this time he was right.

Gloag called, 'Rain's movin' off, sir!'

It was hard to tell the difference, Bolitho thought. There was more spray coming inboard than rain, and the pumps were going busily all the time, so that he guessed a good portion of sea-water had found its way below.

There was a different light, not anything like the sun, and yet the tossing wavecrests were brighter, their deep troughs less grey.

The helmsman cried, 'Steady she goes, sir! West sou'-west!'

Bolitho held his breath. Incredible. In spite of the powerful wind, Gloag had brought her three full points into it, with every sail and spar cracking and booming like a miniature battle.

Hugh Bolitho saw his expression and gave a quick nod. 'I told you, Richard. She handles well!'

A yell from the lookout put an end to speculation. 'Deck there! Ship on the lee bow!'

Peploe, the sailmaker, bustling past with his mates to prepare for the first exploding piece of canvas, looked at the acting-master and grinned. 'Got 'im! We'm to wind'rd of th' bugger now!'

The lookout shouted, 'She's sighted us!'

They stared, fascinated, as the other vessel seemed to expand out of the receding rain like a spectre. She was moving well, the sea creaming back from her forefoot in an unbroken white moustache.

Someone gasped as smoke belched from her quarter, and before the smoke had been thrust aside a ball slammed through *Avenger*'s sails and rigging, ripping holes in the starboard studdingsail and main alike.

'By God, the old fox is still alert!' Hugh Bolitho turned to watch the ball pounding across the waves. He strode to the lee side and trained his telescope on his adversary. 'Load and run out, if you please. I see no need for a challenge. That has already been offered!' He left the *Avenger*'s small broadside to Truscott and said in a quieter tone, 'That was a powerful piece. A nine-pounder at least. Probably put aboard with this in mind.'

Another bang, and a ball whimpered past the taffrail before throwing up a waterspout well off the larboard quarter.

Hugh Bolitho said angrily, 'Run up the colours.'

He watched as the gunner signalled from the foredeck that the guns were all loaded and run out. With the hull at such an angle it had been easy to thrust the six-pounders tightly against their ports, but less easy to fire with any accuracy. The sea was barely inches below each port, and the crews drenched with each savage plunge.

'On the uproll!'

Five tarred hands were raised along the bulwark, five slow-matches poised, hissing, above each touch-hole.

Then, *'Fire!'*

The sharp explosions were closely joined, jarring the deck, probing the ears, as shouting and cheering the crews hauled in their guns to swab out and reload with a minimum of delay.

Above the swaying hull men swarmed like monkeys to repair severed cordage, to take in the studdingsail, which because of the wind's strength had torn itself to shreds. And it had taken only one shot to do it.

Crash.

The cutter shook violently, and Bolitho knew that a ball had at last hit the hull, and possibly close to the waterline.

Bolitho steadied a glass on the other vessel. Instantly her masts and yards sprang alive in the lens, and he saw tiny figures moving around the deck, or working at braces and halliards like the *Avenger*'s men.

He winced as the next puny broadside banged out from the starboard battery. He saw the balls splashing around the *Virago*'s handsome counter, or falling well astern of her. The guns would not bear, but to give the crews a chance

Hugh would have to sail even closer to the wind, and so lose time and lengthen the range. He saw a brief, stabbing flash from the other vessel's quarter, imagined he saw a black blur before the iron ball ripped through the bulwark and tore along the deck like a saw. Men yelled and ducked, but one of the helmsmen was almost cut in half before the ball smashed its way through the opposite side.

Voices bellowed orders, feet slithered in spray and blood as more men ran to tend the wounded, to take control of the tiller.

Virago was drawing away now, and as Bolitho moved his glass still further he saw a patch of green on her poop and guessed it was Vyvyan in the long coat he often wore for riding.

Gloag shouted, ''S'no use, sir! Much more o' this an' we'll lose every spar!'

As he spoke another ball hissed through the shrouds and brought down the other studdingsail complete with boom, cordage and a trailing tangle of canvas. Men dashed with axes to hack it free, as like a sea-anchor it floundered alongside, hampering their progress.

Hugh Bolitho had drawn his sword. He said calmly, 'Make this signal, Mr Dancer. *Enemy in sight.*'

Dancer, used to the instant discipline of a ship of the line, was running to the halliards with his signal party before he properly understood. There was nobody to signal to, but Vyvyan might not realise it.

Even as the signal jerked up to the yard and broke to the wind *Virago*'s master would be advising Vyvyan to change tack, to beat further south for fear of being caught in a trap and driven into Mounts Bay by two instead of one pursuer.

'It's working!' Dancer stared at Bolitho with amazement.

The *Virago*'s sails were in disarray as she edged closer to the wind, her yards braced so tightly round they were almost fore and aft. But more flashes spat from her side, and several lengths of rigging and some shattered blocks joined the litter on *Avenger*'s deck.

A great crash shook the hull, and a chorus of shouts and yells made the seamen scatter as the topmast with yards and flailing stays plunged down, splintering yet again above the guns before lurching over the side.

Hugh Bolitho waved his sword. 'Put the helm down, Mr Gloag! We will steer as close as we can!' As the tiller went over and the great mainsail swung on its boom, obedient to the straining seamen, he added for Truscott's benefit, *'Now! On the uproll!'*

With the range falling away, and fully conscious of their own peril, each gun captain fired at will.

Bolitho gritted his teeth and tried to ignore the terrible cries from the wounded men below the mast. He concentrated every fibre as he watched for the fall of *Avenger*'s ragged broadside.

Then he heard the crack. Across the angry wavecrests and above the din of battle he heard it, and knew one of the six-pounders had found its mark.

And it only heeded one. Under full sail, standing danger-ously into the wind to beat away from *Avenger*'s invisible ally, the sloop seemed to quiver, as if striking a sand-bar.

Then, slowly at first, then with terrifying speed, the complete array of canvas began to stagger aft. The topgallant mast, the foretopmast and yards, driven with all the speed of wind and strain, collapsed along the deck, changing the *Virago* from a thoroughbred to a shambles in seconds.

Hugh Bolitho snatched up a speaking trumpet, his eyes never leaving the other vessel as he shouted, 'Stand by to shorten sail! Mr Pyke, prepare to board!'

Then there was a new sound, rumbling and spreading as if from the *Avenger* herself. But it was her company whose voices mingled in something like a growl, as snatching up their weapons they ran to their stations for boarding.

Dancer said, 'There'll be more of them than us, sir!'

Hugh Bolitho pointed his sword and looked along the blade as if sighting a pistol.

'They'll not fight.'

He watched the range falling away, the sloop spreading out on either bow as if to snare them.

'Now, Mr Gloag.'

The sails were already being taken in, and as the tiller went over again the *Avenger*'s bowsprit came up and into the wind, while between the two hulls the sea was lost in their shadows.

The tiny figures on the *Virago*'s deck had become men, and the faces had sharpened into individuals, some of whom Bolitho recognised, a few he had even seen in Falmouth.

Hugh Bolitho stood at the bulwark, his voice sharp through the trumpet.

'Surrender! In the King's name!' His sword swung like a pointer towards the levelled swivel guns. 'Or we fire!'

With a lurch the two vessels came together, bringing down more broken rigging and spars to add to the confusion. But despite a few defiant shouts not a shot was fired, not a sword was raised.

Hugh Bolitho walked slowly between his men towards the place where he would board. Taking his time, looking for some last spark of defiance.

Bolitho followed him with Dancer, hangers drawn, conscious of the oppressive silence which had even quietened the wounded.

These were not disciplined sailors. They had no flag, no cause to guide or inspire them. At this moment of truth they knew they would not escape, so that personal safety had become all important. To lay evidence against a man they had once called a friend, to face prison rather than a gibbet. Some would even now be hoping to be freed altogether by using lies with no less skill than their cruelty.

Bolitho stood at his brother's shoulder on the *Virago*'s deck, watching the cowed faces, feeling their fury giving way to fear, like the blood that had faded away in the blown spray.

Sir Henry Vyvyan would probably be able to plead for some special privilege even now, he thought. But Hugh's victory was complete all the same. The ship, her cargo and enough prisoners to make Mounts Bay safe for years to come.

'Where is Sir Henry?'

A small man in a gilt-buttoned coat, obviously the sloop's master, pushed towards them, his forehead badly cut by flying wood splinters.

'Worn't my fault, sir!'

He reached out to touch Hugh Bolitho's arm but the sword darted between them like a watchful snake.

So he backed away, while Bolitho and the others followed him towards the poop, which had taken the full brunt of the falling mast.

Sir Henry Vyvyan was pinned underneath one massive spar, his face screwed into a mask of agony. But he was still breathing, and as the sailors stood over him he opened his one eye and said thickly, 'Too late, Hugh. You'll not have the pleasure of seein' me dance on a rope.'

Hugh Bolitho lowered his sword for the first time, so that its tip rested on the deck within inches of Vyvyan's cheek.

He replied quietly, 'I had intended a more fitting end for you, Sir Henry.'

Vyvyan's eye moved towards the glittering blade and he said, 'I would have preferred it.'

Then with a great groan he died.

The sword vanished into its scabbard, the movement final, convincing.

'Cut this wreckage away.' Hugh Bolitho sounded almost untouched by the events and the sights around him. 'Pass the word to Mr Gloag. We will require a tow until a jury-rig can be arranged.'

Only then did he look at his brother and Dancer.

'That was well done.' He glanced at the flag which was

being run up to the *Virago*'s peak, the same one which, although torn ragged by wind and gunfire, still flew above his own command. 'The best Christmas gift I have ever been given!'

Dancer grinned. 'And maybe there will still be something left at Falmouth to celebrate with, eh, Dick?'

As they made their way back to their own vessel, Bolitho paused and looked aft towards the great heap of wreckage.

His brother was still standing beside the trapped body in the long green coat.

Perhaps, even now, he was thinking that Sir Henry Vyvyan had beaten him?

Band of Brothers

'The wings of opportunity are fledged
with the feathers of death.'
Sir Francis Drake

For you, Boo, with my love.

Contents

1

The Way Ahead

Midshipman Richard Bolitho threw up one hand to shade his eyes, surprised by the fierce, reflected glare from the water alongside. He waited while two seamen lurched past him half carrying, half dragging some bulky objects wrapped in canvas toward the open deck and the hard sunlight. After the semi-darkness of *Gorgon*'s between decks, it only added to his sense of unreality.

He calmed himself. *Another day.* For most people, anyway.

He glanced down at his uniform, his best. He wanted to smile. The *only* uniform that would pass muster and avoid criticism. He flicked off several strands of oakum which he had collected somewhere along the way from the midshipmen's berth, his home in *Gorgon* for the past year and a half.

Was that really all it was?

He took another deep breath. He was ready; and it was not just another day.

He walked on to the main deck, adjusting his mind to the noise and outward confusion of a ship undergoing the indignities of a badly needed overhaul. Chisels and hand-saws, and the constant thud of hammers in the depths of the hull, while elsewhere men swarmed like monkeys high above the decks, repairing the miles of standing and running rigging which gave life to a fighting ship and the sails that drove her. And now it was almost finished. The stench of tar and paint, the heaps of discarded cordage and wood fragments, would soon be a cursed memory. Until the next time.

He gazed across the nearest eighteen-pounders, black muzzles at rest inboard of their ports, still smart, disdaining the disorder around them. And beyond, to the land, hard and sharply etched in the morning light: the rooftops and towers of old Plymouth, with an occasional glitter of glass in the sun. And beyond them the familiar rolling hills, more blue than green at this hour.

He tried not to quicken his pace, to reveal that things were different merely because of this particular day. The new year of 1774 was barely a few days old.

But it *was* different.

Some seamen flaking down halliards glanced at him as he passed. He knew them well enough, but they seemed like strangers. He reached the entry port, where the captain was piped aboard and ashore, and important visitors were greeted with the full ceremonial of a King's ship. Wardroom officers were also permitted here, but not a midshipman, unless on duty in his proper station. Richard Bolitho was not yet eighteen, and he wanted to laugh, to shout, to share it with someone who was free of doubt or of envy.

Out of the blue and with less than a few days' warning, the signal had arrived: the appointment every midshipman knew was inevitable. Welcome, dread, even fear: he might receive it with all or none of these emotions. Others would decide his fate. He would be examined and be subject to their decision, and, if successful, he would receive the King's commission, and take the monumental step from midshipman to lieutenant.

He watched a schooner passing half a cable or so abeam, her sails hard in the wind, although the waters of Plymouth Sound were yet unbroken, a deep swell lifting the slender vessel as if it were a toy.

'Ah, here you are, Mr Bolitho.'

It was Verling, the first lieutenant.

Perhaps he was waiting to board a boat himself, on some mission for the captain; it was unlikely he would be leaving the ship, *his* ship, for any other reason at a time like this. From dawn until sunset he was always in demand, supervising working parties, checking daily, even hourly, progress above and below decks, missing nothing. He was the first lieutenant, and you were never allowed to forget it.

Bolitho touched his hat. 'Aye, sir.' He was ahead of time, and Verling would expect that. He was tall and thin, with a strong, beaky nose which seemed to guide his pitiless eyes straight to any flaw or misdemeanour in the world around him. His world.

But his appearance now was unexpected, and almost unnerving.

Verling had turned his back on the usual handful of watchkeepers who were always close by the entry port: marine sentries in their scarlet coats and white crossbelts, a boatswain's mate with his silver call ready to pipe or pass any command immediately when so ordered. The sideboys, smart in their chequered shirts, nimble enough to leap down and assist any boats coming alongside. And the officer of the watch, who was making a point of studying the gangway log and frowning with concentration, for Verling's benefit no doubt.

Bolitho knew he was being unfair, but could not help it. The lieutenant was new to the ship, and to his rank. He had been a midshipman himself only months ago, but you would never know it from his manner. His name was Egmont, and he was already heartily disliked.

Verling said, 'Remember what I told you. It is not a contest, nor an official corroboration of your general efficiency. The captain's report will have dealt with that. It goes deeper, much deeper.' His eyes moved briefly to Bolitho's face but seemed to cover him completely. 'The Board will decide, and that decision is final.' He almost shrugged. '*This* time, in any case.'

He touched the watch fob that hung from his breeches pocket but did not look at it. He had made his point.

'So you had *not* forgotten, Mr Dancer. I am glad to know it, sir.'

As if in confirmation, eight bells chimed out from the forecastle belfry.

'Attention on the upper deck! Face aft!'

Calls trilled, and from across the water came the measured blare of a trumpet. Part of life itself. Colours were being hoisted, and there would be several telescopes observing from the shore and the flagship to make certain that no one and no ship was caught unawares.

Midshipman Martyn Dancer exhaled slowly, and nodded to his friend.

'Had to go back to the mess, Dick. Forgot my protector, today of all days!'

It was a small, grotesque carving, more like a demon than a symbol of good fortune, but Dancer was never without it. Bolitho had first seen it after his ordeal with the smugglers. Dancer still bore the bruises, but claimed that his 'protector' had saved him from far worse.

Verling was saying, 'I wish you well. We all do. And remember this, the pair of you. You speak for yourselves, but today you represent *this ship*.' He permitted himself a thin smile. 'Go to it!'

'Boat's alongside, sir!'

Bolitho grinned at his friend. It was only right that they should be together today, after all that had happened.

Lieutenant Montagu Verling watched them climb down to the launch which had hooked on to the 'stairs' beneath the port. Had he ever been like that, he wondered?

'*Cast off! Shove off forrard!*' The boat, caught on the tide, veered away from the big two-decker's side, oars upright in twin lines, the coxswain gripping the tiller-bar, gauging the moment.

Verling was still watching them. It was not like him, and he was a little surprised by it. The carpenter and the boatswain would be waiting with yet more lists, work to be done, stores or cordage not yet arrived or the wrong sort if they had. For he was the first lieutenant. Right aft, beneath that big ensign curling in a steady south-westerly, the captain was in his quarters, secure in the knowledge that this refit would be completed on time. That would please the admiral, and so on, up the chain of command.

Verling saw the oars fanning out on the launch's sides, like wings, while the crew leaned aft to take the strain.

Perhaps, one day soon . . .

'Give way *together*!'

He swung round, and saw the new lieutenant trying to catch his eye.

It was wrong to harbour personal dislikes in your own wardroom.

He turned and stared across the shark-blue water, but the launch was already out of sight amongst other anchored ships. Suddenly he was glad that he had made a point of being here when the midshipmen had departed, whatever the outcome of their examinations today.

He rearranged his features into the mask of command and strode towards a working party struggling with another tackle-load of timber.

'Take a *turn, you*, Perkins! Jump about, man!'
The first lieutenant had returned.

In spite of the deep swell, the *Gorgon*'s launch soon
gathered way once clear of the two-decker's side. Fourteen
oars, double-banked, pulling in a strong but unhurried
stroke, carried her past other anchored men-of-war with
apparent ease. The coxswain, a tough and experienced
seaman, was unconcerned. The ship had been so long at
anchor during the overhaul that he had grown used to most
of the other vessels, and the comings and goings of their
boats on the endless errands of the squadron. And the man
whose flag flew above the powerful three-decker which he
could see in miniature, framed between the shoulders of his
two bowmen. The flagship. Like most of his mates, the
coxswain had never laid eyes on the admiral. But he was
here, a presence, and that was enough.

Bolitho tugged his cocked hat more tightly over his
forehead. He was shivering, and tightened his fingers
around the thwart, damp and unyielding beneath his
buttocks. But it was not the cold, nor the occasional needles
of spray drifting aft from the stem. They had all discussed
it, of course. Something far away in the future, vaguely
unreal. He glanced at his companion. Even that was unreal.
What had drawn them to one another in the first place? And
after today, would they ever meet again? The Navy was
like that; a family, some described it. But it was hard on
true friendship.

They were the same age, with only a month between

311

them, and so different. They had joined *Gorgon* together, Martyn Dancer having been transferred from another ship which, in turn, had been going into dock for a complete refit. About sixteen months ago. Before that, he had by his own admission served 'only three months and two days' in His Britannic Majesty's service.

Bolitho considered his own beginnings. He had entered the navy as a midshipman at the tender age of twelve. He thought of Falmouth, of all the portraits, the faces that watched him on the stairs, or by the study. The Bolitho family's might have been a history of the Royal Navy itself.

He thought, too, of his brother Hugh, who had been in temporary command of the revenue cutter *Avenger*. Less than two months ago. He and Martyn had been ordered to join him. An odd and daring experience. He looked over at his friend. That had been unexpected, too. Hugh, his only brother, had been the stranger.

He turned to watch the flagship. Closer now, her reefed topsails and topgallants almost white in the glare, the vice-admiral's flag streaming from the foremast truck like blood. And she had been Martyn's last ship. His only ship. *Three months and two days.* But he was here today for examination. *Like me.* Bolitho had served for five years. There would be others today, bracing themselves, gauging the odds. Did hardened, seasoned officers like Verling ever look back and have doubts?

He stared up at the towering masts, the tracery of black rigging and shrouds. Close to, she was even more impressive. A second-rate of ninety guns with a company of some eight hundred officers, seamen and marines. A world of its own. Bolitho's first ship had been a big three-decker also, and even after some four years aboard in that cramped and busy space there were faces he had never seen twice.

The hull loomed over them, the long bowsprit and jib boom sweeping like a lance. And the figurehead, *Poseidon*, the god of the sea, resplendent in new gilt paint which alone must have cost a month's pay. The 'gilt on the ginger-bread', the sailors called it.

The coxswain called, 'Stand by! *Bows!*'

The two bowmen stood and tapped their blades together to signal the crew to be ready. *A ship shall be judged by her boats . . .*

There were other boats at the booms or hooked on to the chains. Bolitho saw a lieutenant gesturing to the launch, heard the coxswain mutter, 'I can see *you*, sir!'

Martyn touched his sleeve. 'Here we go, Dick.' Their eyes met. 'We'll show them, eh?'

Like those other times. Not arrogance or conceit. A sort of quiet assurance; he had seen it in the rough and tumble of the midshipmen's berth, and again in the face of real, chilling danger. All in so short a while, and yet they were like brothers.

'Boat yer oars!'

The hull lurched against fenders and the coxswain stood by the tiller-bar again, his hat in one hand. He looked at the two midshipmen. One day they'd be like that bloody lieutenant up there at the nettings, waving his arms about.

But he said, 'Good luck!'

They were on their own.

The officer of the watch checked their names against a well-thumbed list and regarded the newcomers with a cold stare, as if to ensure that they were presentable enough to be allowed further.

He glanced at Dancer's leather crossbelt. 'Take in the slack.' He looked on critically while Dancer tugged the dirk into place and added, 'This is the flagship, so don't you forget it.' He signalled to a young messenger. 'He'll take you to the captain's clerk. Show you where to wait.'

Bolitho said, 'Are there many here for the Board, sir?'

The lieutenant considered it.

'They're not dragging their feet, I'll say that for them.' He relented a little. 'You will be the last today.' He swung round to beckon to another seaman, and Dancer said quietly, 'I hope we can get something to eat while we're waiting!'

Bolitho smiled, and felt sheer hilarity bubbling up. Like a dam breaking. Dancer could always do it, no matter how tense the situation.

They followed the messenger, the ship reaching around and above them. A teeming world of packed humanity separated only by the invisible boundaries of status or rank.

As a mere boy, it had been like being carried on a tide, with all the bumps and bruises, spiritual as well as physical, you might expect along the way. And the characters, the good and the bad, those you trusted on sight, and others on whom you would never turn your back without risk.

And always busy, ceremonial one moment, court martial the next. He felt the smile on his lips again. And always hungry.

The captain's clerk was a pale, solemn individual, who would have passed as a clergyman ashore or in more suitable surroundings. His cabin was close to the marines' messdeck and stores, the 'barracks' as they termed it, and above the other shipboard sounds they could hear the clatter of weapons and military equipment and the thump of heavy boots.

The captain's clerk, Colchester, seemed oblivious to everything but his own work, and the position which set him apart from the crowded world around him.

He waited for the two midshipmen to seat themselves on a bench half covered by documents neatly tied with blue ribbon. It looked chaotic, but Bolitho had the feeling that Colchester would know immediately if a single item was misplaced.

He regarded them with an expression that might have been patience or boredom.

'The Board today consists of three captains, unlike the more usual practice of one captain and two junior officers.' He cleared his throat, the sound like a gunshot in the paper-filled cabin.

Three captains. Dancer had told him what to expect, to warn him, this very morning, while they had been trying to dress and prepare themselves mentally in the noise and upheaval of the midshipmen's berth. It had seemed worse than usual, and the mess space was further reduced by stores and bedding from the sick quarters nearby.

How had Dancer known about the Board's members?

He did not seem troubled by it, but that was Dancer. His way, his shield. No wonder he had won a kind of respect even from some of the hard men in *Gorgon*'s company.

And from Bolitho's sister Nancy, in the short time Dancer had stayed at the house in Falmouth. She was only sixteen, and it was hard for Bolitho to accept her as a woman. She was more used to the youngsters around Falmouth, farmers' sons, and the callow young men who made up the bulk of the officers at the garrisons in Pendennis and Truro. But it had not been merely his imagination. She and Dancer had seemed to belong together.

Three captains. There was no point in wondering why. A sudden sense of urgency? Unlikely. There were far too many officers in a state of stalemate, with no prospect of promotion. Only war increased demand, and cleared the way on the Navy List.

Or perhaps it was the admiral's idea . . .

He looked over at Dancer, who appeared serenely oblivious.

Colchester said, 'You will wait here until you are called.' He got slowly to his feet, his lank hair brushing the deckhead beams. 'Be patient, gentlemen. Always fire on the uproll. . . .'

Dancer watched him leave, and said, 'If I get through today, Dick, I shall always owe it to you!'

Not so confident, then. Bolitho looked away, the words lingering in his mind. He had thought it was the other way around.

2

Not a Contest

Waiting was the worst part, more than either of them would admit. And here they were shut off from life, while the great ship throbbed and murmured above and around them. The clerk's cabin consisted merely of the screens which separated it from the marines' quarters and stores, and was devoid of ports; the only light came from vents above the door and two small lanterns. How Colchester coped with his letters and files was a mystery.

It was now afternoon, and apart from a brief visit by a young midshipman who had hovered half in and half outside the screen door as a seaman had delivered a plate of biscuits and a jug of wine, they had seen nobody. The midshipman, whom Bolitho thought was about twelve years old, seemed almost too frightened to speak, as if he had been ordered not to confide in or converse with anyone waiting to face the Board.

So young. I must have been like that in Manxman. It had been his first ship.

Even now, *Poseidon* was evoking those memories. Constant movement, like a small town. The click of heels, the thud of bare feet, and the heavier stamp of boots. He cocked his head. The marines must have abandoned their 'barracks' to carry out drills on the upper deck, or some special ceremony. This was the flagship, after all.

Dancer was on his feet again, his face almost pressed against the door.

'I'm beginning to think my father was right, Dick. That I should have followed his advice and stayed on dry land!'

They listened to the rumble of gun trucks, one of the upper deck twelve-pounders being moved. To train a new crew, or for care and maintenance. At least they were *doing* something.

Dancer sighed and sat down again. 'I was just thinking about your sister.' He ran his fingers through his fair hair, a habit Bolitho had come to know and recognise. He was coming to a decision. 'It was such a pleasure to meet her. Nancy . . . I could have talked with her for ages. I was wondering . . .'

They both turned as the door clicked open. Another seaman this time, but the same midshipman hovering at a distance, the white patches on his uniform very clean and bright in the filtered sunlight from a grating above his head.

'Just come for this gear, sir.' The seaman gathered up the plates and the wine jug, which was empty, although neither of them could recall drinking the contents.

He half turned as the midshipman outside the door answered someone who was passing. Friends, or a matter of duty, it was not clear. But it was like a signal.

He looked quickly at Dancer, then leaned over towards Bolitho.

'I served with Cap'n James Bolitho, sir. In the old *Dunbar*, it was.' He darted another glance at the door, but the voices were continuing as before. He added quietly, ''E were good to me. I said I'd never forget . . .'

Bolitho waited, afraid to interrupt. This man had served under his father. The *Dunbar* had been James Bolitho's first command. Well before his own time, but as familiar to him as the family portraits. The seaman was not going to ask any favours. He wanted to repay one. And he was afraid, even now.

'My father, yes.' He knew Dancer was listening, but keeping his distance, possibly with disapproval.

'Cap'n Greville.' He leaned closer, and Bolitho could smell the heavy rum. ''E commands the *Odin*.' He reached out as if to touch his arm, but withdrew just as quickly, perhaps regretting what he had begun.

The young midshipman was calling, 'Tomorrow at noon, John. I'll not forget!'

Bolitho said quietly, 'Tell me. You can rest easy.'

The ship named *Odin* was a seventy-four like *Gorgon*, and in the same squadron, and that was all he knew, except that it was important to this seaman who had once served his father.

The plates and the jug clashed together and the man blurted out, 'Greville's bad, right the way through.' He nodded to emphasise it. *'Right through!'*

The door swung slightly and the young voice rapped, 'Come along, Webber, don't take all day!'

The door closed and they were alone again. He might have been a ghost.

Bolitho spread his hands. 'Maybe I was wrong to let him speak like that. Because he knew my father, I suppose. But the rest . . .'

Dancer made a cautioning gesture.

'It cost him something to come here. He was afraid. More than afraid.' He seemed to be listening. 'One thing I do know. Captain Greville is on the Board, here and now.' He regarded Bolitho steadily, his eyes very blue, like the sky which had begun the day. 'So be warned, my friend.'

The door swung open.

'Follow me, if you please.'

Bolitho walked out of the cabin, trying to remember exactly what the unknown seaman had said.

But he kept hearing his father's voice instead, seeing him. It was the closest they had been for a long, long time.

The young midshipman trotted briskly ahead of them, as if he were afraid they might try to break the silence he had maintained. Perhaps it was policy in the flagship to keep candidates from any contact that might prepare or warn them against what lay in store. It was certainly true that they had seen no other 'young gentlemen' here for the same rendezvous.

Up another ladder and past one of the long messdecks. Scrubbed tables and benches between each pair of guns: home to the men who worked and fought the ship, and the guns were always here from the moment when the pipe called them to lash up and stow their hammocks, to sunset and pipe down. The constant reminder that this was no safe dwelling but a man-of-war.

Dancer was close behind him, and Bolitho wondered if he remembered these surroundings as intensely after so many months. Like his own first ship, the noise and the smells, men always in close contact, cooking or stale food, damp clothing, damp everything. Most of the hands were at work, but there were still plenty of figures between decks, and he saw a glance here and there, casual or disinterested; it was hard to distinguish in the gloom. The gunports that lined either beam were sealed, a wise precaution against the January chill and the keen air from the Sound; as in *Gorgon*, only the galley fires provided any heat, and they would be kept as low as possible to avoid wasting fuel. The purser would make sure of that.

Another climb now, to the impressive expanse of the quarterdeck, where the day seemed startlingly clear and light. Bolitho stared up at the towering mizzenmast and spars, the furled sails, and the ensign he had seen from the launch this morning, still lifting and curling beyond the poop. About seven hours ago, and the ordeal had not even begun. They had talked about it often enough, been warned what to expect, even if they survived the selection process today. Being successful and actually receiving the coveted commission were often two very different matters. A sign of the times, with promotion only for the lucky, and the clouds of war as yet unknown to those of their own age and service.

A tall lieutenant was standing by the hammock nettings, a telescope trained on the shore, and a boatswain's mate waiting close by. Apart from two seamen polishing the fittings around the compass box and the great double wheel by the poop ladders, the deck was deserted. After the confines of the world below, it seemed an almost sacred place.

Bolitho looked at the land. The hills were edged with copper. Hard to believe it would be dark before long. Perhaps the examination had been postponed. Cancelled.

'So. The last two.' The lieutenant had moved, and sounded impatient. 'You know what to do.' He hardly spared them a glance. 'Get along with you.' He was already striding to the quarterdeck rail, straightening his coat as he went.

Bolitho stared at the fresh gilt paintwork, the scrubbed gratings and perfectly flaked lines and halliards. The empty marines' mess, the sound of oars alongside, no doubt at the ornate entry port. The admiral was about to go ashore, or visit another ship of the line in his command.

Their youthful guide quickened his pace past the wheel, and Bolitho saw that the two seamen were packing away their cleaning gear. Down another hatchway where the deck planking was covered with black-and-white chequered canvas, he could see that the hand ropes were smartly pipeclayed, and a marine sentry, or at least the lower half of one, was standing rigidly beside the screen doors of the great day and dining cabin. The admiral's quarters.

'Wait!' Another screen loomed before them, freshly painted, like white glass in the light from the quarterdeck, similar to the one directly beneath them.

Dancer nudged him with his elbow.

'The admiral's on the prowl. And I thought it was all for *us*!'

He was even smiling.

A servant ushered them into a lobby, partitioned from the main cabin by more screens which could be hoisted and bolted to the deckhead if the ship was cleared for action. There were two or three comfortable chairs sharing the deck space with one of the after battery's twelve-pounders.

The cabin servant studied them severely and pointed to a bench by a sealed port.

'When you are called.' He had the stiff, tired face of a man who had seen it all before. Their midshipman guide had vanished.

They sat, side by side. Almost soundless here, the highest part of the ship. There was a skylight almost directly above them and Bolitho could see the mizzen shrouds and part of a spar, the sky holding its light beyond. After all this time, nearly six years of his life in the Navy, and he still had no head for heights. Even now, when the sails cracked and shook and the pipe shrilled *All hands aloft!* he had to force himself to respond.

'When we get back to *Gorgon*, Dick . . .' Dancer was gazing at the screen door. 'I have something hoarded away for this occasion.'

Nervous now, unsure? It went far deeper. He said lightly, 'You'll be fine, Martyn. *Under full sail*, remember?'

Dancer said in an odd voice, 'You'll never know,' but the smile was back. 'Bless you!'

'Mister Midshipman Dancer?'

They were both on their feet, unconsciously, and the screen door was being held partly open by the cabin servant, as if he were guarding it.

There was no time for words; perhaps there were none to say. They touched hands, like two friends passing in the street, and Bolitho was alone.

He wanted to sit down, to gather his thoughts, perhaps in one of those comfortable chairs, as some act of defiance. Instead, he stood directly beneath the skylight and stared up at the mizzen shrouds and the empty sky, and very slowly, an inch at a time, made his mind and body relax, come to terms with this moment. They had even joked about it. Looked sometimes at the lieutenants and wondered if they had ever had qualms, and, in some cases, how they had passed. And again the face and the words of the seaman kept coming back. He should have stopped him there and then. They were all told often enough never to listen to gossip or condone it. In the crowded world of a man-of-war, it could end in face-to-face confrontation, insubordination, or worse.

He concentrated on the screen door. The great cabin was part of, but so completely separate from, this vast three-decker. Here the captain could entertain his particular friends and favoured subordinates, even the most junior if it suited him. Bolitho himself had been invited into the captain's quarters aboard *Gorgon* on two occasions, once on the King's birthday, when as the youngest present he had been required to give the Loyal Toast, and another to wait upon some female guests, and ensure that they did not stumble on the ladders between decks or entangle their gowns while entering or leaving the boats alongside.

He thought of Dancer again. Always so at ease with women, outwardly anyway. It was not something false, or done for effect; Bolitho had known plenty like that. Martyn Dancer was of a different breed, something he had noticed even when they had first met. His father was a wealthy, worldly man, of influence and authority, who had made it plain from the outset that he was opposed to his son's choice of career. *Throwing his wits to the wind*, as he had put it more than once.

And he had seen it in his sister's eyes when she and Martyn had talked and laughed together. And in the watchful glances from his mother.

He walked to the opposite end of the screened lobby and peered through to the big double wheel, at the scrubbed gratings where two or more helmsmen would stand when the ship was under way, and heeling over to her towering pyramid of canvas. Another grating was propped upright by the mizzen, probably to dry, but suddenly reminiscent of those far-off days in *Manxman* and the first flogging he had ever witnessed. It was something you had to accept, a necessary discipline. What else would deter the persistent offender?

Accept, perhaps, but Bolitho had never grown accustomed to it. And yet he had seen some of the older hands bare their backs and boast of their endurance of the cat, as if the terrible scars were something to be carried with pride.

He could still remember standing with the other midshipmen, the very first time he had heard the pipe, 'All hands lay aft to witness punishment!'

He had found himself gripping the arm of another middy, his entire body shaking to every crack of the lash across the torn skin.

And that other stark and brutal memory, which never completely left him, months or even a year after that, when he had been face-to-face with an enemy, unskilled and desperate, and carried bodily by the stamping, cursing crush of boarders across the other vessel's deck. Pirates, smugglers, rebels . . . they were the enemy. Cutlass, pike and boarding axe, their faces masks of hate and anger. Sailors he knew, or thought he knew, stabbing and hacking heedless of the screams, men falling, voices urging them forward.

And then there had been one face, so near that he could smell the sweat and feel his breath, and eyes which had seemed to fill it. He remembered seeing the blade, like a cutlass, and had wanted to cry out; he had been gripping the hanger in his fist as if he were holding on to life itself. The blow to his shoulder had numbed it before the agony began. But the eyes were still staring at him, fixed with shock or disbelief. And then he fell, the weight of his body almost dragging the blade from Bolitho's fingers.

And a harsh voice almost in his ear; he had never discovered whose. 'Leave 'im! 'E's done for!'

Done for. He had killed someone. A lifetime ago.

He could still feel the blade jerk in his fist, as if he had only just been called to action, and seen a human being fall beneath his stroke.

He swung round and found the cabin servant watching him. No sound, no word; he had even lost track of time.

'Come, sir.'

It was too soon. Where was Martyn? But the door to the inner cabin was open. Waiting.

He thought suddenly, wildly, of Lieutenant Verling's words this morning.

It is not a contest.

He strode past the servant and heard the screen door close behind him.

Two tables had been placed end to end across the big dining cabin, behind which sat the three captains of the Board. It was like walking on to a stage with no audience, only the three motionless figures who were framed against the flag captain's private day cabin behind them. The stern and quarter windows held and reflected every sort of light, from the sea below and beyond the poop, to the deepening purple haze of the main anchorage. There were already candles burning, so that the three figures on the other side of the table were almost in shadow.

There was one tall chair facing them. If any uncertainty still lingered in the newcomer's mind, it was quickly dispelled: a sword, complete with belt, was laid across it.

Bolitho stood beside it, and said, 'Richard Bolitho, midshipman, sir!' Even his voice sounded unfamiliar.

He thought fleetingly of Dancer. How had he fared at this table? All it needed was the sword lying across it with the point towards him, and it would be more like a court martial than an interview that might lead to promotion.

'Be at your ease, Mr Bolitho. You are here today because others are prepared to recommend you. Be truthful and frank with us, and my brother officers and I will be likewise.'

Captain Sir William Proby did not trouble to introduce himself; there was no need. An unorthodox, some said eccentric, officer who had distinguished himself in the Seven Years War and in two campaigns in the Caribbean, he had served until recently as acting-commodore with the Channel Fleet. It was rumoured that he was next in line for flag rank.

Bolitho had seen him several times when carrying despatches to his present command, the *Scylla*, a seventy-four like *Gorgon*, but half her age.

The officer sitting on his right he also knew. Captain Robert Maude was comparatively young, with an alert, intelligent face, and he commanded the *Condor*, a sleek thirty-two-gun frigate, and was doubtless envied by many because of it. *Condor* was rarely at anchor for long; even now Maude was glancing through the adjoining cabin, perhaps at the shadows on the water, or the small boat passing the flagship's quarter and showing a solitary lantern.

The third member of the Board sat with one elbow on the table, his free hand resting on some certificates. And a midshipman's log.

My log.

Even if he had never met or spoken with the unknown seaman, he felt he would have recognised Captain John Greville of the *Odin*. He could still hear the voice. *Greville's bad. Right the way through.*

A narrow, pointed face, not unlike that of Verling, but tight-lipped, very contained. The eyes were in shadow.

Proby said, 'In matters of general seamanship your reports read well. It seems you suffer from an acute dislike of heights, but you have overcome it.' A hint of a smile. 'Outwardly, at least. Having taken charge of a landing party with ship's boats, what cover would you prepare if resistance was expected?'

'Round shot, if a gun was available, sir. To give time for my people to move into position.'

Proby opened his mouth as if to answer, and frowned as Captain Greville said sharply, 'Grape or canister would be far more effective, I would have thought.'

'Later, perhaps, sir. But there is too much risk with either of hitting my own men.'

Greville ruffled the corners of the papers. 'A few eggs have to be broken sometimes, Bolitho!'

Proby tapped the table.

'They are *people*, John, not eggs.' But he was smiling as he turned to his other side. 'You have some points on gunnery, Maude? While we touch upon the subject.' Polite, but strangers.

Maude leaned forward, and Bolitho guessed that he was very tall. It would be a constant handicap below decks in a frigate.

'In a large ship of the line, a three-decker,' he lifted his hand, 'this one, for instance. The order to beat to quarters has just been called, and the ship cleared for action. You are stationed on the lower gun deck and in charge of a division. What precautions will you take?' The hand gestured again. 'Consider it.' He was leaning back in his chair now, his head slightly on one side, as if completely relaxed, and Bolitho felt his own tension slipping away in response. Maude's voice, or perhaps his manner, seemed to exclude the others, and ease his uncertainty. It was almost like having a conversation with an old friend.

He said, 'Lower gun deck, thirty-two-pounders, "Long Nines".' The hand moved very slightly, and he went on, 'Nine feet long, sir.' He saw him nod, as if to encourage him. 'Seven men in each gun crew, the captain responsible for giving a set task to each one and assigning a number to each. The lower the number, the greater the skill.'

Proby cleared his throat loudly. 'Suppose this ship is about to engage an enemy to wind'rd? With the deck tilting to the wind, how would seven men manage to haul the gun up to its port? A "Long Nine" weighs a pretty piece, I'd say.'

Bolitho wanted to lick his dry lips. Anything. He answered, 'Three tons, sir.' He waited, but nobody commented. 'I would take men from the gun on the opposite side. With the same precautions to ensure no hands and feet were broken or damaged when the gun recoiled. But bandages should always be close by.'

'You seem to care a great deal for their welfare, Bolitho. But the fight should always come first.'

Bolitho felt his fingers relax. He had not realised that his hands had been so tightly clenched. It was Greville. In some strange way, the challenge was almost a relief.

He said, 'Badly injured men cannot fight a gun, sir. It could delay a complete broadside.'

'But the battle is joined.' It was Maude again. 'Loading, firing, and once more running out. Provided, of course, that *you have enough men*. Is there anything else against which you should guard?'

'Every third shot or so, I'll have the barrel cleaned out, its full length, with the worm and then the sponge. Remove any burning fragment. And to prevent a misfire when a new charge is rammed home.'

Maude nodded. 'Discipline is everything in gunnery, as in most matters in our service. *All orders will be obeyed without question* – I daresay you have heard that a few hundred times since you donned the King's coat?'

Bolitho looked at him. A strong, proud face, not unlike

the sketches of Captain James Cook he had seen in the *Gazette*, accompanying tales of his latest voyages. A man you would willingly serve no matter what.

He said, 'It is far easier to drive than to lead, sir. But I believe that trust is all important. On both sides.'

Maude folded his arms.

'Only then will you get the dedication you need when the odds are against you.'

Proby glanced past him. 'Is that all, Maude?' and swung round abruptly on his chair. 'What the *hell*! I gave strict orders!'

But all three captains were on their feet, and the air was suddenly sharp, blowing from the outside world. The creaking of the rigging was audible now, and the occasional scream of gulls circling over incoming fishermen.

Bolitho wanted to turn and identify the newcomer, who had burst uninvited and unexpectedly into this meeting.

Like waking from a bad dream, he thought, a nightmare: the three captains rigid behind the table, and Maude's height indeed compelling him to bend beneath the deckhead beams.

'Excuse my untimely interruption, gentlemen. My barge is alongside, and I would not wish to keep my cox'n waiting much longer. But I wanted to bid you farewell, and thank you for carrying out these duties, from which we shall all benefit in due course.'

Bolitho flinched as a hand touched his sleeve.

'And who is this? I was assured that you had finished here today.' It sounded more like an accusation than an apology.

Bolitho turned and faced him. He had seen him only once before, when his own boat had tossed oars to the barge and he had had the briefest glimpse of Vice-Admiral Sir James Hamilton, the great man himself. His uniform and lace gleaming in the reflected light, cocked hat casually balanced in his other hand. Half smiling now.

'Cornishman, eh?'

He knew his mouth had moved and he had said something, but it had been like hearing someone else blurting out his name.

The admiral was looking keenly at him. It felt like being stripped.

Then he nodded, as if some thought had dropped into place, some inner reference been made.

'I hope the future is kind to you, er, Bolitho.' He turned away, the contact broken. 'Now I must leave you. I have duties ashore. Events are moving once more.' He reached the door and Bolitho could see the flag captain hovering, with a boatcloak draped carefully across his arm.

For a long time, or so it seemed, they all stood in silence, swaying only occasionally as the flagship pulled at her cable.

Bolitho realised that Sir William Proby was seated once again, his expression a mixture of bemusement and relief.

'An unforeseen interruption, gentlemen.' He paused to listen as calls trilled in the distance, followed by the muffled bark of commands. The admiral's barge was casting off.

'If you have no further questions?' He was not, apparently, anticipating any. He looked at Bolitho. 'Be seated, if you please.'

Bolitho stared at the solitary chair. The sword had vanished.

Proby scratched his quill across a certificate, and said, 'On behalf of this Board, Mr. Bolitho, I congratulate you.' He came around the table before Bolitho could lever himself out of the chair. Proby was a substantial figure, but he had scarcely seen him move.

He was on his feet finally and Proby was shaking his hand and saying, 'We wish you a speedy promotion!' Now it was Maude's turn, shaking his hand abruptly and looking down at him, with a smile he would always remember. He had passed. It might be next month, or a year from now, before he actually received that lieutenant's commission. *But he had passed.* The cabin servant was placing some fine goblets on a tray. But there were only three. He took a deep, deep breath, wanting to laugh, or cry.

It was over. And it was dark beyond the stern windows. He picked up his hat and walked to the door, almost expecting his legs to fail him. *It was over.* He must find Martyn, make sure that . . . He paused and glanced back at the cabin, the hands reaching for filled glasses. Tomorrow they would have forgotten him, put it behind them. It was only another examination.

Captain Greville had not shaken his hand. And he was glad of it.

He saw the bench where they had waited. No turning back. No matter what.

I am a King's officer. Almost. Then he did touch his eyes.

A Favour for the Captain

Lieutenant Montagu Verling stood at *Gorgon*'s quarterdeck rail, his hands on his hips, watching a party of seamen clambering over the boat-tier below him. One of the ship's two cutters swayed across the nettings like an ungainly whale, while Hoggett, the boatswain, gestured with his fist, his voice carrying easily above the noise of other work and the clatter of loose rigging.

'This will not take long.' Verling swore softly as a seaman slithered and fell on the wet planking. It had been raining all night, and now in the grey forenoon the weather showed little improvement. Plymouth was almost hidden in mist, a spire or rooftop showing here and there like projections of a reef.

Bolitho was also watching the cutter, now being moved into position above the tier. At last they were replacing things, and most of the debris left by the refit had vanished. Some lashings remained to be done, and canvas awnings had been spread to protect paintwork and fresh pitch. Between decks, order had already been restored, with stores and spare equipment stowed away, and messdecks cleared of clutter and gear that belonged elsewhere in the hull.

He tried to stifle a yawn, surprised that he had been able to drag himself out of sleep and present himself on deck at the chime of the bell. He turned to peer above the quarterdeck nettings with their neatly stacked hammocks, the cold air wet on his face. Even that did not revive him, and there was a painful crick in his neck. He saw the topmasts of the big three-decker drifting out of the mist at the far end of the anchorage. The flagship; he could even make out the vague dash of colour from her ensign. The bulk of the ship remained hidden by the fog. He winced, but his spirits soared at the memory. Had that been only yesterday? Was it possible?

'Lower away, 'andsomely there!' Hoggett's voice, which seemed even louder on this raw morning.

The cutter began to descend, the men on the tackles taking the strain, feet somehow finding a grip on the slippery planking.

''Vast lowering!'

He heard Dancer give a groan.

'My *head*, Dick. I feel like death!'

Even the Board itself was hard to fix in the mind, like a dream fast disappearing. Only certain moments remained clear: the three figures at the table. An empty chair. And the sudden, startling interruption when the admiral had made his entrance. Perhaps the handshakes remained most vivid in his memory. *We wish you a speedy promotion!*

Then back to *Gorgon*, in darkness, passing an overloaded boat full of sailors, all of whom sounded drunk, probably just paid off from some merchantman. He and Dancer had been unable to stop laughing at the string of curses launched by their own coxswain. Then, in the midshipmen's berth, the heavy silence of some, hunched over written notes, studying or pretending to, by the flickering light of glims, or apparently asleep, being shattered as they had risen as one: a midshipman's salute to any successful candidate for promotion. Hoarded drinks appearing, which had ranged from blackstrap to cognac, helped down by beer from the mess cask, with a mock fight known as 'Boarders Away!' to round off the occasion. It had taken threats of physical violence from the warrant officers' mess to quieten the celebration.

Bolitho cleared his throat, or tried to. And now the captain wanted them aft, in the great cabin.

Verling waved to the boatswain as the cutter finally came to rest on the tier. Even the new paint was unmarked.

He said, 'The captain is going over to *Poseidon* very soon. The admiral has called a conference – all senior captains. Something's in the wind.' He gazed critically at the two midshipmen. 'Under the circumstances, I suppose . . .' He left the rest unsaid.

Bolitho thought of the admiral again, the hand on his arm. *I have duties to perform. Events are moving once more*. Was that the real reason he had interrupted the examination?

Without it, what might have happened? He recalled Greville's sarcasm, his refusal to shake his hand.

He had mentioned it to Dancer, and he had passed it off by saying, 'Greville shook *my* hand, but I could have done without it! I still can't remember half of what I said to them. I was in a daze!' It was something shared after that, real. They had hugged one another, each glad for the other.

And now they were to see the captain. After all this time, he remained remote, almost unknown. And yet nothing had any real purpose without him, without his presence. At any ceremonial, or drill with sails and guns, he was always there, usually with Verling nearby, an extension of himself. He was there to announce any achievement by the ship, or even an individual, and to read the Articles of War before awarding punishment.

Bolitho had once heard a friend of his father's say that when a King's ship was away from the fleet, and free of the admiral's apron strings, all that stood between a captain and chaos were the Articles of War and a line of marines across the poop. And he still recalled his father's quick retort: *'It would all depend on that captain!'*

Only yesterday . . . and yet he could feel the change in himself, sense the scrutiny of the younger midshipmen. As if he represented something, some possibility no longer beyond their grasp. *How does it feel to be one of them?* He was still grappling with his own emotions, and the prospect of a new future.

Verling had tugged out his watch.

'I shall take you aft.' He faced them again. 'Several others failed to satisfy the Almighty yesterday.' He did not smile. 'Not certain what *I* would have decided!'

They followed him aft, not quite reassured.

Captain Beves Conway was standing by a small desk fastening the cuff of his shirt. His dress uniform coat hung across the back of a chair, with his hat nearby. He was preparing for the admiral.

They had passed *Gorgon*'s surgeon as he was leaving, a stooping figure of indeterminate age, with a thin, almost lipless mouth. Bolitho had heard some of the old Jacks say that he would rather bury you than cure you if you ever fell into his hands, but they said that about most surgeons. He wondered what he had been doing for the captain. He had noticed that Conway sometimes held one shoulder stiffly, like now, as he slipped into his coat. A wound he had taken during the Caribbean campaign against the French, he had heard, although others had hinted at a duel fought, of course, over a lady.

He realised that there was another person in the cabin, perched on a chest by the screen, the captain's coxswain. A big, powerful man, always smart and instantly recognisable in his gilt-buttoned coat and nankeen breeches, he seemed to come and go as he chose. More like a trusted companion than a subordinate.

He was holding a drawn sword now, running a cloth slowly up and down the blade. He glanced briefly at the two midshipmen, but nothing more. He belonged. They were merely visitors.

Conway smiled.

'You did well, both of you. Full credit to the ship also.'

Verling said, 'I'll come aft when you're ready, sir.'

The screen door closed behind him. He had spoken to the marine sentry by name when they had arrived at the lobby. A gift, or careful training? It was impossible to know, but Bolitho guessed it was rare enough. He had known some officers who had never cared to learn a name and match it to a face.

He had heard Verling quietly rebuking one of the senior midshipmen, who had since gone to another ship. 'They are people, flesh and blood. Remember that, will you?'

Bolitho wondered if he had passed or failed at his Board.

The captain said suddenly, 'A moment,' and beckoned. 'Come and see *Condor* spread her skirts – a sight that never fails to excite any true sailor!'

They followed him into the main cabin where the stern windows reached from quarter to quarter, and the panorama of ships and anchorage shimmered against the salt-smeared glass like some unfinished painting.

And here was the frigate *Condor*, topsails and fore-courses already set and filling to the wind now shredding the sea mist, her masthead pendant and ensign stiff and bright as metal against the clouds.

Yesterday. Her captain twisting round in his chair aboard the flagship, gauging the sea, the mood of the weather. Impatient to go. And no wonder.

He turned as Conway asked, 'Do you see yourself in command of a frigate one day, Bolitho?'

'Given the chance, sir . . .' He got no further.

Conway moved closer, watching *Condor*'s outline shorten, her yards shifting as she changed tack towards open water and the sea. He said, 'Don't wait to be given the chance. Take it. Or others will.'

He turned abruptly and walked across the cabin. Bolitho wanted to hold the moment, cherish it. This was *the captain*, as he might never see him again. Perhaps older than he had thought, but virile and vigorous, something the streaks of grey at his temples and the crows' feet around his eyes could not flaw or diminish.

He said, 'This damned overhaul is all but finished, thank God.' He looked up and around the cabin, perhaps without seeing it, or seeing it in a way they could not yet understand. 'This lady will be fit and ready for sea again if I – and the first lieutenant – have any say in the matter. After that –' He touched the chair that stood squarely facing the constantly changing panorama. 'Who can say?'

His expression changed and seemed angry, embarrassed. He said almost sharply, 'I have a favour to ask. I've taken enough of your time and the ship's as it is.'

Bolitho saw Dancer gripping a fold of his coat, another habit he had come to recognise, and sometimes understand. It happened when he was surprised, or moved, by something he had not anticipated.

Captain Beves Conway, experienced post captain, who

had seen action and served in most waters where the ensign commanded respect, had a favour to ask?

Beyond these massive timbers, the other world continued to function unimpaired. The trill of a boatswain's call and a shouted command, too muffled to distinguish. The squeal of tackles as another load of stores or equipment was hoisted aboard. A ship preparing for sea. It was what Conway cared about most. Perhaps all he cared about.

He said, 'You will be leaving *Gorgon* shortly on a brief passage duty.' There was a suggestion of a smile. 'Not like your daring adventure with the revenue service, Bolitho. I believe your own brother was in command on that occasion. A family affair, it would seem.' The smile was gone. 'But it will stand you in good stead when you are finally commissioned. Mr Verling will give you the details.'

It was like a fist striking out of nowhere.

Conway was leaving the ship. Giving up command. And it was all he had.

'A new midshipman is joining tomorrow forenoon. His name is Andrew Sewell, and he is fifteen years old.' He glanced from one to the other, suddenly relaxed, as if some weight had been lifted from him. 'A mere boy compared with you seasoned mariners. He has everything to learn, and it was his father's dearest wish that he should follow his family's tradition and become a sea officer. His father was a great friend of mine, perhaps my best, but, alas, now dead . . . Just offer him a hand when it is needed. Will you do that?' Like a challenge. 'For *me*?'

Bolitho turned as Dancer asked, 'First ship, sir?'

'Not his first.' Conway looked at the reflections rippling across the curved deckhead. 'He has served for two months in *Odin*, Captain Greville, and before that in the *Ramillies*, with the Downs Squadron.'

He looked from one to the other. 'I know, from your behaviour and your reports, and what I have seen for myself, that you are well suited to your profession. Maybe because you come from very different backgrounds, or in spite of it. It might be said that young Andrew Sewell is totally unsuited, a victim of circumstances.' He shrugged, and Bolitho saw the flicker of pain in his face.

The marine sentry stamped his feet, somewhere beyond the screen. Verling must be back, and was waiting.

Conway said, 'My old friend is dead. It is the last thing I can do for him, and perhaps the least.'

His coxswain had appeared, his hat beneath his arm, and Conway's sword in his fist. No words: like an understanding between them.

Dancer offered, 'My father was firmly against my going to sea, sir.'

Bolitho nodded. 'And I never had any choice, sir.'

Conway held out his arms as his coxswain deftly clipped the sword into place.

'So be it, and I thank you. Young Andrew must learn that you do not necessarily have to leave your own deck to confront an enemy.' He shook hands gravely with both of them. 'May good fortune go with you.'

He half turned, as if unwilling to leave. His coxswain had

already departed, and Verling's shadow stood across the outer screen.

'When you return to the ship your new orders may be waiting for you. If not, then be patient.' He picked up his hat and visibly squared his shoulders. He was in command again.

The two midshipmen waited without speaking, listening to the shouted commands and, eventually, the calls as the side was piped and Conway's gig pulled away. Then Dancer murmured, 'Whatever ship I join, I'll never forget *him*.'

They left the great cabin in silence, passing the same marine sentry, their weariness, headaches and sore throats forgotten.

Bolitho considered the passage duty Conway had mentioned. Probably helping to move another ship to different moorings, for some refit or overhaul. And after that . . . He glanced over at Dancer. They would be parted. It was the way of the Navy.

Like Conway. Saying goodbye; the hardest duty of all.

4

Hotspur

Martyn Dancer gripped the launch's gunwale and pointed across the larboard bow.

'There she is, Dick! The *Hotspur*! I'll not want to leave this beauty when the time comes!'

Excitement, or sheer pleasure: Bolitho had not seen him like this before. Perhaps strain and uncertainty, which he had always been able to conceal, were at last giving way.

Bolitho felt it, too. The *Hotspur*, which had not even been discussed until today, as if it were a sworn secret, was a topsail schooner, small if set against any frigate or brig; but her style and lines would catch any real sailor's eye immediately.

She was lying at her anchor, and rolling evenly in the swell, showing her copper, bright in the forenoon sun, and the rake of her twin masts. A thoroughbred, and said to be new and untried, straight from her builder.

But the ensign flying from her gaff and the few uniforms moving about her deck were identical to those they had left astern in *Gorgon*, and all the other men-of-war that lay at Plymouth. She was a King's ship.

It was difficult to accept the speed of the events which had brought them here. From the moment they had reported to the first lieutenant, their feet had barely stopped. Until now.

Verling had explained, almost curtly. They were to be part of a passage crew, not to move some hulk or ship awaiting overhaul, but to deliver *Hotspur* to the authorities in Guernsey, as a replacement for an older vessel used in the waters around the Channel Islands for patrol and pilotage. It was another world to them.

And an escape, after all the waiting and doubt, and then yesterday's climax. Again he felt the exhilaration run through him, like his friend beside him. Dancer was pointing at the schooner again, calling something to the cutter's coxswain. And it was the same coxswain and boat's crew which had taken them to the flagship. He heard Dancer laugh and nudged him sharply with his elbow. This sense of light-hearted freedom and excitement would cut no ice with Verling, who was sitting silent and straight-backed by the tiller. The first lieutenant was always very strict when it came to behaviour in boats, maintaining that the ship would be judged accordingly, as every middy soon learned when he came under that disapproving eye.

But even Verling seemed different. It was something in the air, from the start of the day when the hands had been called to lash up and stow their hammocks.

Bolitho had seen the captain speaking with him just before the cutter had cast off. Maybe it was only imagination, but Conway, too, seemed altered, unlike that brief interlude in the great cabin; the mood of defeat, almost valediction, had vanished, and the old Conway had returned. Bolitho had seen him clap Verling on the shoulder this morning, had even heard him laugh.

There were rumours, of course. In a hull crammed with some six hundred sailors and marines, there were always those. But this time there was substance; the reason for the captains' conference, they said. More trouble in the colonies, particularly in Boston, Massachusetts. Unrest fuelled by increased taxes and repressive legislation from London had taken a more aggressive form, too often clashing with the local administration and so, eventually, the military. Although the British were hardened to war and the threat of rebellion, the infamous memory of what had come to be called the Boston Massacre had left a far deeper scar on the public conscience than might have been expected; a radical press had made certain of that. Bolitho had still been serving in *Manxman* when it had happened, and remembered poring over accounts in the news-sheets. A crowd of young people disturbing the peace on a winter's night and coming face-to-face with soldiers from the local garrison, common enough here in England, but more incendiary in a colony chafing under what it believed to be unjust taxation, and seeking a louder voice in its own affairs. At a different time, perhaps a different man might have diffused the situation, but the officer who was present had been convinced that only a show of force would disperse the crowd, and the resulting volley of shots had killed half a dozen of the troublemakers. It was hardly a massacre, but it was bloodshed, and the echoes of those muskets had never since been allowed to fade.

But to those who lived and all too often died on the sea, it meant something else: the need for readiness. Ships to be brought out of dock and stagnation, men to be found to crew, and, if required, fight them. And perhaps officers of merit and experience, captains like Conway, would view any unrest in America as a fresh chance of personal survival. Bolitho had heard his own brother Hugh say as much during their time together in the revenue cutter *Avenger*. Just weeks ago, and it already seemed like an eternity.

His brother had been reserved, almost unknowable, and not only because he had been in temporary command. He looked over at Dancer. It was strange; he had heard Hugh speaking earnestly and intently to him on several occasions when they had been on watch together. Two people who could have so little in common. And yet . . .

'They've seen us at last! Thought they'd bin so long at anchor they'd forgot what they joined for!'

That was the cutter's other passenger, 'Tinker' Thorne, *Gorgon*'s senior boatswain's mate. There was no yarn that might be spun around him that could not be true. It was impossible to guess his age, although Bolitho had heard that Tinker had served in one ship or another for twenty-five years. Originally from Dublin, a Patlander, as all Irishmen were nicknamed by the lower deck, it was said he came of gypsy stock, and had begun life mending pots and selling fishing gear on the roads. He was not tall, but stocky and muscular, with skin like old leather and fists that could handle any unruly hawser or argumentative seaman before you could guess the next move. He was watching the *Hotspur*, her tapering masts rising now above the double-banked oars, his expression amused and a little critical. His eyes were bright blue, like those of a much younger man looking out from a mask. Admired, respected, or hated, 'It's up to you, boyo,' as he was heard to say when the occasion arose.

He shifted around on the thwart and said, 'Let some other Jack take the strain while we're away, eh, sir?'

Nobody else in the ship could speak so offhandedly to Verling.

Verling was still looking astern. His face was hidden, but his thoughts were clear enough.

'I hope so, Tinker. If we've forgotten anything . . .'

'Ah, even the cook knows what to do, sir.'

Bolitho watched them with interest. It was important that *Hotspur* was in safe hands until she was delivered to her destination; and Verling had despatches with him, from Conway and probably the admiral. It seemed significant, and would do Verling's own chances of promotion no harm.

But every pull of the oars was taking Verling away from the ship, and the life he cared about most, and like Bolitho's brother Hugh, he had become unfamiliar. It was like meeting a stranger.

He returned his attention to the schooner, larger and heavier than he had first thought, but with a grace any true sailor would relish.

Tinker Thorne saw his eyes, and grinned.

'Old John Barstow is the finest builder in the West Country, that he is. A strange one an' no mistake, swears to God he's only once sailed out of sight of land, an' that was when he was caught in a fog off the Lizard, if you can swallow that!'

The coxswain brought the cutter smoothly alongside, with oars tossed and a bowman ready with his boat hook.

Verling seized the ladder and said, 'You can carry on, 'Swain. Watch those tackles when you stow the boat on the tier. It's all new. Untried.'

'Aye, sir. I'll keep a weather eye on things.'

He might have been mistaken, but Bolitho thought he and Tinker winked at one another. But Verling was turning to look once more at *Gorgon*.

A small side party had assembled on the schooner's deck, and a net was rigged to hoist any personal gear on board.

They waited for Verling, as senior in the boat, to leave first, and Dancer murmured, 'Look who's here, Dick. Surely he's not coming with us?'

It was Egmont, the newest and most junior in *Gorgon*'s

wardroom. He raised his hat in salute as Verling climbed over the gunwale, while the side party came stiffly to attention, or tried to. The schooner was no two-decker and the seamen were more used to *Gorgon*'s massive bulk than a hull that seemed alive in the offshore current. Egmont almost lost his balance, but managed to blurt out, 'Welcome aboard, sir!'

Verling returned his salute coolly and paused to look forward along the deck. Bolitho could not see his face, but guessed he was missing nothing, not even the young lieutenant's discomfort and anger. And, he saw, he had no difficulty in keeping his balance.

Verling said, 'I trust everything is in hand, Mr Egmont. I see that the boats are stowed, so nobody is still ashore?'

Egmont straightened his back. 'As ordered, sir. Ready for sea.'

Bolitho knew he was being unfair to Egmont, but it sounded like a boast, as if he had manned and prepared the *Hotspur* for duty single-handed.

Verling snapped, 'Where is Mr Sewell, our new midshipman? He should be here.'

Bolitho glanced at Dancer. Verling was back in his proper role. He even remembered the midshipman's name, when he could hardly have found time to meet him.

Egmont licked his lips. 'Below, sir. Being sick.' He licked his lips again. Just the mention of it in this choppy sea was having its effect.

Verling had not missed that, either.

'Dismiss the hands. We shall go aft. I trust the chart and

sailing instructions are ready, too?' He did not wait for an answer, but pulled out his watch and flicked open the guard with his thumbnail. 'So be it. The tide is right – we shall weigh at noon,' and to the thickset boatswain's mate, 'Carry on, Tinker. You know your men.'

'Picked 'em meself, sir.'

Even the use of his nickname seemed correct and formal. Only Verling could have carried that off.

He stopped in his stride. 'Stow your gear, then report to me.' He saw Dancer peering around and added calmly, 'This is no line-of-battle ship, Mr Dancer. I expect you to know every stay, block and spar by the time we drop anchor again!'

The deck lurched as the schooner snubbed at her anchor cable, and Dancer said quietly, 'Wind's getting up. Shan't be sorry when we do get under way.'

'A moment, you two!' It was Egmont, recovered, it seemed, from his performance earlier. 'I know both of you have just satisfied the Board – yesterday, wasn't it? And you heard what Mr Verling said. Remember it well. Board or no Board, there'll be no passengers on this deck, *I'll* make certain of that. Now stow your gear and be sharp about it!'

They watched him turn away and gesticulate at some seamen, his words lost in the wind. Dancer shrugged.

'He needs a bigger ship, that one, if only for his head.'

Bolitho laughed.

'Let's go and find our fellow middy. I suspect it wasn't only the motion that made him vomit!'

Verling paused on the after ladder, his eyes level with the deck coaming.

It would be good to get away from the endless overhaul, clearing up disorder and making the ship, his ship, ready to take her place again, in response to any demand.

In *Gorgon* he was still the first lieutenant. Transferred to any other ship, he would be just another member of the wardroom, with seniority but no future.

He felt the hull shiver again, heard the clatter of loose rigging. She was alive. Eager to go.

He touched the shining paintwork. *So be it, then.*

As Tinker Thorne had firmly declared, the men chosen for *Hotspur*'s passage crew were all skilled and experienced hands, who would be badly missed if their old two-decker was suddenly ordered to sea.

Bolitho recognised most of them, and felt a sense of belonging which was hard to understand, although he had often heard older sailors describe it.

The initial unfamiliarity was gone at the moment of weighing anchor, with the first pressure of bodies leaning on the capstan bars, and the slow *clank, clank, clank* as the pawls started to respond. All spare hands thrusting in time to Tinker's hoarse commands. Midshipmen as well; even the cook in his white smock.

Two men on the wheel, others waiting to 'let go an' haul!' when the anchor broke free of the ground. Every piece of rigging joining the din, blocks taking the strain, ready for the canvas to fill and take command.

Verling stood by the compass box, his body poised for the moment of truth.

Clank, clank, clank, slower now.

A seaman, right forward above the bowsprit, peered aft and cupped his hands. Even so, his voice was almost drowned by the noise of wind and rigging.

He had seen the stout cable, now taut like a bar, and pointing directly at the stem. *Up-and-down.*

Then, 'Anchor's aweigh!'

It was something Bolitho would never forget. Nor want to. The sudden slackness on the capstan as the cable came home, the deck tilting, so steeply that the lee scuppers were awash as the hull continued to heel over.

It was exciting, awesome; not even in the lively revenue cutter *Avenger* had he known anything like it. The great sails cracking and filling to the wind, spray sluicing over them like icy rain. Feet sliding and kicking against the wet planking, gasps and curses from men bent almost double in the battle against wind and rudder.

Bolitho had watched plenty of smaller craft getting under way in a brisk wind. It had always fascinated and moved him, like seeing some great seabird spread its wings and lift from the water.

Even through and above the noise, he could hear Verling's occasional commands, could imagine him down aft by the wheel, angled against the tilt of the deck, watching each sail and the moving panorama of the land, blurred now as if seen through wet glass.

And over all Tinker Thorne's voice, urging, threatening.

'Catch another turn on that pin, Morgan! Move your bloody self, will you!'

Or, 'What d'you mean, Atkins, you *think*? Leave that to Jacks with brains!'

Bolitho saw the land, a white tower or beacon, bursting spray, rocks along the headland. A ship, too. Moving, anchored, or aground, it was impossible to tell. He knew Verling had put two leadsmen on either bow, a necessary precaution when leaving harbour for the first time, but it would take more than lead and line to save them if they misjudged the next cable or so.

'*Over here!*' Tinker again. 'You as well, Mr Bolitho!' He was even managing to grin through the spray streaming down his leathery face. 'Remember what you was told, *no passengers*!'

Despite the movement and confusion Bolitho found he could smile, even laugh suddenly into the spray. The deck was steadier, the snaking halliards and braces stiff and taut in their blocks, and each great sail throwing its own pale reflection on the churning water alongside.

'Steady as you go!' Verling now, probably watching the final spur of headland. 'That will be Penlee Point.' He almost slipped, but a hand reached from somewhere and steadied him. The face he knew, but all he could gasp was, 'Bless you for that!'

The seaman ducked to avoid another snake of wet cordage as it hissed around its block and grinned. 'Do the same for me!' The grin widened. '*Sir!*'

The sky beyond the shrouds and hard canvas seemed

clearer, the motion still lively, but easier. Men were pausing at their work to look for a friend, relief, pride, something of each on their faces. Across the quarter the headland had fallen away and lost its menace. This time.

Bolitho gripped a backstay and took a deep breath.

Beyond the straining jib and staysails was open water: the Channel. He felt Dancer lurch against him, his hand on his shoulder.

Yesterday seemed a long way away. They were *free*.

5

Envy

Bolitho clambered through the main hatch, and seized a stanchion as he steadied himself against the angle of the deck and waited for his vision to clear. The night was pitch black, the air and spray stinging his cheeks, driving away all thoughts of sleep. And that was the odd thing, that he was still wide awake. It was eight o'clock, and a full eight hours since *Hotspur* had weighed anchor and struck south into the Channel. The thrill and confusion, groping for unfamiliar cordage and becoming more accustomed to the schooner's demands in a brisk north-westerly wind, had settled into a pattern of order and purpose.

They were divided into two watches, four hours on, four off, with the dogwatches giving a brief respite in which to devour a hot meal and fortify themselves with a tot of rum. It all helped.

Verling was handing over the watch now, his tall shape just visible against the sliver of foam beyond the lee bulwark. 'Sou'-east-by-south, Mr Egmont. She should be steady a while now that the topsails are snug.' The merest pause, and Bolitho imagined him staring down at the junior lieutenant, making sure that there was no misunderstanding. 'Call me *immediately* if the sea gets up, or anything else happens that I ought to know.'

Bolitho moved closer to the wheel and the two helmsmen. He could see the bare feet of one, pale against the wet planking. During the first dogwatch he had seen the same seaman blowing on to his fingers to warm them against the bitter air, but he was standing barefoot now with no show of discomfort. He must have soles like leather.

Another shadow moved past the wheel and he saw a face catch the glow from the compass box: Andrew Sewell, the new midshipman. They had scarcely spoken since they had come aboard; Egmont had seen to that. Fifteen years old, Captain Conway had said. He looked younger. Nervous, shy, or possibly both, he was a pleasant-faced youth with fair skin and hazel eyes, and a quick smile that seemed only too rare. He had helped Bolitho lay out some charts in the precise way that Verling always seemed to expect. It had been then, in the poor light of the main cabin, that Bolitho had seen Sewell's hands. Scarred, torn and deeply bruised, never given the chance to become accustomed to the demands of seamanship. Deliberately driven seemed the most likely explanation; it was common enough even in today's Navy. He remembered the captain's obvious concern for him, perhaps not merely because of his dead father.

Bolitho reached out impulsively and touched his elbow.

'Over here, Andrew! A bit more sheltered!' He felt him start to pull away, and added, 'Easy, now.'

Sewell let his arm go limp.

'I've just been sick again, Mister . . .'

' "Dick" will do very well.' He waited, sensing the caution, the doubt. Sewell did not belong here. *Suppose I had felt like that when I was packed off to sea in* Manxman?

He looked up and watched the fine curve of the great sail above them. Not shapeless now, and pale blue in a shaft of light as the moon showed itself between banks of scudding cloud. And the sea, rising and falling like black glass, reaching out on either beam. Endless, with no horizon.

Bolitho tugged the rough tarpaulin coat away from his neck. It had rubbed his skin raw, but he had not noticed.

He said, 'This could be the middle of the Atlantic, or some other great ocean! And just us sailing across it, think of that.'

Sewell said, 'You mean that,' and hesitated, 'Dick? How you truly see it?'

'I suppose I do. I can't really explain . . .' Something made him stop, like a warning, as he felt Sewell move slightly away.

'Nothing to do, then?' It was Egmont, almost invisible in a boatcloak against the black water and heavy cloud. 'I want a good watch kept *at all times*. Have you checked the deck log and the set course?'

Bolitho replied, 'Sou'-east-by-south, sir. Helm is steady.'

Egmont turned towards Sewell.

'Did I hear you spewing up again? God help us all! I want you to check the glass yourself. Let every grain of sand run free before you turn it, see? I don't want you warming the glass every time, just so you can run below and dream of home. So do it!'

He glanced at the wheel as the spokes creaked again.

'Watch your helm, man! And stand up smartly, stay alert!' He swung away, the boatcloak floating around him. 'What's your name? I'll be watching *you*!'

The seaman shifted his bare feet on the grating.

'Archer.'

Egmont looked at Bolitho. 'I'm going below to check the chart. Watch the helm and call me if you need advice.'

He may have looked at the helmsman. 'And, Archer, say *sir* when you speak to an officer in the future!' He strode to the hatch.

Bolitho clenched his fist.

Then try to act like one!

He heard Sewell gasp, with surprise or disbelief, and realised that he had spoken aloud.

But he smiled, glad he was still able.

'Something else you've learned in *Hotspur, Mister* Sewell! Don't lose your temper so easily!'

Andrew Sewell, aged fifteen, and the only son of a hero, said nothing. It was like a hand reaching out, and he was no longer afraid to take it.

The helmsman named Archer called, 'Wind's gettin' up, sir!'

He jerked his head as the wet canvas rattled and cracked loudly above them.

Bolitho nodded. 'My respects to Mr Egmont . . .' The mood was still on him. '*No*. I'll tell him myself.'

Tired, elated, angry? Sailors often blamed it on the wind.

He reached the hatch and called back, 'Remember! *No passengers!*'

The wheel jerked sharply as both helmsmen gripped the spokes and put their weight against it, but the one named Archer managed to laugh.

'Easy does it, Tom. Our Dick's blood is on the boil. He'll see us right!'

Vague figures were moving to each mast, the watch on deck, and ready for the storm.

Andrew Sewell had heard the quick exchange between the two men at the wheel and felt something quite unknown to him. It was envy.

The next few hours were ones even the old Jacks were unlikely to forget. A blustery succession of squalls became a strong wind that had all hands fighting each onslaught, bruised and blinded by icy spray and the waves that burst across the bulwarks and swept down the scuppers like a tiderace. All through the middle watch the storm continued its assault, until even the most vociferous curses were beaten into silence.

But when the clouds eventually broke and a first hint of dawn showed itself against straining canvas and the crisscross of shining rigging, *Hotspur* was holding her own, with not a spar or shroud broken.

Bolitho had remembered Tinker Thorne's admiration for her builder, Old John Barstow, *the finest in the West Country*; he had clung to those words more than once in the night when the sea had smashed against the hull or sent men sprawling like rag dolls in its wake.

Tinker's voice had rarely been silent, and his sturdy form was everywhere. Dragging a man from one task and shoving him into another, putting an extra pair of hands on halliard or brace, or bullying another too dazed to think clearly, to add his weight to the pumps.

And Verling was always there. Down aft, holding himself upright, while he watched the relentless battle of sea against rudder, wind against canvas.

A few men were injured, but none seriously, with cuts and bruises, or rope burns when human hands could no longer control wet cordage squealing through block or cleat.

And as suddenly as it had begun, the wind eased, and it was safe to move about the deck without pain or apprehension.

Bolitho heard Verling say, 'Another hour, Mr Egmont, and we'll get the tops'ls on her. The wind's backed a piece. I want a landfall on Guernsey, not the coast of France!' Calmly said, but he was not joking. 'Check and report any damage. Injuries, too. I'll need it for my report.' He patted the compass box. 'Not bad for a youngster, eh?'

Egmont hurried forward, his boatcloak plastered to his body like a mould. In the poor light it was hard to gauge his reaction to the storm.

''Ere, sir.' Bolitho felt a mug pushed into his frozen fingers. 'Get yer blood movin' again!'

Rum, cognac, it could have been anything, but it began to work instantly.

'Thank you, Drury – just in time!' The seaman laughed. Like Bolitho, he was probably surprised that he had remembered his name.

Dancer joined him by the foremast and clapped his shoulder.

'Well, that's all over, Dick!' His smile was very white against wind-seared features. 'Till the next time!'

They both looked up. The masthead pendant was just visible against the banks of low cloud, flicking out like a coachman's whip, but not bar-taut as it must have been for the past few hours.

Dancer said, 'I'll not be sorry to see the sun again!'

'*Here?* In January?' They both laughed, and a sailor who was squatting by the forward hatch while his leg was being bandaged stared up at them and grinned.

Tinker had heard Verling's words to Egmont, and Bolitho saw that he was already mustering some of his topmen, getting ready to loose the topsails. *Hotspur* would fly when that was done. Like the great seabird of his imagination.

'Go below, one of you, and fetch my glass!'

Bolitho called, 'Aye, sir!' and nudged his friend's arm. 'You stay and watch for the sun!' Dancer's coat sleeve was heavy with spray.

Dancer saw the question in his eyes and shrugged. 'I put my tarpaulin over one of the injured.'

Bolitho said, 'You would!'

It was deserted below deck, although he could hear men shouting to one another as they put new lashings on some of the stores *Hotspur* was carrying as additional ballast. He paused to listen to the sea, sluicing and thudding against the hull. Quieter now, but still menacing, showing its power.

He found Verling's telescope, just inside the tiny cabin which would be the new master's domain and, when necessary, his retreat.

Verling's coat was hanging on a hook, swaying with the motion like a restless spectre. When *Hotspur* anchored again, he would go ashore as a well-turned-out sea officer, not as a survivor. It was impossible to see him in any other light.

He stiffened, surprised that he had not heard it before. Sewell's voice, husky, even cowed.

'I *didn't*, sir. I was only trying to—'

He got no further, cut short by Egmont, angry, malicious, sarcastic.

'What d' you mean, *you couldn't help it*? You make me sick, and you still believe that anybody will ever accept *you* for a commission?' He was laughing now; Bolitho could see him in his mind. Barely out of the midshipmen's berth himself, and he was behaving like a tyrant.

'I've been watching you, and do you think I've not guessed what you're trying to do?' There was another sound. A slap. 'And if I see you again . . .'

Bolitho did not know he had moved. It was like the actors in the square at Falmouth; they had all watched them as children, had cheered or hissed to match the mimes and poses.

Egmont swinging round to stare at him, mouth half open, cut short by the interruption, one hand still in the air, after the blow, or preparing another. Sewell, leaning against the curved timbers, covering his cheek or mouth, but his eye fixed on Bolitho.

'What th' hell are you doing here?'

Almost as if he had imagined it. Egmont quite calm now, arms at his sides, swaying to the motion, but in control. And the young midshipman, saying nothing, his face guarded, expressionless. Only the red welt by his mouth as evidence.

Bolitho said, 'I came for the first lieutenant's glass.' It was like hearing someone else. Clipped, cold. Like Hugh.

'Well, don't just stand there! Take it and go!'

Bolitho looked past him. 'Are you all right, Andrew?'

Sewell swallowed, and seemed unable to speak. Then he nodded and exclaimed, 'Yes, of course. It was nothing, you see—'

Egmont snapped, 'Hold your tongue!' and turned to Bolitho again. 'Go about your duties. I'll overlook your insolence this time, but . . .' He did not finish it, but swung round and left the cabin.

They stood facing each other, without speaking or moving, the sounds of rigging and sea distant, unintrusive.

'Tell me, Andrew.' Bolitho reached out to take his arm, and saw him flinch as if he expected another blow. 'He *struck* you, and just before that . . .'

He got no further.

'No. It would only make things worse. D'you think I don't know? What it's like – *really* like?'

Bolitho felt the anger rising like fire. Egmont's shock when he had burst into this cabin, and then as quickly, his recovery and arrogance. He could still feel Sewell's arm; it was shaking. Fear? It went deeper than that.

He said, 'I'll come aft with you right now. Mr Verling will listen. He *has* to. And in any case—'

But Sewell was shaking his head.

'*No*.' He looked at him directly for the first time. 'It wouldn't help.' Then, quite firmly, he pried Bolitho's fingers from his arm. 'He would deny it. And . . . so would I.'

Someone was shouting; feet thudded across the deck overhead. He still held Verling's telescope in his other hand. Nothing was making sense.

Sewell was fumbling with his coat, trying to fasten his buttons, not looking at him now. 'You will be a good officer, Dick, a fine one. I see the way they respect you, and *like* you. I always hoped . . .'

He moved abruptly to the door, and to the ladder beyond.

Bolitho stood very still, his anger giving way to a sense of utter defeat. Because of what he had just seen and heard, and because it mattered.

There were more shouts, and he found himself on the ladder as if it were an escape. But he kept seeing Sewell's face, and his fear. He needed help. *And I failed him.*

On deck, it seemed nothing had happened, routine taking over as seamen jostled at their stations for making more sail. *Hotspur* had altered course again, the canvas shivering and cracking, the main and gaff topsails taut across the bulwark, throwing broken reflections across the water alongside.

'Loose tops'ls! Lively there!'

Verling called, 'Give it to me!' He seized the telescope and trained it across the weather bow. 'Thought you'd fallen outboard. Where the hell were you?' He did not wait for an answer or seem to expect one, and was already calling to men by the foremast.

Egmont was near the wheel, shading his eyes to peer up at the topsail yards. He glanced only briefly at Bolitho before returning his attention to the newly released sails as they filled and hardened to the wind. Disinterested. Bolitho heard Sewell's voice again. *He would deny it. And so would I.*

'All secure, sir!' That was Tinker, eyes like slits as he stared at the small figures on the yards, groping their way back to safety.

Most of the sea was still hidden in darkness, but the sky was lighter, and in so short a time the vessel had taken shape and regained her personality around and above them, faces and voices emerging from groups and shadows.

Bolitho felt the deck plunge beneath him, exuberant, like the wild creature she was. *Hotspur* would make a fine and graceful sight even in this poor light, with all sails set and filled, the yards bending like bows under the strain.

'Now that was *something*, Dick!' It was Dancer, hatless, his fair hair plastered across a forehead gleaming with spray.

Verling said, 'Send half of the hands below, Mr Egmont. Get some food into them. And don't be too long about it.' His mind was already moving on. 'Two good masthead lookouts.' He must have sensed a question, and added, 'One man sees only what he expects to see if he's left alone too long.' His arm shot out. 'Mr Bolitho, *you* stand by. I need some keen eyes this morning!' He might even have smiled. 'This is no two-decker!'

Bolitho felt his stomach muscles tighten. Even the mention of climbing aloft could still make his skin crawl.

Verling was saying, 'Take my glass with you. I'll tell you what to watch out for.'

Dancer said softly, 'I hope I'm as confident as he is when I'm told to take a ship from one cross on the chart to another. Nothing ever troubles *him*.'

They went below, and suddenly he grasped Bolitho's arm and pulled him against the galley bulkhead.

'I've been thinking. You remember what Captain Conway said about young Sewell's experiences in previous ships? One of them was the *Ramillies*, wasn't it, in the Downs Squadron? Where everything started to go against him.'

Bolitho said nothing, waiting. It was as if Dancer had just been with him. Then he said cautiously, 'What about *Ramillies*?'

'Something I heard a minute ago made me stop and think. Surprised Conway didn't know.' He turned as if to listen as someone hurried past. 'Our Mr Egmont was a middy on board at the same time as Sewell. A bully even then, to all accounts.'

More figures were slipping and clattering down the ladder, jostling one another and laughing, fatigue and injuries forgotten until the next call.

Bolitho said, 'Then I've just made an enemy,' and told him what had happened.

Someone ducked his head through the hatch. Bolitho could see his face clearly despite the lingering gloom between decks.

'What is it?'

'Mr Verling wants you on deck, sir.' A quick grin. ' "Fast as you like", 'e says!'

In the silence that followed, Dancer said lightly, 'Then I'm sorry to say Egmont's made another enemy. He seems to have a talent for it.'

They reached the upper deck together. There was more cloud than earlier, rain too.

Dancer exclaimed, 'Thunder! Not another storm, I hope.'

Bolitho looked at him. The bond between them was even stronger.

'Not on your oath, Martyn. That was cannon fire!'

6

No Quarter

The deck seemed unusually crowded, all thought of rest and food forgotten. Some men were in the bows, peering or gesturing ahead, calling to one another, voices distorted by the wind. Others had climbed into the shrouds, but the sea was still dark and empty. And there was no more gunfire.

Verling said, 'Due south of us.' His eye lit up as he gazed into the compass. 'Dead ahead, if I'm not mistaken.'

'At least we can outsail 'em, sir.' That was Tinker.

Egmont snapped, 'We're not at *war*, man!'

Verling glanced at him. 'We take no chances, Mr Egmont. Today's handshake can easily become tomorrow's broadside.'

Dancer murmured, 'What do you think, Dick? Heavy guns?'

Bolitho shook his head. 'Big enough. There was no

return fire.' Ships meeting by accident, a case of mistaken identity in the darkness and foul weather. These were busy trade routes where almost any flag might be sighted. And the possibility of war was never forgotten. *Shoot first* was often the first rule.

Smugglers, privateers, or local pirates, every deepwater sailor had to take his chance.

Bolitho looked over towards Verling and tried to see it as he would. Facing an unknown threat, considering his own responsibility. The officer in charge . . . He had heard it said all too frequently. Do wrong and you carried the blame. Do right, and if you were too junior, others reaped the praise.

Deliver Hotspur *to her new command, and return to Plymouth without unnecessary delay.* The orders were plain enough. Maybe Verling was weighing the choices that might lie ahead. Fight or run, as Tinker had suggested. *Hotspur* carried two small bow-chasers, six-pounders, quite enough to deal with trouble in home waters. But no shot had yet been brought aboard. And her four swivel guns would be useless in any serious engagement.

Verling had made up his mind.

'Stand by to shorten sail. Reef tops'ls and take in the gaff tops'l.' Another glance at the compass. Bolitho could see his face now without the aid of the lamp. The sky was clearing, the clouds purple towards the horizon, when it was visible.

He heard Egmont ask, 'Shall we fight, sir?'

Verling was gesturing to Dancer. 'Fetch my logbook,

then stand by me.' He seemed to recall the question. 'We've no marines to support us this time. Break open the arms chest.' He did not even raise his voice.

He looked at Bolitho. 'Up you go. Sweep to the sou'-east. Take your time. Remember what you saw on the chart.'

Afterwards, Bolitho recalled how each point was allowed to settle in his mind, take shape. So calmly said when Verling's entire being must have wanted to ram his meaning home, or even to snatch up the glass and claw his way aloft himself. In case he was mistaken. When Bolitho and the other midshipmen had gathered around *Gorgon*'s sailing master, old Turnbull, for their regular instruction in navigation and pilotage, or when they were struggling with the mysteries of the sextant, they had often been warned about the first sight of land. Turnbull had reminded his youthful audience, 'An error in judgement is no excuse at the court-martial table!'

He reached the foremast shrouds as Verling shouted, 'Shorten sail!'

Men were already at their stations, handling lines and tackles as if they had been serving *Hotspur* for months, not days.

Bolitho climbed steadily but slowly, making sure each ratline was underfoot before he took his weight with his arms, Verling's heavy telescope thumping across his spine. He heard Tinker call after him, 'Don't drop *that*, me son, or the sky'll fall on you!'

How he could find time to joke about it was a marvel. Tinker was everywhere, and at once. Ready to help or threaten without hesitation. He should have been promoted to warrant rank; there was not a strand of rope or strip of sail he could not control. But in twenty-five years at sea, he had never learned to read or write.

Bolitho reached the upper yard, and could feel his heart banging against his ribs. *Too long in harbour. Getting soft . . .*

The lookout already curled in position, his arm around a stay, turned and peered at him.

'Mornin', sir!' He jerked his thumb. 'Land, larboard bow!'

Bolitho swallowed and forced himself to look. Sea and haze, an endless expanse of choppy white crests. But no land.

The lookout was one of *Gorgon*'s foretopmen; more to the point, he had been chosen by Tinker for the passage crew.

He gasped, 'Tell them, Keveth! No breath!'

He swung the telescope carefully around and beneath his arm, even as the lookout yelled to the small figures below. With a name like that, he must be a fellow Cornishman. Two wreckers up here together . . .

He opened the telescope with great care, waiting for each roll and shudder running through his perch, causing *Hotspur* to vibrate from truck to keel.

Land, sure enough. Another careful breath, gauging the moment. The sea breaking; he could feel the power and height of the waves, but when he lowered the glass to clear his vision there was nothing there. *But it was there*. The blunt outline of land, sloping to a point which defied the waves. Like the little sketch in Verling's log.

Jerbourg Point. Who or what was 'Jerbourg', he wondered.

He made his way down to the deck and hurried aft, slipped and almost fell, lightheaded, as if drunk or in fever.

Verling listened as he blurted out everything he had seen. He was conscious of his eyes, his patience, as he described the landfall.

All he said was, 'Well done.'

Egmont said loudly, 'I'll note it in the log, sir.'

Bolitho said, 'The lookout, Keveth. *He* sighted it first, sir. Without a glass!'

Verling glanced at both of them, as usual missing nothing.

'A good hand, that one. A fair shot, too, when given the chance.' The hint of a smile. 'And should be. He was a poacher before he signed up with a recruiting party. One jump ahead of the hangman, I shouldn't wonder.'

'Deck there!' It was the masthead again. The poacher. *'Wreckage ahead, larboard bow!'*

Verling did not hesitate. As if he had been expecting it; as if he knew.

'Stand by to lower a boat. Two leadsmen in the chains.' His hand shot out. 'Good ones, Tinker. This is no coastline for chances.'

Egmont asked, 'You know Guernsey, sir?'

'I've sailed close by before.' He was looking towards the land, which was still invisible. 'It was enough.'

He walked to the hatch. 'Wreckage. Wind and tide make their own landfalls, for *us*, eh?'

Dancer commented softly, 'My God, he keeps a cool head!' He clasped Bolitho's arm. 'Like another ancient mariner not a cable's length away!'

It seemed to take an age for the drifting fragments of wreckage to become clearly visible, more scattered, and reaching out on either bow. There was absolute silence now, the seamen very aware of their kinship with these pathetic remnants which had once been a living vessel.

Verling was on deck again, and stood with his arms folded, watching the sea, and the strengthening blur of land which had almost been forgotten.

Hotspur had shortened sail once more, so that her shipboard sounds in the silence added to the atmosphere of uneasiness, with the creak and clatter of loose rigging, and the groan of the rudder and yoke-lines as the helmsmen fought to maintain steerage way.

Verling said, 'I think both boats will be necessary. It will save time. Not that there is much to see.' He was thinking aloud, as if questioning each thought as it came to him.

Even Tinker's voice seemed subdued as he watched the first boat being hoisted and swung above and over the gunwale.

Verling said, 'You leave now, Mr Egmont. See what you can discover. Small craft, I'd say.'

Egmont leaned over the side as some larger fragments of timber bumped against *Hotspur*'s side.

Bolitho felt a chill run through him. It was, or had been,

a cutter as far as he could tell. Like *Avenger* . . . There was part of a mast now, and torn sail dragging half submerged, like a shroud.

The first boat was pulling away, with Egmont in the bows, leaning over to signal his intentions to his coxswain.

Verling called, 'Now you, Bolitho.' He had his glass up to his eye again, but trained on the spur of land, not the splintered remains drifting below him. 'Take Sewell with you. Stay up to wind'rd if you can.'

He felt as if he were being cut off, abandoned, once the boat was in the water and the headrope cast off.

'Easy, lads, keep it steady!' He had taken the tiller himself and waited for the oars to pick up the stroke, each man feeling the mood of the sea, trying not to watch the schooner as she fell further and further astern.

At least the wind had eased. Bolitho felt the salt spray on his mouth and soaking into his shoulders. Sewell was crouched down beside him, his back half turned; impossible to see or know what he was thinking. Hard to believe that the confrontation in the cabin had ever happened. Only this was real.

He winced as the boat dipped steeply and more spray burst from the oars. This was no cutter or gig built for the open sea.

'*There!*' Sewell's arm shot out. 'Oh, God, it's one of them!'

Bolitho stood up, holding fast to the tiller-bar to keep his balance.

'Bowman! Use your hook!'

The seaman had boated his oar and was poised in the blunt bows like a harpoonist as more wreckage surged above a trough.

'Oars! Fend off, lads!'

It was as if a complete section of the wreck had risen suddenly and violently from the depths, like some act of retribution or spite.

An oar blade splintered and the seaman pitched across his thwart, the broken loom still grasped in his fists. Surprisingly, nobody shouted or showed any sign of fear. It was too swift, too stark. Not just one corpse, but five or six, tangled together in a mesh of torn canvas and broken planking.

It lasted only a few seconds, before the corpses and their tangled prison rolled over and dipped beneath the sea.

Only seconds, but as they fought to bring the boat under command again, the grim picture remained. Staring eyes, bared teeth, gaping wounds, black in the hard light. And the stench of gunpowder. Like the splinters and the burns: they had been fired upon at point-blank range.

Bolitho tugged at the tiller-bar. 'Back water, starboard!' He felt the sea sluicing around his legs, as if the boat had been swamped and was going down.

He heard Sewell yell, 'More wreckage!' He was clambering over the struggling oarsmen, thrusting his legs over the side to fend off another piece of broken timber. Then he must have lost his footing, and slithered bodily over the gunwale, his face contorted with pain.

The seaman who had been in the bows flung himself

over the thwart and seized his arm, just as Bolitho managed to bring the boat under control.

Nobody spoke; nothing mattered but the slow, steady splash of oars as they regained the stroke and gave all their strength to the fight. Only then did they turn and peer at each other, more gasps than grins, but with the recognition that, this time, they had won.

Bolitho eased the tiller very slowly, feeling the effort of each stroke, knowing they were in control.

Sewell lay in the sternsheets, the trapped water surging across his legs, his lip bleeding where he had bitten through it. Bolitho reached down and wrenched open his coat. His breeches were torn; it must have happened when he had used both legs to kick off that last piece of wreckage. But for his prompt action, the boat might have foundered.

There was blood, too, a lot of it. He could feel the torn skin, the muscle under his fingers clenched against the pain.

He exclaimed, 'You mad little bugger!'

Pain, shock, and the bitter cold; Sewell was barely able to form the words.

'I was drowning . . . I couldn't h-hold on. My fault . . .'

He cried out as Bolitho knotted a piece of wet rag around his leg, the blood strangely vivid in the grey light.

Bolitho pulled some canvas across his body and shouted, 'You saved the boat! Did you think we'd just *leave* you?' He was gripping his shoulder now, as if to force him to understand.

'I just wanted to . . .' He fainted.

Bolitho swung the tiller-bar against his ribs until the impact steadied him.

'Enough, lads! Give way, *together*!'

The boat lifted and swayed as the blades brought her under command again. Bolitho clung to Sewell's sodden coat to ease the shock of each sudden plunge.

He heard himself gasp, 'I *know* what you wanted! I'll remind you when we get back on board!'

Someone yelled, ''Ere's *'Otspur*, sir! Larboard beam!'

Bolitho wiped his streaming face with his wrist, his eyes raw with salt. A blurred shape, like a sketch on a slate. Unreal. He tugged at Sewell's coat and gasped, 'See? We found her!'

The rest was a confused daze, the schooner's shining side rising over them like a breakwater, muffled shouts, and figures leaping down to take the strain and fasten the tackles for hoisting the boat into what suddenly seemed a stable and secure haven. He felt a fist thumping his shoulder, heard Tinker's familiar, harsh voice.

'Well done, me boy!' Another thump. 'Bloody well done!'

Then, almost choking over a swallow of raw spirit. Rum, cognac; it could have been anything. But it was working. He could feel every scrape and bruise, but his mind was clearing, like a mist lifting from the sea.

And Verling. Calm, level, a little less patient now.

'What did you find?'

It was all suddenly very sharp. Brutal . . . Like the end of a nightmare. Even the sounds of sea and wind seemed muffled. The ship holding her breath.

'They were all dead, sir. Killed. Point-blank range.' Like listening to somebody else, the voice flat and contained. 'No chance. Taken by surprise, you see.' He could see their faces, the savage wounds and staring eyes. Not a drawn blade or weapon in sight. *Cut down.* 'Grape and canister.' He broke off, coughing, and a hand held a cloth to his mouth. Only a piece of rag, but it seemed strangely warm. Safe.

He knew it was Dancer.

Verling again. 'Anything more?'

Bolitho licked his raw lips. He said, 'There were two officers. I saw their clothes.' The image was fading. 'Their buttons. Officers.'

Verling said, 'Take him below.' His hand touched Bolitho's arm briefly. 'You behaved well. Anything else that comes back to you . . .'

He was already turning away, his mind grappling with other questions. Bolitho struggled to sit up.

'Sewell saved the boat, sir. He might have been killed.'

Verling had stopped and was staring down at him, his face in shadow against the fast-moving clouds. '*You* did nothing, of course.' Somebody even laughed.

Bolitho was on his feet now. He could feel the deck. Alive again. He should be shivering. Holding on. He was neither.

Dancer was saying, 'When I saw the boat, I thought . . .' He did not continue. Could not.

Bolitho held on to a backstay and looked at the sea. A deep swell, unbroken now but for a few white horses. No wreckage; not even a splinter to betray what had happened.

And the dark wedge of land, no nearer, or so it seemed. And yet it reached out on either bow, lifting and falling against *Hotspur*'s standing and running rigging, as if it, and not the schooner, was moving.

Dancer said, 'Young Sewell seems to be holding out well. I heard the lads say you saved his skin, or most of it. He'll never forget this day, I'll wager!' He added bitterly, 'Of course, Egmont's boat found nothing!'

They were standing in the cabin space, although Bolitho could not recall descending the ladder. Here the ship noises were louder, closer. Creaks and rattles, the sigh of the sea against the hull.

Bolitho turned and stared at his friend, seeing him as if for the first time since he had been hauled aboard.

'We might never have known, but for the gunfire. It was the merest chance.' He held up his arm and saw that the sleeve was torn from wrist to elbow. He had felt nothing. 'We can't simply sail past and forget it, as if nothing has happened!'

Dancer shook his head. 'It's up to the first lieutenant, Dick. I was watching him just now. He'll not turn his back on it.' He regarded him grimly. 'He can't. Even if he wanted to.'

Someone called his name, and he said, 'We'll soon know. I'm just thankful you're still in one piece.' He was trying to smile, but it eluded him. Instead, he lightly punched the torn sleeve. 'Young Andy Sewell has you to look up to now!'

He swung away to find out who had called him. 'That makes two of us!'

Bolitho stood by the cabin door, and tried to calm his thoughts, put them in order. Fear, anger, relief. And something else. It was pride.

'Ah, here you are, *sir*!' It was Tinker, almost filling the space. He had a cutlass under one arm, and was holding out a slim-bladed hanger with his other hand. 'More to your fancy, I thought.' He was grinning, although watching him keenly. 'Mr Verling's orders. Seems we're goin' after the bastards!'

Who? Where? With what? It had never been in doubt.

Feet thumped overhead and Bolitho heard the impatient squeal of blocks, the flap and bang of canvas free in the wind. *Hotspur* was under way once more.

Verling's decision, right or wrong. For him, there was no choice.

Tinker nodded slowly, as if reading his thoughts. 'Are ye ready?'

Bolitho could hear Verling's voice, Egmont's too. But he was thinking of the staring, dead faces in the water.

He fastened the belt at the waist and allowed the hanger to fall against his thigh.

Tomorrow's enemy. He said, 'Aye. So be it.'

7

Command Decision

Lieutenant Montagu Verling stood by the cabin table, his head slightly bent between the deck beams, his face in shadow. The fingers of his left hand rested only lightly on the table while his body swayed to the schooner's motion. Even that seemed easier; you could almost feel the nearness of land. Something physical. Outside, the sky, like the sea, was grey, and the wind, although steady, had dropped. The sails were heavy with rain and spray.

Here in the cabin, the light was no better, despite a couple of lamps. Verling's chart was spread almost directly beneath the small cabin skylight, strangely clear as it appeared to move slowly from side to side with each steady roll.

Bolitho saw the brass dividers in Verling's right hand move again, the points tapping the chart. Perhaps he was reconsidering, ensuring he had forgotten nothing, sifting fact and speculation.

Bolitho glanced at Dancer. The quill in his hand had hesitated, poised over his log and the record of events he was keeping for Verling. Achievement, or a legal defence; all would depend on the next few hours.

Verling had turned slightly, and the angle freed his features of shadow. He looked calm and alert, as if he were quite alone here, and this was just another day.

Bolitho wanted to turn and look once more around the cabin, record the images in his mind, and the others who were sharing this moment. Dancer, opposite, with the open log, the ink on the page already dry, the writing, the sloping, cultured hand he had come to know so well. He could imagine it that of a captain, perhaps even a flag officer, making some comment for posterity on the occasion of some great battle at sea. Beside Dancer, staring at the chart although his eyes were scarcely moving, Lieutenant Egmont, the corners of his mouth turned down. What was he thinking, feeling? Impatience, doubt, or fear?

And Midshipman Andrew Sewell, lying propped on a bench seat, his bandaged legs thrust out, his eyes tightly shut. When he awoke from the oblivion of pain and rum, he would be different, *feel* different. Another chance awaited him. He might even come to accept the life he had not chosen, lived though it must be in his father's far-reaching shadow.

The door creaked, and without looking Bolitho knew it was Tinker Thorne blocking the passageway, sharing the meeting but, as always, with an ear tuned to the ship, the sounds of sea, wind and rigging clearer to him than any chart or conference of war.

Bolitho touched the hanger that lay against his leg. And they were *not* at war. That must be uppermost in Verling's mind at this very moment. He looked up, and realised that Verling was staring directly at him, but when he spoke it was to all of them. And to the ship, which should have been delivered to St Peter Port on Guernsey's east coast today, as stated in his orders.

'It is obvious that whatever vessel was responsible for so ruthless and unprovoked an attack on the cutter was already engaged in some unlawful mission. Smuggling is too commonplace between these islands and the mainland to provoke such an attack, or the murder of unprepared sailors and their officers.'

Egmont said, 'I didn't see them, sir. But if Mr Bolitho says otherwise—'

Verling interjected, 'You will *what*?'

In the silence that followed, he tapped the chart with his dividers.

'You don't have to be told that these are dangerous waters. Among these reefs and shallows, pilotage is often a dire necessity, even for visitors familiar with this coast-line.' His eyes returned to Bolitho. 'Those men who were killed had not been preparing to fight or to withstand an attack, correct?'

Dancer's pen was moving again, the scratching quite audible above the sounds of the hull and the sea.

'Correct, sir.'

Verling nodded. 'Which is *why* they were killed. Because they recognised the other vessel.'

'Local smugglers, sir?' He shook his head. 'Then why the force of arms, the point-blank range?'

Egmont cleared his throat and said stiffly, 'Mistaken identity perhaps, sir?' When Verling did not answer, he hurried on, 'We can proceed to St Peter Port and hand over *Hotspur* as planned. Warn the garrison – they can send troopers overland, or maybe there will be some local patrol vessel armed and ready to deal with this intruder.' His eyes flicked over Bolitho. 'Smuggler, or the like.'

Dancer laid down his pen and said quietly, 'I learned a good deal about local trade, sir. My father used to instruct me on the subject. Gin from Rotterdam, brandy from France and Spain, rum from the West Indies. Some five to six million gallons of it were imported each year.' He looked up at Verling, the blue eyes very clear. 'And tobacco from Virginia. All for sale to our own traders,' he paused, 'and smugglers. It made St Peter Port rich. Adventurous.'

Egmont said scornfully, 'I don't see that your boyhood lessons in "local trade" can be of any interest here!'

Dancer did not look at him; he was speaking only to Verling. 'My father also dealt with a number of ships which traded in tea.'

Egmont looked as if he were about to burst out laughing, but stifled it abruptly as Verling said, 'You have a good brain, Mr Dancer. I can see why your father had a rather different course charted for you.' He banged the table with his knuckles. 'Ships familiar with these waters, but suitable for the ocean as well. And big enough to carry powerful guns for self-defence,' he looked around the cabin, 'or murder.'

He swung away from the table. 'Call all hands. We will change tack directly. Then have the people lay aft. They shall hear what we are about, and what I intend!'

He strode to the adjoining cabin and closed the door.

Dangerous, reckless; many would say irresponsible.

Bolitho looked over at Dancer, now closing the log.

Certainly the bravest.

Bolitho tightened his neckcloth and winced at the water running on his skin, soaking his shoulder. Rain or spray, it made no difference now. He stared along the glistening deck, beyond the foremast and flapping canvas to the land, the rugged outline of which seemed to stretch from bow to bow. It, too, was blurred by a heavier belt of rain sweeping out to meet them.

Verling was taking no unnecessary chances, with topsails reefed and a minimum of canvas, and a leadsman in the chains on either bow.

Even now he heard one of them call out, *'No bottom, sir!'*

Plenty of room for any shift of tack. So far. But he knew from the chart how swiftly that could change. There were sandbars, and a scattered necklace of reef less than a mile distant.

He glanced over his sodden shoulder at the helmsmen, eyes slitted against the downpour as they peered up at the shaking canvas and the vague shadow of the mast-head pendant, barely lifting in the wind. Verling was close by, hands behind his back, hat pulled low over his forehead.

What was he thinking now? The seamen at their stations, wet and shivering, were probably hating him, although an hour ago, even less, he had seen some of them nod with approval; a couple had even raised a cheer. The grim remains of the cutter and its crew had been stark in each man's mind.

This was different. Sailors took risks every day, although few would admit it. They obeyed orders; it was their life. But suppose Verling was wrong, and he was taking an unnecessary risk with *Hotspur*, and the life of every man aboard?

He watched Verling walk unhurriedly to the weather bulwark and back to the compass box.

One day that might be me. Could I do it?

He felt, rather than saw, Dancer move across the slippery planking to join him.

'D'you think we're too late?'

Dancer was closer now, his voice just loud enough to be heard over the downpour and the shudder of rigging.

'Not unless they turned and ran immediately after the attack. But they must know these waters well.' He stared towards the land as a tall column of surf rose against a darker backdrop, before falling slowly.

Soundless, like a giant spectre. 'They'd not last a dogwatch otherwise!'

Bolitho shivered, but found a strange comfort in his friend's words.

Dancer looked round as Egmont's voice cut through the other noises. Men were already running to obey his orders.

'*He'll* probably be proved right in the end.'

He bit his lip as the call came aft again from the chains.

'*By th' mark ten, sir!*'

Bolitho imagined the leadsman feverishly coiling in the wet line and preparing for another heave. He tried to picture *Hotspur*'s keel dipping and lifting through the depths of grey sea. Ten fathoms. Sixty feet. Safe enough. So far . . .

'No bottom, sir!'

He let out a sigh of relief. No wonder experienced sailors treated the Channel Islands with such respect and caution.

Verling strode past them, one hand covering the lens of his telescope. Perhaps he had changed his mind. Remembered tomorrow in St Peter Port, this might seem an act of reckless folly.

'Mr Egmont, we will come about directly! Muster your anchor party.'

He had not changed his mind.

'*By th' mark seven!*'

Verling had trained his glass on the spur of headland, legs braced as he gauged the distance and bearing. Bolitho saw his face as he turned to watch the seamen crouching on the forecastle above the cathead. *Hotspur* was already coming about and into the wind, sails in confusion and, suddenly, all aback.

'Let go!'

Bolitho tried to see the chart in his mind; he and Dancer had pored over it and gone through Verling's notes until they almost knew them by heart.

The cable was still running out, the anchor plunging down, and down. A sandy bottom here, sheltered in its way by the same reef which had thrown up an occasional giant wave.

More men were scampering to secure sheets and braces, the deck swaying heavily as the anchor's fluke gripped and the cable took the full strain.

Dancer had his hand to his mouth. He had cut it at some time, but he was already running to add his strength to the others'.

Tinker cupped his hands. 'All secure, sir!'

Hotspur had come to her anchor, her masts tall against sullen cloud. Even the wind had dropped, or so it seemed. Bolitho looked at the land. Once only a pencilled cross on Verling's chart; now a blurred reality through the lens of a telescope.

He wiped the stinging spray from his eyes. So hard to believe. It was no time at all since he had first seen *Hotspur*, and had heard Dancer say, 'I'll not want to leave this beauty when the time comes!'

And that would not be long now, no matter what diversion delayed them. The way ahead was clear.

He heard Egmont shouting names, saw Tinker standing

at his elbow, nodding or making some encouraging comment as a man responded and snatched up cutlass or musket.

He had seen all this before, and should be hardened to it. Eyes seeking out a friendly face: those you fought for when battle was joined. But he was still not used to it, and was moved by it. Perhaps he was not alone, and others felt it also, and concealed it.

Someone muttered, 'I'll lay a bet them bastards is watchin' us right now, as we breathe!'

Another laughed. 'Not if I sees the scumbags first!'

Was that all it took?

And suddenly there was no more time left. One boat was hard alongside, swaying and lurching in the swell, men clambering down sure-footed, as if it were part of a drill.

Verling stood with his back to the sea, as if unwilling to let them go.

He said, 'Find out what you can.' He was looking at Egmont, as if they had the deck to themselves. 'I must know the strength and position of the enemy. But remember, no heroics. If you cannot find or identify the other vessel, stand fast until I send help, or recall you.' His glance moved only briefly to Bolitho. 'It is important. So take care.'

Egmont half turned, and swung back.

'It might take hours to make our way across to the anchorage, sir.'

'I know. There is no alternative.' He reached out as if to touch the lieutenant's arm, but decided against it. 'I shall be here. Conceal the boat as soon as you get ashore.' He saw a seaman signalling from the bulwark, and said curtly, 'Off with you.'

Bolitho scrambled into position but hesitated as Dancer leaned towards him, his face only inches away.

'Easy does it, Dick. Glory can wait,' he was trying to grin, 'until *I'm* with you!'

And then Bolitho was in the boat, wedged against the tiller-bar with Egmont beside him. The boat was full, two men to an oar, the bottom boards strewn with weapons and some hastily packed rations.

He heard Tinker shout, 'Cast off! *Easy*, lads!' He would be remaining aboard, hating it. But Verling was short-handed, and if another squall found them or *Hotspur* was forced to up-anchor for some reason, Tinker would be the key to survival.

The oars rose and dipped, slowly but steadily. It was going to be a hard pull.

Egmont shouted, 'Watch the stroke, damn you! Together now!'

Bolitho looked over his shoulder. *Hotspur* was already beyond reach.

Egmont said, 'Take over, will you? Steer for the ridge.' He swore under his breath as spray dashed over the stem and drifted aft. It was like ice. 'Of all the damn stupid ideas . . .'

He did not finish it.

Bolitho tried to guess what lay ahead, and to hold the image of the coastline fixed in his mind.

He called, 'Be ready with the boat's lead-and-line –' and paused, fixing a name to the face. 'Price, isn't it?'

'Indeed it is, sir! And I'm ready!' He sounded as if it were a joke, and the Welsh accent was very pronounced.

He heard Egmont mutter something. Anger or anxiety, he could not tell. He was a stranger, and would always remain so.

And Verling: was he having second thoughts now that he had set his plan in motion? Suppose there was no other vessel, no 'enemy'? He would be reprimanded for hazarding *Hotspur* to no purpose. And if he had sent a landing party into real danger, the blame would be immediate. He recalled Verling's face when he had turned to watch *Gorgon* as they had weighed anchor at Plymouth. As if something had been warning him, too late.

The small boat's lead splashed over the side.

'Three fathoms, sir!' A pause. 'Sandy bottom!'

Egmont said nothing, and Bolitho called, '*Oars!*'

The blades halted like stilled wings and the boat idled ahead, the men staring aft at the two uniforms by the tiller.

It was even darker here, more like sunset than afternoon. Just shadow, cloud, land and sea like a wasteland, a heaving desert.

Bolitho tensed and leaned forward, one hand to his ear.

Egmont snapped, 'What is it?'

How many times? How many shores? He felt the stroke oarsman watching him, both hands gripping his loom.

The gentle, regular surge of water on the sand.

He said, 'Give way together! Easy all!' Then, to Egmont, 'The beach, sir.'

And now the land was real, a fine crescent of hard, wet sand and a tangled mass of trees, almost black in this dull light. Like Verling's chart and the scribbled notes he had gathered from somewhere.

'*One* fathom, sir!'

Bolitho felt his mouth go dry.

'Oars! Stand by to beach!'

The sound of the water was louder, and he could see bright phosphorescence streaming from the blades as they glided silently into the shallows.

Then men were leaping over the sides, to control the hull as it ground on to the hard, packed sand; others were running up the beach towards the trees, one of them dropping on to his knee, a musket to his shoulder.

No shouted challenge, or sudden crash of gunfire: the sounds of failure, and of death.

Only the lap of water against the boat's stranded hull, and the hiss of a breeze through the leafless trees.

To himself, Bolitho murmured, 'We did it, Martyn!'

To Egmont he said, 'Shall we cover the boat, sir?'

'Not yet. We don't know if . . .' He appeared to be staring down the beach, beyond the grounded boat, as if he expected to see *Hotspur*. But there was only darkness.

Then he seemed to come out of his trance and said, almost brusquely, 'We must get into position on the ridge, if there proves to *be* one. We will be able to see across the bay.' He stared at Bolitho. 'Well?'

'We could send scouts on ahead, sir. Tinker picked out some good ones. Fair marksmen, too.'

Egmont said, 'It won't come to that, for God's sake. We've got twelve seamen, not a troop of marines!'

He eased his pistol against his hip, marshalling his thoughts.

'We'll move off now. Those scouts – fetch them. And I want the boat shifted nearer the trees, and properly hidden.' He called after him, 'And check those supplies!' He kicked irritably at the sand. 'I can't do everything!'

The trees seemed to move out and around them, the seamen keeping abreast of Bolitho as he trod on firmer ground, the sounds of water on the beach already fading. The thrust and tramp of bodies and the occasional clink of weapons seemed deafening, but he knew it was only imagination. Maybe they were keeping too close together, the habit of sailors thrown ashore, away from their crowded element. It was their way.

He thought of the brief confrontation aboard the flagship. A lifetime ago . . . And the sudden reality of that word. *Trust*.

He quickened his pace and sensed the others following suit on either side of him. Right or wrong, they were with him.

8

Lifeline

'This is far enough. We'll stop while we get our bearings.'
The lieutenant stood by a fallen tree, the pattern of his
buttons oddly bright in the gloom. Bolitho remembered the
corpses he had seen trapped in the submerged wreckage. A
chilling reminder.

Egmont added tartly, 'And keep them quiet! They're like
a herd of damned cattle!'

Bolitho looked at the sky, the clouds moving steadily but
more slowly now, and closer at this height above the sea, on
the crest of the ridge or nearly so. He wanted to stamp his
feet, which were like ice despite the long tramp over rough
ground, uphill for most of the way since they had hidden the
boat. And so quiet, not even the murmur of surf any more,
only wind and the rustle of dead leaves, the clink of metal or
a muttered curse from one of the stooping shadows.

He realised that Egmont was close beside him, could see the oval of his face, hear his breathing. Calm enough, giving nothing away.

He said, 'It will be steeper on the far side. It leads right down to the bay.' He was brushing the front of his coat with one hand as he spoke; a few dead, dry twigs clung to it. It was like seeing him for the first time; he had always been so smart, not a thread or clip out of place. Because he was so new to the rank, or because he still needed to prove something? So different from the unexpected outbursts of anger, or the hostility he had displayed in the cabin. When he had struck Sewell in the face.

'You told me you've detailed two hands as scouts? Can you vouch for them?'

'Keveth and Hooker, sir. When the names were selected . . .'

Egmont snapped, 'Never mind what Tinker Thorne said. What do *you* think?'

Bolitho pressed his knuckles against his side to control his irritation.

'I'd trust them, sir. Hooker was brought up in the country, and Keveth too, before he volunteered.'

Egmont might have been smiling.

'And he *is* a fellow Cornishman, I believe? Say no more.' He moved to the edge of the rough track, looking back towards the sea. 'We shall make our way down to the bay shortly. Those two men will scout ahead. Don't ask them, Bolitho. *Tell* them. This may be a waste of time, but it may not, and I'll not have any slackness, is that clear?'

Bolitho swung round as several voices let out a collective gasp of surprise or dismay.

Just one light had appeared, moving against the black curtain of sea and sky. Tiny, a mere pinprick, but after the stealth and scent of danger it seemed like a beacon.

Egmont said, 'Hold your noise!' He was feeling his pocket, as if for his watch. '*Hotspur*'s riding light. To show others that we are here upon our lawful occasions, if anyone else is fool enough to be abroad at this time!'

Someone muttered, 'The 'ole bloody world'll know by now!'

Egmont moved away from the edge. 'And take that man's name! Any more insolence and I'll see the culprit's backbones at the gangway when we rejoin *Gorgon*!'

Bolitho followed him along the track. They were on the downward slope, and he thought he could feel the sea's nearness, the protection of the little bay he had seen on the chart. When he glanced back, the tiny light had vanished, masked by the fold of the ridge. Like having a line severed, the last link with the small, personal existence they had come to know. And depend on . . . a sailor's faith in his ship.

Egmont was saying, 'Watch your weapons! Keep them covered!'

Keveth, the keen-eyed foretopman who had begun life as a poacher, murmured, 'Ready when you are, sir.'

The second man, Hooker, one of *Gorgon*'s gun captains, raised his fist.

'We won't move too fast for you, sir!'

Bolitho could see his teeth in the darkness. As if he was sharing some private joke, reassuring him of something.

They walked a few yards and they were completely alone.

Keveth turned and said softly, 'Just *us*, see?' He drew a finger across his throat. 'Anyone else gets this!'

How long, how far, Bolitho lost count. He heard the sea, a slow and heavy rhythm like breathing, and the faint ripple of water running over rocks.

Keveth said, 'Bill Hooker's gone off to smell 'un out. Good lad.'

Bolitho forced each muscle to relax. Two Cornishmen on this godforsaken piece of coast, which even now was so hauntingly reminiscent of home. If Keveth took it into his head to leave him, he could simply melt away.

'I bin thinkin', sir. When you gets your new ship . . .' Keveth was still beside him.

Bolitho smiled. 'I haven't got one yet.'

'Ah, but when ee do . . .' He broke off, his hand sliding through some wet gorse like a snake. '*Still!*'

But it was Hooker, bent double, grinning when he knew he had found them.

Keveth said, 'Thought ee'd swum back to the ship, my son!'

Bolitho had seen the glint of the dagger before he slipped it back under his coat.

Hooker took a deep breath and slumped down on the ground.

'I *seen* 'er, sir!' He nodded, as if to convince himself as well. 'I got down to the beach. There was a rift in the clouds, an' there she was!'

Keveth exclaimed, 'Bloody saphead! Some 'un might have seen ee!'

'Thought they 'ad. Two of 'em almost trod on me!' He laughed shakily. 'Near thing!'

Bolitho reached over and gripped his arm. He could feel him shivering.

'Tell it as it happened. What you saw, maybe heard. Then we'll go back and tell the others.' He waited, allowing his breathing to slow, and said, 'You did well. I'll see that it's not forgotten.'

Keveth murmured, 'He *will*, too, Bill.'

'I kept close to them rocks, just like you said.' He was looking at his friend, but speaking to Bolitho. 'It was as black as a well, an' then there was a break in the clouds to the nor'-west – even saw a few early stars. Then it was gone.'

Bolitho was aware of Keveth's irritation.

'What sort of vessel is she? Square-rigged, fore and aft? Take your time.'

It was hard to remain calm, contained, but any sign of impatience or doubt and Hooker's recollections would be scattered. He thought of Egmont back there in the darkness, doubtless fuming with frustration and cursing Verling for sending him out on this pointless quest. *A waste of time.* What Hooker had to say now would change everything.

Hooker said deliberately, ' 'Tis a brig. I'd swear to that,

sir. All canvas furled an' snugged down for the night, I'd say. But she's anchored so far out, it was 'ard to be sure.'

Keveth nudged him.

'Keep goin', Bill. You're doin' handsome.'

Hooker did not seem to hear him. He continued in the same unemotional tone, reliving it. Feeling the menace, alone on the beach.

'There were two boats on the sand, another one moored farther out, in the shallows. Bigger'n the others, one mast, sail-rigged.' He banged the ground with his hand. 'Lee-boards, I'm almost sure.' Another nod to himself. 'Small coaster, I reckon.'

Just the kind of vessel for a dangerous rendezvous. And there would be hundreds of such craft around the islands or used for trade along the French coast.

Hooker continued, 'They was arguin', do you see, sir? Shoutin' some o' the time. I thought they was near comin' to fists or worse.'

Keveth prompted, almost gently, 'English?'

Hooker stared at him, as if it had not occurred to him. 'Some was. Others could 'ave bin French. I ain't sure. But the ones with the coaster was cursin' the crew from the brig. Anchored too far out, one was yellin'.'

Bolitho got to his feet. That had to be the key. *Too far out.* Whatever was being unlawfully traded or moved to another rendezvous, and was worth cold-blooded murder, had to be shifted *now.*

He said, 'Hazardous or not, they have no choice.' He thought of *Hotspur*'s isolated riding light. Neither did Verling.

He looked at Keveth, who was also standing now, his carefully wrapped musket over one shoulder.

'I'll have you relieved as soon as I can. We'll go and find the others.'

Keveth hesitated, as if some sharp comment was hanging on his tongue. But he said, 'I'll be here, sir. The lieutenant will be wantin' a boat's crew, I'm thinkin'.' He added firmly, 'I'd like to keep with you,' and wiped his grubby chin with the back of his hand. *'Sir!'*

It was only a short time before they found the others, but long enough for the truth to become clear to him.

A boat's crew was needed without delay. Verling must have known it even as he was grappling with each doubt. If he had waited until dawn, the mystery ship would have sailed, despite the risks in these shoal-ridden waters. The alternative was the end of a rope.

And the smuggled cargo which had reached this far?

He recalled Dancer's quiet speculation. It was certainly neither rum nor tea.

Egmont waited for Bolitho to stride up to him.

'Well?'

Impatient, anxious, even excited? For once, he was hiding his emotions.

'Hooker has had a quick sighting, sir. A brig, anchored well out.'

Egmont glanced at the seaman in question.

'Anything else? Got a tongue, has he?'

Hooker swallowed hard.

'There was men on the beach, boats as well.' When

Egmont failed to interrupt he continued in his round country accent, but there was nothing slow-witted about his observations. Bolitho had watched him at numerous drills aboard *Gorgon*, as gun captain of one of her long eighteen-pounders; his brain was fast enough.

Egmont waited in that enigmatic silence, and then said, 'Some were French, you think?'

Hooker shrugged. 'I thought they was, sir.'

Egmont looked at the sky. 'Probably locals. They speak a Norman-French patois here. No better breeding ground for smuggling on the grand scale.' He broke off, as if surprised at himself for sharing his opinions. He regarded Bolitho coldly. 'If the vessel is anchored far out, and it seems wise in these waters, that will mean they must begin loading their contraband straight away. No time to lose. Two boats, you say?'

Hooker spread his hands. 'An' the coaster.'

Egmont folded and unfolded his arms. 'The brig would have one, maybe two more. All the same . . .'

Bolitho said, 'A long haul, even so.'

Egmont stared past him, watching or listening to the trees.

'Wind's livelier. They might not have noticed that aboard *Hotspur*. More sheltered beyond the point.'

Bolitho said, 'Mr Verling will have given strict orders—' He got no further.

'I know that, damn it! But he won't have any idea of the timing needed. *I* shall deal with that immediately.' He swung round and looked at the huddle of dark

shapes, crouching on the cold ground or in the shelter
of a few salt-bitten trees. 'I want a boat's crew *now*.
Hooker, you lead the way. You can tell Mr Verling
what you told me.' He checked him with his hand. 'And
make sure you get it right, man! It will be upon your
head!'

Bolitho felt the anger churning at his guts. No word of
praise or thanks, only a threat of recrimination. He recalled
Keveth's words. *I'd like to keep with you.* He had already
guessed, known, that Egmont would be returning to
Hotspur with a boat's crew. In the shortest possible time. It
made sense. And yet . . .

Egmont was looking at the sky again. 'Take charge until
you receive further orders. Observe their movements, but
remain out of sight.' He turned away. 'Select five hands to
stay with you. I shall manage with the other half of the
party.'

Someone muttered, 'Done, sir. I've picked our lads.'

Bolitho forced himself to concentrate, to blot out the
glaring truth. He was being left behind, with only five of
the original landing party. Keveth had known; so,
probably, had Hooker.

The voice at his elbow was that of Price, the big
Welshman who had been the boat's leadsman on their
passage to the beach. He was known for a rough and
irrepressible sense of humour, not always appreciated by
Tinker, the boatswain's mate.

'That's long enough!' Egmont was watching the small
group of figures breaking up, separating into two sections,

a few grins and remarks here, a quick pat on a friend's shoulder there.

Hooker paused for the merest second by Bolitho.

'I'll pass the word to Mr Dancer, sir.' That was all. It was enough.

Egmont's people were already moving back beneath the trees at the foot of the ridge. In two hours he would be in the boat; in three or thereabouts, in *Hotspur*'s cabin.

He left without a backward look. Was that how it had to be?

Will I be expected to behave like that when – if – my chance comes?

Price was still beside him. 'Well, there you are, see. The cream always comes out on top!' One of the others even laughed.

Bolitho said, 'Let's find a scrap of cover – I think I felt more rain. This is what we'll do.'

For an instant he believed he had imagined it.

But he had not. He was in charge. And he was ready.

9

In the King's Name

Richard Bolitho pressed down on both hands to take the weight of his body and ease the pain in his legs. He was wedged between two great shoulders of rock, worn smooth by the sea. He could hear the slap and sluice of trapped water somewhere below his precarious perch, like a warning, sharpening his mind. The tide was on the make, or soon would be. That would mean climbing higher, losing contact, or worse, any protection he and his small party had gained.

He leaned forward once more. He had lost count of how many times he had repeated the movement, staring at the faint curve of the beach and the ungainly outline of the lugger Hooker had described, more at an angle now, pulling restlessly at the anchor which prevented her from grinding on to this treacherous shore.

He closed his eyes and tried to focus his thoughts. At first, when Keveth had guided him to this point, he had feared immediate discovery. Every loose pebble, or the splash of feet across wet sand, had sounded like a landslide, *a herd of cattle* as Egmont had so contemptuously called them. But the dark, scrambling figures, the occasional shouts of instruction or anger across the water had continued uninterrupted. The two longboats had been loaded and had pulled strongly away from the beach. It would take several journeys to complete the transfer of the lugger's cargo. It had probably been their original intention to moor directly alongside. *Too far out.*

It was that important even now. Important enough to kill for.

He tensed as sand splashed into the water below him, and realised that the curved hanger was already partly drawn, the hilt cold in his fist. But it was Keveth, and he had not even seen him until he was here, only an arm's length away.

Keveth had turned and was looking down towards the beach.

Then he said, 'One of the boats is comin' back now.' He was breathing evenly, apparently at ease. 'Next load'll be ready to move directly. Heavy work, no doubt o' that!'

Bolitho heard the creak of oars; men jumping from the boat to guide it into the shallows, somebody barking an order. It could have been any language.

'Did you see what they're carrying?'

Keveth was watching him; he could almost feel his eyes.

'Guns.' He was peering at the beach again. 'I knew 'twas summat heavy. I seen muskets stowed like that afore.' He let his words sink in. 'New ones, anyway.'

Bolitho stared into the darkness; the blood seemed to be pounding in his ears like the sea beyond these rocks. No wonder the prize was worth the risk. Worth human life.

And yet there must be houses, perhaps farms quite close by . . .

Keveth must have read his thoughts.

'Well, ee d' know what 'tis like at home. Nobody sees nowt when th' Brotherhood is out.'

But all Bolitho could think of was the shipment of guns. Where bound? And destined for whose hands?

There had been rumours. The more radical news-sheets had openly used the word 'rebellion' in the American colonies ever since the Boston Massacre. And only days ago one of the lieutenants in *Gorgon* had claimed it was the subject of the admiral's conference. Even Captain Conway had mentioned it.

It had seemed so distant, so vague. Another quarterdeck whisper. But if true . . . just across the water, the old enemy would be quick to encourage any such insurrection.

Keveth was on his knees, peering once more at the beach.

''Nother boat comin' in. Must be a load o' muskets. Th' lugger's leeboards is well above th' line.'

Bolitho glanced up at the sky. Hooker had seen the first stars. There were more now, and the torn clouds seemed to have gathered speed. He thought of *Hotspur*'s riding light, unreachable beyond the ridge. And of Egmont, brushing dead leaves from his coat. He had once heard someone remark that Egmont's father was, or had been, a tailor at one of the naval ports. That might explain . . .

He pushed it away and said, 'It's up to us.' He tried to shut out the other voice. *It's up to you.* 'The tide's on the make. They'll be weighing anchor before we know it.'

Keveth said, 'I dunno much about such things, but us Jacks ain't supposed to. Rebellion or freedom, *we* obey orders an' that's all there is to it. It's which end of the gun you're standin' at that counts in th' end!'

Bolitho stood up suddenly to prevent himself from changing his mind, one hand against the rock to take his weight. He could feel his heart thudding against his ribs.

'I must get nearer.' He thought Keveth would protest. Now, while there was still time. He was outspoken enough; he had proved that. Sharp and clear, like a lookout's view from the topsail yard. Five seamen, who could just as easily turn their backs as obey a direct command that might end in death. And who would know? Or care?

Keveth looked at him in silence, and Bolitho thought he had not heard. Then he moved swiftly, reaching out towards his face, as if to strike him. But he was touching one of the white patches on Bolitho's lapel. 'Better hide them middy's patches. Stand out like a priest in a brothel.' He folded the collar deftly. 'Best be goin', then.'

Bolitho felt him grasp his elbow as they descended from the rocks: unreal, and strangely moving. And not once had he called him *sir*. Which made it even stronger, because it mattered.

Perhaps this was madness, and it was already too late.

But through it all he could hear Martyn's voice, just before he had climbed down into the boat and cast off from *Hotspur*'s side, a thousand years ago . . .

Glory can wait. Until I'm with you.

He said, 'You *are*.' Then he joined the seaman who had once been a poacher, and together they stared at the pale, coffin-like shapes which had been hauled on to the sand.

Even in the shelter of the rocks, he could feel the increasing thrust of the wind. A long, hard pull for the men in the boats, even with extra hands.

Keveth pointed. ''Nother box.'

Bolitho saw the shape being lowered over the side of the lugger, heard the squeak of block and tackle and the louder splashes of men wading through icy water with the next load of muskets. No shouts or curses this time. They were probably breathless.

He asked, 'How many hands still aboard, d'you think?'

'Three or four. Enough for th' winch, watchin' th' anchor cable as well. If that parted . . .'

He ducked as someone shouted, but nothing else happened. The box had been manhandled further along the beach and on to firmer sand. The would have the wind against them all the way back when they came for the next load.

Bolitho pushed the hair from his eyes. The last one, perhaps.

He said, 'Might be the time to act.' He recalled Egmont's words when they had landed. *Don't ask them. Tell them!*

He tried to gauge the distance from the rocks to the moored lugger. They would have to wade through the water, farther than they thought. He knew he was deluding himself. The tide was already coming in, noisier now with the wind in its face.

'When the other boat shoves off . . .' He touched Keveth's arm. It did not flinch. 'We'll board her.'

He saw another pale shape jerking slowly down the side close to the leeboard. Hooker would have described all this to Verling. What would the first lieutenant be thinking? If he had listened to Egmont, *Hotspur* would be snugged down in St Peter Port by now, and somebody else would be responsible, reaping the praise or the blame.

Bolitho considered the others in this small party. Price was a steady, reliable hand, in spite of the humour so often aimed at his superiors. The other three he knew only by sight, and in the daily routine, and in the past few weeks he had not seen much of that. He thought of his brother Hugh, in temporary command of the revenue cutter *Avenger*. A stranger. And yet Dancer had spent a lot of time with him. Getting on well together, it had seemed.

Don't ask them. Tell them. Even that sounded like Hugh. He said, 'Are you with me?'

Keveth did not answer directly, but turned to listen as the second boat was pushed and manhandled into the water. Then he unslung the carefully wrapped musket from his shoulder and said, 'Work for old Tom 'ere, after all!'

He faced the midshipman again. 'All the way, *sir.*'

It was time.

Bolitho was aware of the others pressing around him, could feel their breathing and, perhaps, their doubts.

'We'll board her now, before the boats come back. This wind will carry us out. After that we can stand clear and wait for *Hotspur.*'

'Suppose the tide gets other ideas, sir?'

Bolitho put a face to the voice. Perry, an experienced seaman who had been with him when they had found the dead boat's crew. Tough, withdrawn. But observant. If the wind dropped, the lugger would run hard aground as soon as the cable was cut.

Price said, 'I've seen boats like this one before, sir. No keel to speak of – they use the leeboards if they need steerage way. Used to watch the Dutchmen when I was over on the Medway and they came across the Channel.'

Another voice. His name was Stiles. Younger, and aggressive, said to have been a bare-knuckle prizefighter around the markets until he had decided to sign on. In a hurry, it was suggested.

'Will there be a reward?'

Bolitho felt the winter wind in his face, wet sand stinging the skin. At any moment the chance might desert them. At best they might be able to drift clear of the shore until *Hotspur* up-anchored and made an appearance. The lugger would provide enough evidence for any future action.

He said bluntly, 'It's our duty!' and almost expected the man to laugh.

Instead, Stiles replied, 'That'll 'ave to do, then!'

The remaining seaman was named Drury, a sure-footed topman like Keveth. He had been flogged for insolence, and Bolitho had seen the old scars on his back once when he had been working in the shrouds aboard *Gorgon*. Curiously, he had been among the first hands selected by Tinker for the passage crew. As boatswain's mate, Tinker himself had probably dealt out the punishment.

Drury said thoughtfully, 'Might get a tot o' somethin' to warm our guts if we make a move right now!'

Bolitho felt someone nudge him. It was Keveth.

'See, sir? They'm good as gold when you puts it like that.'

Bolitho faced the sea and tried not to hear the hiss of spray along the beach. Then it was surging around his legs, dragging at him like some human force as he strode towards the lugger.

They would fall back, leave him to die because of his own stupid determination. And for what?

It was like a wild dream, the icy sea dragging at his body, and surging past the lugger which seemed to be shining despite the darkness, mocking him.

He slipped and would have been dragged down by the current, out of his depth, but for a hand gripping his shoulder. The fingers were like iron, forcing him forward. And suddenly, the blunt hull was leaning directly over him, the pale outline of the leeboard just as Hooker had

described it, and the loose hoisting tackle dragging against
him, caught on the incoming crests. Like those other times,
in training or in deadly earnest, he was scrambling up the
side, using the hard, wet tackle and kicking every foot of
the way. He felt metal scrape his thigh like a knife-edge,
and almost cried out with shock and disbelief as he lurched
to his feet. He was on the lugger's deck.

'Cut the cable!'

But the cry of the wind and the surge of water alongside
seemed to muffle his voice. Then he heard a thud, and
another, someone yelling curses, and knew it was Price's
boarding axe taking a second swing.

He felt the deck shudder and for an instant thought they
had run ashore. But the hull was steady, and somehow he
knew it was moving, free from the ground.

A figure seemed to rise from the very deck, arms waving,
mouth a black hole in his face. Yelling, screaming, unreal.

And then a familiar voice, harsh but steady. 'Oh, no, you
don't, matey!'

And the sickening crack of a heavy blade into bone.

Bolitho gasped, 'Fores'l!' But he should have recognised the confusion of wet canvas, already breaking into
life.

He staggered across the deck, towards a solitary figure
grappling with the long tiller-bar. It was Drury, with a
cutlass thrust through his belt.

'Steady she is, sir!' He laughed into the wind. 'Almost!'

There was a small hatch, and Bolitho saw that he had
nearly fallen into it. Two more figures were crouched on a

ladder, shouting; perhaps they were pleading. Only then did he realise that the hanger was in his hand, and the blade was only a foot away from the nearest man.

He yelled, 'You two, bear a hand! *Now*, damn you!'

His words might have been lost in the noise of wind and flapping canvas, but the naked blade was clear in any language.

Price was calling, 'She's answering, sir! We'll tackle the mains'l now!'

Bolitho stared at the sky, and saw the big foresail swaying above him like a shadow.

'Are we all here?' He wanted to laugh or weep. Like madness.

Keveth shouted, 'Large as life, sir!'

There was a muffled splash and he added, 'That 'un won't bother us no more!'

Bolitho tried to sheathe the hanger in its scabbard, but felt Keveth take it gently from his hand.

'Don't need this for a bit, sir.' He was grinning. 'We've taken th' old girl!'

Bolitho moved to the side and stared at the choppy wavelets below him. He was shaking badly, and not because of the cold. Or the danger. And it was hard to think, and make sense of it. They would winch up the mainsail and steer a course clear of this rocky coastline.

At first light . . . But nothing would form clearly in his mind, except, *we did it*.

Below deck they might find more muskets, evidence which would justify *Hotspur*'s actions.

And ours.

Tomorrow . . . He looked at the stars. He was no longer shivering. And it was tomorrow now.

He heard someone else, 'Too bloody late, you bastards!' and the immediate crack of a musket. But even that was distorted by the wind and rigging.

Then Keveth, sharp, angry, 'Get under cover an' reload *now*, you mad bugger! You'll 'ave a dead charge on your 'ands with the next shot!'

There were shouts and another shot and Bolitho remembered that the boats were out there, lost in the swell as they pulled towards the beach. Another few minutes and they would have foiled any attempt to board the lugger, and there would be corpses rolling in the tide to mark their folly. He ran to the side and peered past the tiller. It was not imagination. He could see the vague outline of the ridge, edged against the sky, where before there had been solid blackness. Clouds, too, but the stars had gone.

Keveth called, 'That'll show the bastards!' But he was staring after the one who had fired his musket. 'They'll be comin' for us – they've nowhere else to turn to!' He waved his fist to drive the point home. 'Listen!'

The rattle and creak of loose gear seemed to fade, and in a lull in the wind Bolitho could hear the slow, regular *clink, clink, clink*, like that last time, when they had left Plymouth. The pawls of a capstan, men straining every muscle against wind and tide to break out the anchor. The brig was making a run for it. Those in the boats, even their own hands, were being abandoned. There were no rules for the smuggling fraternity but *save your own neck first*. He banged his fist on the bulwark, the pain steadying him.

The brutal truth was that *Hotspur* might still be at anchor, unwilling to risk any dangerous manoeuvre on the mere chance of an encounter. He recalled Verling's parting words. *No heroics.*

He joined Drury by the tiller-bar and leaned his weight against it. He could feel the heavy shudder, the power of the sea, and tried to guess at their progress. Without more sail and time to work clear of the bay . . . He shut his mind to the ifs and the maybes. They had done better than anyone could have expected. Hoped.

'The brig's weighed, sir!' Another voice said, 'Cut 'er cable, more like!'

Either way, the smuggler was making sail. If she worked around *Hotspur* or avoided her altogether, her master would have the open sea ahead, and every point of the compass from which to choose his escape.

And even if there was further evidence below deck, what would that prove? The two cowering wretches who had pleaded for mercy when Keveth and his mates had swarmed aboard would certainly go to the gallows, or hang in chains on the outskirts of some seaport or along a coastal road as a grisly warning to others. But the trade would never stop while men had gold to offer. Personal greed or to sustain a rebellion, the cause mattered little to those who were prepared to take the risk for profit.

He heard a cry from forward: Stiles, the prizefighter, poised high in the bows, one arm flung out.

Bolitho wiped his face. It was not a trick of light or imagination. He could see the young seaman outlined against the heaving water and occasional feather of spray, and then, reaching out on either side, an endless, pale backdrop of sea and sky.

Then he heard Stiles' voice. Clear and sharp. *'Breakers ahead!'*

'Helm a-lee!' He saw the tiller going over, one of the captured smugglers running to throw his weight with Drury's to bring it round.

Bolitho saw Keveth staring at him, as if telling him something, but all he could think was that he could see each feature, and that he still had his musket, 'old Tom', across one shoulder. As if all time had stopped, and only here and this moment counted for anything.

Stiles was stepping down from his perch in the bows, still watching the sea and the lazy turmoil of breakers. Not a reef, and at high water it would be little more than shallows. A sandbar. But enough.

And here too was the brig, her courses and foretopsail already set and filling to the wind, even a small, curling wave at her stem. Moving through the grey water, her hull still in darkness. Like an onlooker. Uninvolved.

'Pass the word! Stand by to ram!'

It could have been someone else's voice.

More of a sensation than a shock, the most noise coming

from the flapping canvas as the handful of seamen ran to slacken off all lines and free the winch.

They had ground ashore, with hardly a shudder. When the tide turned again she would be high and dry.

Bolitho walked aft and watched the brig, heeling slightly as she altered course, her sails hardening, a masthead pendant whipping out like a spear.

The seaman named Perry shook his fist.

'We did our best, damn their eyes!'

'Not enough . . .' Bolitho flinched as someone gripped his arm. *'What?'* And saw Keveth's expression. Not shock or surprise, but the face of a man who could no longer be caught aback by anything.

He said quietly, 'An' *there's* a sight, sir. One you'll long remember.'

It was *Hotspur*, lying over to the wind, casting her own shadow like a reflection across the whitecaps. She had skirted the headland, so closely that she appeared to be balanced across it.

Keveth swung round. 'Wait, sir! What're you about?' He was staring up at him as Bolitho ran to the side and climbed into the shrouds.

'So that he'll know!' He was unfolding the collar of his coat, until the white midshipman's patches were clearly visible. 'Give me my hat!'

He reached down and took it without losing sight of the brig. Verling would see him, and know what they had done. That this fight had not been so one-sided after all. That his trust had not been misplaced.

But who did he really mean? *So that he'll know* . . .

'Boat! Larboard quarter!'

Price turned away. 'Easy, Ted! It's our lads!'

He looked up at the midshipman in the shrouds, one hand holding his hat steady against the wind. To others, it might look like a salute. They would not see his torn and stained uniform across the water. But they would see him. And they would not forget.

Bolitho heard none of it, watching the two sets of sails. On a converging tack, the land rolling back like a screen. There was light on the water now, a faint margin between sea and sky, but hardly visible. Or real.

Hotspur made a fine sight, *the bird unfolding her wings.* Ready to attack.

Too far away to see any movement, but he could hold the image clearly in his mind. Swivel guns manned, puny but deadly at close quarters. *Hotspur*'s two bow-chasers would be empty, useless. Someone would answer for that. Later, perhaps, when they read Verling's log. Written in Martyn's familiar hand.

And bright patches of scarlet as if painted on a canvas: Verling had hoisted two ensigns, so that there could be no mistake or excuse. *Hotspur* had become a man-of-war.

He heard the boat come alongside, voices, excited greetings. Then silence as they all turned to watch the two vessels, almost overlapping, *Hotspur* graceful, even fragile, against her adversary.

There was anger now, alarm too, at the far-off sounds of

shots, like someone tapping casually on a tabletop with his fingers.

Hotspur must have misjudged her change of tack, as if, out of control, she would drive her jib boom through the brig's foremast shrouds. But she had luffed, and must surely be almost abeam. Then there was a brief, vivid flash, and seconds later the sharp, resonant bang of a swivel gun.

The seamen around him were suddenly quiet, each man in his mind across the grey water with his friend or companion, and at his proper station. This was like being rendered helpless, cut off from the only world they knew.

Keveth said, 'What the *hell*! If only . . .'

The two vessels were still drifting together, sails in disarray, as if no human hands were at the helm of either.

There was a great gasp, mounting to a combined growl, like something torn from each man's heart. Just a small sliver of scarlet, but it was moving slowly up the brig's overlapping mainyard, and then it broke out to the wind. To match the two flags flying from *Hotspur*'s masts.

Bolitho could not tear his eyes away, despite the wild burst of cheering, and the hard slaps across his shoulders.

'That showed 'em!' and 'That made the murderin' buggers jump!'

One seaman, the boat's coxswain, was trying to make himself heard.

'I'm to take you aboard, sir! Mr Verling's orders!'

Bolitho seized Keveth's arm and said, 'You're in charge, until they send someone to relieve you.' He shook him gently. 'I'll not forget what you did. Believe me.' He walked after the boat's coxswain, but paused and looked back at his own small party of sailors. Price, the big Welshman; even he was at a loss for a joke now. Perry, Stiles, and Drury, who was still standing by the stiff and motionless tiller-bar, his face split by one huge grin.

Then he was in the boat, faster and lighter now without the weight of extra hands sent by Verling. Rising and plunging across each rank of incoming waves, and all the time the tall pyramids of sails seemed to draw no closer. Only once did he turn to gaze back at the beached lugger, and the small cluster of figures by the stern.

'Stand by, bowman!'

He hardly remembered going alongside, only hands reaching out and down to assist him aboard: familiar faces, but all like strangers. He wanted to shake himself, be carried by this moment and its triumph and thrust the strain or uncertainty, or was it fear, into the retreating shadows.

He could still feel their hands pounding his shoulders, see their grins, and Keveth's pride and satisfaction. The victors.

He stared around, and across to the other vessel's poop. The wheel was in fragments, the bulwark pitted and broken by the single blast of canister from *Hotspur*'s swivel. There was blood, too, and he could hear someone groaning in agony, and another quietly sobbing.

He saw Egmont, back turned, his drawn sword across his shoulder, quite still, as if on parade.

'This way, sir!' A seaman touched his arm.

He saw some of them pause to glance at him, and young Sewell, his rough bandage still dangling from one leg. Staring, raising his hand to acknowledge him, his face changed in some way. Older . . .

Verling was by the compass box, hatless, and without a sword.

'You did damned well,' he said.

But Bolitho could not speak, or move. As if everything had stopped. Like the moment when the scarlet ensign had appeared above the brig's deck.

He saw that Verling had a bandage around his wrist, and here, also, there was blood. Beyond him, splinters had been torn from the deck. Like feathers, where those few shots had left their mark.

Verling said, 'If there was any way . . .' He broke off, and gestured abruptly at the hatch. 'He's in the cabin. We did all . . .'

Bolitho did not hear the rest.

He was down the ladder and in the cabin, where they had sat and waited. Talked about the Board and the future.

Dancer was on one of the bench seats, his head and shoulders propped on some cushions. He had been watching the door, perhaps listening. Now he tried to reach out, but his arm fell to his side.

There was one lamp burning in the cabin, near the same skylight beneath which Verling had been standing during that final discussion. The light was moving unsteadily as the hull nudged against the captive vessel alongside, and gave colour to Dancer's fair hair, but revealed the pallor of his skin and the effort of his breathing. There was a small red stain on his shirt.

Bolitho took his hand and held it between his own, and watched his eyes, trying to keep the pain at bay, or to experience it himself. Like all those other times.

'I came as soon as I could, Martyn. I didn't know . . .' He felt the hand move in his, attempting to return his grip.

He said, 'You're here now, Dick. All that matters.'

Bolitho leaned over him, shielding his face, his eyes, from the light. He could barely hear the words.

The hand moved again. Then, just one word. 'Together.'

Someone spoke. Bolitho had not known there was anybody else in the cabin. It was Tinker.

'Best leave him, sir. He's gone, I'm afraid.'

Bolitho touched his friend's face, gently, to wipe away some tears. The skin was quite still. And he realised the tears were his own.

Somewhere, in another world, he heard the trill of a boatswain's call, the response of running feet.

Tinker was by the door, blocking it. In his years at sea he had seen and done almost everything. In ships as different as the oceans they served, and with captains just as varied. You became hardened to most things. Or you went under.

He had heard the new activity on deck. He was needed now, more than ever. The prisoners to be put to work, both vessels to be got under way again. Maybe a jury-rig to be fitted aboard the brig's steering as the helm had been shot away. The first lieutenant had no doubt been yelling for him already.

But it was the here and now that required him most.

'Listen, me son. Soon, maybe very soon, you'll be standin' into a new life. You have their respect, I've seen you win it, but that's only the beginning. You'll make friends, an' you'll lose some of 'em. Sure, that's the way of it. It's a sailor's lot.'

The calls were silent, the feet on deck were still. The hard, leathery hand touched his torn sleeve very briefly.

'Just think of the next watch, an' the next horizon, see?'

Bolitho turned by the door and glanced back. He could be asleep. Waiting for the next watch.

He felt his lips move and heard himself speak, and the words were dry and controlled, and the voice unfamiliar.

'I'm ready. When you are.' He looked at the door again. 'You'll never know.'

The way ahead. *Together*.

Captain Beves Conway swung away from the stern windows of his day cabin and called, 'Have him come aft directly, man!'

He had been watching the thirty-two-gun frigate *Condor* enter harbour and drop anchor with a minimum of fuss and delay; it was what he would expect from a captain like Maude. Always busy, always in demand. He cocked his head to listen to his own ship's routine, and almost sighed with relief. The disruption of overhaul was finished, until their lordships insisted on another; the constant comings and goings of working parties and dockyard experts and the noise, smells and personal discomfort were being inflicted on some other vessel, and His Britannic Majesty's Ship *Gorgon* could now show even a frigate a thing or two if required. Freshly blackened standing rigging and gleaming paintwork were shining brightly, despite a morning so cold and misty that even the usually restless gulls seemed content to float upon the anchorage like discarded wreaths.

The screen door opened a few inches, and the lieutenant said, 'Mr Bolitho, sir. He has apologised for the state of his uniform.' He said it without a smile, unlike Verling. It felt strange to have another officer standing in for him until his return from Guernsey. Verling would be fretting over the delay. He would have heard all the latest news from the colonies when *Condor* had called at St Peter Port with the admiral's despatches.

It would be good to have him back as first lieutenant. Although he might feel quite differently about it, after his brief but exciting flirtation with the schooner *Hotspur*.

Conway glanced at the letters lying open on his desk; they had been sent across from *Condor* within minutes of her anchor hitting the bottom.

One letter had been from his old friend's son, Midshipman Andrew Sewell. He was still with Verling and the passage crew in Guernsey, but the short, simple note had seemed like a reward, something which had warmed him more than he would have believed, or hoped.

The door opened, and Richard Bolitho walked into the cabin. This was only just February, and much had happened since their last meeting, the Board held in the flagship, which was still moored in exactly the same position as the day when several 'young gentlemen' had been required to face their tormentors. They all had to endure it, and laughed about it afterwards. The fortunate ones, anyway.

He strode to meet him and clasped his hands.

'So good to see you again, my boy! I want to hear all about the capture of the smugglers, and the contraband you helped to seize. It will carry some weight, I can tell you, with their lordships, and above!'

He guided him to a chair and the table where a servant had laid out some wine and his best goblets.

'I arranged for you to take passage in *Condor*. I hope it was a pleasant, if uneventful one?' He did not wait for a reply; he rarely did. 'I know you will have a good deal to do, and I shall not delay you unnecessarily. My clerk will take care of the other matters.'

Bolitho leaned his back against the chair. The same ship; even the weather, cold and grey, had not changed. The houses of Plymouth, like the ranks of anchored ships, were still half shrouded in mist. It had seemed to take an eternity for the frigate to make her entrance and anchor.

And yet only days had passed since it had begun. When they had climbed aboard *Hotspur*, a lifetime ago.

He glanced down at the breeches someone had loaned him, and at the makeshift patches on his coat. Reminders, like the cuts and bruises on his body.

The captain had poured the wine himself and was smiling down at him.

'I am very proud of you, Richard. One of *my* midshipmen.' He raised his glass. 'No need for you to be delayed when it could be avoided. I had a word with the flag captain.' He was refilling his glass, although Bolitho did not recall tasting the wine. 'And I wanted to do it myself.' He pulled open a drawer and took out an unsealed envelope. 'You are free to leave the ship and complete your arrangements.'

He watched him take the envelope, the 'scrap of parchment' they all joked about. Afterwards.

'Your commission, Richard. None better deserved!'

Bolitho saw his goblet being refilled. And still he could taste nothing.

It was here. The moment, the impossible step. He had seen some of the frigate's midshipmen glancing over at him during their brief time together. All so young, like Sewell . . . although Sewell had seemed suddenly mature.

And his first appointment. *You are herewith directed and commanded, upon receipt of these orders . . .* The rest was blurred.

But it was a frigate, named *Destiny*.

Conway was saying, 'I shall delay you no longer.' He looked over at the desk. 'Young Andrew Sewell has told me what you did for him. It helped him more than you can know. His father would have been obliged to you, had he been here himself to thank you.'

Bolitho stood up; there were voices in the outer cabin. He was grateful for the interruption, and so, possibly, was the captain.

He said, 'Martyn Dancer was a great help to him, sir. They got on well together.'

Conway walked with him to the screen door, and impetuously put his arm around Bolitho's shoulder. Afterwards, the cabin servant remarked that he had never seen Conway do anything like it, and it was never repeated.

Conway said, 'Then my thanks are to you both.' He looked again at the stern windows. 'God be with you when you join *Destiny*,' and he paused. 'As a King's officer.'

Out on the broad quarterdeck the air was still misty, but there was a gleam on the water, as if the sun were about to break through.

He would go to Falmouth and tell his mother and sister. It would have to be a brief visit, and he was glad of that also.

He looked around the familiar decks, and at the groups of seamen and marines.

This was the past. Ahead lay the new horizon.

Colours Aloft!

Alexander Kent

SEPTEMBER 1803

Vice-Admiral Sir Richard Bolitho finds himself the new master of the *Argonaute*, a French flagship taken in battle. With the Peace of Armiens in ruins, he must leave the safety of Falmouth.

What lies ahead is the grim reality of war at close quarters - where Bolitho who will be called upon to anticipate the overall intention of the French fleet. But the battle has also become a personal vendetta between himself and the French admiral who formerly sailed the *Argonaute*.

Bolitho and his men are driven to a final rendezvous where no quarter is asked or given.

arrow books

Form Line of Battle

Alexander Kent

June 1793, Gibraltar

The gathering might of revolutionary France prepares to engulf Europe in another bloody war. As in the past, Britain will stand or fall by the fighting power of her fleet.

For Richard Bolitho, the renewal of hostilities means a fresh command and the chance of action after long months of inactivity. However, his mission to support Lord Hood in the monarchist-inspired occupation of Toulon has gone awry. Bolitho and the crew of the *Hyperion* are trapped by the French near a dry Mediterranean island. The great ship-of-the-line's battered hull begins to groan as her sails snap in the hot wind.

'One of our foremost writers of naval fiction'
Sunday Times

TO FIND OUT MORE ABOUT

Alexander Kent

Visit www.bolithomaritimeproductions.com
or you may wish to subscribe to
The Bolitho Newsletter.

To join our mailing list to receive *The Bolitho Newsletter*,
send your name and address to:

The Bolitho Newsletter
William Heinemann Marketing Department
20 Vauxhall Bridge Road
London
SW1V 2SA

If at any stage you wish to be deleted from *The Bolitho Newsletter*
mailing list, please notify us in writing at the address above.

*Your details will be held on our database in order for us to send
you *The Bolitho Newsletter* and information on Alexander Kent,
Douglas Reeman and any of our other authors you may find
interesting. Your personal details will not be passed to any third
parties. If you do not wish to receive information on any other
author please clearly state so when subscribing to the newsletter.

arrow books

Man of War

Alexander Kent

Antigua, 1817, and every harbour and estuary is filled with ghostly ships, the famous and the legendary now redundant in the aftermath of war. In this uneasy peace, Adam Bolitho is fortunate to be offered the seventy-four gun *Athena*, and as flag captain to Vice-Admiral Sir Graham Bethune once more follows his destiny to the Caribbean.

But in these haunted waters where Richard Bolitho and his 'band of brothers' once fought a familiar enemy, the quarry is now a renegade foe who flies no colours and offers no quarter, and whose traffic in human life is sanctioned by flawed treaties and men of influence. And here, when *Athena*'s guns speak, a day of terrible retribution will dawn for the innocent and the damned.

'One of our foremost writers of naval fiction'
Sunday Times

arrow books

Relentless Pursuit

Alexander Kent

It is December 1815 and Adam Bolitho's orders are unequivocal. As captain of His Majesty's Frigate *Unrivalled* of forty-six guns, he is required to '*repair in the first instance to Freetown Sierra Leone, and reasonably assist the senior officer of the patrolling squadron*'. But all efforts of the British anti-slavery patrols to curb a flourishing trade in human life are hampered by unsuitable ships, by the indifference of a government more concerned with old enemies made distrustful allies, and by the continuing belligerence of the Dey of Algiers, which threatens to ignite a full-scale war.

For Adam, also, there is no peace. Lost in grief and loneliness, his uncle's death still avenged, he is uncertain of all but his identity as a man of war. The sea is his element, the ship his only home, and a reckless, perhaps doomed attack on an impregnable stronghold his only hope of settling the bitterest of debts.

'As ever, Kent evokes the blood and smoke of battle in crimson-vivid prose'
Mail on Sunday

'A splendid yarn'
The Times

arrow books

Sloop of War

Alexander Kent

SPRING 1778

The year marks a complete transformation for Richard Bolitho and his future in the Royal Navy. It is the year that the American War of Independence changes to an all-out struggle against British rule – and the year when he takes command of Sparrow, a fast, well-armed sloop of war.

As the pace of the war increases, the Sparrow is called from one crisis to another; and when the great fleets of Britain and France converge on the Chesapeake, Bolitho must be ready to come of age in a sea battle that will decide the fate of a whole continent.

'A splendid yarn'
The Times

arrow books

The Only Victor

Alexander Kent

FEBRUARY 1806

The frigate carrying Vice-Admiral Sir Richard Bolitho drops anchor off the shores of southern Africa. It is only four months since the resounding victory over the combined Franco-Spanish fleet at Trafalgar, and the death of England's greatest naval hero.

Bolitho's instructions are to assist in hastening the campaign in Africa, where an expeditionary force is attempting to recapture Cape Town from the Dutch. Outside Europe few have yet heard of the battle of Trafalgar, and Bolitho's news is met with both optimism and disappointment as he reminds the senior officers that, despite the victory, Napolean's defeat is by no means assured. The men who follow Bolitho's flag into battle are to discover, not for the first time, that death is the only victor.

arrow books

To Glory We Steer

Alexander Kent

JANUARY 1782

Captain Richard Bolitho is ordered to take the frigate *Phalarope* to the Caribbean, where the hard pressed royal squadrons are fighting for their lives against the combined fleets of France and Spain and American privateers.

It should have been a proud commission for Bolitho, but *Phalarope* has been driven to near mutiny by her previous commander. Bolitho sets about restoring the ship's pride. Caught between inner conflict and the broadsides of the enemy, the great battle of the Saintes provides captain and crew with the ultimate chance of redemption.

'As ever, Kent evokes the blood and smoke of battle in crimson-vivid prose'
Mail on Sunday

arrow books

ALSO AVAILABLE IN ARROW

With All Despatch

Alexander Kent

SPRING 1792

England is enjoying a troubled peace, with her old enemy France
still in the grip of the Terror. In harbours and estuaries around the
country, the fleet has been left to rot, and thousands of officers
and seamen have been thrown unwanted on the beach.
Even a frigate captain as famous as Richard Bolitho is forced to
swallow his pride and accept a minor appointment to the Nore.
With his small flotilla of three topsail cutters he sets out to search
for the most brutal gang of smugglers England has known, the
Brotherhood – a gang with men of influence behind them and a
secret, sinister trade in human misery.

'One of our foremost writers of naval fiction'
Sunday Times

arrow books

ALSO AVAILABLE IN ARROW

Success to the Brave

Alexander Kent

Spring, 1802

Richard Bolitho is summoned to the Admiralty to receive his orders for a diffcult and thankless mission . . .

The recent Peace of Amiens is already showing signs of strain as old enemies wrangle over colonies won and lost during the war. In the little 64-gun *Achates*, Bolitho sails west for the Caribbean, to hand over the island of San Felipe to the French.

But diplomacy is not enough . . .

'One of our foremost writers of naval fiction . . .'
Sunday Times

arrow books